NAKED JESUS

Jery Tillotson

Copyright © 2021 Jery Tillotson Books

All rights reserved. No part of this publication may be reproduced, distributed, or transmitted in any form or by any means, including photocopying, recording, or other electronic or mechanical methods, without the prior written permission of the publisher, except in the case of brief quotations embodied in critical reviews and certain other noncommercial uses permitted by copyright law. For permission requests, write to the publisher, addressed "Attention: Book Rights and Permission," at the address below. Published in the United States of America

ISBN 978-1-953904-22-5 (SC)

Jery Tillotson Books
#219 60 Caledonia Rd
Asheville, NC 28803
www.jerytillotson.com

Ordering Information and Rights Permission:

Quantity sales. Special discounts might be available on quantity purchases by corporations, associations, and others. For details, contact the publisher at the address above.

For Book Rights Adaptation and other Rights Permission. Call us at toll-free 1-888-945-8513 or send us an email at admin@stellarliterary.com.

Contents

PART ONE The Mountain Messiah 8
- CHAPTER ONE 1941 10
- CHAPTER TWO 21
- CHAPTER THREE 60

PART TWO The Boys 69
- CHAPTER ONE 70
- CHAPTER TWO Eighteen Years Later, Brandon 76
- CHAPTER THREE 96
- CHAPTER FOUR Tommy 111
- CHAPTER FIVE 120

PART THREE Return of the Messiah 155
- CHAPTER ONE 156
- CHAPTER TWO 182

PART FOUR Tommy Barnes Discovers Life 249
- CHAPTER ONE 250
- CHAPTER TWO 269

PART FIVE "We're Brothers" 289
- CHAPTER ONE 290
- CHAPTER TWO 299
- CHAPTER THREE Events Now Raced to a Climax for Both Men 323

PART SIX Diana Lives Again! 331
    CHAPTER ONE 332
    CHAPTER TWO 338
    CHAPTER THREE 363
    About the Author 372

Also by Jery Tillotson

- **White Gods**
- **I, a Man**
- **Writing as 'Jason Fury'**
    - *Wild Boys of the Swamp*
    - *Eric's Body*
    - *Naked Fury*
    - *The Rope Above, the Bed Below*
    - *His Eyes Were Dark, He licked His Lips*
    - *Screams of Pan*
    - *The Secret of Jimmy X and Other Tales of*
    - *Gay Macabre*
    - *The Kiss of King Kong*
    - *Orgy*
    - *Nights of Fury*
    - *Coming in Spring, 2021: The Strange Case of Kurt James*

- **Writing as 'Andrea D'Allasandra**
    - *Death House*
    - *The Creaking Door and Other Tales of Madness*
    - *Horror House*
    - *House of the Screaming Clowns*
    - *The Master of Hell Mountain*
    - *Run Fast, My Wolf Boy*

- **Writing as Kandy Kristmas**
    - *Doofus the Little Christmas Boy*

- **Writing as 'Big' Bill Jackson**
    - *Eighth Wonder*

This is a work of fiction. All of the characters, backgrounds and events proposed in this novel are the products of the author's imagination or are used fictiously.

NAKED JESUS. Copyright 2015 by Jery Tillotson. All rights reserved. Printed in the United States of America. For information address the author at his website: www.jerytillotson.com.

First published by iUniverse, 2015-2016

"If a man dies, shall he live again?
All the days of my appointed time will I wait, till my change come."

— Job

PART ONE

The Mountain Messiah

"Millions of years before dinosaurs roamed the earth, there flourished on this planet titanic civilizations that vanished because of tremendous cataclysms."

"Most extraordinary were the Mourians who worshipped the deity of Mouria. This being was both male and female as were her followers. An extraordinary priest helped Mouria rule. Love was preached to all. When a mighty flood covered most of the globe, a hundred of the Mourians ended up on the highest mountain peak in North Carolina. It is now called Mt. Mouria. And then these survivors also vanished, but the all-powerful priest (there may be one more) is still believed to exist, resting eternally in a special cavern within Mt. Mouria—where he awaits resurrection for the return of Mouria. Jesus Christ has long been believed to be this exalted person. Vesaria is the village that evolved there."

From *Lost Prehistoric Worlds*.

— Dr. Norma DuPree

CHAPTER ONE

1941

On a Sunday evening in February, the North Carolina mountain village of Vesaria cowered beneath a terrifying black storm.

A hellish torrent of huge hail stones and enormous bolts of lightning were unleashed. Ferocious winds ripped the trees out by their roots and destroyed many log cabins.

More horrific than any of this is the sky turned a blood red that churned into a massive whirlpool above the terrified residents through the night.

Had harm finally come to the powerful Mountain Messiah?

All the phone lines were down. Because of the ferocity of the storm, no one dared venture out of their homes.

Emmanuel Trident had declared from the pulpit just that afternoon that should anyone endanger his family, and especially that freakish half-man, half-woman wife of his that hell would wipe out the community that he had transformed within two years.

Starting a century ago, Vesaria had devolved into a dark, sinister place, full of incest, brutality and murders.

Everything was grim, charcoal looking, with no color anywhere. A permanent thick layer of dirty clouds hung like an umbrella over this once-vibrant town. Artists and writers had once flocked here. Flower gardens grew everywhere. Food grew in abundance. Animals thrived here. Life was good if you worked hard. People helped out one another.

But then, the violent backwoodsmen and criminals moved into the thick forest behind the village. More and more joined these jobless, sadistic men who never bathed, never combed their matted hair or wiped their filthy butts after using the primitive outhouse.

They thought nothing of raping their boys and girls and then trading them around to other drinkers of moonshine. Christmas was when the prettiest child was gifted as a present to a neighbor—to be used by the father and his sons to enjoy in dirty beds. Sometimes it would be spring by the time the favorite returned to his own family—by then, though, the pretty boy or girl had become diseased, exhausted and was kicked out into the woods to die alone.

They chose scriptures from the Bible to justify their violence. As members of the Ku Klux Klan, they greatly enjoyed riding out into surrounding areas to lynch a black person or a queer. These were human vermin that God said to destroy. The sadists proudly called themselves the God Squad.

They were considerably taken aback when one morning this do-gooding stranger, Emmanuel Trident, appeared with a group of twenty-five local men and women. All were armed with family rifles. They were all members of his newly formed place of worship: The All Souls Church of the Mountains.

Standing big, fearless and determined with a cold wind blowing his white robe, his mane of thick hair, Emmanuel Trident gave these outlaws a warning: if they ever came down to the village anymore to start trouble, there would be a mob of both men and women ready to fight them.

No longer were these brutal goons going to intimidate respectable people by beating them up, destroying property, stealing merchandise, and trying to grab little children to take back to the log cabins for unspeakable attentions.

The God Squad's chief, Houston Badgett, listened to the unwanted visitors and spat out a stream of tobacco juice from his blackened lips. With his unwashed hair, his dirty face with moles, his gray mouth with no teeth, he shouted for these intruders to leave him and his folk alone.

"Don't none of you tell me what to do!" he grunted. "We lives our lives according to the Bible. It tells us to punish and kill the God-doomed. Niggers. Faggots. They all need to be wiped away—and we're good Christians who'll do it."

"You do it," warned this Mountain Messiah, "and you'll pay for it in the worst way that would even impress your fairy-tale God."

But even these mountain misfits had to admit to themselves that this Emmanuel Trident, who looked like a giant and acted like somebody from another planet, certainly did awe them. Especially those strange, very light green eyes of his just blazing at you.

#

With his coming, this dynamic newcomer was instrumental in having the community's businesses paint their buildings with vivid colors of orange, pink, blue, emerald and gold. Polished windows set off the snow-white curtains. Beautiful flowers hung in large baskets over the entrance.

"Color! Color!" he exulted. "Make it all beautiful! Here's buckets of paint the colors of persimmon, red apples, grapes, corn, wheat, black and silver."

He created a food bank where he paid from his own pocket the farmer's produce and the baked goods and fruit preserves brought in by the women.

A free clothes building was established where all residents could choose from attractive, warm clothing that had been cleaned and shoes polished. A library was created on the second floor of Polly's Little Snack Shop. It became the most popular spot in culture-starved Vesaria. It was filled with people who wanted to read the daily newspapers, magazines, books, while school kids researched topics for their classes.

A hearty fire roared in the hearth. Cups of hot coffee or apple cider were available for pennies. The floors of pine were kept shined. Blue curtains hung in the windows. The residents loved the cleanliness and coziness of their new library.

A Laundromat was created with seven new machines and racks for drying clothes that could be used for free by anyone. The manager and her assistants kept the place spic and span and were paid good wages for their work.

The mountain minister encouraged the more wealthy farmers to hire men, women, and their children so they could at last have some money of their own.

He kicked the ass of old Parson Pickwick out of town. He was the only minister in Vesaria but he had long drained his followers of their money and patience. This senile old pervert had the reputation of defiling young boys and girls. He was a close crony to the vicious backwoods men up in the dense forest.

And then this charismatic Messiah created his own church: The All Souls Church of the Mountains.

He resembled a powerful god from books of myth. With his mane of dark hair hanging to his mighty shoulders, a trimmed beard and moustache to frame his handsome face, his eyes stunned everyone: they were a light, lustrous lime—like sparkling ocean water. Yet, they blazed with energy, with life and with great warmth for everyone.

When he looked at you, it was like he saw everything within.

He would appear at the podium of his church, wearing a luxurious robe of white linen, made by the female members of his congregation. Then he would step down—throw aside the robe—and he was buck naked!

Only a slender panel of silk covered his male endowment. His mighty torso rippled and gleamed with virility. And when he turned around, there was more shock. His posterior was completely revealed—but on his back there gleamed a fabulous tattoo of a face. Was it an image of him—or-- Jesus Christ?

His sermons were strange at first: he discussed how the ancient deity of Mouria was the only true god to worship. Mouria was a hermaphrodite—with both sexes as part of her body. She had ruled that only love, peace and harmony would be allowed in her mighty civilization one hundred million years ago.

She would return again soon to Mt. Mouria where the last of her worshippers were last seen—to create a society here that was harmonious and loving to people of all genders.

#

While the violent thugs of the woods loathed this extraordinary stranger—his church members worshipped him. They felt safe in his towering presence. His teeth dazzled, his jaw-dropping eyes reflected his warmth and love, and his magnificent body made everything around it stable and good.

But then he met the white nigger, the village freak, the hermaphrodite known as Diana DuPree—who, like the god Mouria, had both male and female body parts. That's when the mutterings grew louder—and then even some of this Mighty Messiah's most faithful flock began to desert him.

Now, as the powerful winds screamed against their windows, many of the residents cowered in their homes, worried that maybe those sadistic hillbillies had finally done what they had been muttering they would do for the past year—to destroy this unwelcome religious man and his freakish wife.

#

He had just suddenly appeared out of nowhere following a ferocious blizzard two years before.

With dark hair reaching his shoulders, his six foot five frame was covered by a white Cossack robe of beautiful wool. A full beard hid most of his handsome face. A striking cape of fur, with a matching hat protected him from the cold. His feet were encased in leather sandals.

With a wooden staff, he was just suddenly there on Main Street of Vesaria. He was first seen, leaning against a building, as if exhausted.

Mrs. Pim was walking with her neighbor Hattie McGuire on the windy side street between Polly's Little Snack Shop and Heron's Grocery Store when they witnessed this amazing sight.

"It was supernatural," the two women informed everyone along Apple Lane where they lived. They could not believe their eyes when this very striking and handsome apparition just suddenly appeared.

He was dressed so strangely for Vesaria that he naturally stood out. He was a gleaming figure in his white and gold against a backdrop of gray, black and cocoa. No one wore color in the village of Vesaria.

When asked if he needed help, he said "I'm very thirsty and hungry because I've come from a long way." He pointed toward the treacherous Mouria Gorge, the vast abyss that had no road or paths.

He never said where his home was located. And everyone wondered how he could have climbed up the sheer face of the steep mountain. His lightly gold skin glowed with an inner radiance. There was no sign of dust or sweat that happens to most humans after a long trip by foot.

Beside his wooden staff, he carried a leather bag that bulged with gold nuggets and precious stones. Attached to his leather belt was curiously a small hand whip.

One of the more eagle-eyed women, feisty Mrs. Pim, who became one of his most passionate followers, vowed that she noticed white scars on his palms and feet. It looked as if, she would say, and pause dramatically, that his scars resulted from nails being driven into his flesh. Maybe he had hung from a cross.

To her and later the followers there was no doubt in their minds: This was Jesus Christ returned to Earth—to clean up the garbage of Vesaria and make this once mountain paradise glow again.

He instantly enticed them into joining the new church he was planning: the All Souls Church of the Mountains.

It was held first in a deserted railway shack with a leaking roof. Kerosene lanterns provided light but immediately, this stranger attracted dozens of residents desperate for inspiration and faith.

In good weather, Emmanuel Trident encouraged the residents to bring out their stringed instruments and provide mountain music on the main sidewalks.

Soon, tourists were coming here just to hear bearded men and women in gingham dresses play their zithers and fiddles and banjos as they performed long forgotten mountain music. A group of cloggers was especially popular

When a hat was passed around for tips, dollar bills were abundant. The entertainers were delighted to have some money in their pockets for once. They could even afford a meal in Polly's Little Snack Shop.

Polly Morgan, who owned the popular eatery, became so busy with diners that she added a large extension and hired twelve more people. She brought in her talented nephew who was a noted chef in Atlanta, to take over the kitchen of her establishment.

Her menus now offered seasoned steaks, meats of all kinds, vegetables straight from the gardens of the village and her very popular banana pudding and peach cobbler. Her large fluffy biscuits were part of every meal served along with a small bowl of hot milk gravy.

The variety of wine and alcohol drinks offered by the red-haired Polly brought in even more patrons. Two young mountain brothers—Mark and Bart-- became popular bartenders. Their fresh charm and expertise in concocting drinks (Polly sent them to a bar workshop in Atlanta) was so effective that their tips were large enough for them to buy a cheap but dependable Ford. The fact that the boys were unusually handsome attracted car loads of pretty girls and gay men from out-of-town.

An abandoned warehouse was turned into a beautiful movie theater. The Morning Star Cinema was renovated and refurbished by Emmanuel Trident and his followers. Local artists were hired by the preacher man to paint murals on the interior walls. The exterior became a glowing pale orchid and pink. A majestic stage curtain of burgundy velvet was donated from a theater in Savannah, Georgia.

First run movies were shown. An elaborate concession stand offered home-made goodies, wine and beer and soda pop. For a little more money, one could purchase delicious fried chicken, hot dogs and hamburgers. For an extra dollar, patrons could sip cocktails, moonshine or a variety of mountain made wine. The staff worked proudly in their wine-and-gold uniforms. Their salaries were outstanding.

Because of this dramatic change for the better, the villagers, even the children, helped build for Emmanuel Trident the one-story All Souls Church of the Mountains out of rock and timber.

The old women outdid themselves in creating beautiful cushions made from fur and lamb's wool that were fitted into the pews.

Within six months, this extraordinary stranger had turned the dead-end little Vesaria into flourishing fields of wheat and corn. When he was called to the home of Sara Clodfelter, her child was dying of suffocation. Emmanuel pressed his hand on the infant's head—and it survived.

No one was surprised. They believed totally that this miracle worker was the Holy One who had returned to Earth and he chose Vesaria for his resurrection. Word spread fast about this miracle throughout the mountains. When the new church opened its doors for the first time, there were more than one thousand worshippers hoping for admission.

#

On the first Sunday in his new church, Emmanuel Trident stepped out from behind his podium and standing before the packed pews he suddenly threw off his robe. This produced a collective gasp.

He was totally naked except for a silken pouch that was wrapped around his impressive manhood. There was a dramatic stir among the worshippers and several couples quickly rose up and rushed out of the church.

His massive arms, thighs and chest amazed everyone. Enormous pectorals bulged out like a pair of buttocks. His stomach was flat and displayed a chiseled abdomen. Around his wrists and his mighty biceps coiled gleaming bracelets in the form of copper serpents.

"Look at me!" he shouted and beat his chest. Holding his fists high, he roared: "See me? I'm a Man! This is who I am! I'm not ashamed of showing you Mouria's temple! Neither should you blush and cringe in horror. You see a structure created by a higher power and it's this edifice that has brought me here to you—to protect and guide you! Look at me and feel my love for you!"

Now he turned his back toward the congregation and a second wave of shock swept over the church members for their leader revealed his rear that was covered by nothing. Not only that but an amazing tattoo of Jesus Christ—or himself for the two looked exactly alike—covered his rippling back.

The colors were like no one had ever seen for a tattoo. They glowed richly and the eyes in the face appeared to be staring straight at them and saying: "Behold, do not be afraid! You are in the presence of fantastic good!"

His message to them that day was shocking because it was like nothing they had ever heard before. Most had no use for the Bible. Parson Pickwick had worn them all down with his shrieking warnings that since they were all sinners, then they were all heading to hell.

Now, they suddenly sat up and listened.

"There is no god except for Mouria. All of you have heard of the legend of the Mourian Indians. They weren't fantasy. They really existed on this mountain top but were forced to leave by the maggots who called themselves pioneers.

"Mouria is greater than any other God because she sees the world from the eyes of both male and female. All her Indians were like her. She had two extraordinary priests who she sent out when necessary to destroy evil and replace it with good. Jesus Christ was born of Mouria and became her powerful priest. And we know what happened to him."

"One day you'll understand the meaning of my words."

His words left the church members stunned—for it seemed that he was saying that their Christ was born of the bizarre Indian god Mouria! This was certainly something to chew over in their minds.

And then he sang a song. There were no words. The holy man had merely explained that the song was millions of years old. He asked everyone to just open their minds and listen to the sounds

Holding his strong arms aloft, he sang intensely music that had no words. His eyes glowed and his body moved as if he were expressing an out-of-body melody. Everyone listening suddenly imagined pink and white clouds, trees swaying in strong winds, a vast ocean of cobalt blue and tangerine shades, roiling beneath a radiant light of rose and silver.

Some claimed later they could make out creatures with wings that fluttered around flowers and mountains. These beings possessed both male and female sexual parts.

When asked for the title of this eccentric gem, the singer said it was pronounced Aka.

"Tens of millions of years ago, Aka was the universal song that expressed love and solidarity with one another. One sang it when entering a new country so the populace there knew you were friends."

#

Many were convinced Preacher Trident could even control the clouds, now the sun filtered through occasionally to create a beautiful haze of silver in winter and gold in spring and summer.

As has been mentioned, however, there was that one shadow that hung over this extraordinary stranger from the beyond: his intimate friendship and then his marriage to the creature often called the White Nigger.

CHAPTER TWO

All residents were aware that this bizarre creature known as Diana DuPree was actually an Adam DuPree—a beautiful blonde man who lived like a woman. Or was it the other way around? Everyone knew it was fact that he grew up a youth in Vesaria until he was educated at the most expensive private schools in America.

When he returned, he let it be known Adam DuPree no longer existed. He was now Diana DuPree—with a female body and garb to prove it.

There was an air of mystery as to why the former DuPree boy would choose to return from being educated in the nation's top universities to the lonely life of a hostile mountain village.

Yet, he would be a fool to ignore the majestic chalet of rock left to him by his world-famous mother, Norma DuPree, the feisty, fearless archaeologist. The property set literally on the edge of Mouria Gorge. A rare visitor said a path from the back porch ended abruptly at the edge of the drop that ended far, far below in the canyon. A stranger could easily walk over into oblivion.

From what was known, his very wealthy ancestors had developed Mt. Mouria and mined it for wood and minerals.

Upon the tip of the mountain was perched the village of Vesaria. A male descendant, Tyler Dupree, married the extraordinary Norma Teasdale, who specialized in ancient civilizations and Egypt in her appearances at Harvard, Yale and Blackwood Institute.

She was a feisty redheaded dynamo who acted like no other woman anyone had ever seen. She smoked, drank, went off on archaeological digs in Egypt, Africa and China.

When her husband died, he left his widow tens of millions of dollars and Norma DuPree traveled for years, always returning to the chalet to bring artifacts and treasures from around the world.

Her home became internationally famous. Visitors wrote memoirs of their unforgettable stay at Chalet DuPree.

There were turrets and dormer windows and balconies. Magnificent stained glass windows enhanced the image of the mansion as being a cathedral of beauty. She had a staff of twenty-two who took care of her home, her kitchen, her prize-winning horses and lavish gardens maintained by three landscapers.

She was generous in her gifts to the village. A beautiful school was constructed that would contain all twelve grades. Free breakfast and lunch were included for all students. She paid for paving Main Street. Numerous children were given a four-year scholarship to any institute of higher learning that they wanted. Her staff was paid so well that most had built beautiful homes with electricity and running water.

Yet, her most passionate endeavor was exploring the treacherous Mouria Gorge. She became known as an authority on the Mouria Indians and the deity they worshipped: Mouria. Her scholarly articles on these subjects appeared in academic magazines. Publications like *Ladies Home Journal, National Geographic* and *The New York Times* featured her.

The author was considered more beautiful than any movie star. A famous photo showed her wearing safari garb, sitting behind the wheel of a jeep, a cocktail in one hand, a cigarette in the other, jewelry glittering around her throat and wrists, while behind her posed nearly fifty naked tribesmen.

The widow told her interviewers that she was determined to discover the fate of the Mourian Indians who just suddenly vanished literally overnight.

They had dwelled where the village of Vesaria later emerged. Brutal invaders had come and tried to wipe out the strange Mourians. When their priest, who may have been Jesus Christ, sensed what was being planned for them---total destruction—word swept over the one hundred member tribe.

Like their ruler, all Indians were physically both sexes and considered beautiful beyond description. They were neither men nor women. They were both.

On the day of the massacre, enemies discovered a deserted village and not a trace of the inhabitants or their animals. This became one of America's most tantalizing mysteries.

Mouria's Gorge was known to have numerous natural made caves but as Norma DuPree wrote, she was convinced that there had to be one paramount cavity into which the Indians had vanished. This had to be their vast secret temple—where miraculous rites were performed.

One magical secret was the preservation of their extraordinary priests from age and death. They could be sent into a trance to hibernate for thousands of years and the subject would grow neither old nor dead.

Some of their leaders, she lectured, could still be reanimated from this trance when a special mystical signal was given. Norma DuPree made headlines when she even stated that Jesus Christ was one of these exalted leaders.

#

One October morning, the mistress of Chalet DuPree told her house staff that she was exploring in Mouria Gorge again and not to expect her back for several days.

"I am going to discover the Mourian Temple today," she said fiercely. "If not, then I give up. I'll know it's hopeless, but something whispers in my ear—this time, success!"

Her faithful housekeeper, Hilda, and her husband, Oscar, who acted as both chauffeur and security chief, watched her climb over the edge of Mouria Gorge.

She took along enough water and food for a week.

A week later, she reappeared and it was obvious to the house staff that something profound had happened. She literally radiated joy. She was transformed by some experience she wouldn't describe. She merely said:

"I found it! I found it!"

Nine months later, she had her only child. The husband was never discussed. There were rumors from the beginning that this offspring was very strange physically: that it was a male, but it had female genitalia, too. From all accounts, the child resembled mostly an alarmingly beautiful girl. The mother declared that "Adam" would be treated as a boy until he was eighteen. Then he would flower into female hood as "Diana."

Until he was sixteen, Adam was taught at home. His mother hired two rugged and very handsome mountaineers who were brothers—Aaron and Josh-- to teach her high spirited son the ways of the mountains and how to protect himself for—as she explained bluntly to the two guardians—"he will need to protect himself more than most boys."

Before she hired them, she screened the two men carefully, as she did with the rest of the faithful household, and when she decided they could be trusted, they learned the truth—that their enchanting and mischievous charge was both female and male. His curls were gold, his eyes were a crystal blue and he was as spirited as a young colt. They were to always treat him as a boy.

The brothers never blinked an eye. Aaron, whose dark locks were touched with silver, smiled in understanding when the mother informed them of this condition.

"Whatever he is, we're his father now."

"We'll love him like he was one of our own," nodded Josh, whose wheat-hued hair and staggering good looks had earned him many an admiring look from the ladies,

Both men were powerfully built and cut logs and wrestled just for the fun of it. They had both served in the military, fought wild bear and cougars and enjoyed nothing more than to battle twelve-foot alligators in the coastal swamps.

When the boy was introduced to his two rugged protectors, Aaron said: "You're our son from now on." Josh added: "And you might be our daughter, too." That prompted both the child and the mother to laugh in delight.

Adam was taught to shoot and hit a squirrel right off a tree branch. He learned to fight with his fists, to use martial arts and to expertly shoot a bow and arrow, ride a horse and to roll his own cigarettes. Villagers became used to seeing the lively tow-headed youth racing his horse around the village, with his ever-present companion's right behind him.

While camping, he could make a fire from stones, hunt and cook his own food and kayak expertly in the nearby dangerous waters of the Black River.

When Adam turned sixteen, the handsome Aaron met with the mother and declared:

"I want to marry your son. He wants it and I definitely want it. I see him more as a woman now than a man."

Mrs. DuPree was secretly thrilled at the proposal for Aaron was seen as a powerful and beautiful man by her and the villagers. She answered:

"He's only sixteen years old. He's also half woman. How could you have a happy marriage with someone so—so complicated?"

Aaron responded "With Adam offering both sexes, it should make our lives more interesting than most married couples."

Josh also met with Mrs. DuPree an hour later and said: "I want to marry your daughter."

Norma Dupree smiled for Josh was equal to his brother in having a wise and forceful nature and whose extraordinary good looks made him a much desired companion by the single women in Vesaria.

This time she replied: "He's also male. Surely, you're aware of that, aren't you?"

"I would love her and him equally well."

With much graciousness, Norma DuPree turned down both men but advised them to not become discouraged. One never knew what the future might bring. She wanted her phenomenal offspring to see the world and meet other people before settling down.

It was said that the two big brothers wept when Adam went off to private school. They had fallen passionately in love with him. The youth and his guardians spent their last night together in the woods to mark the sad occasion.

The boy was sent off to military academies where the other cadets treated him with spite—at first. When they ganged up on him for the first time, they were shocked when their "sissy pussy" became a whirling force of ferocity. Several ended up with black eyes and others with sprained hands.

No one bothered him again. Some were even said to have become passionately in love with the "golden-haired girl-boy." Yet, no one there ever saw him naked. He lived off campus in a private apartment of much luxury. The faculty was dazzled with his brilliant mind and extraordinary artistic talent. They predicted the world would know him as a great artist in the near future.

Before even graduating, Adam was already selling his work for thousands of dollars.

Since sixteen, he had strapped down his budding breasts. He had no beard to shave. His skin was so flawless that his girlfriends begged for his beauty cream.

No one knew if he was joking when he told his admirers "To have skin like mine, you take the semen of three men each night and smear it on your face and hands."

Those who knew him said he would have no trouble finding three men who would eagerly supply him with this rare elixir. As always, he lived luxuriously in his own apartment and visitors said that he didn't try to hide his penchant there for beautiful gowns and robes and make-up. It was like he was tired of hiding his feminine self.

Female breasts had grown larger on him. Behind his scrotum, a woman's vagina had formed. He began to use it with some of his most fervent admirers.

The more he allowed his female side to flourish in private, the greater number of swains hung around him. They had never met someone so extraordinary and intoxicating. He could be a hell-raising fighting boy one minute and the next; he could slink up to you with his beautiful mouth moist and inviting words and give you a hard-on.

His effeminacy was what attracted men to him in the first place, while equally repulsing his enemies. But—as the brats in military school discovered, one didn't mess with this unpredictable young artist. His use of martial arts in real life became well-known. He had sent more than one thug to the hospital with an astonishing array of self-defense moves.

He had proven amazingly productive in turning out extraordinary paintings and statues. His work consisted of drawing exaggerated visions of the human body in gaudy colors with giant eyes and mouths and coiling and twisted hair-dos. An exhibit of his at college sold out. Banks and hospitals and corporate businesses vied for his work. He began signing his work "Diana DuPree."

Toward the end of his college days, he no longer tried to hide his blazing duality. His future in the art world was assured. He would never want for anything because of his sales and because of his mother's huge fortune.

His days of living as a male were over. He wanted to be a woman from now on and he didn't have to change a thing. It was always there.

"That's who I am now," he told his friends and faculty members just prior to graduation. "When you see the name of Diana DuPree on a piece of work, that's the new me."

Aaron and Josh were ecstatic when this new creature finally returned home after graduation just as his mother lay dying. Norma DuPree had never failed in her support of her strange offspring.

Diana was in her mother's grand bedroom suite when Norma DuPree motioned her only child to bend closer to hear her whisper:

"For my sake and for yours—remain in Vesaria until you're twenty. Someone will come here to this house—someone very special and I want you to be here when he comes. Feel free to travel but when near your twentieth birthday, be here. If this man fails to show up, then you can go wherever you want to."

Still beautiful in her mid-years, Mrs. DuPree coughed and said in a softer voice:

"You and Mouria Mountain are related. The Indians—they didn't go off and die. They moved to within the mountain for there's a whole world there, invisible to outsiders. They taught millions of years ago the secrets on how to preserve life—how to keep their priests in a state of animation—even when they're tens of thousands of years old. These holy men know when it's time to awaken and appear on Earth and try to spread love…that's the secret of the mountains, my darling Diana."

Her coughing worsened. Diana was about to phone the doctor when her mother motioned her to remain close. From beneath her pillow, she withdrew a narrow leather holster emblazoned with strange Indian symbols.

From this sheath, she pulled out a gleaming dagger. Its handle intrigued with its peculiar curves and designs. Its central figure was an image of Mouria.

"This is yours," whispered the dying woman. 'I found it in one of the caves where the Indians once lived. Keep it with you always. One day you may need it. Should it fail, make certain your descendant receives it. It can change your life—or the one of your child."

As Diana studied this striking weapon, her mother reached for her nightstand and found a jewel-encrusted box. From this she withdrew a small color photograph.

Her daughter stared at the dramatic face of a man who resembled Jesus Christ. He was looking down into the lens. His smile was radiant. Dark hair hung down on either side of his face. It was his amazing eyes, though, that stunned. Thick, dark lashes framed orbs that radiated a light emerald sparkle. Even from the picture, his eyes stared right into her soul.

"He—is your father!" The dying woman explained. "We met in the cave. You—will meet him again. It's pre-ordained."

Mrs. Flores died that night. Diana had the strange photo laminated in hard plastic and she inserted this into the sheath of the dagger.

Was this man one of the legendary Mourian priests her mother was so obsessed with? Could he actually be the Messiah?

"Could my father be Jesus Christ?" she asked in wonder.

That was too bizarre to even consider seriously. Yet, Diana had often heard her mother state as a fact that this was a strong possibility. That night, she attached the holster and the knife onto a narrow leather belt and would wear this souvenir from the mountain every day of her life.

#

So, Diana resigned herself to staying here in her mother's chalet but in a community she loathed.

For by now, Adam had completely become a female in his dress and body and attitudes.

Her dramatic gender transfer was fascinating fodder for her followers and reporters. They all portrayed her as someone who was just masquerading as a female as a publicity ploy, a lark, something like dressing up in clothes of the opposite sex to shock the prudes.

She knew, however, that her physical appearance would prove outrageous to many and during her first few months at home, vandals left signs that she was not wanted here.

Her expensive car was ruined, red paint was splashed on her front door, and windows were broken. This had occurred when Diana and Josh and Aaron had gone shopping for steaks and other gourmet delights in nearby Asheville.

To beef up security, Diana's two protectors hired their three rugged and ravishing young nephews to join them. Ted was a red-haired Adonis with freckles and a powerful body that left a trail of broken hearts. Sammy had worked as a carnival strongman and his dark locks surrounded a rugged face with wide-opened eyes of innocence. Ashley was a slender but well-muscled sexpot who flirted with anything on two legs—with gender making no difference. Like their two magnificent uncles, this trio had all served in the military.

Before they were hired, Diana met with them, along with their uncles, and after getting their promise of secrecy; they were shown her physical attributes. She was at the apogee of her beauty. Her breasts were firm and shapely. Her male equipment was modest, as was her female area. There was no hair down there as there was none on her body. Her skin was beautifully smooth and fair. She moved with a slight wiggle to her hips which her protectors certainly noticed. With her gleaming locks hanging over her shoulders she said with a smile:

"This is me. I'm Diana DuPree—with an extra part thrown in."

Like their uncles, these young bucks were shocked at first. Their mouths had fallen open and their eyes widened. They had only known two sexes: male and female. It had never entered their fantasies that there could be extraordinary people—who could be both.

Fortunately for them, either male or female, Diana DuPree dazzled them.

They were entranced.

They were a unique breed of male like Aaron and Josh. Growing up in the wilds of Mt. Mouria, they had spent much of their lives in silence, living in the woods, guarding their cattle and goats through long nights and thinking much of nature. They had seen too much wild life sex to be appalled by anything that others might consider unnatural. They were schooled at home with parents who were college educated. Their reading material ranged from Tolstoy, Edgar Allen Poe and Oscar Wilde. Their favorite philosophers were Socrates, Xiphrona and Kilpure. They were addicted to comic books, too, and Superman and Flash Gordon were two of their favorite heroes.

The three new hires were excited and titillated to have such an extraordinary person as their boss.

This team of five muscle gods was big, strapping and outstanding in their physical beauty. All wore cowboy hats and gear and gay visitors were stunned to see these fabulous looking men, stripped to the waist, washing the cars or taking care of the horses. Norma DuPree was known all across horse country for having a breed of priceless animals.

The Chalet DuPree also became famous for its spectacular flower garden that extended to the very cliff of Mouria Gorge. Three landscape artists worked to make the floral extravaganza a showstopper. In the right weather, the mansion dazzled with its thousands of pink and white and crimson blooms.

In their spare time, the five warriors boxed, wrestled and helped maintain the property. They competed to see who could impress their beautiful boss the most.

Diana saw them as a bunch of beautiful wild animals. They acted on instinct and were primitive in some ways but they were passionate in their devotion to her. She saw their expressions as pure and innocent. They all possessed the quality of being little, impish boys. These overgrown urchins loved to laugh and play tricks on each other.

They boasted that they would kill anyone who wanted to harm Diana DuPree.

These five mountain men often brought her beautiful bouquets of wild flowers they picked in the woods. Sometimes they gifted her with strikingly carved figures of animals. Her protectors created jewelry for her out of rocks and wood. They vied for the chance to pose in the nude for her life studies.

Visiting artists were beyond thrilled when their hostess brought in her boys and had those all strip down to their skin to pose. Diana laughed heartily when the "boys" would playfully go into their strong male poses.

Aaron, who was considered the most beautifully rugged and muscular of them all, became a great favorite of Helmet Antonioni, a well-known sculptor from Venice, Italy. His statue of a naked Aaron created a sensation when put on exhibit in Manhattan. The artist used no coy fig-leaf to cover his model's outstanding attributes.

When Helmet Antonioni visited Diana DuPree, she always gave him the rear bedroom of the chalet that had its own private staircase. Aaron was often seen visiting the foreigner late at night—and not leaving until morning.

Diana kept her mother's staff and added two extra maids, a second cook and another laundress because she enjoyed entertaining weekend guests. Villagers became used to seeing expensive cars parked at the rock chalet.

Diana's visitors were delighted to visit such a unique artist in this rural, mountainous little village. This was before the arrival of Emmanuel Trident and the landscape was bleak and dramatic—a perfect backdrop for such a complicated artist as Diana DuPree.

Diana had built a cozy clubhouse for her five men behind the house. In this beautifully decorated building, the "boys" had their own private bedrooms and bathrooms, along with a well-stocked fridge and their bed linen was changed each day with starched sheets and pillow cases.

In their den, they had the latest in radios, record players, albums, endless games to play, checkers, chess, the latest magazines, comics and books.

They shared their meals with their mistress and these gatherings were full of laughter and teasing and catching up. Diana told one friend that eating with the posse was like being with a bunch of "savage, glorious young panthers. They eat voraciously and drink prodigiously. They love to cut up and tease me. I can see the love in their eyes for me."

After work, these handsome huskies sat around the fireplace bunkhouse and discussed how much they loved Diana DuPree. They pondered ways to prove their devotion and what kind of gifts she might enjoy.

Like their handsome uncles, each of the new trio of bodyguards were invited into her bedroom. They were spellbound by her love-making and the fact that she was both male and female inflamed their passion even more.

They became obsessed with becoming her main lover.

But then, she and the Holy Man met, and everything changed.

It was a damp and raw afternoon. Strangely overhead, columns of light had pierced the thick bank of bruised clouds. It looked like celestial searchlights shone down because of some paramount event about to happen.

Diana DuPree had just returned to Vesaria after spending six months away.

She had explored Tangier, Morocco, Russia, Budapest and Tibet. She had hoped to learn more about the deity, Mouria, the one that had made such an impact on her mother.

To her disappointment, only Tibet had a few of the priests who gave her any ideas about that long vanished civilization. All they could tell her was that Mouria was expected to return to this world sometimes in the very near future. Her spirit was alive, as was her main priest. He was kept in a state of animation, his body never changing, until resurrected by a magical signal was sent to him to awaken.

A month before returning to Vesaria, she had explored Manhattan for her future home. She was moving to New York City to settle down and devote her energies to becoming a successful artist.

Diana found a magnificent penthouse in the very ritzy area of Manhattan known as Gracie Square. It was located in the tony section of the vast city described as the "Silk Stocking" neighborhood. Her private elevator took her up to her twenty-first floor aerie. Marble floors and glass walls contained three levels. She had a glorious view of the East River.

She had delighted in furnishing her stunning home with extraordinary tapestries, lamps, statuary draperies. Her closets were now filled with luxurious furs, gowns, lingerie. On her balcony were lounge chairs and tables for cocktail parties she planned to throw. She had made many new friends in Gotham. They were totally aware of her sexual duality and this made her even more fascinating. Her paintings were now being exhibited in several prestigious art galleries on Madison Avenue.

In just two months, she would move there. Her chalet would be kept for her occasional visits.

When she got off the train in Asheville, her five protectors gave her a joyous reception. All the time she was away, they wrote her weekly, their letters full of the new Mountain Messiah who was transforming Vesaria.

What excited her was that this charismatic stranger was a messenger of Mouria. His sermons praised this god that had obsessed Norma DuPree. This was certainly significant. And when they showed her the re-vitalized downtown, she was delighted and her interest piqued: Was this the stranger her mother had said would visit her?

When they came to the steel gate that began the circular drive to the mansion, Diana asked to be let out of the car. She needed the exercise and she wanted to enjoy, possibly for the last time, a look at the house where she had grown up in. She wrapped herself tightly in a luxurious cape of mink fur. A matching hood protected her face from the bitter cold and dampness.

She had just turned twenty. The stranger had never shown up. So Diana planned to waste no more time in a place she hated. She was excited about becoming a New Yorker. While there, she had met with her mother's attorneys. They assured her that her enormous fortune would steadily grow because of shrewd investments.

Diana had also written her own will. Her inheritance would go to her offspring, should she have any. If not, she wanted her wealth to go into a permanent foundation, one that would award outstanding art and fashion talents.

As she came closer to the front entrance, though, she stopped *a*nd her breath quickened.

There *he* stood, bigger than life, wearing a beautiful cloak and hat of fur. Dead leaves danced around him.

Now, he grinned charmingly at her and nodded his head.

"May I presume you to be Diana DuPree?"

"I'm Diana and you don't have to introduce yourself. I've been hearing all about you, Emmanuel Trident. In fact, I've been waiting for your visit."

Saying nothing, he bowed his head slightly and then looked up to stare into her face. Diana was startled by the luminous glow of this man's emerald hued eyes. They glistened warmly and stared straight into her own.

Diana's pulse raced. This was *the* man she was destined to meet.

Over her shoulder, she laughed at the excitement of her protectors. On this cold day, they all wore cowboy hats, jackets and snug jeans. They had definitely recognized the preacher and were beside themselves. He was their hero.

"Reverend Trident, I believe that five of your most ardent fans would like to say hello."

They eagerly clasped his hand and he charmingly greeted them and asked about their health.

"Your men make my church choir sound like mighty angels," he smiled. "They truly have outstanding voices."

"I'm sure I'll be okay with our visitor, boys" laughed Diana. "You can go about your business."

Her five bodyguards gave high yelps as they trotted to their clubhouse.

"It's baking day, Reverend Trident, so I'd love for you to join me in seeing what the cook has prepared for us."

Together, they crossed over the threshold of Chateau DuPree.

#

Inside the house, the air was redolent of freshly baked bread and other delectable goodies. The staff had finished their work for the day and had all gone home.

Emmanuel Trident dwarfed everything because of his tremendous size.

"What a beautiful home you have here, Miss DuPree."

'Please call me Diana—and thank you. I'm comfortable here. This was my mother's house.

"This is amazing!" the visitor said sincerely. "It's like a combination art gallery, museum and personal den."

Indeed, thanks to her mother, the large den brimmed with stunning antiques and furnishings from Tibet, Africa, India, Egypt, and the Orient. Masks and tapestries covered the dark wood walls. On small tables glistened African and Indian figures and jewelry. Ancient deities from Egypt and China were carved from wood and rock.

A fire crackled in the large fireplace. Small lamps with crystal hoods of ruby, emerald and gold glowed around the snug chamber. Cherry incense perfumed the air.

One huge painting hung over the hearth. It was a brilliantly colored canvas that showcased a strange looking image—a dreamy figure that had female breasts and modest male genitalia.

"That's my vision of Mouria—the Indian deity. My mother talked about Mouria so much when I was growing up."

"Your mother, I hear, was a brilliant explorer and archaeologist. I would love to have met her and discuss Mouria."

In the kitchen, Diana was followed by her guest who sat in the eating nook. It was round and lined with windows that looked down into the dizzying canyon below.

"Have you ever had Russian Tea—my mother used to make it for me. I think you'd like it."

"Yes, indeed. I'm a little tired of coffee."

"And here's a freshly baked Red Devil's cake and some donuts my cook just baked."

She had thrown off her fur cape to reveal a flowing gown of chocolate hued wool belted at the waist with a red and gold belt. Her flaxen hair glowed like a cape of moonlight. Turquoise jewelry glistened at her throat, wrists and fingers.

Her visitor had also pulled off his cloak and hat.

He was a breath-taking sight and for a moment, she said nothing.

"Excuse me for staring, reverend, but I didn't know you were so—so big!"

'You can stare. I'm used to it. It helps me in my sermons."

She had known many men before returning to Vesaria and even those who lived here. Each of her male guardians was passionately in love with her—they told her this and their love-making was intense and wonderful.

This visitor triumphed over them all in his exhilarating machismo.

His skin was so outstanding: gleaming, glowing, as if lit by an inner fire. His dark hair hung to massive shoulders and was clean and shiny and streaked by gold. Diana loved beauty—in her clothes, jewelry, furnishings. She had never seen it exemplified so powerfully in a human being. His eyes were iridescent, lashing with emotion in their jade hue.

He enjoyed with gusto the refreshments and had several refills of Russian Tea, two large slices of cake and he consumed the platter of cookies. When she made him a huge sandwich of ham, cheese, tomatoes, pickles and lettuce, he swallowed it down, followed by several mugs of homemade beer she had made by a local brewery.

"Because of my size," he smiled, "I seem to need so much fuel to keep my engine running."

Sitting on the sofa before the fire in the den, they sipped the heady cherry liquor her staff made. Diana enjoyed the warm glow the drink infected her with and she began to pour out her feelings with no inhibitions.

She sensed she could confess to him anything and it wouldn't shock. Since she now fully believed that this man was the one her mother had forecast, Diana felt it important that he know how she felt about her life.

'You know what some call me in the village. I've heard the names all my life. Freak. Faggot. White Nigger."

"White Nigger? You should wear that label proudly—because it means people who call you that are frightened and confused because they know you're special and they never will be. The god Mouria was half man and half woman. She was the duality of self that's in all of us. See, she would be called a White Nigger, too, if she was alive."

He spoke those words softly, but with intensity. She was surprised to find her cheeks wet with tears.

"Sorry," she whispered. "I've never confessed my feelings like this to anyone."

He closed his eyes briefly in understanding.

"Why did you come back to such a primitive place like Vesaria," he asked. "You seem made for a teeming metropolis—like New York, Chicago, and Los Angeles?"

"When my mother was dying, she made me take a vow to live here until I was twenty—because a very special stranger would visit me."

"And you're how old?"

"I was twenty three days ago—and now I'm moving to New York City while keeping this place as my second home."

He had moved closer so their bodies touched. His body heat was intense. Diana smelt a haunting scent that emanated from his vast body, a delicious aroma of wood, musk, and citrus—of warm, clean flesh.

"Perhaps I've come at just the right time," he murmured. "Please—show me who you are. Don't be afraid. Don't be shy. You'll find I accept everything for what it is. It might help you. And you couldn't surprise me."

Slowly, and reluctantly, she stood up and faced him.

"I'm frightened—I've never done this with anyone I didn't love."

"Don't be afraid of me," he murmured soothingly. "This might be the most important moment in your life."

She undid her wool gown so that it dropped to the floor.

This was followed by her lingerie of gold lace and silk.

Her gleaming hair hung down her back and over her shoulders.

"Beautiful!" whispered Emmanuel. "You look unreal."

He was spellbound. His fingers were gentle as they touched her breasts, her modest male genitalia and those that made her female.

He used his mouth to taste these physical wonders until he lifted his radiant face up to gasp in astonishment: "You're *Mouria*! She didn't die. She came back in you!'

"I'm afraid I'm very human but with a few major differences."

His clothes dropped to the floor now and he encouraged her to explore his magnificent torso.

She was staggered by his naked physique.

Her five member posse was outstanding in their dazzling bodies.

Emmanuel Trident, though, was like someone unreal. She had never beheld such incredible proportions of the male form.

Her hands greedily inched over him—his amazing pectorals that she caressed like they were woman's breasts...the flatness of his chiseled stomach...the glorious endowment that she used both hands to hold and fondle and to watch it grow steadily in size...the beauty of his rear-end and the deep cleft.

She was dizzy from ecstasy when he picked her up easily and took her to bed. Afternoon turned into night before they settled into the relaxed afterglow of intense sexual action.

He ravished her as both male and female—with his lips greedily kissing her in all her hidden corners and crevices. He demanded she do the same to him. He was so vast; it took considerably much longer to delight in the phenomenal magnificence of his fleshly terrain. His skin was hot and salty and smelt like an ancient perfume that haunted one long after.

When he lay on his back and she took control of his front, his powerful torso rippled and danced as his breathing quickened. His already gleaming flesh sparkled with sweat that emphasized all of his amazing bulges and ridges.

When he guided his enormous endowment into her, she stilled herself for pain—but incredibly, he was so skillful a lover that she felt nothing but ecstasy.

As he bent over her, his hips moving in steady rhythm, she looked up into his face that was radiant with delight and something much more. His orbs of jade were hot and glittering with passion and joy.

As they lay there silently, still breathing heavily from the intense love-making, Diana felt like she was floating into a new dimension. Everything around her sparkled and vibrated and she experienced for the first time the sensation of being with someone extraordinary.

She asked that he come live with her.

He said he would marry her first and the next day, they drove into Asheville and were united by an Episcopalian preacher. That afternoon, Emmanuel moved his few belongings into her place. His presence turned the lonely abode into one that simmered with intense eroticism.

Diana's employees were astounded and then thrilled, too. They were all great fans of the dazzling Naked Jesus, as he was called by many—and the fact that he was now living with their beloved mistress excited them, as well. Even her five male protectors were ecstatic.

Their idol now lived with their beautiful lady. They felt like they were the luckiest men in Vesaria. To them, a family was formed with Emmanuel Trident the powerful head of the household. He was one man they did not mind at all in looking up to. He treated them like his brothers and he proved this when he galloped off with them on their hunting trips.

He wouldn't discuss at all his past or where he had come from. He merely smiled at her questions and ignored them although he did make a most tantalizing statement:

"What if I *were* Christ? He was resurrected, remember, from the dead. Perhaps no matter how many times he died—he'll return for a special reason."

"And the reason."

He stared at her tenderly. 'Perhaps it's you. Maybe you're more special than you think. Perhaps you're here to bring one or more special beings into the world. If that happens, we'll see the real resurrection of Mouria and the Messiah."

Diana had shown her husband both the gleaming Mourian dagger and the strange photo.

"This is my father," she explained. "The man my mother met in one of the caves. He looks like Jesus Christ. And he also looks amazingly like you."

Emmanuel Trident studied the photo and handed it back with the suggestion of a smile.

"The world is stranger than we can imagine."

When he took her to bed, Diana thought: Emmanuel is the face in that photo. He is my father—and he could well be Jesus Christ.

#

The residents of Vesaria were shocked at the news: their Naked Jesus was now married to the White Nigger!

Most residents tolerated the beautiful Diana DuPree. Even though she had funded free meals at the school she had built, no one could think of approaching her. She was, after all, known to be a physical abomination.

Members of the All Souls Church of the Mountains, though, put their dark feelings about her behind them. They wanted to meet and see for themselves what was so attractive that their earthly savior had chosen her, of all people, to be his wife.

The mountain thugs, though, were enraged that this union had taken place. When they got drunk on moonshine in the afternoon, there were curses and shouts of how they could not let live such an unholy couple. Some could read their Bibles. These few men pointed out passages that said it was the right thing to do to eliminate such desecrations from Earth.

If they were true God-fearing American men, they had to rise to the occasion. Let the world see that Vesaria did not tolerate sinners like the Tridents. They were worse than the niggers and queers that they had lynched over the years.

#

Emmanuel Trident saw many of the children destroyed by hideous sexual infections—with their faces half gone, their teeth rotted out, their tongues protruding and gaping sores around their orifices. The doctors he hired could do nothing for them. They were literally being eaten up by venereal diseases.

"The men—fathers, brothers, neighbors—did this," muttered one of the visiting nurses who treated the children. "Nothing we say to them changes anything. They've done this for decades."

The young minister's warnings to the men were received with mutterings and stares of sheer hatred. There wasn't nothing wrong about what they were doing. They were real men who acted like real men. It was their right to take what they wanted. It had always been so. These were the men who hated Emmanuel Trident because he preached against the abuse of anyone—but especially children. He knew what went on up here in the hills and he was going to stamp it out.

And so more ammunition was added to the conviction that these enemies needed to act now to destroy him and all those close to him. Especially that abomination who was now his wife—that freak who wasn't a man and who wasn't a woman but a monster of nature.

A White Nigger.

#

The sensational success of Emmanuel Trident in both his preaching and his civic work had spread beyond the mountains.

Each Sunday, there were a thousand and more who gathered around the church, hoping to find a seat. The regular members were always admitted first—and then five hundred out-of-towners.

None of the visitors were disappointed in their visit to the church.

They were thrilled to see this glorious giant suddenly emerge from a small door near his pulpit.

Wearing a flowing gown of white or gold, he stood still, welcoming everyone.

And then he came out from behind the podium and descended five steps into the audience. There the minister stood right beneath a golden spotlight. All other lights dimmed until one saw only this spellbinding creature.

Suddenly, he yanked off his robe and tossed it aside.

There he stood, then, in all his glory—a long-haired god with the most powerful looking physique they had ever beheld, completely exposed—except for a sliver of gleaming silk that hid the essentials. Equally exciting was the dynamic delivery of words from this Mountain Jesus.

His messages broke all the rules that one usually heard in churches around America on Sunday mornings.

"Where did Jesus Christ come from? Certainly not from some ordinary set of parents. Mouria sent him here! It was Mouria who commanded him to cleanse the earth of evil and depravity. He had the psychic power of being able to shrink in size until he was almost an infant. Possibly he was flown to Bethlehem on one of the flying machines known only to Mouria. And then he grew up and worked hard to finally bring peace and love to people. But what did he get in return? There were no thanks. This is what always happens to celestial beings who try to work with men. Sometimes they succeed. Often, though, the mob takes over. They don't want change. They want to soak in the old ways, the evil ways. Satan is already here in many people. The Satans of the world are the ones who murder, maim, lie, destroy and torture. You'll see proof of it again—soon!"

#

With Emmanuel Trident now master of the house of the household his wife's many friends from the art world treasured an invitation for the weekend. All were entranced with Mrs. Trident's magnificent, charismatic and charming spouse. The ravishing five protectors certainly added to the abundance of male flesh that was always on full display.

Wearing beautifully created tunics of vivid, sparkling colors, Emmanuel Trident created a fanatical cult of admirers. No one had ever met anyone like him before. It was like encountering a fabulous comic book hero who was genuinely interested in each person. They couldn't get enough of him.

One of Diana's most famous guests, the artist Victor Santoro, insisted on painting a huge portrait of Emmanuel Trident.

During the master's visits, he spent several hours each morning, painting his subject. Emmanuel Trident wore absolutely nothing at the Italian's request. Diana and her Boys came by to watch the artist at work.

They were spellbound by the nude form of the Mountain Jesus as he sat beneath a small gold light. He was like living sculpture.

He relaxed on a low rock, with his hands gripping the large stone behind him and his massive chest thrust out. His head was thrown back and his face dazzled with its celestial illumination. The background was a dramatic rendering of a dark storm, with bolts of yellow lightning.

For his reward, Victor Santoro was invited by Emmanuel Trident to ride out with him one afternoon into the thickly wooded area near Vesaria. The cook prepared them a basket of food and wine.

When they returned the next morning, the artist was radiant and strangely quiet. His only comment was: "It was the greatest few hours of my life. I was with a human god who could very well have been Jesus Christ—wearing no clothes and no inhibitions."

#

A year after Emmanuel Trident moved into Chalet DuPree, he lay with his wife on their goose-feathered bed. Snow lay thick outside their large windows. Burning logs in the large hearth sent red and gold shadows that danced over the magnificent master bedroom.

The Holy Man was grateful for the snow for it kept the busybodies from invading his privacy.

Emmanuel Trident touched the gleaming mane of hair of his radiant companion who smiled at his touch.

Next to the bed were two cradles. In them peeped the faces of twin boys.

Yet, each infant was totally different from the other. One had white hair, just like his mother with gentle eyes of blue, while his sibling had jet curls and lively green eyes.

The household staff and especially The Boys were thrilled. No one had any indication that their mistress was even pregnant.

Now, they would come in like gentle giants and stare in rapture at these new little creatures to be watched over. The blonde child was called Neil and the dark haired imp was named Todd.

Emmanuel knew the village was rocked—at the news that he and his strange wife had conceived such beautiful little infants. This was not supposed to happen—not to a Holy Man and his Unclean Thing companion.

But it had—and he sensed it was time to move on. Vesaria was slowly reverting to what it was before he came.

A growing group of Parson Pickwick followers were spreading trouble here and painting a black picture of him. Another bunch of bitter and warped residents who were shocked by his unorthodox teachings—and especially his fleshy displays of nakedness—had joined the troublemakers.

While he had enjoyed strong support from many of the villagers, the ones who had left his church were vicious in their disapproval.

He had done all that he could in this remote community.

The minister and his wife decided to move in the next few months to Diana's magnificent penthouse in Manhattan. They would transport The Boys and the household staff to live with them.

All the most valuable furnishings in Chateau DuPree—the paintings, sculptures, tapestries, carpets, lamps and so on—would be shipped there.

The Tridents would give the chalet to the village to use as a school or learning center. As they made plans for the big move, they also continued gathering around the piano after supper each night and singing.

One of the great pleasures of Chateau DuPree was vocalizing.

When Emmanuel Trident married Diana DuPree and moved in, he introduced his bride and The Boys to the joys of singing.

They were spellbound by the master's extraordinary style of singing. His voice was strong, tremulous and intense. Tears would run down his cheeks when he crooned a religious ballad or a mountain tune.

They discovered that Diana had a beautiful pure soprano and the five men had fine, strong voices, too. Together, they learned to harmonize smoothly on old mountain ballads.

With Diana performing on the piano, Emmanuel played the violin and Aaron and his cohorts did well on the bass fiddle and banjo and flute. They gave themselves a name: The Tridents. They brought their talents to the All Souls Church of the Mountains and proved to be a tremendous hit. Recording equipment was installed in the chapel. On the weekends, the musical group rehearsed and began to issue 78 rpm records under the banner of Mountain Magic.

These recordings were sold for very modest fees. A visiting recording executive from Atlanta who had heard about the outstanding musical talent arranged for the singers to record an album of old mountain ballads. Among them were "On the Banks of the Ohio," "John Riley," and "Geordie.' The album was called "The Tridents Sing Mountain Magic!"

The outstanding little musical group did what they did for fun. They had no plans for turning their talents into a theatrical success.

After much pleading from concert promoters, the group gave their consent to perform in the big Blue Mountain Music Festival held each October in the city of Knoxville, Tennessee.

The Tridents had agreed that the two songs they would perform would be a rollicking original square dance number, "Dancin' Maggie McGee,' and the more lyrical but haunting, "Black is the Color of My True Love's

Hair." If there should be demands for encores, the group also rehearsed a dozen other tunes.

On the night of October 13, 1941, the Tridents stepped upon the large stage before an audience of 9,000. They had come from everywhere and included fans and talent agents.

No one there knew or cared about the personal drama surrounding the Tridents back in Vesaria.

Their entrance upon the stage brought strong applause. Diana wore a gold gown spattered with sparkling cherry hued sequins. Red roses were intertwined into her long hair.

Emmanuel and The Boys were all attired in snug fitting leather britches and white shirts opened wide upon their brawny chests. Their long hair gleamed on their shoulders. Their beards and moustaches were neatly trimmed.

From the first note, the audience went wild. Diana DuPree sparkled with her platinum hair and beautiful features. The men, though, caused the female audience members to jump up and dance. These Vesaria males all moved sexily in rhythm—undulating their hips, their shoulders and arms as they harmonized. They stomped their feet in rhythm when they belted out 'Dancin' Maggie McGee' many audience members leaped out into the aisles to dance along with the rollicking tune.

Emmanuel Trident's strong voice caused each song to soar to the back rows. When he sang, he didn't try to be smooth and sweet and calm. He roared out his notes, with his raw energy affecting the whole group. They all lost their inhibitions and let it rip.

There were screams for encore after encore. Because of the hot lights, the men stripped off their shirts to display their outstanding upper torsos. Their leather britches were cut very low so their upper hips were on display. Sweat sparkled on their smooth skin. If possible, the women screamed more hysterically.

The Tridents won that night's top award. Recording executives from all over the country all wanted to sign this beautiful group up to lucrative contracts.

All of this was for naught because after the horror that hit Vesaria, no one on the outside wanted anything to do with this evil mountain village.

There was no one there to sing anything.

#

While the Tridents performed to their roaring audience, back in Vesaria their enemies gathered in an old stable on the edge of town.

Now was the time to strike and return Vesaria back to what it was before this so-called Messiah arrive.

There were fifty men and women present. They were all members of the Ku Klux Klan that included the vicious hillbillies. It had been a long time since they had lynched niggers and queers in surrounding towns. They were all thrilled to contemplate watching again the bodies twitching at the end of a noose and then burned to ashes in a big bonfire. The children always loved this part of the lynchings.

Among the loudest agitators was old Parson Pickwick who had sneaked into Vesaria wearing a disguise? He knew there were good men and women in the village who would love to string *him* up!

 He told the gathered criminals that twenty or thirty other Klansmen in other towns wanted so badly to don their white robes and go out into the countryside and clean up God's mistakes. And Diana DuPree was very definitely an abomination that the good Lord wanted exterminated.

And these murderers didn't want anybody calling them Ku Klux Klan members.

They were the God Squad.

#

Emmanuel Trident was acutely aware that the haters in Vesaria were spreading their poison about him, his church and his family and they were doing it in a visible way.

Someone had sabotaged the Social Center by setting it afire several times in a month. Food was stolen and the washing machines were being wrecked.

The free clothes section had been ruined by cans of red paint being spattered everywhere. The sewing machines were nearly destroyed.

Vesaria was fast receding to its old, evil self again.

Some members of the Holy Man's Church had relatives who lived in dark evil. These faithful worshippers reported their suspicions to The Boys and these protectors passed on the information to Emmanuel Trident. He was not surprised but he was bitter that all the good things that had started to happen in Vesaria were now vanishing.

He gathered everyone at Chalet DuPree and warned them of possible danger. Diana DuPree was already well aware that hostility was steadily building in parts of the village.

Emmanuel Trident and the Boys gave each of the household a rifle, a revolver and bows and arrows and taught them how to use these weapons.

These twenty-one men and women—who worked in the house, the yards, the stables--were passionately devoted to their master and mistress.

They vowed that they would be prepared for any danger that might come. In their spare time, they practiced shooting and throwing spears at targets and practicing how to protect themselves from enemy fire.

Emmanuel installed a tall pole in front of the mansion to which he attached a large brass bell.

If anyone saw anything to suggest danger, they were to ring the bell.

#

For two days before the coming Sunday, the sky was the topic of fearful talk.

Vesaria was used to violent blizzards in February. But there was something scary and unreal about the purple clouds overhead.

An ominous quality of bilious green and black blurred into the grape-hued layers of clouds. Bolts of lightning flashed here and there. Some of the old-timers said they could make out images in the cloud formations that closely resembled the face of Satan. Something terrible was about to happen.

The feisty Mrs. Pym, the most faithful of followers in the church also sensed something monstrous was fast approaching. She went to each member of the congregation and told them to be prepared for battle. "If you've got an axe, a rake, a rifle, be prepared to use it. I don't think I'm being overzealous. We've seen how that mountain scum up in the woods has acted before. They're just hankering to put on their bed sheets again for more trouble."

She and the other worshippers had little faith in getting the law to come to Vesaria. Since there was no one in the village who wore a badge, they had to depend on enforcement from the Asheville Sheriff's Department, seventy miles away.

#

An eerie illumination of milky emerald touched the landscape. No one in Vesaria had ever seen such a light.

As the first worshippers entered the All Souls Church that Sunday, a sharp wind suddenly began to whistle around the building. It made some of the worshipper's think of a woman's shrill scream.

Above the church, the clouds were now starting to swirl rapidly in a bizarre circular pattern, like a monstrous whirlpool, as the sky became steadily darker.

For a moment, though, church members forgot about the outside elements when they realized that the preacher's wife had finally brought in the two twin boys.

Diana DuPree glowed in a flowing dress of light pink silk with a matching wide-brimmed hat and slippers. Her little boys were asleep in their bassinette. The infants looked so tiny, yet both were unusually beautiful.

They were dressed in gowns of cashmere, with animals and fairies embroidered in the lace trim.

Beaming down at them was her husband who filled the church with his powerful virility and strength.

The small choir sang a special hymn that their preacher had written for them. As a church song, some worshippers were struck by its hint of doom:

"*For we can see only what the sun shows us,*

"*While in the shadows, our sight is dim.*"

Emmanuel Trident stepped forward.

As was customary by now, he tossed aside his white Cossack gown and flexed his incredible body. Out-of-towners were shocked beyond speech when they saw how naked he looked—except for the flimsy sarong of gold cloth that only emphasized his impressive manhood.

They were spellbound, as were the church members, by his electrifying presence. It was as if his flexing and his bulging muscles were to reassure them that he was their protector. Nothing would dare harm with such a mighty warrior standing over them.

None there would ever forget this magical moment. His lightly gold skin gleamed and rippled with each movement. He raised his muscular arms up in the air.

"I am a man!" he cried. "Look at me! I'm your Jesus Christ come to life. He never died and here I am! See my mighty power?" He struck his fists on the massive pectorals, the bulging biceps, and his flat stomach.

"But I must now speak of something serious. I hear there are strong rumors in town that there are people who want to destroy me and my family and my church. This would prove to be fatal to you, too.

"Let me say this and don't any of you ever forget it. Remember this and tell your children what I say. I promise you that starting at this very moment— if my enemies do bring harm to me and my loved ones, then the whole town of Vesaria will be destroyed! A plague of horrible proportions will wipe out every living thing here. No man, woman, child or animal will survive. Vesaria will become only a memory. It will become a ghost town that the world will avoid."

There was much stirring and whispering at these shocking words. Worshippers looked around and at each other. They became quiet as their leader continued:

"If all these rumors are false, and no one means harm to me and my family, then Vesaria will continue to flourish like never before. But should the opposite occur and evil reigns—then all of you and everything living will be dead within two weeks."

"Now, let us pray."

His words were like a machine gun shot bullets that exploded in the minds of the congregation. Some had also heard the whispers of death plots against the minister but these church members thought they were only the grumblings of the usual trouble-makers and town scum or followers of Parson Pickwick. They were always muttering and fighting and shooting at each other.

Perhaps there was something to it, though, for him to preach about them.

The minister's church members vowed to become his bodyguards. Nothing would harm him with them around. Sitting on the front row was Mrs. Pym and her three beautiful young daughters. She looked around her, nodding her head as if saying: "Okay, you heard it yourself. Get ready for battle!"

Sitting next to her on the bench were Mark and Bart—the two handsome bartenders at Polly's Little Snack Shoppe. Their expressions were grim for they, too, had heard all the rumors at the bar. They would drive home in their beat-up jalopy and grab their rifles to protect their minister.

When the services finished, the worshippers fled from the church because the sky looked even more horrifying. Tremendous black clouds swirled above and the eerie green light had become more visible. It had become twisting plumes like an army of monstrous snakes.

When Emmanuel Trident and his family arrived home, Aaron and the four other guardians raced up in their jeep.

"We heard some bad news, Reverend! We don't know how many there are but we heard those scumbags are recruiting people right now to cause some bad trouble for you and Miss Diana! They might be heading here right this minute!"

Aaron ran to the alarm bell and began to ring it over and over. The men and women from the stables and the gardens ran up to the chalet. They all grabbed their weapons and stationed themselves at the windows and doors.

"I'll call the sheriff in Asheville," said Diana.

Everyone heard her pleading with the sheriff on the phone but then she hung up and said: "I can't believe it. He said he's tied up now and will come later."

What none of them knew was that Sheriff Bailey Shortcut was first cousin to the notorious Parson Pickwick. This lecher had already described in detail to his cousin all the things he and his mob planned to do to the Tridents. For when the sheriff hung up the phone, he leaned back in his chair with a big grin and smirked to a dozen of his deputies:

"Well, it's finally gonna happen. We'll get rid of that White Nigger and her fake do-gooding preacher boy. Wish I was there."

#

"Emmanuel, take your family and get away," demanded Aaron. "We'll ride with you until you're safe. The others will stay here and protect the place."

Saying nothing, Emmanuel Trident hurried his wife into their car. Hilda, the faithful housekeeper, bundled the infants into their bassinette and jumped into the back. The vehicle was packed with weapons for such a getaway.

In the doorway of the mansion, Emmanuel shouted for everyone present: "Protect yourselves!" he shouted. 'You can run for it now or stay here. We'll be back."

"Go!" shouted one of the stablemen. "Get out before it's too late. We're staying."

Above them, tremendous clouds whirled and writhed and now a terrifying reddish glow, the color of blood, began to seep into the layers of twirling terror. The grotesque sky now became a celestial maelstrom, of steadily revolving layers of clouds.

Before the group had traveled far, they beheld a fearful sight at the steel gate that led into the drive.

A mob of dozens of white-sheeted men on horses and in trucks appeared before them at the gate. They formed a terrifying barricade.

With wild whoops and shouts, the Klansmen crashed through the metal barrier. Nearly fifty men and women and even some children were all covered in white and they headed furiously toward their victims.

A group of cars quickly surrounded Aaron and his men.

Another mob raced up to the Tridents but Emmanuel dodged them and veered to the left. Both he and Diana and Hilda were taking aim and shooting the closest Klansmen. Diana expertly knocked men off their horses with her bow and arrows. In the backseat, Hilda was also shooting at the attackers and saw them slump over in their jeep.

As the others closed in, though, she whipped out a rifle and began firing with deadly accuracy. Emmanuel Trident drove his car straight into a row of Klansmen, knocking them all from their horses with great screams.

Suddenly, several cars entered the drive and out jumped twenty or more church members. Men, women, even children brandished a few rifles and pitchforks. The children carried tree branches and rakes.

Mrs. Pym and her three daughters fired their rifles and watched two of the thugs fall from their horses. Next to them were Mark and Bart whose expert aims brought down three more of the savages.

But they and the others were instantly trapped by Klansmen, run over by cars and some of the men stopped to smash in their faces with baseball bats and machetes. Mrs. Pym and her daughters were now unrecognizable. Their faces and bodies were crushed by horse's hooves and truck wheels. The two bartenders were beheaded and mutilated.

The Tridents were outnumbered. Hilda was grabbed by her hair and one woman used her machete to scalp her. Diana whipped out her Mouria dagger and began to slice and pierce every enemy around her.

A mob of shrieking attackers dragged Emmanuel Trident out of the car and stripped off his clothes. They carried the struggling minister to a large cross that one of the Klansmen had erected on the edge of Mouria Gorge.

"Ha!" shrieked Parson Pickwick. "Here's our fine Mountain Jesus now!"

A dozen attackers dragged Diana DuPree by her hair over to a noose that was thrown over a tree limb.

"My babies!" she shrieked. "Don't hurt my little boys!"

And at that moment, the nightmarish mass of clouds parted above them and some of the attackers screamed when they saw the flaming sky staring down. It was like no sky any of them had beheld.

It was like the giant eye of God was glaring down at them.

Giant bolts of lightning began to strike everywhere.

CHAPTER THREE

A group of FBI agents sat nervously—and somewhat frightened--in Polly's Little Snack Shop on the main street of Vesaria. They barely touched their coffee and slices of apple pie.

The horrendous stench that had enveloped the village since the preacher and his sons disappeared four days before made the thought of food repulsive.

There was no one on the sidewalks of the village. Rags were stuffed around the doors and the windows to keep the nauseating smell out. The few people the agents had seen covered their mouths and nostrils with handkerchiefs and scarves. To breathe this hideous air was like sucking glue-like death into your lungs.

No one knew where the gag-inducing odor came from but it was so intense that it soaked into one's food, clothes and the very air. It oozed out of drinking water and from cups of hot coffee. Bedclothes drank in the stomach-churning aroma until people slept on bare floors.

It covered the eyeballs with a stinging layer of pain, as if it were corrosive acid. Residents were filling up the town clinic so badly that new patients were being ambulanced to Asheville and Black Mountain.

Even animals were falling over and dying. The old timers said the smell was worse than rotting flesh and cesspools from outhouses and decaying food.

Strangely, though, visitors to Vesaria were not affected. It was like a sinister hand was directing this ghastly vapor into the bodies of every villager and animal. Only they suffered with horrific boils, churning stomachs, inflamed lungs.

The agents felt like they were in the midst of some nightmarish scenario that had no basis in reality. Everything about this tragedy was so horrific that they couldn't compare it to anything they had ever investigated. It was like something out of a pulp horror magazine. Their training had certainly never prepared them for this.

The indescribable smell began the day after Emmanuel Trident and his two little boys, vanished after the massacre at Chateau DuPree.

Diana DuPree's naked body was found hanging by a noose thrown over a tree limb near her home.

Her killers had violently cut out her genitalia and tied it to her head like a horrific bonnet. Her breasts were sliced off. The killers had slit her mouth up from ear to ear to resemble a Halloween grin. Her golden hair blew in the strong winds. Her beautiful feet dangled above the mutilated corpses of her five protectors, her bodyguards, the ones known in town as the White Nig's Pussies.

They had all been beheaded. Near them were placed their heads with their male organs stuffed into their mouths. Their arms and legs were chopped off so the pile of human limbs was high.

A crude wooden cross leaned nearly to the ground not far away. Emmanuel Trident had been nailed to it—just like the crucifixion of Jesus Christ. Big nails still showed remnants of flesh where the hands and the feet were positioned.

The body had vanished, though. Did the mob have second thoughts and thrown it over the cliff?

At the crushed gate to Chateau DuPree were the bullet-ridden and slashed bodies of a dozen or more villagers who had attempted to save the Tridents. A woman known as Mrs. Pym and her three daughters had been mutilated beyond description. They were all scalped. Even the children who had bravely fought the enemy with rakes and baseball bats and even fishing poles were all trampled by horses and then run over by vehicles. All their bones were broken.

And in the stables, the dozen of prize horses were also butchered—with their eyes gouged out and their heads left lying on the ground.

Corpses of Klansmen were also scattered around the grounds, still clad in bed sheets, like store dummies. And how bizarre was it that a hellish storm that turned into a tornado had broken out, just as this attack was going on? Trees were uprooted, houses in Vesaria were destroyed, and tremendous bolts of lightning were striking all over the damned place.

Everyone agreed the sky had turned a nightmarish red of swirling clouds, just like a celestial whirlpool—as if the end of the world had finally come.

The spectacular chateau was no more.

Dynamite had reduced it to rubble. More than twenty bodies of the mansion's staff were massacred. They were all scalped, their fingers and toes chopped off, their throats slit, their eyes gouged out. All were sexually mutilated and ten were beheaded.

The celebrated flowers and garden of Chateau DuPree had been ripped up like a lunatic brat had dug up every inch of soil.

Everything reeked of sheer evil. It was like these human demons had gone completely crazy with total, blinding hatred.

The monsters had rapidly fled the scene.

They had time, though, to dynamite the All Souls Church of the Mountains.

All signs of Emmanuel Trident legacy were obliterated. All of his good work—the Social Center, the free Laundromat, the free clothes room, the food kitchen, the library, even the beautiful little movie theater-- everything was wiped out.

But where were Emmanuel Trident and the two baby boys?

"Nobody knows anything," sneered head FBI agent Timothy Snyder. "You've got a famous preacher and two children who just suddenly vanish off the face of the earth. A world famous artist like Diana DuPree is lynched and mutilated like she was a black man. And then you've got five guys who worked for her who were castrated and beheaded. And nobody knows anything!"

"Of course we *know* who did it!" snorted agent Kevin Grubb. "That gang of diseased mountain scum and a mob of Klansmen, that old pervert Parson Pickwick. And don't forget there were woman seen who were just as hellish as the men. Can you believe this?"

He and the other lawmen were from the city of Asheville, seventy miles away. To them, Vesaria was always just a dot on the map where nothing ever happened. There wasn't even a stop light here.

And now they had this big-time missing person's scandal going on. It was making headlines all over the nation because the murdered woman, Diana DuPree, was damned famous in the art world. She and her family were becoming hotly popular in the music field, too, as the religious singing group, The Tridents.

The girl's mother was a world-wide expert on the Mouria Indian cult.

Even that Yankee paper, the *New York Times*, was covering this mess. One of its headlines said it all: "Mountain Massacre: Firebrand Preacher, Artist Wife, and Sixty More Murdered!"

Part of the scandal was the shocking lack of action by the sheriff's department in Asheville. He and his men could have prevented all of this from happening.

One newspaper disclosed that Sheriff Bailey Shortcut received an urgent call the afternoon of the attack from Diana DuPree begging for help—and he had hung up with a laugh.

Another informant claimed that the despicable lawman and all of his deputies had bragged about their refusal to help out a fucking cocksucker and her fake preacher husband. In a favorite bar hangout for the sheriff and his men, one of the waitresses said the whole gang tried to outdo the other in mincing around and flipping their wrists like they were homosexuals.

Worse, it was also discovered that the sheriff was the bosom buddy of his cousin, Parson Pickwick, who was at the top of the list of suspects.

The sheriff had protested that he and his department were given a raw deal in the media. They were busy that night—investigating the rumor there was moonshine still near the city.

There was a petition going around to oust him from office and to indict him for murder. The FBI was investigating the sheriff's strange reluctance to answer the call for help.

The lawmen and the reporters had been using Polly's Little Snack Bar as their headquarters for several days and had grown fond of the owner, the red-headed Polly Parker. She didn't care if they smoked and she kept their coffee mugs filled. The shock of losing her adorable bartenders—Mark and Bart—in such a nightmarish way was too much to bear. Many of her closest friends were among those butchered near Chateau DuPree.

She herself looked worn and exhausted. Her sudden and persistent cough worried the lawmen. This is how the plague affected people.

On this dismal afternoon, she stood behind the counter and said "I want you gentlemen to hear something. The Holy man and his wife and her protectors had formed a singing group, The Tridents. They made some recordings. Here's one of them. Just listen."

She placed a big, black record on a player and there was a hissing sound and then a small musical group performed the opening chords to "Dancin' Maggie McGee!"

Everyone listened to the dazzling performance of The Tridents as they launched into the old mountain ballad

'Now listen here, and we'll let you hear

A song that you'll notice comes from here

Here's Miss Maggie, Dancing Strong,

That's all she does, All Day Long!

Dance Sweet Maggie, Yeah

Dance and dance all day...

The listeners tapped their feet and nodded their heads for it was like a brilliant ray of sunshine had entered this dark room. The voices were ebullient, excited and full of life.

When the song ended, Polly said "And now here's one that's completely different. It's my favorite. It's 'Black Is the Color of My True Loves Hair.'"

This time the voices were quieter but no less intense. The harmony was thrilling and as the bleak words were sung, the listeners realized that they were hearing the voices of the doomed. All the singers were either dead or considered so.

"Weren't they wonderful?" Polly said quietly. "It was like you were hearing Jesus and God all rolled up one group. I hope their killers die the worst way possible. The way they carved up the DuPree woman, beheading her guardians, actually crucifying that wonderful holy man—I'm glad the plague is killing them off."

She suddenly covered her face with her hands and sobbed.

The table of lawmen stirred uncomfortably. They had, indeed, interrogated a mob of suspects at the town clinic and they all looked like they were at death's door.

All men and women were yellow with a strange fever. They all coughed so much they could hardly make their denials. They spat great gobs of blood and dark brown phlegm. They were wracked by violent bowel movements. Horrible looking boils covered their bodies. Their eyes were mustard brown. And now the hospital staff were being decimated by the same disease.

Everyone in Vesaria now heard of the Holy Man's terrifying prophecy. There were no doubters anymore.It was horribly identical to the plagues one read about in the Bible.

What startled the FBI even more was that the notorious Pastor Pickwick's body was found in a hotel room in Marietta, Georgia, where he was hiding. A maid found his yellow and boil-encrusted corpse and she ran screaming—not only because of the hideous condition of the old reprobate but the horrible stench in the room.

Other mountain men—who were known to be members of the massacre—also died just a day after the bloodbath in the identical matter. Nightmarish pustules covered their bodies and their flesh turned the color of old egg yolk. Thirty or more backwoodsmen from South Carolina had also died mysteriously in hideous fashion. Their corpses emanated the terrible stench that left hospital staff and funeral home directors retching.

Before one of the suspected killers, Houston Baggett, died in the clinic, he had gasped to one of the nurses a death bed confession of what occurred during the massacre. She scribbled it down and hurried to read it over the phone to the FBI agents:

"It was a bloodbath...about sixty of us murdered them all and those bunch of goody church members that tried to help them out...twenty of us grabbed the white nigger and pulled her out of the car and she had some damned dagger that cut us all up but ole Pastor Pickwick was crazy to get to her and after we stripped her naked we discovered she really was a goddamned freak of nature...some woman grabbed the two baby boys and said, 'I'm takin'em' and God only knows where she took'em...that fuckin' Mountain Jesus—took about twenty of us to strip him naked and hammer them nails into his hands and feet...and about that time, that sky looked like blood and lightning was hitting all around us and I heard the man on the cross cry out a curse that sounded like, 'Curse them all, Mouria—make them all suffer.''

"And then the storm hit and I looked up at that man we had just nailed to the cross and who was dead and I realized that he really was the Messiah...oh, God have mercy....he really was Jesus Christ all the time...and we...we killed him... again!"

When the FBI rushed to the clinic to question the man, his tongue had slid out of his mouth like a huge maggot filled with stinking piss...his eyes bulged out of his head and he breathed no more. His boil-encrusted flesh had turned the hue of rancid butter.

By now, the plague was actually visible to the human eye. The FBI said it was a very light hue of dirty amber. It curled in the air like tendrils from an octopus.

Although a number of people moved out of Vesaria, they later died in horrible agony like those who had already passed on.

No one could escape it. Pet dogs and cats were found in yards and on sidewalks—all stiff and contorted. And the sheriff of Asheville and his deputies—who had refused to help out the Tridents—also perished within a week. The curse knew where to find its targets.

Lawmen and media people quickly got the hell out of Vesaria. For by this time, not even gas masks could keep the poison from seeping in.

After a month, the village of Vesaria was classified as a disaster area by the governor of North Carolina

#

Over the decades, articles appeared about the legacy of Diana DuPree and her tragic fate. Several TV stations in the early fifties did in-depth reporting about the mystery of Emmanuel Trident and his curse.

The recordings made by The Tridents and a newsreel of their success at the Blue Ridge Mountains Music Festival were now in much demand.

And the two baby boys? Were their corpses really moldering beneath the mountain soil? Or, was the rumor true that they may have survived and were living somewhere under different names.

The case of the missing Emmanuel Trident and his sons was never solved and this mystery became part of the folk lore of the mountains.

In history books, it was known as The Vesaria Massacre.

PART TWO

The Boys

CHAPTER ONE

"Let our television crew take you on a frightening true journey tonight, up to the highest peak in North Carolina—Mt. Mouria--and visit the sinister ghost town of Vesaria. For it was here, in 1941, that a ghastly plague struck this beautiful site. Every living thing died. This was foretold by an astonishing stranger, Emmanuel Trident, who was called the Naked Jesus for his extraordinary resemblance to Jesus Christ. He had warned his enemies that should any harm come to him or his family, then the entire village would be wiped out. This mysterious holy man was nailed to a wooden cross by members of the Ku Klux Klan. His body vanished within hours. His wife, Diana DuPree, who was rumored to be of both sexes, was lynched, his supporters were murdered and the twin sons vanished. Let us try to sift through the legend tonight and see what really occurred. You will be astonished by what we discovered."

Edward R. Murrow, *See It Now*, October 13, 1954

A week after the disappearance of Emmanuel Trident and his two infant twins, a minister and his wife in a nearby town of Fairview rejoiced in the adoption of their beautiful baby boy.

At home with the glowing infant, Edith Flores proudly showed him off to her neighbor, Beth Sizemore.

"Law me, Edith, if she isn't just the purtiest thing I've ever seen."

"It's not a *she*, Lillian! It's a boy. Here, I'll just pull his diaper down a little"

The two women had talked for over an hour about this new addition to the Flores family. Edith Flores and her husband, the Reverend Vernon Flores wanted so much to have a son but they couldn't conceive. So, the adoption agency had come through with this beautiful infant.

No, the couple had no idea where it had come from but it was certainly the prettiest baby to be found anywhere.

What was interesting was that this adorable child had a twin brother who was also there to be adopted. Yet, they looked totally different. The Flores adoptee was radiant with light, blonde hair and blue eyes. This other twin was very quiet but cute with dark hair and striking eyes of light mint.

"I couldn't adopt them both," Edith Flores now explained, "and besides there was something a little strange in the way the second boy looked at me. He—he just didn't smile like my little angel."

"He looks like a prince," grinned the visitor. "He sure doesn't look like any trailer park trash or someone raised in a back woods. Have you picked him a name?"

"His name will be Brandon Flores. Maybe people might call him Brandy but I could live with that."

"Brandon?" repeated Beth Sizemore and rolled the name around in her mouth like a piece of candy. "Why not something more boyish. Like Michael or William—"

"Brandon is his name and Brandon it will be! One day you'll see him a star baseball and football player. A champion swimmer and boxer and wrestler. Oh, he'll be the most boyish boy in town."

"How does your husband, Vernon feel about your new addition?"

"Oh, he's thrilled—I guess. He never says much because he saves it all for the Sunday sermon."

Beth said nothing for she shared most neighbors' opinion of Vernon Flores.

He was a Baptist preacher who gave the most boring sermons in town. Nobody could remember much afterwards about him or his droning, colorless addresses. He was so skinny and bland and transparent that he was like a shadow. He flitted around because his wife did all the talking and socializing.

When she was upset, everyone around her instinctively avoided her.

More than one neighbor thought she should be the preacher, and her husband a gray clerk in a department store.

Her screaming tirades against the good preacher still scandalized the neighborhood after eight years. Her vocabulary contained curse words that no one had ever heard before—the weirdest being "fuck hole."

This was, unfortunately, her favorite nasty word and her voice was so loud when she screamed it that some neighbors were horrified when their youngsters began to scream in the same tone, "Fuck Hole!"

The visitor, like most people who knew the preacher's wife, was very careful what she said to the new mother. For Edith Flores was a force of nature when she was on the war path.

Large, big-boned, a mass of dark hair was worn on top her head. When agitated, though, it came loose and flowed around her broad shoulders like a mass of black snakes. She resembled a woman wrestler or a truck driver. When the church built a new home for the Trevor's, whose home was destroyed by fire, Edith Flores was often seen picking up heavy sides of wood as if they were cardboard.

Now, the new mother pulled up the child's gown and studied his tiny male equipment. The visitor thought this was gross and realized that there was something about Edith Flores that was a little off.

She was a preacher's wife but she wore loud, garish colors in both make-up and attire and she could be incredibly crude and could be counted on to tell the most graphic, sexual joke to be heard. And she always shook with laughter after telling her joke—like she had just done the cleverest thing imaginable.

Beth got up to leave and glanced with pity at this adorable little morsel of humanity.

Would he fit into the Flores household—and with a mother who was so obsessed with having a "real boy"?

After the visitor left, Edith Flores lifted the infant's nightgown again and this time peered closely at the area behind the boy's little set of genitalia. That area was strangely glowing and pink protruded slightly. Was this normal? The examining doctor assured her there was nothing wrong. A newborn was always flushed all over in the strangest places. The mother pressed her mouth on this area and kissed it. There, that was for good luck and good health.

#

Eighteen miles away, in the mountain community of Pineville, another married couple beamed down at their newly adopted boy.

"He looks like he could be part Indian," said Myrtle Barnes to her husband, Woodrow. "Look at how his black hair just glows. And those eyes! Aren't they amazing? They're such a striking light green. He's going to be a lively little boy."

"I can see him being a boxer," nodded Woodrow "Woody" Barnes who had always wanted to be a Golden Glove boxer. "He's sturdy and strong for a three-month old."

"Wonder what happened to his parents?" Myrtle murmured. "I couldn't imagine giving up a cute little boy like him. What'll we call him?"

"I thought we'd agreed to call him Tommy. Tommy Barnes. That's a good name."

"His skin is so beautiful. A little bit olive but glowing. He came from good stock."

The twins had been found on the doorsteps of the St. Luke's Charity Home in nearby Vienna, North Carolina.

The two tots were wrapped in exquisite cashmere blankets. Their little gowns were handmade and embroidered with flowers and birds. They weren't "trash" babies as the usual ones were labeled. These were mostly from poor women who just wrapped their unwanted spawn in paper sacks or the nearest towel or pillow case they could find. It's a wonder they weren't thrown down the holes in country backhouses or trailer parks.

Where were the parents of these beautifully attired little bundles of joy? If so much time was spent making them look wonderful in their finery, then such a parent wouldn't dare leave them on the cement steps of a foster home at four o'clock in the morning.

Myrtle Barnes was a slender, neurotic woman who had fantasized of having a baby but she couldn't conceive. Her husband, Woody, was very understanding so adopting was the way they wanted to go.

He was a sweet, boyish man of twenty-eight and although a little husky, stayed in good shape since he was a forest ranger.

He had joyfully helped Myrtle create a nursery for their first child.

Their neighbors came by to see the Barnes new baby.

More than one experienced a strange experience when they gazed down at the wide, staring eyes of Tommy Barnes. They were a startling mint hue and sparkled.

He was so quiet. It was like he just knew what you were thinking.

Some neighbors wondered if Myrtle was really prepared to raise a child.

She was known to have nervous spells and had even been committed to a private sanatorium a year ago because of a mental breakdown. Many wondered what could have brought on her meltdown since her husband treated her like a princess.

He was known to regularly do the house cleaning in the morning before he headed for his job as a forest ranger. Neighbors knew that his wife spent a lot of time all day in bed, "resting," because her nerves were shot. She offered no explanation as to why her nerves were shot.

The new mother studied this new family member very intensely.

She felt nothing but horror. Her doctor and even her minister had told her bluntly that she should not have any children—either born to her or adopted. She wasn't mentally equipped to have a child.

Her extreme moods and nervousness were obvious to anyone who knew her. She would never pick up this infant. She might drop him or kill him. If it cried, then, oh, Lord what was she to do? Her hubby would have to do it all.

The other reason she insisted on adopting a child was because she hated the pitying looks of the women in her church. While they had children, she was the only one without one.

Now, she could hold her head high and smile proudly because she was now the beaming mother of a boy child named Tommy Barnes.

Suddenly, she began to weep. She couldn't control herself. She hurried back to her bed and pulled the covers over her head.

CHAPTER TWO

Eighteen Years Later, Brandon

Brandon Flores dipped his brush into the blob of red oil paint and created an eye that leered out from the white canvas like a demented sun.

That looked striking since the other orb of the face was a ghostly lavender with specks of gold.

His painting was complete now. He stood up to study it and he felt good: another bizarre mask in his series of striking visages. This one would really stand out on the wall of the Fairville National Bank which had four other paintings of his in prominent view.

Each one had rewarded the young artist with $5,000. Private art collectors had also purchased a dozen of his other striking exercises in vibrant fantasy.

I'm eighteen years old, he thought. And I've already got more than thirty thousand dollars in my bank account.

Even better he was also creating and selling cutting edge frocks that were lapped up by his women friends. They were urging him to take this new activity seriously and become a fashion designer.

He had merely sketched some designs for dresses and skirts and tops. His close friend, Kitty LaSalle and her family down the street, had taken the drawings, had a group of her lady friends to sew and create them with the ladies later strutting their stuff on the catwalk, wearing his creations, in a charity fashion show.

. A fashion editor from Charlotte had seen the exhibit and show and ran a major feature on him: *Picasso Is Alive and Well in Fairville: Meet the 18-year-old Genius!*

Now, he was thinking of how to mass produce these clothes and get them into stores.

All of this was happening so fast and he still felt dizzy at the fact that four months ago, he had been rewarded the coveted Diana DuPree Scholarship—an honor given out only once during the past twenty years.

It was strangely fitting, though, since he had been obsessed with the whole extraordinary Vesaria Massacre since he first heard about it.

The whole mystery was more exciting than any of the Nancy Drew Mysteries that he devoured. The dramatic appearance of the charismatic Emmanuel Trident...the powerful belief that he was truly Jesus Christ, returned to Earth and to clean up the village of Vesaria.

Then he met and married the extraordinary Diana DuPree who was considered a hermaphrodite, the birth of twin sons...the horror of the couple being butchered...the vanishing of both the father and the twin sons.

Perhaps, thought Brandon, I could be one of the boys. I look amazingly like Diana DuPree, judging from her pictures. The same light blonde hair, large blue eyes, and an artistic nature.

He brushed a hand over his chest. My breasts are getting bigger. They were not so large that they drew attention—but in the mirror, they were becoming slightly rounder, more plump. His nipples were unusually large and pink.

I'm more woman than man, he thought as he had countless times over the years. He felt no shame. He sensed that this extraordinary convergence of two genders in one body contributed to his artistic triumphs.

Fate has cast me into a path that can lead to spectacular success, he thought dramatically.

I was adopted in February, 1941. I had a twin brother who was taken by another family. We were both discovered on the steps of a charity hospital just hours after the Vesaria Massacre happened.

There *has* to be a connection between me and Vesaria.

#

His bedroom door flew open.

Edith Flores stood there with her fists on large hips. Her thick, dark hair was arranged in a bun with enough strands escaping to give her a disheveled look. Sweat gleamed on her large face.

"Why haven't you sat the table and started supper?" she snarled. "Your Daddy wants his supper on time. It's past five o'clock."

"I'm busy."

"Busy, my damned ass! Put away all that junk and get moving!"

Brandon didn't look up. A brush dripping with orange-gold paint created a dramatic burst of color on the face on his canvas that already resembled a circus of hues.

His mother suddenly bolted forward, grabbed a paint brush from a jar of turpentine and tried to smear it upon her step-son's canvas.

Brandon knocked her hand out of the way.

"Don't you even think of ruining my work—like you used to do," he warned her.

The woman had regained her balance. Her face flushed purple while her hands clenched and unclenched. She was preparing for battle.

Brandon recognized her expression. He removed a thick Billy club hanging above his desk and slapped it across his palm.

"You hit me and I'll hit you worse," he warned. "And then I'll call the police again."

"Goddamn you!" Mrs. Flores muttered. "It was the worst mistake we ever made when we adopted you that day instead of your brother."

"Why don't you run an ad in the paper and ask somebody to bring you a live, red-faced bully for a son. You'd like that wouldn't you? God wouldn't let you have children and he had good reason. Your living mistake here will be off to college in four weeks so then I won't have to live anymore with a woman like you. Now get out of here. I'll be down in a few minutes."

His foster mother's mouth had grown tighter. She knew now what this freak was capable of doing. She didn't want the police to come here like they did three years ago.

"Just you wait," she muttered. "God will punish you. We have a Christian house here—"

"Okay!" he shouted. "God, I'm waiting to be punished. Just get this woman out of this Christian bedroom!"

#

Before the young artist put his brushes aside, he glanced at his window which looked down on the small backyard of the house next door.

Brandon took a deep breath and felt excitement race through him.

The new neighbor was working out again.

Dick Brown and his fat wife had moved in three weeks before. He worked at the nearby furniture factory down the road. His wife, Linda, was a checkout clerk at the Piggly-Wiggly.

The handsome newcomer had begun performing his calisthenics and weightlifting in the small patch of a backyard just a few days ago. He was naked, except for a daringly brief black speedo.

Dick Brown's muscles were impressive, with large pectorals, strong arms, shoulders and legs.

Wearing his hair in a dark helmet, the man's face, as was his body, deeply tanned. His mouth, though, was small and cupid-shaped.

Now, he lay on his back on the wooden plank that served as his amateur gym. The heavy barbell he clutched rose up and down. Each time his flat stomach sank in and out. Brandon could glimpse the beginning of his pubic hair.

Just at that moment, Dick Brown looked up, saw the voyeur, and winked at him along with a grin.

Brandon fell back—surprised but thrilled.

He knew I was watching him! And he didn't mind!

#

When Brandon was fifteen, his mother demanded he join the church group to go visit the big circus in town.

"You're going or I'll wear you out with my broom," she seethed. "I'm sick and tired of you acting more like a freak homo every day. Everybody's talking about what a weirdo you are and I'm putting a stop to it."

Brandon had no doubt that this was true.

His height was only five feet five. From a distance, he resembled a beautiful little girl with whitish-blonde curls, flawless complexion and he swished when he moved. The bullies whistled at him and taunted him: "Miss Brandy, is you a girl or a boy? Tell us, pretty little Brandy?"

He hated sports, never allowed himself to get dirty, loved studying fashion magazines like *Glamour, Harper's Bazaar* and had rather play with girls than boys.

His mother was enraged.

She told him and everyone that she wanted her son to be a "real boy," to wrestle and "mix it up," and be a star of the ball field or the basketball court. Edith Flores openly jeered at his effeminacy and told her lady friends how she should buy "the freak son" lacy dresses and under panties.

Brandon remembered one incident three years ago. The church where his father preached had just let out on this Sunday noon. Edith Flores was gossiping with some friends when Brandon walked by.

"Oh, look, everybody. He's not wearing his skirt and blouse today. Why not, Miss Brandy."

Brandon went up to her and said: "I need one of your sanitary napkins, Mommies Pop. My bra's too small. Can I buy a bigger one?"

The lady friends gasped. Mrs. Flores' face turned purple.

"Just wait when I get you home."

Her beating lasted a long time. Brandon heard later neighbors had heard his screams and called the police. The callers were told there was nothing the cops could do. And besides that, Mrs. Flores was a preacher's wife.

What she or his enemies couldn't deny was that his artistic talent was outstanding. Even in the first grade he was already painting, drawing, creating fabulous gowns that he had seen in the old Technicolor movies with Betty Grable and Judy Garland.

Mrs. Flores was horrified. It wasn't normal for a "boy" to do things like drawing dresses, elaborate hair-do, painting in lipstick and mascara on his characters.

She destroyed his work and laughed about it.

Brandon began hiding his creative efforts with his neighbor, Kitty LaSalle and her handsome husband, Antonio. They were convinced he was a prodigy and would be famous someday.

The couple, along with several other families up and down the block, made Brandon their permanent baby-sitter. They rewarded him with lavish fees and with occasional treats at fancy restaurants and a visit to the movies. He was so witty and friendly that the children, in particular, loved to be around him. Even the husbands laughed at his imitations of his mother and movie stars like Bette Davis and Marilyn Monroe.

#

The church bus was filled with kids he hated and adult chaperones. The boys and girls were always jeering at him. The boys called every name they could think. Homo. Cocksucker. Sissy Britches were just a few. Lately they had added "Marilyn" to the names because as he matured, his startling resemblance to the golden-haired movie star, Marilyn Monroe, was obvious to everyone.

The boys would now wait for him in the school hallway and when he came near, they'd all unzip themselves and wave their tinklers at him, saying: "Come and get it...we know you want it, Miss Fag Ass Flores."

His step-mother loved these outings where she could joke and laugh and sing songs.

"To the circus...to the circus," she sang out, "La, la, la. Haaa, o boy are we gonna have fun today."

Wearing a green dress with big red roses, she led the group of twenty young people and adults straight to a tent that bore an enormous banner: *Freak Show*.

"We gotta go see these freaks!" she whooped. "Me wants to see the Alligator Man and…"

The tent was filled with sweaty faced fun lovers. Brandon held back. He sensed something bad was going to happen here. He knew his mother well by now. Nothing was too outrageous for her to try and torture him.

"Over there!" sang out Edith Flores. "The Man-Woman. Woo, we gotta see this thing."

On a podium sat Mary Jane, The Man-Woman. This creature was actually a petite person who wore a man's tuxedo on one half of its trim body and a woman's gown on the other. The top had been pulled down to expose a modest breast.

"Brandon, get on up here," yelled his mother. "I want you to see this thing. Somebody bring him up here."

Two of the boys roughly pushed him up to the stand where his mother stood.

"Look, Brandon," she hissed. "This is you. You're a freak and here's a freak. You're both alike. God couldn't make up his mind when he made this freak. Ha, ha, ha! Same with you."

The Man-Woman stared down at Edith Flores.

"Ma'm," she said in an unusually strong voice. "Am I hearing what I hope I'm not hearing? Are you making fun of me and your little son?"

"Oh, Lord, ha, ha, I guess I am!" brayed Edith Flores.

The Man-Woman suddenly leaped from her chair and landed straight on top of Edith Flores. The performer yanked at the trouble-maker's hair and slapped her across the fac.

Brandon's mother resembled a female wrestler as she tried to sit up, only to be knocked down again by the Man-Woman.

The barker hurried up to pull the two figures apart.

"What's happening here, Mary Ann?"

The Man-Woman calmly brushed the saw dust from her costume and mounted the stand.

"This mother insulted both me and her little boy."

"She's not my mother," Brandon aid loudly. "I'm adopted."

"Goddamn you miserable freak!" shouted Edith Flores. "I'm suing you and this fucking circus! The very idea of attacking me, a preacher's wife."

The creature looked down at Brandon and everyone was startled when she smiled down at him—and he smiled back.

"I'm glad this dirty-assed bitch isn't your mother," said Mary Ann. "You deserve a lot better than her."

"Fuck you!" roared Edith Flores. "I'll have your ass thrown into jail."

The other church members watched this drama play out with dropped jaws—certainly being entertained by something so bizarre but listening to the minister's wife talk like a truck driver.

As the circus manager explained, Edith Flores could bring suit against the big top but it would mean publicity for everyone.

"I'll think about it," fumed Edith Flores.

But after everyone went home, she got out her leather belt and began to beat and slap her outspoken son.

"You lousy freak!" she panted. "Embarassing the hell out of me!"

The minister came out of his study and watched his wife flog the poor child again.

"Hurry up with the whipping, honey. Brandon needs to start fixing us our supper."

He returned to his study where he was working on his Sunday's sermon about "How Important It Is to Love."

As Brandon lay curled up on the floor and his mother rested before she began another round of making him scream for mercy, it was like he suddenly saw himself from above.

He heard an inner voice saying: "You coward. You lay there and take it and all you do is wail and cry. You deserve it for not fighting back. You're a special person. Fight back!"

Quickly, he got to his feet and hurried out the front door with his mother hollering for him to return for more punishment.

He walked the ten blocks to the police department and asked to see Chief Turlington. He was a nice, older man who had spoken at school about the evils of drugs and drink.

He and several other officers were curious about this pretty preacher's son who had blood streaming from his mouth, nose and ears.

"My step-mother is trying to kill me," he said in a rush of words. "She's been beating me non-stop and I can't take it anymore. See? Here's scars on my arms and neck. Please help me."

The chief and his deputies were startled by what they were hearing and seeing. This kid was so beautiful—like a golden-haired choir boy.

The police chief had also felt guilty for not delving into the complaints about child abuse that the neighbors of the Flores family had been calling in for several years.

Twice the police chief did sent a deputy to check on the weird little Flores boy but Edith Flores had laughed it off and said her son was prone to nerves and nightmares. She always offered the visitors a slice of cake and coffee for their troubles. And she was the wife of a Baptist minister.

Captain Turlington put Brandon into his police car and drove to the pastor's residence. The boy was shivering and breathing rapidly.

Edith Flores grinned when she saw the police chief but glared at her son.

She denied Brandon's accusations and said he was just a nutty, spoiled brat who liked to spread lies.

"Those aren't lies," snapped Chief Turlington as he pointed out the streams of dried blood on the victim's face, throat and his white jersey. The captain warned that if Brandon reported another beating, then charges would be filed against Edith Flores for child endangerment.

She raised her arms dramatically above us and wailed: "Oh, Lord, why are you visiting me with evil lies by an ungrateful brat. Punish this evil-doer, O Lord!"

The Reverend Ed Flores also protested: "We want our son to make us proud and live a Christian life."

"Trying to beat up and murder your son's not very Christian," drawled Chief Turlington.

Outside the house, the kindly man instructed Brandon: "Come back with me to the station. I have something for you that might help you out in the future."

At the station, Brandon was given a short baton of hard wood.

"Wear this with you always—under your shirt, up your sleeve. But when someone tries to beat you, knock them in the head with this—and they'll stop bothering you. Don't be gentle. Hit'em hard."

The next afternoon after Brandon returned home from school, hands suddenly grabbed him from behind and slammed him to the floor.

"Thought you'd spread lies about me, didn't you?" hissed Mrs. Flores. She raised her foot to kick her son in the head but to her shock, he grabbed her ankle and pulled her to the floor.

He stood over her now and slammed the Billy club against her head, her face, her shoulders, and her body.

She shrieked and hobbled from the kitchen to fetch her husband.

He came out of his study with his pipe in hand.

"What's the meaning of this, son?"

"Knock the hell out of him, goddamn it!" shrieked his wife.

"You'll never use me for a punching bag anymore," Brandon spat and tapped the club up and down on the palm of his hand. "You try it again and I'll beat the holy shit out of you."

He had squared his shoulders. Some invisible force was guiding him along. He could feel strong hands on his shoulders and he was sure his guardian had whispered: "Great! Keep it up! Never let them touch you again!"

And from then on, his mother didn't beat him up—although her put-downs were vicious. Brandon ignored her.

And now, he thought, in four weeks, he would be out of Fairville and enjoying a new life at Blackwood Institute.

#

Beside his bed, he had taped a copy of the last photograph taken of Emmanuel Trident and his wife. He was naked, except for a swath of gleaming silk that barely hid his manhood. This "Mountain Jesus" was a powerful, muscular figure, with enormous pectorals, arms and legs that made him resemble Superman.

Diana DuPree shimmered with silver and ivory. Her gleaming mane of hair was a light blonde, almost white. She was often described in articles and books as resembling a gorgeous movie star. Her gown was designed in the Grecian fashion and it may have hidden her physical abnormalities: The sexual organs of both male and female.

She was shown with her twin sons in her arms. Their features were obscured by a lace blanket. Husband and wife stared out, smiling, only a day before they were slaughtered.

Perhaps I'm one of those twin boys, the young artist thought many times. He, too, looked feminine, with light, gold hair and a girlish way of walking and acting.

His breasts had grown more prominent and his lips full and beautifully formed. I'm going to be a woman someday, he thought, because he read the newspaper articles about Christine Jorgenson, a man who had undergone surgery to become a man.

In one of Brandon's favorite books, *Great Unsolved Mysteries*, a whole chapter had been devoted to the Vesaria Massacre.

"What happened in Vesaria on February 21, 1941, is still so incredible that even today, societies and cults and considerable scholarship have expended much energy in trying to separate fact from fantasy.

"What startles us today is that nearly everyone in the mountains were convinced that Emmanuel Trident really was Jesus Christ. These believers included regular mountain people, lawyers, judges, professor's even scientists. He was an exact replica of the Messiah with a mane of dark hair, beard and moustache, luminous light green eyes and a blazing radiance that exuded from him to those around him.

"So we have to seriously ask the question today: Was this really the Christ—who returned to bring peace to a dark place—only to die again? The noted anthropologist, Norma DuPree, the mother of the murdered Diana DuPree, wrote extensively that she was convinced that the powerful priests of Mouria still slept in suspended animation in one of the hidden caverns that dot the face of the Mouria Gorge."

#

Dick Brown and his wife were invited for supper at the pastor's home next door.

Brandon prepared the menu: meat loaf, mashed potatoes, corn and lima beans and for dessert, a lime cream pie.

Afterwards, everyone sat on the screened porch and chatted.

Brandon tried not to visually rape the handsome Dick who wore unusually short shorts and a white tee shirt. His muscular torso was showcased while his wife, Linda, resembled a piglet, thought Brandon.

"That was a real nice meal you fixed, Brandon," nodded Dick Brown. "Not many boys know how to cook."

"He might can cook," cut in Edith Flores, "but he can't play sports or wrestle or do all the things a real boy does. He's a sissy."

"Ha, ha," retorted Brandon "I'm a sissy whose earning my own money with my paintings and fashion designs and who also won a four-year scholarship, all expenses paid, to Blackwood Institute."

"You don't say," Dick Brown said. "I didn't know we were living next door to an outstanding artist."

"Don't make him feel special," snorted Mrs. Flores. "He's conceited enough. I should make him some dresses to take along to college. He's sissy enough."

"Oh, please do, Mommie!" mocked Brandon. "And don't forget my garter belt, my padded bra and my Kotex. I need some silk pink panties for school so my boyfriends will like them."

Linda Brown gasped while her husband burst out laughing.

"Woo, you are funny," snickered Dick Brown. "You got some paintings you could show us?"

"Sure," smiled Brandon and jumped to his feet. "Let's go upstairs to my studio."

#

When they came to Brandon's bedroom, they paused while the occupant took out a key from his pocket to use on the padlock.

"You lock your door?" asked Linda Brown.

"Oh, yes. I had to. Because someone kept sneaking in and tearing up my work. So, I was forced to buy me a lock."

"He's full of shit," muttered Mrs. Flores.

The bedroom was small, hot but packed with many oil paintings and boxes of brushes, tubes of color, crayons and charcoal pens. In the corner, an electric sewing machine was covered with a stack of dresses. Several of them hung on hangars. They were all wheat colored with colorful jolts of color.

"Wow!" gasped Dick Brown. "You really are a busy artist."

"Weird, too," muttered his wife. "I don't think I'd want these on my walls."

The artwork emphasized faces of all shapes and designs and colors. All possessed bizarre eyes that were slanted, closed, bulging. An orb that resembled an explosion of tangerine and strawberry might look sideways. A mouth would be opened in a scream. Hair was a thick mane of rainbow colors that might turn into serpents.

One large ink and charcoal picture stood out. A creature was depicted with the left side the nude image of a man. The right side revealed a nude female. The face was a blob of umber and gray.

"What the hell is that filthy thing?" muttered Edith Flores. "I'm getting rid of it."

She reached to tear it from the wall but Brandon knocked her hand away.

"Don't touch it!" he demanded. "That's the deity of Mouria that Emmanuel Trident worshipped. It stays there."

"Goddamn homo!" hissed Edith Flores before stomping out of the room. She was followed by Linda Brown and the pastor.

Brandon sensed that his next door neighbor was standing very close. And then a strong hand tightened on his shoulder.

"I'm glad you can dish it back like that," the man said softly. Brandon turned to look up at him.

"I work out a little each afternoon," smiled Dick. "Would you like to join me? I'm used to having company when I exercise. I could show you a few moves."

#

"Ready to make some muscles?"

"I'm your eager pupil. Let's go."

They were alone in the small backyard of the Browns.

Dick said his wife worked until four p.m. at the Piggly Wiggly.

Brandon's step-parents were spending the afternoon visiting some nearby nursing homes and to study the Bible with the residents.

Above the man and the youth, the sky was a deep, smoky blue with giant billows of clouds.

Brandon had chosen his outfit carefully. His top was lavender with white poodles all of which he had made himself. His shorts were a snug white and his sandals came from Rose's Five and Dime Store.

His mentor was a sultry sight. Dick Brown was nearly nude except for his black briefs.

Brandon had never been so close to a man who was so unclothed and so handsome. His fantasies of lust were those he saw in bathing suit ads or in the movie magazines. He had watched Tarzan and Bomba movies and drooled over all that exposed flesh of male beauties.

And now, he was actually in the close, sweaty company of a flesh-baring male.

"Now watch me work on my arms and stomach," said Dick Brown.

Laying back on the wooden plank, he lifted a barbell up and down. Brandon studied intensely the way the chiseled stomach moved, how the large pectorals swelled up and how the low-cut speedo moved so close to that forbidden area of a man's body. Less than an inch lower, Dick Brown's male organ would be glimpsed.

As they worked together on several more exercises, Brandon had a chance of studying his neighbor more closely. His eyes were a watery blue with heavy lids. His mouth was small and heart-shaped. Dick Brown had only a few teeth: they were located at the front so that his cheeks appeared sunken.

These were not weaknesses for Brandon. They enhanced his appeal as a strong, virile man who did hard labor at the furniture factory and his muscles were needed for his labors.

"Let's go into the house for something cold to drink," gasped Dick Brown as he dropped the heavy barbell to the ground.

Inside the kitchen the young artist was startled at how drab it seemed. There was nothing there except for a plastic table and two plastic chairs. Garbage was piled high in the corner with much of it flowing onto the floor. Coffee grounds and egg shells and orange peel looked as if they had lain there for a long time.

On the counter cockroaches raced everywhere.

"What are we drinking today?" asked the host. On the table were several packages of Kool-Aid. A small scrap of paper was taped above each one with the name of the day spelled out.

"It's Raspberry Day! See, Brandon, for each day of the week, I drink a different flavor. I've got Lime and Orange and Cherry—and it's real cheap, too. Two packages for twenty-five cents."

He went to the refrigerator and withdrew a white plastic pitcher and poured the red beverage into two large purple glasses.

"Mm, I loves my Kool-Aid," sighed Dick Brown. "Mm, good!"

He said he needed to shower but Brandon could look at Dick's scrapbooks in the meantime.

The den was dank and dark. A sheet hung over the two small front windows. On the coffee table lay a thick scrapbook. It contained numerous photos of Dick Brown's physique modeling in various contests.

"I'll be out in a jiffy," he said and vanished into the bathroom.

Brandon was excited to see his neighbor, again nearly naked, in his small bikini briefs, while his well-oiled torso rippled for the cameras. Dick Brown's hair was thicker and curlier and he sported a moustache in some of the images.

"How you like those pics?"

Dick Brown had trotted out of the shower. He wore just a white towel around his waist. He sat next to his visitor, his still moist body pressed up close to him.

"That's me in Hogansville, Georgia, a year ago," Dick Brown explained eagerly as he pointed to himself in a red brief and grinning at the camera. A blonde woman with large boobs was shown squeezing his biceps.

"You look amazing, Dick" nodded Brandon.

"Well, gotta get ready for work," the muscular man said. "One day you could look like that, if you'd work at it."

"Not me," Brandon replied. "That's for real he-men like yourself. You'll find me in the audience as a body worshipper."

"Hm?" Dick smiled. "Oh, I see what you mean. Ha, ha, at least you're honest son. Guys like me need pretty boys like you. You're an artist."

#

That Sunday, Brandon sat in the small choir of the Fairville Baptist Church as he had done since he was eight.

His father was preacher there but his foster son had long ago tuned him out when it came to sermonizing.

It was always the same. Everybody was a sinner and so everybody was going to hell unless they did all these things to please an invisible deity named God.

On this occasion, though, the budding atheist had perked up to listen to that morning's sermon.

A young, handsome ministerial student, Brock Adams from Wake Forest College, was the visiting speaker. With a shock of dark hair, a strong voice and a trim torso, he was a welcome change from the gray, monotonous Reverend Ed Flores.

"I've been thinking of the Vesaria Massacre for a long time," he began, which instantly caught Brandon's attention. "We all know that a strange man name Emmanuel Trident appeared in Vesaria one afternoon. Written accounts describe him as looking—and acting—like our Jesus Christ. He's remembered as exuding a dazzling radiance. He did good there but the dark forces took over. He was actually crucified, his wife lynched, his two little boys vanished. A plague devastated the village with everyone dying.

I'm not describing a fantasy. These events can be found in countless books. Scholars have written about it.

"But if he were to return again today, right here, how would you know? He could well be disguised, yet he would be different enough, in a positive way, that you sensed he must be of an extraordinary birth. He could be the new trash collector, your new next door neighbor, the man who fills up your gas tank or repairs your TV. You might just go up to him and ask: 'Are you the one?' It's that easy. Are you the one, is the question that he would answer truthfully."

#

A resurrected Jesus Christ could be anyone!

Your TV repairman…your next door neighbor.

What if Dick Brown—could be the Messiah in disguise? Brandon knew this was ludicrous but the artist loved to fantasize incredible backstories for people who interested him.

I'm going to ask Dick Brown point blank one day: "Are *you* the one?"

CHAPTER THREE

The next few days were busy ones for Brandon.

He presented his three original paintings to the president of the Fairville First Bank in a ceremony that was covered by the local media.

Fairville's Art Prodigy
Sells Three Paintings

— By Janice Hickman

"France had its own Picasso but the city of Fairville has an artist even better. And that's the talented, eighteen-year-old Brandon Flores.

"In a ceremony yesterday at Fairville National Bank, its president, Robert Metcalfe, presented the prolific young prodigy with a check for $30,000 for the trio of striking paintings that show the artist's trade-mark faces.

"We here at the bank believe we have made a wonderful investment by an outstanding artist who will become famous someday soon," the bank president told the illustrious crowd.

"On the same afternoon, a fashion exhibit was held at the Fairview Country Club that displayed some of the young artist's original clothing designs. He said his women friends in his neighborhood helped put his creations together.

"A parade of striking dresses impressed the packed ballroom. All twenty originals were sold. They were priced at one hundred dollars each and the creator said designing fashions will be a strong part of his repertoire in the future, including his artwork. There was a strong demand from everyone present for more original fashions.

"Brandon won the much coveted Diana DuPree Scholarship. His expenses during his four years at Blackwood Institute will be completely covered.

"Brandon said he felt a powerful connection with the tragic Diana DuPree. He told this reporter that he hopes to make the late artist and philanthropist proud of what he hopes to accomplish in the future."

#

The local TV station also showcased the art prodigy by running a flattering interview and visit with Brandon later that week.

He was shown in his bedroom working on several canvases and also at his electric sewing machine as he created his own design of women dresses.

"Not many young men your age are interested in these artistic endeavors," the male reporter pointed out. "You've probably had some bullying among your classmates for doing this and not playing sports."

"Of course," shrugged Brandon. "But I don't allow peer pressure or opinion bother me. I'm doing what I like to do. I'm going to be a big name one day in the future. I don't think you'll hear anything about these boys who make fun of me."

#

Before he went to bed at night, Brandon enjoyed working on his portrait of Dick Brown.

He was shown naked, with greatly exaggerated genitalia. The artist now added long, dark hair, a moustache and beard.

"He could well be The One," thought Brandon. "I'm going to ask him point blank and see how he reacts.

#

He received an impressive letter that week from a Bruce Jasmine, a famous agent who represented several big names in the fields of music and art. His office was in Asheville, North Carolina where he headed the prestigious Jasmine Associates that had a sixteen member staff.

"I just read a wire story about your accomplishments and if you're interested, I think it would benefit both of us if we could get together and chat about your future. I could represent you in the fields of art, sculpture and especially fashion. I think you're on your way to becoming a phenomenal talent in the art and fashion worlds. I'll be contacting you again after you've settled into life at Blackwood Institute."

A business card with a photo imprinted on it was enclosed and presented the handsome image of Bruce Jasmine. A mop of ginger curls framed a macho, intense face with dark eyes.

Brandon biked to the library where his dear friend, Amanda, the head librarian, helped him research Jasmine and Associates.

What they found made them both smile, Young Bruce was a multi-millionaire who lived in a beautifully restored Victorian mansion in Asheville. It was staffed by a dozen servants.

Several photos showed him bare-chested as he boxed "for fun," kayaked in white rapids, raced his motorbike over the sands of the Kalahari Desert, and in one startling image, he posed with a group of Amazon natives as they all held up a monster anaconda.

The shot that Brandon zoomed in on was a naked Bruce, who wore just a brief bikini, enjoying cocktails at the last Cannes Film Festival in Italy. Dark shades hid his eyes and he held his drink up to the camera—while all around him were scantily clad starlets.

Bruce Jasmine handled some of the brightest stars in the art and fashion worlds.

There was Jamara Toccobi, the Argentina artist and sculptor, whose minimalist fashion and sculpture decorated the homes of the super-rich. Teddy Boy and the Scandals, the red hot boy band from Great Britain, whose daring experiments in pop and rhythm and blues was revolutionizing the music world.

Chobowa, the Oriental man, whose nude dancing galvanized Broadway crowds every night.

Amanda hugged her friend.

"Oh if you get this Bruce Jasmine behind you now, at the beginning, it's no telling how far you'll go. The stars are aligned for great fortune and recognition."

"I'm being guided by two spirits," Brandon nodded. "I feel like they're with me at all times."

#

"Too hot for anymore exercise," Dick Brown said. "Let's get out of the sun."

He wiped a towel over his chest and nipples and slid it down beneath the waistband of his black briefs. Whenever he did these things, his eyes were always focused intently on his young admirer. A curious half-smile touched his cupid-shaped mouth.

Both of Brandon's parents were at the church where the "Christian Kiddie Summer Program" was ending.

If possible, more bags of rotting garbage had fallen onto the floor near the sink. More cockroaches scurried around the counters. Dick Brown appeared oblivious to these repulsive conditions as he poured orange Kool-Aid into tall plastic glasses.

He had picked two tomatoes from a basket on the floor and without washing them off, bit hungrily into them. Juice and matter burst upon his chin and chest. He let the crimson wetness remain on his skin without drying it away.

"Wanna see some pictures I just added to the album? You can look at 'em while I shower."

Brandon heard his host splashing in the shower while humming a tune. The den looked starker than before. There was only a sofa covered with plastic and the cheap coffee table. On the wall was a dime store picture of a Parisian café, with figures sitting around the tables.

The small living room was stuffy and hot to a suffocating degree. No air came from the locked windows behind the bed sheet. Brandon's fresh outfit of purple jersey and black shorts quickly clung wetly to his body. He smelt the rotting food from the kitchen and wasn't surprised to see a rat dart behind the sofa.

The scrapbook revealed more images of Dick Brown wearing nothing more than a big grin and a sliver of nylon to hide his male essentials.

"How you like them apples, huh? Huh?"

Dick Brown stood right above his guest, wearing only a towel. His crotch was just a few inches from Brandon's face.

"You always look amazing, Dick."

The host held two large tomatoes in his hand.

He pulled a plastic chair across the room so that he sat opposite his guest.

"Ever see any bigger than these?" he asked in a quiet, whispery tone.

He had placed the red vegetables between his thighs and right up against his privates beneath the towel.

"See how big and juicy they look? Want to taste them, little boy? They can be yours if you work hard for them."

Brandon trembled at this sudden revelation of his neighbor. So far it had been just an older man showing a younger male how to exercise.

Now, the pattern had dramatically changed.

"What—what do I have to do?" murmured Brandon.

Dick ran fingers over the scarlet globes and glanced up under his brows: "Crawl over here on your hands and knees and maybe I'll let you enjoy them."

"Crawl over--?"

"Do it now, honey, or you'll not be getting God's gift to women."

It was like an oven had been turned on because now the intense heat was almost painful. Brandon had to wipe the sweat from his eyes before he fell to his knees and slithered toward this prize that he had fantasized about. A big naked man, giving the dreamer his torso.

"Act like you really want these two big balls of happiness. Sound like a pig. Make pig noises. Oink. Oink."

"Oink," repeated Brandon as he crawled nearer to the prize. Then he blurted aloud: "Are you the one?"

The host blinked his eyes slowly. "Am I—the one? Shit yeah—to my wife, I'm the only one."

Brandon was now at the knees of his dream lover. The two tomatoes hid the human goodies that only Dick Brown possessed.

"Don't use your hands to touch 'em," commanded the host. "Just use your mouth. Now chow down, boy!"

With two warm thighs on either side of his face, Brandon chomped down on a tomato. Juice exploded onto his face. He pushed his face further, for the ultimate prize but the owner covered that with his fingers.

"Just one more 'mater to go and you'll be home free. You'll finally have that stuff I know you been dreaming about. I seen your look. Can't fool me. You want ole Dick Brown in the worst way. I seen you jus' eating me up with your eyes. Lots of people do that. It's okay. I don't mind. I gives them what they want."

Once more, the youth tore up the other vegetable with his teeth, so that his face was splashed with wet pulp and juice.

"You're nearly there!' chortled Dick Brown. "Just another inch...another inch...and you'll see why they call me a sperm bull."

Brandon trembled as his mouth pushed hard against Dick Brown's fingers when suddenly...

"Opps, gotta get ready for work!"

Dick Brown jumped up and stared down at the figure who was still on his knees.

"You'd better clean up all that 'mater stuff from your face and get on home now, son."

Brandon didn't move. He suddenly saw Dick Brown for the sadist that he was. A veil had lifted and with it the illusion Brandon had spun about his fantasy god.

He wasn't handsome and his face was pinched and drawn. When he smiled, he only had a few teeth in front. His muscles all looked fake and artificial. The thin lips of that heart-shaped little mouth were now stretched upward into a big smirk.

"You bastard!" hissed Brandon as he got to his feet and used his shirt to dry off the red juice and pulp from his face. "You *tricked* me! You sonofabitch!"

"Hey now, let's not throw a hissy fit. It was just a game, see? That's all it was. You're a sissy boy and it's pretty clear what you wanted all along and I promised your Mama..."

"Oh, good God! So she was in on this, that dirty assed bitch."

He moved closer to his tormentor: "From this day on, you're cursed Dick Brown. Within four weeks, you'll see what I mean. You're cursed—now go to hell. And you're gonna die real soon!"

A flicker of uneasiness crossed Dick Brown's face. "Say now, let's calm down a little. Here, you wanna squeeze my balls, go ahead. I won't tell your Mama."

He dropped his towel and cupped his testicles like they were prize jewels.

"Take your balls and drop dead, Dick Brown. And you'll be dead very, very soon."

#

Brandon silently moved to the Brown house where a light shone in their bedroom window. The darkness was thick and sultry. His parents were watching *The Ed Sullivan Show* on television.

Several times before, he had made this clandestine trip but a sheet always hung over the window and he could see nothing.

Tonight, though, a corner of the sheet had caught on something so that the voyeur could clearly see the interior of the bedroom. A thick crepe myrtle bush also formed a barrier for the voyeur to hide behind.

Like the rest of the house, the chamber was barely furnished.

There was a bed, covered with dull looking sheets. A naked bulb hung above. A large bushel of vegetables stood against the wall. A cardboard box served as a nightstand. Used Kleenex and a bottle lotion covered the top.

Linda Brown suddenly entered the room.

Her flab was barely contained in a bra and see-through nylon panties. Her head glistened with rows of metal curlers. Brandon wondered why she used curlers. Every time he glimpsed the woman her hair was like a dull greasy rug that hung down her back.

With a tall can of beer in one hand, a long cigarette held between her fingers on the other, she plopped down on the bed. A belch made her stick her tongue out.

And then appeared her better half—only this was a Dick Brown no one in town had ever seen.

A woman's bra was stretched across his chest. Lipstick was smeared over his lips and purple mascara around his eyes. He resembled a monster from a cheap horror movie.

"You are cursed!" he trilled and plopped down beside his wife. "I curse you Dick Brown! You'll be dead in four weeks."

"Ha!" whooped Linda Brown. "I'd love to have seen that fag on the floor and dying to squeeze your nuts."

"That poor little cocksucker was just shaking all over because he thought I was going to let him suck me. I woulda broken the queer's fuckin' neck if he'd tried to."

Brandon shuddered as he heard himself described by these two giggling low life's. He refused to leave, though. *I'll learn from this. These dregs will teach me a valuable lesson of how brutal people can be.*

The wife had put her beer and cigarette aside and now she moved so that she lay supine before her husband. Her face rested in his lap while her fat ass greeted the young peeping tom.

Her head bobbed up and down. Dick Brown's mouth opened into a black hole. He stuck his tongue out and wriggled it. His wife placed two large tomatoes between his thighs—just the way her husband had positioned them for the hidden on-looker earlier that day.

The woman's face worked furiously over the vegetables. She raised her head briefly to glance up at her husband's face. Her's resembled the victim of a terrible car wreck. Crimson pulp and juice covered her features, glistened in her hair and on the metal curlers.

She resumed her frantic gobbling only this time her spouse groaned: "Eh, Linda, slow it down a little...you...you're biting me too hard...too hard, I told you...those metal curlers are cutting into me...Linda...I...Oh, God!"

His scream made both his wife and the watcher jump.

"You—you fuckin' bitch—you—you cut my balls! Where's my balls! You goddamn bitch—my balls are gone!"

"Wha—what--?" babbled his wife. Her eyes bulged white against the scarlet mask of tomato remnants. Brandon had to clamp hands over his mouth so they wouldn't hear him howling. The woman looked like a fat clown in a black Minstrel show.

Dick Brown stood up on the bed, clutching his crotch with both hands. His lower torso was doused in red. Tomato pulp and blood dripped thickly from his genitalia area.

"They're gone!" he screeched. "You chewed my fuckin balls off, you bitch!"

"No, no," gurgled his wife. Her hands dived into the pulpy red mass on the bed. "No, that can't be!"

"Gone!" cried Dick Brown as he kept staring at the area of his body where his testicles had once hung.

Now there was nothing there.

#

For the next two weeks, Brandon could barely repress hysterical laughter as neighbors discussed the tragedy of Dick Brown.

He had been rushed to the emergency room where it was discovered that he had somehow slashed a main artery and had lost a tremendous amount of blood. Taken to the nearby town of Pineville, he had nearly died. Then peritonitis set in and his condition worsened.

His wife described how her dear husband had slashed himself by accident with a pair of new gardening shears. Since two of the main nurses at the hospital were from the patient's home town, they quickly learned the truth. It quickly spread over Fairville.

When Dick Brown returned home, his fellow workers and church members visited him with magazines and food.

Brandon refused to set foot in the Brown residence at first. On the third day, however, the young artist agreed to accompany his parents to pay their condolences.

The former body builder's bedroom was filled with the former workers of Dick Brown from the furniture factory. Some of Linda Brown's co-employees at the grocery store were there, too.

Even Brandon was shocked at the drastic transformation of the strutting peacock to this cavernous looking creature who lay in his bed.

A dramatic loss of weight had caved in his cheeks so that his eyes bulged out. His facial skin was pulled back so dramatically that the tip of his gray tongue protruded between the thin lips. They resembled those of a lizard.

His muscular torso now looked thin and spindly in the striped, cotton pajamas.

He smiled weakly as the Reverend Flores and his wife stooped over him to wish him well.

The room fell silent when that weirdo artsy kid, Brandon Flores, appeared, dressed all in black, like he was attending a funeral. His amber-hued hair, his gold and pink coloring set him apart from the care-worn faces of the others. His jet outfit also contrasted to their jeans and flannel shirts and hunting hats worn by the others.

The patient's wife, Linda, who sat in a chair against the wall, made a snorting sound of derision when she saw him. She looked at the other visitors and shook her head, as if saying: "Can you believe this queer?"

"Hello, artist!" Dick Brown murmured. "Wondered why you haven't been over."

"Really, Mr. Brown? *Really*? I've brought you something that I hope will make you feel better."

From a paper sack, he withdrew two large tomatoes. He placed one on either side of the invalid's hips.

"There—don't they look round and juicy—the kind every red-blooded man or woman would want! Yes, even God's gift to women!"

"What the hell?" muttered Linda Brown?

"You—you brought me 'maters?" gasped Dick Brown. "Why?"

"Just what are you up to?" queried Edith Flores.

"Oink! Oink! Mmm, sooo good!" Brandon laughed.

Brandon turned and left the room. Behind him he heard Linda Brown cursing him: "That goddamned freak."

Brandon also heard Dick Brown say to the Reverend Flores: "Mr. Preacher Man, can you remove a curse?"

#

One week later, a pickup truck parked in front of the Brown's house. The few furnishings were brought out and packed up in the vehicle. Linda

Brown said she and her sickly husband were moving in with her grandmother in a small farmhouse in South Carolina.

Later, Brandon heard his former heart-throb had died of peritonitis. He told his relatives he had been cursed by someone but he wouldn't explain why he had been chosen for this terrible fate.

#

Twenty or more people gathered around Brandon on a windy afternoon in late August as he prepared to leave for college.

They had been his neighbors for eighteen years. They had all befriended him as they knew only too well the hell he experienced while living at the parsonage.

They had brought him beautiful sweaters, toiletries, a coffee maker, an electric clock, all the things he might need in his dorm room.

The children he had babysat so many times had made him paintings and sketches. His women friends presented him with tins of cookies and cake and candies.

They were convinced that he was going to be famous one day. Some of the women had regularly treated him to a hot meal when life with his stepmother became intolerable. They had remembered his birthday, gave him big bonuses along with a regular check for babysitting the kids. Their genuine affection for him helped him survive nightmarish days in the Flores parsonage.

Kitty LaSalle and her good-looking husband and three teenage children all embraced him with tears flowing in abundance.

"You're going to the top," smiled the pretty sandy-haired Kitty. "Don't forget us old fogies."

Her husband, Antonio, also squeezed Brandon close to his hard body.

"You're like our own son," he smiled. "Anytime you want to come back home, you can stay with us."

As Brandon prepared to get into the car, Edith Flores came out of the house. She had avoided the festivity surrounding her unwanted step-child but now she had decided to do the motherly thing. She was one happy woman—to finally rid her life of this sissy freak.

Everyone fell silent as they watched the preacher's wife approach her step-son with a big grin on her face.

. Jiggling her shoulders and batting her eyes comically she grinned: "Well, ain't cha gonna give your own Mommie a farewell hug? Huh? Huh?"

She stuck her face close to his, pooched out her lips and closed her eyes. To show her neighbors how witty she was, she shook her ass, too.

"Sure Mommie. Here ya go!"

Edith Flores wasn't prepared for the powerful slap that sent her reeling backwards. She fell so hard to the ground that her skirt flew up and everyone saw she wore piss-stained white drawers.

The car driven by Reverend Flores was already pulling away by the time she got to her feet. She chased the vehicle a little way before she wheeled upon the neighbors and screeched: "Did'ja see that? That ungrateful cocksucker knocked his own mother down! And none of you lifted a hand to help me!"

The crowd moved away and went to their homes where they could discuss with relish the dramatic kiss-off to his hated mother from a radiant young prince who would be famous one day.

#

Brandon barely heard his father's weak "Good luck, son."

This dull man had been a piece of furniture in the house that no one remembered. He barely spoke and wanted to be alone while he smoked his cigars and read the daily newspaper.

Brandon was supposed to catch the twelve-forty express train to Blackwood Institute.

As he gathered his luggage and hurried to the platform, one of his boxes fell to the ground.

Before he could stoop to pick it up, a powerful young man handed it to him. Brandon looked up into a pair of stunning eyes of luminous light green. Thick dark lashes surrounded these beautiful orbs.

"Oh, thank you, thank you," Brandon said.

Brandon couldn't move for a moment. This stranger was like an extraordinary young giant with a trimmed beard and moustache. He resembled a radiant Jesus Christ.

"Glad to help you out," replied Tommy Barnes.

He felt an electrical jolt as he stared down into the sparkling blue eyes of Brandon Flores. Had they met somewhere before?

They parted—with Brandon hurrying to board his train, and Tommy Barnes heading toward the end of the platform where he and thirty other Army recruits would be bussed to boot camp.

CHAPTER FOUR

Tommy

Tommy Barnes was a superstar at Pineville High School. He stood out from the other mountain boys like Goliath among David. He was Hollywood handsome, thought girls and women, and his jet-black curls framed a face both beautiful and rugged. His features were those of a mature man with a five o'clock shadow darkening his chin and upper lip. No matter how closely he shaved, his stubble appeared by two in the afternoon.

Most striking were the sparking eyes of a glistening emerald, filtered through sparkling water. Thick lashes of jet surrounded these stunning orbs. Girls would stop him in the hallway and politely ask: "Tommy, can we see your eyes?" And Tommy would comply sweetly as he stood and listened to his admirers who would say: "Unbelievable! Tommy they're so beautiful—like you." He never joked about this or snickered. The other guys dared not tease him about it, either.

His powerful, young body astonished with its amazing muscles, strong arms and back and he moved with a beautiful gait. At home, his trophies from weight-lifting competitions across the South crowded two shelves.

Everyone knew, too, that he was adopted and that his foster mother spent most of her time in bed. She complained of "nerves" and her husband coddled her as if she were a big baby.

The neighborhood gossip, though, suggested she was frightened of her foster son. His largeness suggested dominance, so it was said. Myrtle Barnes confided to one relative that she wished she and her husband had never adopted Tommy Barnes. They should have chosen the blonde twin.

The attitude of his foster parents never seemed to bother Tommy. He went his own way, was sweet and friendly to all others. He mowed the lawn of neighbors for free, went grocery shopping for four of the invalid residents down the street and would not hear of being "tipped" or given money. As an Eagle Scout, he was the role model for those scouts below them. He gave them good advice. They confided in him their most secret thoughts. They saw him not as an eighteen-year-old muscle god. He was quiet, wise and strong.

It was so strange to see him now and remember that for several years he was the fattest boy in town.

#

As a child, he grew his own garden because, "I want to have lots of food that's good for you and doesn't cost anything for my parents."

His garden was recognized as an outstanding success. His parents were surprised, too, because now they had an over-abundance of beautiful tomatoes, squash, corn, potatoes, onion, and okra, in addition to watermelon and honey dew melons. The amateur farmer was seen eating these home-grown goodies like they were popcorn.

He waddled around the small town like a moving blimp. Mean kids called him Fatso. Elephant Boy. Big Boy.

And then, all those layers of fat gradually vanished. Tommy began to exercise each day, began to run, to work out with barbells and weights in the school's' gym. To everyone's astonishment, he had become big, beautiful and extraordinary.

His glossy dark curls touched his massive shoulders.

And that face! More than one thought how much he resembled the pictures of Jesus Christ.

If he grew a moustache and beard, the comparison would be astounding.

But it was the body that fascinated everyone. No student at Pineville High had ever had such a magnificent physique.

His pectorals were enormous. They bulged out like twin pillows and each was capped with a thick nipple. His waist was trim, his arms outstanding. Yet, Tommy refused to follow a routine where the veins stood out and his torso became "shredded."

He developed a natural looking physique that looked as if he had just evolved from working hard on a farm. Still, what he had made heads turn whenever he passed by.

When his drama class planned to stage the drama, *Olden Gods*, Tommy Barnes was cast in the major role of Jupiter. Since there was no budget for costumes, the cast was asked to whip up their own creations using bed sheets.

On the first night, Tommy refused to let anyone see what he wore behind stage. An over-sized robe covered his torso.

When the curtains parted, however, and Tommy was spotlighted as he stood alone at the top of a staircase, the audience gasped—then applauded.

He was naked except for a very brief sarong that barely covered his manhood. His beautifully oiled body rippled with power, with astonishing muscles and in classical proportions. His shoulder-length hair, his trimmed beard and moustache made everyone think of one figure: Jesus Christ.

When his admirers told him of this comparison, he was pleased. He was known to carry a small portrait of Jesus Christ in his wallet. This experience of being admired by an audience was a powerful one for the youth. It was like, he thought, I've done this all before—many times—

appearing naked before a crowd of admirers and I preached to them—but what did I preach?

Everyone in school knew that he was religious—but they weren't exactly sure in what way.

As a child, he had attended every sermon at the Pineville Methodist Church. He sang in the choir and when he was asked to sing solo, he amazed both himself and the worshippers with a beautiful, intense voice. He remembered with delight how the words—and the music—just seemed to come forth from his throat.

His vocalizing proved another reason why he had become so well-known in Pineville. Other churches asked him to sing and his performance of such religious hymns as *Beneath the Cross of Jesus* and *The Old Rugged Cross* had congregations weeping as the result of his stunning renditions.

His many fans marveled at his vocal prowess and tried to explain to others what it was about this Apollo's singing that made him outstanding.

"It's like," said Betsy Gallimore, the most fervent of Tommy's fans, "he's singing beautifully—but there's a subtle level of intense warmth beneath it all."

In his senior year in high school, he stopped attending his church and he told his teachers the Bible didn't answer the questions he wanted addressed.

For instance, why didn't the Holy Book even mention those titanic civilizations that had existed millions of years before the dinosaurs?

In his anthropology class, taught by a brilliant young professor, Dr. Mattie Olson, Tommy became fascinated with the work of Dr. Norma DuPree, the famous explorer and anthropologist. She had written extensively about these long-forgotten worlds that had been ruled by such ancient deities as Zanzothrope, the god of air and war.

Of unusual interest was the half-male, half-female god, Mouria, the hermaphrodite power that ruled tens of millions of people.

Dr. Mattie Olson then led the class into the unsolved mystery of the Vesaria Massacre. To enhance the myriad riddles of this tragedy, an hour-long documentary was shown.

The film was introduced by the teacher who said: "You're about to watch probably the most fascinating unsolved mystery in America: the Vesaria Massacre. Even today, serious scholars argue whether Emmanuel Trident was actually Jesus Christ—who had returned to Earth and settled into the mountain community of Vesaria."

As the low voice of the narrator introduced the film, there were some gasps as the film clips and photographs revealed a near-naked Emmanuel Trident as he conducted a sermon. His magnificent torso looked surreal—the way his powerful muscles flowed together in beautiful harmony. A light sheen of sweat emphasized the stunning proportions that could be compared to heroic deities in books of fairy tales.

His voice was strong, beautifully intense, and he urged the worshipper to think of Mouria—as the real god of this world.

There were more motion picture moments that showed the students Diana DuPree, a luminous, dazzling person as she accompanied her husband as he made his way among his congregation.

The famous "Diana's Posse," the five glorious looking men, who were the bodyguards—and quite probably lovers—of their mistress had posed for the camera. They were all shirtless, muscular and laughed at some secret joke. A segment showed the Tridents performing at the Blue Ridge Music Festival and then the religious leader and wife showing off their new twin sons.

The final segment of the film depressed the students. A camera panned over the wind-swept ruins of Chateau DuPree, where Emmanuel Trident and his beautiful bride lived with their children. The charred remains of the All Souls Church of the Mountains...the blown-up rubble of the Social Center, the movie theater, the library...of everything.

The documentary ended with a startling close-up—in vivid color—of Emmanuel Trident.

The Mountain Messiah faced the camera, bare chested, smiling, as the wind ruffled his thick hair. Behind him the sky was cobalt blue. Closer the camera moved until only the astonishing eyes of iridescent jade filled the screen.

When the lights turned on, no one could speak for several seconds.

Tommy and the others were profoundly moved by this tragic ending to a group of vibrant personalities who had once lived in the mountain community of Vesaria.

"So what happened to the twin boys—and to their father?" asked the teacher. "The father was last seen nailed to the cross—but somehow overnight, his body vanished. One theory believes he was actually a great priest of Mouria—and there is a sacred temple built into the steep wall of Mouria Gorge where he managed to return to and now rests in suspended animation. And as to the boys? Were they murdered—or were they saved? If so, where could they be now?"

First one, then others, all turned to look at Tommy Barnes.

"Tommy, that was you up there on the screen!" gasped Doris Bruner, another of his most fervent admirers. "Emmanuel Trident could be your father."

The rest of the class joined in, excited and fascinated by the uncanny similarity between their classmate and the mesmerizing Emmanuel Trident.

Tommy blushed and tried to laugh it off. Yet, he was as astonished by that final shot of the face of the mythical Emmanuel Trident as the class was.

The teacher also looked his way. Dr. Olson had raised her brows, as if asking, "Well, are you the son of Emmanuel Trident?", but a slight smile softened her expression.

When the school bell rang for the changing of classes, Tommy waited until everyone had left the classroom before he approached the teacher.

"Could I talk to you in private, Dr. Olson? About what we just saw?"

She smiled. "Most certainly. I'm free for the next hour. Let's go to my office."

Her small office was crowded with stacks of books. She poured herself and Tommy two mugs full of strong coffee. Tommy took several of the homemade cookies she offered.

"Dr. Olson I'm still in a state of amazement—after seeing that documentary."

He described how alien he felt toward the world—not in a hostile way, but it was like he was misplaced.

"I keep seeing myself naked, in front of hundreds or thousands of people—preaching to them. In my dreams, I often see this powerful looking man, who wears no clothes, and a beautiful blonde woman. She also has male genitalia. They're saying something to me which I can't understand. And so just now, I watched that film—and it was like seeing the people in my dreams again."

He explained that he and his twin brother were found on the steps of a charity hospital in February, 1941—just hours after the Vesaria Massacre.

The young teacher listened with growing excitement as Tommy continued to talk. When he finished, Dr. Olson leaned forward.

"Okay, I'm going to say something that might shock you more. I received my master's degree as a result of my thesis, which was an investigation into the Vesaria mystery. I spent two years going through hundreds of photographs of the major principles, read a thousand or more articles on the subject, listened to the Tridents singing on their records. And so when I first saw you here, I was shocked. You're the very embodiment of Emmanuel Trident. I feel there must be a connection between you two."

Tommy fell back in his seat. "Wow!" he gasped. He shook his head in disbelief.

"And here's something I've never said aloud. I'm really convinced that Emmanuel Trident—*was* Jesus Christ! I know, it sounds like something from a fantasy magazine, but--everything points to it. I really believe that Mouria had several phenomenal priests. One was the Messiah. He may be in that sacred magical cavern, still alive but in suspended animation. I wish some explorers would investigate this. If they found this cave and its inhabitant, it would rock the world."

#

Tommy was dumb-founded by all that was happening. It would be up to him to investigate this mind-boggling theory and find an answer.

He visited the local library and researched the whole Vesaria legend. There were cults now around the world that were composed of scholars, students, ordinary people who were devoted to keeping the spirit of Emmanuel Trident alive.

One such group was located in Atlanta, Georgia. For two dollars, they would send you a whole packet of articles and photos of the tragic religious man. The big attraction was that one of these pictures was of the crucified man in full color.

When Tommy received his large envelope from the Emmanuel Trident Association, he was thrilled to see the beautifully restored image of the Mountain Jesus—in lush hues.

He was shown naked, except for his frontal panel, with his arms raised up to a stormy sky. His eyes glowed in luminous agate.

Tommy stripped naked and devised his own skimpy apparel from a strip of towel. He oiled his body up and aped the picture before a floor to ceiling mirror in his bedroom.

"We're exactly alike!" he thought. "He and I are duplicates."

The boy's torso was as well developed as that of his idol.

What can I do about this, he wondered?

In the meantime, the students who had watched the Vesaria documentary, spread the word that Tommy Barnes was an exact replica of Emmanuel Trident.

Some began to refer to him affectionately as Tommy Trident.

The young Adonis heard this name and he shrugged

Jesus Christ returned to Vesaria, he decided. His name was Emmanuel Trident.

I must find a way of proving that.

While keeping this in mind, he threw himself into playing football, in weight lifting. He competed in a body builder competition in Black Mountain. As usual, he had to wear a special jock strap to keep his over-abundant manhood "toned" down. Still, his black speedo bulged out enough to shock some of the judges. Overall, though, they were amazed to see a mere eighteen-year-old man looking so incredibly muscular and mature.

CHAPTER FIVE

One night Tommy was reading the newspaper when his eyes lit up. Evangelist Buster Scoggins was bringing his ministry to the nearby town of Alabaster for three months.

Tommy had grown up watching the *Buster Scoggins Religious Show* on TV. The very handsome, former wrestler was a galvanizing sight as he bound around the stage and sang with his fifty member choir.

His show always ended with him stripping off his shirt, to reveal a tanned, well-muscled upper torso. He would fall to his knees and with tears trickling down his cheeks, he pleaded for viewers to send in money to help the poor of the world.

And right after his evangelical show ended, his even more popular—*Buster's Bible Stories*—would begin. These were very well produced, thirty-minute episodes, where unusually beautiful men and women would enact a Biblical event or a modern day story centered around the power of love and Jesus Christ.

What made these mini-dramas so popular was that the performers were forever stripping naked. If they emerged from a forest pool, it was obvious the actors wore no clothes. A strategically placed tree limb, or bush, would obscure the hot spots. If they got out of bed, a sheet covered the essentials.

Tommy wished he could be in one of these sizzling entertainments. He would definitely attend one of the revival shows.

#

"You are now safe here in my company," sang out Buster Scoggins to the thousand or more worshippers before him. Ten million viewers watched him on live television.

The people who were fans of Buster Scoggins now crowded the enormous tent in Alabaster—plain men and women, many children, and sitting on the front row was Tommy Barnes.

He was delighted with the warmth of the crowd, the refreshing stream of cool air from the giant air-conditioners above, the fifty-member choir attired in their gowns of purple silk.

Most of all, Tommy bathed in the warmth that radiated from the powerful man on stage now.

Buster Scoggins was a very handsome man of forty-eight. He wore his expensive suit of wheat-hued linen with ease. His ten years as a vastly popular pro-wrestler, "Bustin' Bruisin' Buster" had gifted him with dynamic charisma and a torso which he regularly displayed to the delight of his fans.

There were numerous newspaper and magazine pictures of him wearing a skimpy black speedo while lounging by a pool or preparing to jump into the water. Images of him—all sweaty, teeth bared and his muscles bulging from his wrestling days—were collector's items.

He appeared on the cover of muscle magazines that displayed his hard, gleaming torso in all its splendor. His black bikini contained some impressive manhood.

Now, he bounded around the stage, microphone in hand, as he asked everyone to "drop" their problems into his lap.

"Just think real hard—Ole Buster is here to guide and protect you—and drop them ole troubles with me, and I'll take care of you."

Toward the end of the program, Tommy sat forward when the religious leader said; "Any of you men folk who think you've sinned, come forward and let me whip them out forever. Don't be shy. You'll sleep better tonight."

This was another popular feature of his shows: whipping away, with a short leather whip, the sins of male attendees.

Men began to stand up and move down the aisle toward the stage. Several handsome young ushers were there to guide them to the presence of Buster Scoggins.

Tommy was the third one in line and he nodded his head eagerly as the evangelist called out:

"Let me...let me...let me whip out your sins and make you clean again."

He had yanked out from the podium a leather hand whip that he snapped in the air.

Tommy Barnes was the center of everyone's attention, especially that of Buster Scoggins.

The religious leader was used to seeing good-looking men—both from his wrestling career and even now, as an evangelist.

This stunning Adonis, though, was like a super star from the movies. When he ripped off his jersey and let the evangelist nip the powerful shoulders and back, everyone in the tent applauded and cheered. The whipper had signaled his photographer to get as much film on this penitent as he could.

Tommy whirled around and left the stage rubbing his raw shoulders and lower back.

More young male staffers gathered around him: "Are you okay? You need any lotion?"

Tommy merely smiled and returned to his seat. Those near him patted his sore back and said things like: "God bless you...You've been saved!"

Buster Scoggins ended his show with the ripping off of his jacket, shirt and even his pants.

Clad only in a pair of silk boxer shorts, the color of gun metal, he made an exciting figure as he clasped his hands and rocked back and forth while wailing: "Only you can save the starving children of Ethiopia! Please find it in your heart—and give!"

When he stood up, he waved at his fans, bunched up his muscles and posed mockingly like Hercules. His fans cheered. The choir belted out "Give Me That Ole Time Religion."

On his way out of the tent, Tommy went up to one of the male ushers. "I'd like to work for the evangelist. How do I apply?"

The worker was a good-looking college student. He looked Tommy up and down and whistled: "Woo, I think he'd definitely hire you but he gets hundreds of requests each day. But to really put it over, you'd need to do something damned dramatic. Be a little outrageous. Reverend Scoggins likes anything that shocks. Use your body. You've got plenty to work with."

Right after Tommy left, the evangelist' main assistant, Charlie Moss, hurried out of the tent. He went up to the college student.

"Have you seen a big, handsome young man with dark hair and green eyes?"

After being told this young giant had left, Charlie Moss, moaned.

"No, no! The chief wanted to meet him!"

#

Two nights later, Buster Scoggins was busy at work in his spacious office that overlooked the rolling lawn of his rented mansion.

He was just a few miles from Pineville, a place he had always enjoyed visiting for its small-town ambiance, the friendly folk and low-cost of living.

He had so many TV appearances, revival meetings, and a trip abroad to check on his various charities, that he knew it would be a busy year for him. His incredibly popular television series, *Buster's Bible Stories* grew steadily with millions of fans.

A knock on the door and his personal assistant, Charlie Moss, entered.

"Reverend Scoggins, there's someone whose here to see you on a matter of life and death."

Without looking up from his paperwork, Buster snorted "Aren't they all, Charlie? Why should I see this person? I've got tons of work to do. We're making so much money I don't know what to do with it." "I think you'll want to see this person. He is most unusual. I would suggest looking at that photograph on your desk. Your Billy Big Boy to be precise."

On the preacher's desk were several candid shots of some of his most attractive followers that were present every night here in Alabaster.

. They were given names by the evangelist, such as Sunshine Sue, Billy Big Boy and Earth Angel.

Billy Big Boy showed a striking photograph of a shirtless Tommy Barnes, being whipped, his powerful chest gleaming with sweat and his angelic face of an Apollo lit up with an inner fire.

"Oh, my God—you mean—?"

Charlie flashed a significant smile: "The one and only. And wait until you see him."

"Bring him in!"

The door to his plush office opened and in stumbled a bizarre figure.

The youth bore a heavy wooden cross on his powerful shoulders. Long ringlets of dark hair hung over his face. He wore no shoes. His clothes were tattered enough to show that this young giant suffered abrasions and bruises and cuts. Mud spattered the remnants of his clothes.

To top it all off, heavy chains hung down from his neck.

"I've sinned, Good Preacher," the figure spoke wearily. "I'm here to do penance."

Buster was genuinely shocked at this sight. Not only by the dramatic appearance of the sinner—but at the physical size of the penitent. He didn't look like a madman. He resembled a troubled young soul who visibly trembled.

"Good heavens, son, you look like you're nearly dead. Let me help you off with that cross and chains. Have you come far?"

"I've walked here from Pineville. I started out a day ago. I've had no food or drink. I'm here to do penance for all my sinning."

"What is your name, son?"

"Tommy Barnes."

"How have you sinned?"

"I've had nasty thoughts non-stop. I can't stop thinking about sex."

As the evangelist helped remove the heavy cross and the chains, Tommy Barnes stood up straight. His powerful torso was clearly outlined beneath the rain-drenched rags.

Thrilled to his toes, the evangelist pressed a button and his personal assistant came in.

"Charlie, get this poor sinner a big tray of food and lots of water. He's nearly dead."

Charlie turned away with a sly smile on his face. Rarely did someone this unusual—and attractive—break the norm and stand out from the usual sinners.

"Here, my boy," clucked the evangelist "We need to get you out of these filthy clothes and give you a bath while your food is being prepared." He put his arm around his visitor and nearly swooned as he guided the visitor into the adjoining luxurious bathroom. Tommy stood several feet taller than the preacher and his body heat, despite the cold rain, was extraordinary.

"You've come all this way to have your sins driven out of you?" Reverend Scoggins asked eagerly.

"I want to be flogged and flogged until I'm cleansed of all my sins. I've still got a heck of a lot of sinning in me. Please help, me, dear Lord."

Although Tommy had never suffered a moment in believing he had "sinned," he was tickled, though, to be physically close to this dynamic celebrity. Fate had brought him here, Tommy believed. This was a relationship that could prove profound.

"I'll certainly help you cleanse yourself, young man. You're the type of sinner I look forward to helping out."

Over the past two decades, Buster Scoggins had "helped" countless sinners—but only those men and women who were young and good looking. All were grateful for his aide. Trading their bodies for endless hours of pleasure was a very small price to pay for what he did for them. And the evangelist was generous in giving his protégées their due.

He gave them money, scholarships, sharp legal advice, valuable contacts in the professional world. They performed on his television episodes of *Buster's Bible Stories* and were seen by tens of millions of viewers. To both him and these supplicants, it was a good and fair exchange.

The evangelist and the newest lost soul entered a bathroom that was the size of most living rooms. Everything glistened in gold and white. A huge sunken bath took up a corner of the room.

"Now, you step out of those clothes, young fellow, and I'll prepare you a nice, warm bath. After you've eaten, we can talk."

While he adjusted the water temperature, Buster watched his visitor remove his clothes. It was like watching a professional stripper. Tommy slowly and painfully pulled off his shirt. Then he peeled down his trousers and stepped out of them. He wore no underwear and now he wrapped a hand around his amazing endowment and shook it slightly to loosen it up. It was like he possessed a pink and tan thermos bottle of flesh.

The evangelist was stunned anew.

Tommy stood unmoving for a moment, as if giving his host a chance to look him over.

"Unbelievable!" whispered Buster Scoggins in awe. "Simply unbelievable."

This young sinner could have been a mighty gladiator from ancient Rome. All that was lacking was a shield and a helmet.

With the minister's arm around his waist, Tommy slipped into the soapy water and let his head dip below the surface. When he came up for air, his jet hair hung boyishly over his face.

A knock on the door and Charlie pushed a cart laden with food into the bathroom.

"If there's anything else you want," the secretary said softly to Tommy, "please let me know. I'll just take the visitor's clothes and put them through the washer and dryer."

Tommy chose that moment to stand up and his glorious young body gleamed like living marble. Charlie's mouth fell open and he look bug-eyed at the evangelist.

"Jesus—I mean, Good grief, but he looks like Samson!"

For the first time, Tommy grinned and this enhanced his air of a bad but beautiful little boy. He stepped out onto a mat and the secretary and the evangelist eagerly helped dry him off. Buster Scoggins took a long time to make certain the massive genitalia and the buttocks were dry. This caused the boy's phallus to visibly thicken.

The secretary left to return with a white robe.

"This is the biggest I could find."

"Are you referring to the towel or what young Tommy has weighing between his thighs?"

Tommy snickered for the first time. When he put the robe on, it was still too small and the hem came up high on the thighs. The evangelist took him into his private bedroom where everything was in the hues of silver and white. Charlie pushed the food cart into a corner where a dining room table was set up and placed the food there before leaving his boss and the visitor alone.

Tommy sat down and hungrily consumed the ham and cheese sandwiches, the fried chicken and mashed potatoes and the banana ice cream sundae. He gulped down several glasses of iced water.

The evangelist sat across from him spellbound and saying little.

The youth's face was striking in its quiet beauty. Eyes sparkled jade and opened wide and deep set beneath black brows. The mouth was full and sensuous but most compelling was the look of sheer innocence. A dark stubble shadowed his cheeks and jawline.

In a corner of the vast bedroom rose a podium and on this was positioned a large wooden cross. Manacles of steel gleamed at the top and the bottom. Only rarely had the minister found a sinner worthy of being flogged. Now, the most beautiful of them all had arrived from nowhere and Buster Scoggins was excited to start the physical chastisement. This was what this strange creature wanted and the evangelist was just the expert to do it.

"We'll start right now. Stand up, Tommy, and throw aside your robe."

The sinner jumped to his feet and threw off his robe.

Standing there, with his feet wide apart and his head thrown back, Tommy's physique gleamed from the fresh bath. In his twenty years of being an evangelist, and having counseled hundreds of gullible fools, Buster Scoggins was convinced that this extraordinary youth was like a gift from God.

His pronounced resemblance to Jesus Christ was also striking.

"Tommy, go up to that cross there on the podium."

The young buck obeyed and Buster followed him.

"Put your wrists within those clamps there and I'll lock them."

After his wrists were secured, the same thing was done to his ankles.

Tommy looked like he was to be crucified.

The evangelist picked up his hand whip that he used at his revivals.

"Prepare yourself, Tommy, to be cleansed. Cry out all you want. But don't ask me to stop."

"Whip me, Preacher, whip me! Don't go easy on me! I'm a man! I can take it!"

Usually the minister used very light strokes to prepare the penitent and gradually built up the intensity.

In Tommy's case, though, he had made it clear that he wanted an extreme cleansing and he wanted nothing gentle about it.

The thongs of the whip flayed across the highly mounted rear-end of Tommy Barnes.

He shuddered and shook his head but said nothing.

Another lash made his beautiful flesh shiver. This was followed by louder blows of the whip.

While this was going on, Charlie the secretary slipped in to watch this ritual.

His mouth fell open again when he saw the massive young torso of this young Hercules shivering and flinching under the beating.

"Let me do it," he whispered to Buster Scoggins.

The evangelist handed his assistant the whip and Charlie stepped forward and delivered a series of strong, intense lashes. Tommy cried out and cried out: "Harder! Harder! I'm doing this for Jesus."

Tommy's backside was rosy with welts and swellings. His flayers helped him from the podium and onto the king-sized bed of the evangelist.

The whippers both applied soothing ointment to the bloody welts.

As they did so, Tommy writhed and moaned quietly. He was growing aroused again and the evangelist quickly slid a bath towel beneath the penitent's hips. This proved wise since Tommy ejaculated again.

Tears wet his cheeks and a smile of dazzling beauty lit up his face.

"Yes, yes, that feels good and I know Jesus is watching."

Now, Tommy grabbed the evangelist and pressed him close to him.

"You've saved me, Mr. Scoggins! I can feel the sin leaving me!"

Buster Scoggins pressed his face against Tommy's powerful chest, ran his hands up and down the rippling back, the highly mounted buttocks.

"I'll want you to return home but I'll let you borrow one of my cars. And you can come and visit me each day that I'm here. Would you like to work for me? I think you would fit in nicely."

By the next week, Tommy Barnes was now part of the evangelist corps of strong, young men who acted as ushers and the security force.

Unlike the other members of this team, Tommy drove one of the boss's new cars and rarely did he return home.

Roy and Myrtle Barnes had given up trying to figure out their complicated, be troubled son. His room was kept in order and occasionally he returned home.

He explained to them that he had gotten a great job working for the evangelist which amazed them. They knew that he had once been feverishly religious and then suddenly lost interest.

But now, they had no idea he had traveled so far. The name of Evangelist Buster Scoggins was famous all over Dixie. He was like a movie star.

Their son certainly seemed to be successful in his job. The car he drove gleamed black and expensive. He wore costly clothes that were of the latest fashion. He paid his parents thirty dollars a week, even though he was a rare guest these days. He explained that all the male ushers and security guards slept in a dormitory behind the Scoggins rented mansion.

Frankly, Myrtle Barnes was relieved that he was avoiding his home. He had become so physically powerful that he scared her. She saw him as a human gorilla, rather than a flesh and blood youth that she and her husband took in.

There was another incident that made her wary of this young man.

One night, eleven years ago, the foster mother had an intense dream. She could remember everything about it. She saw herself floating from her bed and glided to the bedroom of Tommy.

The door opened by invisible hands. The boy lay on his back, naked, but on either side of him stood two magnificent looking people. Both were nude. On his right was a radiant woman with long, gold hair and an angelic face. Her breasts were modest. Down where her pubic hair should be, she showed a man's organ.

On the other side, a powerful looking giant also stood. His dark hair touched his shoulders. He was built like a fantastic character from a book of Roman gods. Sparkling eyes of lime stood out in the shadows.

Both creatures were murmuring something to Tommy. He rose up in the air. The dream visitors leaned down and kissed him.

Myrtle had awakened with a start. She got out of bed and fearfully opened the door to her son's bedroom.

He lay alone, under the covers. A sweet wind stirred the curtains covered in images of horses and cowboys.

That was real, she thought. It wasn't a dream. But what did it mean?

#

As a senior, Tommy would graduate in just a few months. He visited several of the college representatives who had come down for College Day.

These men and women were startled when he visited them—for in no way did he resemble the usual eighteen-year-old innocent. The dark stubble on his face, the luxurious mane of black hair that touched his shoulders, his very size and the obvious musculature—all represented a grown adult male.

Football and basketball recruiters were determined to sign him up for scholarships but to their dismay, he showed zero interest in being a jock.

#

Dressed in his jet uniform, hat and boots, he looked impressive enough to quell any troublemaker attending the revival services.

Several times a week, Tommy visited the evangelist for his ritual whipping.

The pattern never changed.

He doffed his clothes and ascended the steps up to the whipping dais.

Naked now, he was manacled and shivered in delight with the flaying of the whip against his white butt.

After one flaying, Tommy relaxed as the evangelist massaged the soothing cream into his raw skin.

And Buster Scoggins said something that made the young sinner suddenly sit up in great excitement.

"It's truly amazing," observed the preacher, "but I've been trying to think of whom you remind me of and now I know. Emmanuel Trident. The Mountain Jesus. The preacher who vanished mysteriously with his wife and two little boys from the village of Vesaria eighteen years ago."

Tommy quickly sat up and grabbed his benefactor by his arms.

"Emmanuel Trident? Did you know him?"

"I can tell you about the time I went to Vesaria and spent the day with the Mountain Jesus."

#

Buster Scoggins was a lusty eighteen-year-old youth who drove his beloved Aunt Tabitha to Vesaria to see what all the excitement was about.

"The day was beautiful," remembered the evangelist. "Windy, crisp and we'd been hearing about this Naked Jesus, as some called him. We got to this beautiful All Souls Church of the Mountains really early and got the last two seats.

"And suddenly there he was. It was like an explosion. The chapel was shadowy, with burning candles, with this soothing choral music and a side door opened and Emmanuel Trident appeared.

"He looked uncannily like Jesus Christ only this guy was enormous—way over six feet five or six. Thick dark hair that he wore long, a moustache and beard. And then, he threw off his robe and everyone just gasped.

"He was totally bare-assed, except for this narrow strip of velvet he wore over his privates. Wow. Talk about a powerful god—he resembled Super Man. And then he began to talk, and his magic grew with his intense words.

"He told us about how this prehistoric deity, Mouria, had once ruled a world that vanished millions of years ago. This god and all the countless subjects were hermaphrodites. Half women, half male. They achieved incredible arts, flying machines and there was a panel of extraordinary priests. One of them was Jesus Christ. Toward the end of the sermon, the Naked Jesus brought out a small hand-whip. A dozen men from the congregation came up to the podium. They removed all their clothes as if there was no one there. And Emmanuel Trident gave each one a thorough whipping to wipe out their sins. Then another male worshipper appeared and he gave the same whipping to Emmanuel Trident. That carried over to what I do now. Everyone loves to see me flaying the hell out of ordinary men folk.

"I saw later Mrs. Trident, or Diana DuPree, who was reputed to be a replica of Mouria. And a month later, all was destroyed in the massacre."

Tommy was silent as he soaked in this new account of the Vesaria mystery.

"We've got to go to Vesaria!"

"We will but first I'm going to turn you into a star."

To his amazement—and delight—Evangelist Buster Scoggins discovered that his extraordinary protégée had proven to be the hit of his revival shows. For this, the minister showered his golden boy with hefty checks and bonuses and a wardrobe ordered from Manhattan.

At first, Tommy Barnes was hired as a security guard and a greeter.

Dressed in his snug khaki uniform and hat, the handsome youth was affable and sweet to everyone. The children, girls and women loved him. The men admired his outstanding looks. With Tommy nearby, everyone felt safe. His sense of serenity and his powerful virility soothed everyone near him. He could have been an award-winning Eagle Scout. The boy you'd want your daughter to marry. The adorable kid you'd want for a son.

He made a sterling impression for the Buster Scoggins Revival Show.

From there, the powerful young guard was promoted to the stage where he stood, all dressed up in an expensive suit and tie, and took the microphone to sing in a pure baritone a traditional hymn.

Tommy had greatly enjoyed singing in the high school's choral group. He was often selected to sing solo and was always thrilled to see the effect his talent had on an audience.

Now, those watching him in the revival tent and over television were in the tens of millions.

. With the choir backing him up, he proved to be even more dynamic. Even Tommy was surprised when he was asked to sing and out came this beautiful sound.

What enthralled everyone, especially the evangelist, was this amazing kid didn't try to ape the popular pop artists. He didn't close his eyes and click his fingers and do all that fake stuff. He stood before the microphone and sang like he meant every word. His young voice was intense and emotional and sometimes tears ran down his cheeks.

When he sang "O, Holy Night," he poured so much emotion into it that his backup choir could barely perform because of their sobs.

The evangelist was excited to see that the audience behaved the exact way. Men, women, young kids all sobbed and wailed. When Tommy finished, there were screams and cries of delight. The applause went on and on.

He feigned nothing.

Buster realized that his glorious discovery had a natural stage magic.

His outstanding looks alone made him a natural for TV. Tommy let his dark hair grow out so that it touched his strong shoulders. He cultivated a dashing moustache and beard. His emerald-hued eyes looked wonderful on the new color TVs.

So much fan mail poured in for this new sensation that the evangelist had to hire an extra secretary to handle it. Yet, Buster Scoggins hid all of these outpourings. He wanted no one to distract this glorious young gladiator from his work with the Scoggins Ministry.

From their first encounter, the evangelist was convinced that Tommy Barnes would be a natural for the tremendously popular *Buster's Bible Stories* television episodes. In addition to being superbly produced, costumed and photographed in the preacher's studio behind his house, the story lines always featured the best looking women and men to be found.

The productions were noted for their adult themes and partial nudity of the performers. Buster knew just how far he could go so that his shows were never banned. Yet, they caused plenty of comment from his critics. His faithful followers loved them.

Now was the time that Buster could show the world what a staggering hunk of muscle he had in the fascinating youth from Pineville. A new episode aired each month, right after his televised evangelical tent meetings. In constant syndication around the world, each showing showered Buster Scoggins with endless profits.

The cast cost almost nothing. Buster knew of many very beautiful women and very handsome men who were eager to work for free on these shows because the exposure was an actor's dream.

And the secret ingredient of their tremendous popularity—besides the religious themes—was sex.

There was no dialogue because Buster narrated the stories. Occasionally he enjoyed making a cameo appearance where he liked to show off his handsome body. In one story he might appear as a near-naked guard or a gladiator. In another scene, he might wear just a loincloth.

His followers loved to recognize him and they'd whoop:" There's Preacher Scoggins."

For Tommy, the evangelist came up with the perfect story. He would portray the mighty Samson who is betrayed by the vicious Delilah.

On the day of the filming, Tommy was locked up with Buster Scoggins and Gregory LaGrande, a flamboyant man from Atlanta who was to prepare Tommy to look like Samson.

"Here is your wardrobe!" teased the designer and held up a tiny little loincloth. "Hope you won't catch cold."

"That's my wardrobe?" asked Tommy. "Wait'll you see what I have because I think you'll have to make the pouch a little bit bigger."

""Oh, we'll squeeze you in somehow."

Tommy stripped naked in his dressing room and came out to where Buster and Gregory LaGrande eagerly awaited him.

The evangelist had warned the wardrobe man to be shocked. And he was.

For a moment, the costumer was too stunned to say anything. Tommy stood before him in all his glory with his fists on his hips. He threw his head back and laughed like a naughty little boy at the reaction of the designer.

For Gregory LaGrande had slapped a hand over his forehead and gasped: "Good God Almighty! Are you for real? Holy shit. I've never ever seen a boy with a body like yours. And that includes what's hanging there between your thighs like a loaf of bread. . Is that for real"

Tommy flapped his equipment playfully and Buster Scoggins howled:

"See? I told you."

"Ah!" sighed the costume design in mock passion. "You've got soooo much to work with, Tommy boy."

A narrow panel of leather barely covered the cleft of the buttocks. The front panel was cut down to the pubic area. When he came upon the small stage, his co-star, Myrna Lloyd, and the crew were all amazed. Tommy was bigger and better than any Samson they had ever seen in the movies.

The film was made quickly. The two performers had no lines to speak since it was completely narrated later by Buster Scoggins. Tommy was fitted with a wig of thick curls. When the actress cut them, he had passed out from too much wine.

Buster Scoggins made certain the camera traveled over every inch of Tommy's torrid physique. In one scene, he sat in Delilah's bedroom with his legs spread apart and his crotch bulging out. In the scene of his shearing, Tommy lay sprawled face down on Delilah's bed.

The camera lovingly photographed his highly mounted buttocks, his broad back with rippling muscles, his powerful arms and legs.

As an inside joke, Buster Scoggins disguised himself as a vicious guard.He had Tommy manacled to the wall. His back panel was abbreviated even more so that his rear was virtually exposed. It was sprayed with water to give it a sweaty look.

Buster yanked out his whip and began lashing Tommy's behind with such force that the crew became nervous. This Samson groaned and undulated his hips as his buttocks shivered with each blow. When the scene was finished, Tommy was released and rubbed his rear while flashing a wicked grin at his flogger.

"You were so gentle this time," he joked. "You're getting old."

When the episode was finally televised a month later, it created a sensation. TV stations were deluged from viewers who wanted them to telecast the episode again. Most wanted to know how they could contact that "heavenly Samson." What added to the intense eroticism of this episode, wrote hundreds of fans, was the adorable, angelic look of this dynamic young Samson.

He had the face of an angel and a body by God.

TV technicians across America made duplicate copies on film and did a brisk business selling these bootlegged prints to women and gay men. These edited episodes showed Tommy in his flogging scene and sitting with his crotch bulging out and another hot picture of him lying on his stomach with his rear-end prominently visible.

Buster Scoggins cleverly made photos of Tommy's most revealing poses and these were sold at his evangelist meetings by the thousands. Even the blue noses couldn't complain. This was Samson. It came from the Bible. Men didn't wear too many clothes back then. How could you disapprove of that? Tommy had created salivating fan clubs without ever saying a word.

When Tommy appeared at tent revival meetings he was deluged with people wanting his autographs.

To follow up on this sensational success of "Samson and the Temptress," Buster decided to really push the envelope for his next Mini-Story.

This time he would make his masterpiece: "Adam and Eve."

For Eve, he hired a large busted stripper from Atlanta, Brenda Brannigan, who wanted to go legit. A religious role might put her on the road of professional respectability.

For the costumes, Tommy's would be a very large silken pouch to hold his male equipment. His ass would be completely exposed. Eve would wear a long wig with strands pasted over her breasts. To protect her lower region, a flesh-colored G-string was chosen.

The production would rely on strategically placed plants and tree limbs and bushes to hide the essentials.

When Tommy walked easily onto the set, his co-star, Brenda Brannigan was speechless.

She wore a robe. Tommy wore absolutely nothing.

"Oh, my God!" she gasped. "I think I've gone to heaven already."

She found all kinds of reasons for caressing her co-star—on his pectorals, his shoulders, his rear. When her fingers inched toward the private area, Tommy politely turned away.

She complained to the cameraman during breaks "Is this kid homo or something? Not many men pass up a chance to touch my titties."

In the first scene, the two performers emerged from a forest pool and were filmed from the waist up. When seen, no one noticed Eve. All eyes were on the magnificent torso of young Tommy. In scene after scene, his rippling display of virility outshone his co-star. His black curls dramatically enhanced the beauty of his wide-eyed expression of innocence. The sparkling of his iridescent eyes, framed by thick lashes, stood out because of the expert photography.

Buster Scoggins cleverly had Tommy photographed full-frontal with a carefully placed tree limb or bush hiding out the area that viewers were to salivate over. When his backside was on full display, which was often, a wisp of hanging moss or a large plant leaf barely hid the cleft. But it was clear to the viewers—this kid was buck naked!

When released, this sizzling episode became even more of a spectacular success than Samson and Delilah. Some stations refused to air it. When Buster pointed out to them that viewers saw nothing explicit— "Go to the beach and you'll find people more naked than my Adam and Eve—the holdouts gave in and saw ratings go through the roof.

As before, Tommy Barnes proved to be a phenomenon. By now, Buster Scoggins was receiving offers from big-time talent scouts. They were thrilled by this vibrant youngster who had the potential to become a major star. They couldn't get over his quality of little boy naïveté. He had a marvelous way of moving, like a ballet dancer and a wild animal. His fabulous body surpassed that of Steve Reeves and Mark Forest—the two most popular movie Hercules in the world.

There was also an intangible glow of magical flesh impact. Tommy stood out in every frame of film. He had a radiance and a wonderful expression of pure innocence touched by a dash of carnal roughness.

Buster never let Tommy discover how popular he was.

He wanted to keep his magnificent boy toy in the dark and all to himself.

The preacher never showed his young star any of the offers from agents and studios or the thousands of fan letters. Quite a few included lonely, overweight or underweight women naked with their legs spread. Even more showed overweight and underweight men with their erections prominent.

All offered him everything they had—if he would only come and love them up.

While working before the camera was fun, Tommy was now obsessed with visiting Vesaria and being in the same place that his new idol, Emmanuel Trident, had lived and probably died.

The boy was fascinated with the rare recordings by the Tridents in l941 that Buster Scoggins still treasured.

Together they listened to the beautiful sound and voices of these poor doomed souls.

'Just think," Buster Scoggins would say softly before he put the record on the turn table. "You'll be hearing people who were murdered twenty-five years ago."

Sometimes the youth burst into tears after hearing these ghostly voices.

"It's so sad!" he sobbed. "So terribly sad! If only I had been there to protect them! Why did God destroy them? Why?"

On a gray, freezing morning, the evangelist and his protégé got into a big, black van and began their journey to Mt. Mouria and the ghost town that was once Vesaria.

Tommy got behind the wheel while Buster Scoggins put baskets of food in the rear. He poured both himself and Tommy big mugs of steaming hot coffee.

Three hours later, they came upon the turn-off that took them up higher to Mt. Mouria. Then another road led them through thick woods and finally they found the sign: Vesaria 9 miles.

As the woods became thicker, the sky grew increasingly overcast. At one point, they slowed down to look at the treacherous Mouria Gorge. Its tremendous depth suggested a primordial abyss where monsters could roam in the tree-covered ground.

A sense of old sorrow seeped into the car and before they entered the little village, they paused to read a green, government warning sign:

"You are about to enter the village of Vesaria, which was decimated in 1941 by a virulent virus. Although the site has been declared safe now, please be advised that you enter this area at your own risk. The U.S. Government and the North Carolina Government cannot be held liable for any illness that may result from your visit."

#

The main street they came upon was empty and dead.

Old leaves and scraps of paper blew in the strong wind. Slowly they drove past boarded up old shops. Past Ned's Hardware Store, Polly's Little Snack Bar, Queenie's Beauty Parlor, Troy's Barbershop, and the Vesaria Food Store.

The two men got out of the car.

All the store windows were encrusted with years of dirt. Most panes were shattered. Visitors had left graffiti. Someone wrote "Ned Loves His Rita—Virginia Beach, 1948." Another had scratched into the wall; 'Fuck this place!" And one scrawled: "Burn in Hell!"

It was ghostly with only the wind gusting against the dead stores.

'Just think," Buster murmured, "these streets used to be filled with people, especially on the weekends. It was a thriving little community here. In good weather, some of the men got out their fiddles and banjoes and played blue grass. Pots of red and yellow flowers hung out over the entrances and swung in the breeze."

Signs that the village had been visited by the curious could be seen in cigarette butts, crushed beer cans, candy wrappers, a potato chip bag—all discarded on the cracked sidewalks.

Tommy had taken out the map he had carefully sketched from library records.

"Let's go find the church of the Mountain Jesus."

They got back into the car and cruised around several little lanes before they came upon a large pile of rubble. Someone had made a wooden sign that read:

"Former site of the All Soul's Church of the Mountains. It was destroyed by mongrels in 1941, the same year of the plague."

The two men picked through the pile of rotting wood, rocks, and broken glass.

"It's all coming back so clearly to me," said the evangelist, "I actually sat here in 1941. I can see Emmanuel Trident even now. Powerful, massive, beautiful."

Tommy was silent, then he returned to the car and stripped naked.

He climbed onto the top of the rubble and held his hands out on either side.

"I've been waiting for this moment," he said. "I think I would have thrived here. I feel like I've been here before."

As the frigid wind blew against him, he pounded his strong chest with his fists:

"I am a man!" he shouted to the wind. "Look at me! Look at my powerful body! My name is Emmanuel Trident! I brought you gifts and progress and things that could make your life better here in Vesaria! And what did you give me? You gave me death and destruction of my family!"

To Buster Scoggins, it was a spellbinding experience—to be reminded of how beautiful Emmanuel Trident was—and now this young boy looked so much like him that he could have been his son. And he sounded exactly like the Mountain Jesus!

Those words struck the visitor for they were so true! Emmanuel Trident had brought joy and prosperity to this little community. And how did it repay him? It was the same with Jesus Christ. He was murdered for his attempts to bring understanding and compassion to the unwashed mass.

The evangelist fell to his knees and wept.

He cried for the memories of that golden day when he witnessed the Naked Jesus in action--and of the horrible tragedy that befell that beautiful Mountain Messiah and his little family.

A strong hand touched his head.

"You can feel the power of the Mountain Jesus, can't you? It's like he still lives here."

Tommy wore only his leather sandals and he could have stepped right off the pages of the old Bible.

Together, the two men knelt in prayer for all the lives that were gone before their time. The younger man shed his tears, too, for instead of feeling fulfilled that he was now in this cursed village, he felt deep sorrow. When they stood, the two men embraced for a long time as the wind whined around them.

Without dressing, Tommy said it was now time find the home of the doomed Tridents.

Buster consulted the map and they followed it for nearly a mile until they came upon another hill of rubble.

Another sign read:

"The rock home where Emmanuel Trident lived with his wife, Diana DuPree and their little twin boys. The house was destroyed by ghouls soon after the Mountain Jesus and his sons vanished—never to be seen again."

Visiting the destroyed church was difficult. Yet, seeing how small-town rage had resulted in the destruction of this once beautiful house was much worse. This was where real people lived and slept.

"Those goddamned animals," muttered Tommy. "What was so bad about Emmanuel Trident that they had to wipe out his home and family?"

"A mob never cares about human lives. They destroy everything in its wake. They just followed the path of the killers. I'm glad the plague wiped them out. I hope they all fried in hell for it."

Tommy went to a small patch of greenery behind the house. Two scrawny rose bushes were all that was left of the much praised garden that Diana DuPree had grown. Tommy had read that her flowers made this place the most beautiful in the North Carolina Mountains when she was alive. It was like a reflection of her soul, she had told someone. All that beauty blowing in the wind made her feel fulfilled.

While his companion watched, Tommy knelt down and dug out a narrow hole in the ground.

Then he lay face down so that he could fit his phallus into the opening.

He humped his hips and rotated them until he gasped as he orgasmed.

When he stood and wiped the debris away from him privates, Buster asked him what was he trying to do?

'I've planted my seed here. One day I'm going to return here and live here and start a new village. A new church dedicated to Mouria."

"I think you will, young Tommy. I'm proud of you."

Near the pathetic little garden yawned the canyon. They peered over the edge and felt dizzy. The ground far, far below was hidden behind mist.

Tommy said: "Emmanuel Trident could actually be living beneath us, in one of those caverns. He was a high priest of Mouria—and they knew how to preserve someone immortal intact until a mystical signal was sent to resurrect them."

"I've always believed Emmanuel Trident was really Jesus Christ."

#

Buster drove the car out onto the deserted road that led out of Vesaria. He frankly wanted to get away from the place because of its intense desolation and doom. He found a narrow logging trail and he followed it for a few minutes before he parked.

He and his passenger opened the baskets and enjoyed the food and coffee.

When they put the baskets back into the trunk of the car, Tommy removed something near the spare tire and shook it playfully at his companion:

"I think we've got a few minutes where you need to punish me."

Buster laughed for the first time during the trip. He took the small whip from Tommy's fingers and made his voice stern:

"You will indeed be punished, my young sinner! You put your hands up against the car and you stick your butt out where I lash the living hell out of it!"

Tommy had never dressed after stripping naked at the ruins of the church. Eagerly, he obeyed the preacher's command and braced his hands on the back of the van.

Buster came up from behind and for a moment stared at the naked boy before him. It was almost mystical the way his torso glowed pale and powerful here in the darkening day, in this frigid air, with the wind slicing their flesh.

He raised the whip and proceeded to flay the buttocks of Tommy Barnes for several minutes until they had become a glowing pink.

"There, you sinner! That should keep you cleansed of sin for a few hours."

Tommy rubbed his rear and grinned: "A few hours? By then I'll be filled with sin again that I'll have to go straight to hell."

The evangelist brought out his pot of skin cream and rubbed it into Tommy's welts. His fingers slid down between the young Apollo's thighs and grasped the heavy genitalia. It felt warm, strong, thick, muscular—just like it's owner.

This time, though, the young sinner didn't object when the evangelist wrapped both hands around his equipment.

Buster Scoggins got to his knees, his hands grasping this wondrous gift.

Tommy threw his head back and shouted against the wind

'I'm Emmanuel Trident! From this day forward, I am his disciple."

#

Roy and Myrtle Barnes prepared a late graduation supper for their son.

Rarely had Tommy visited them in the last six months. All his time was devoted to working for Evangelist Buster Scoggins.

The few times he did show up, it was obvious to the parents that their complicated foster son was transfigured.

His face glowed and his eyes had a faraway expression. He said little to them but when he did talk, it was like he was talking in riddles. What was clear is that he had become obsessed with a place called Vesaria.

"Emmanuel Trident….he was really Christ who returned to inspire a small town to clean up its act…to love one another…and he was butchered in a massacre…his wife was lynched…the two sons vanished…"

Tommy had sensed early on that his presence made both his foster parents nervous and anxious.

Myrtle Barnes would not sit near him. She would mutter an excuse and rush to her bedroom where she pulled the covers over her head. Woody Barnes would stare at this astonishing young giant with a confused expression on his face.

Tommy never did the things the forest ranger had fantasized his only child would do. Sure he played football, won all kinds of trophies for body building. He did all the hard work around the house: painting it, fixing a stopped up toilet or sink, taking care of the yards.

Woody just didn't know how to talk to him.

His expensive clothes and car came from his sponsor, Buster Scoggins. He paid the youth big money.

It was both a profound shock when the Barnes turned on the TV one night to watch *Buster's Bible Tales*—and suddenly they beheld their foster son—buck naked—as he portrayed Samson!

The mother let out a screech and clutched her chest. Woody Barnes had jumped to his feet and stared without speaking as he watched the camera move up his son's nude torso, lingering on the bulging crotch, then studying the thick nipples on the immense pectorals.

And all those close-ups devouring the ravishing young Samson's startling eyes. They were wide open, looking so innocent, with the thick lashes framing them like two precious gems.

The couple was equally astonished when fellow church members and neighbors were lavish in their praise. To them, Tommy Barnes had become like a movie or TV star. He did not even suggest an eighteen--year-old youth. He moved and had the gravitas of a mature man. His blazing beauty and powerful sex appeal was acknowledged by even his critics.

Pineville residents were amazed at what had happened to Tommy Barnes. They knew he was called "odd-ball," "weirdo", "Jesus Freak," "Muscle Head." But now—here he was—appearing in those Bible stories and always naked!

What kind of parents brought him into the world?

So for this graduation meal, the mother had prepared all the dishes that she thought Tommy would enjoy—but even here, she wasn't sure. He had always eaten everything she had served and thanked her politely. To her, it was like preparing a repast for a stranger. She couldn't conjure up the motherly feelings she thought she should have for Tommy was still a stranger from the first day he entered this house as an infant.

Now, they set down for his senior supper and all was quiet.

Tommy had dressed neatly in khakis and a green tee shirt which brought out the sparkling mint of his eyes.

The family now talked quietly of different things until the father spoke up:

"So, what are your plans, son?"

"I'm joining the Marines."

Myrtle nearly dropped her cup of coffee.

"The Marines? I've never heard you talk about the Marines. Why?"

"Yes, son, there's nothing wrong with the Marines—but I was thinking you might study religion at one of the Bible colleges?"

"I don't know what I really want. I can't find what it is I'm looking for. So—I might as well see some of the world. I want rigid discipline. I like rough stuff and I think basic training would be fantastic. Someday I want to live in Vesaria. Bring life back to it. Maybe I could become the new Emmanuel Trident, that Mountain Jesus who was murdered."

Myrtle Barnes began to weep quietly. Her tears were not in sadness for a departing son who would be away for years. She cried for joy. At last, this fake-son would be gone—and she would finally have her solitude back. She wouldn't have to share her husband's attention any longer between her and this foster child.

When Tommy left his parents, he got into the new car that Preacher Buster Scoggins had given him and drove quietly away. He took nothing from home with him.

He didn't kiss his mother or hug his father. He held out his hand and shook theirs—just like a stranger might do.

"Thank you for letting me share your home for eighteen years."

Myrtle Barnes went upstairs and for several long minutes stood in the doorway of her foster son's bedroom.

It was as simple and unadorned as a monk's cell. What secret life he may have enjoyed, one saw no evidence of it here. The bed was neatly made up with its tartan blanket and two big pillows. On the wall was a framed picture of Jesus Christ.

Shelves groaned beneath all the trophies he had won over the years for body building. It was like they no longer meant anything to him.

Curiously she went to his nightstand and found a small notepad in the drawer, next to a long dead mosquito.

On the front page her son had printed boldly: *Property of Tommy Barnes."*

Several words were written on the second page: "Emmanuel Trident…expiation. Pray and forget…Vesaria."

The third page presented a black and ink sketch of a strange figure that looked at first like a man, and then a woman. The male part faced left, the feminine side looked right.

Beneath it, Tommy wrote: *Mouria!*

The name was underlined heavily in black pencil.

"I love you! I love you! Mouria—you're mine!"

Was Mouria a secret girlfriend of Tommy's? If so, why did she resemble this ugly creature?

#

When he gave the Scoggins family the news of his upcoming departure, they were dumb-struck.

Buster put his hands over his face and rocked back and forth.

"Oh, Lord, no, not the Marines, son! I thought you would stay with me and we could grow even bigger with you by my side. I could make you so rich! I could make TV shows that starred just you as Jesus Christ!"

Betty Scoggins and their four children all wept. Tommy had been a delightful addition to their lives for the past year. The kids loved to rough house with their wonderful companion. He could carry them all on his strong back. They loved to be tossed into the air and caught in a pair of powerful arms.

He was the comforting companion to Betty Scoggins when she wanted to go out at night to a movie or have a late supper with some girlfriends. Tommy was always an adorable addition to her lady buddies who flirted outrageously with him.

#

On TV that Sunday night, millions watched as their favorite preacher brought his boy star to the podium.

"And now, all my followers, I have some sad and some good news. Many of you have seen this fine-looking young man with me for the past year. He's found the Lord and he's been a valuable asset to my ministry. But tomorrow, Tommy Barnes will join the Marine Corps—a fitting calling for a true American boy. And now, Tommy would like to say goodbye."

There was a collective moan and gasps. Tommy Barnes was like an adorable kid brother or son. Because of that wide-eyed expression of sheer innocence, many were concerned for his morals. He was a prime candidate to be swallowed alive by some shameless Jezebel. The more cynical visualized endless lines of men who were probably waiting to turn him from virgin to lust object.

His appearances in the *Buster Scoggins Bible Stories* had turned him into a major star. The young girls and the gay men had pictures of him in all his undress all over their walls.

And now, TV cameras showed a radiant young man dressed in a simple shirt of white silk and black velvet slacks.

"My mentor, our evangelist Buster Scoggins, has been like a father to me and he's broadened my education of the world since I've known him. I'll be sad to leave you but I'm eager to serve my country, just as I'm proud to be a member of the army of God."

While he spoke, the choir and the orchestra performed softly in the background. The song was *Nearer My God to Thee...*"

And then Tommy began to sing in his beautiful, deep baritone. Those who heard him and choir join together never forgot that moment. They remembered it for their children as one of the great moments in their lives.

All lights dimmed until only a single golden glow with amber gel focused on his him.

His voice was so rich and sincere, that many wept as he sang out the words:

Nearer my God to Thee...

Nearer to thee...

E'en though it be a cross

That raiseth me

Still all my song would be

Nearer my god to thee

Nearer my God to thee

Nearer to thee..."

When the last words faded away, there were sounds of much weeping. Even the choir, who adored this magical young man, could barely finish the song as strong emotions took over.

Before he left the podium, Tommy ripped open his shirt and tore it from his body.

It was like he was transformed into a supernatural figure.

He raised his fists and his face upward as he cried out.

"I am a Man! Look at me! I can be your Jesus Christ because I am the man who will return one day and lead you all--because *I am the one!*"

A great cry rose up from the enthralled crowd:

"Hallelujah! You are the *one!*"

PART THREE

Return of the Messiah

CHAPTER ONE

"So what do you think of our naked boy? Pretty sexy, huh?" Misty glanced at Brandon Flores and then back at the nude male model.

"I've seen better," Brandon joked. But in reality he hadn't. He was still a virgin. Only in his mind did he have wild and endless sex with his movie Tarzans and Bomba the Jungle Boy...

Wearing nothing at all, the object of all eyes was trim and slender with an average endowment. Sandy curls framed a boyish face. With one knee brought up under his chin, his testicles hung loose as they rested on the stool. Brandon could see him easily skate-boarding or surfing in the ocean.

It was obvious that he had made an impression on most of the girls, with some of them nudging each other. It wasn't every day that you walked into a classroom from the snow outside to find a cute guy sitting on a stool casually exposing what Mother Nature had gifted him with and which was usually hidden.

Yet—Brandon felt a surge of unease as he studied this pretty creature. After his nightmarish experience with Dick Brown, he secretly hated all men he had seen naked in the showers or the occasional exhibitionist in the hallways of the dorm. The boys had taunted him, swiveling their naked hips and saying things like, "Come and get it, prissy boy! Maybe I'll let you play with it you got $50..."

Dr. Patterson, the art professor, had wandered around the class, making comments and suggestions. He paused beside Brandon and remarked: "Ah, very, very nice Brandon. You've gotten the lines of the body fine—and I like the way you've worked on the background, too."

Brandon's sketch showed the model in all his naked glory but the face was what made the picture standout. The facial features were shadowed with meaning and a slight smile played on the young man's face.

"Brandon always stands out," gushed Missy and chomped her gum.

Dr. Patterson, a handsome, silver-haired man, raised his brow and nodded.

"He's certainly got the talent and I just hope he learns to continue to work on it and use it."

Nearby students heard the conversation and now they came over to see what Brandon had done.

"Oh, wow, your picture is so great!" one of the girls sighed. "As usual."

"You're our Picasso!"

"Oh, stop it. All of you are just as good in your own way."

Yet, after a half year here at Blackwood Institute, he could barely hide his growing frustration and extreme boredom. He was wasting precious hours here when he could work on his own projects and make more money in a moth than many of the art faculty made in a year.

He had moved out of the raucous dorm and away from the vicious fraternity boys into a beautiful loft on the edge of the campus. It occupied a well-kept concrete building with a sparkling river running just below.

He had numerous rooms where he could spread out his insanely busy projects. One chamber housed his wildly popular fashion line of dresses and accessories he was creating. Another room was used for his sculpture and another for his paintings.

His handsome and gung-ho art agent and manager, Bruce Ramsey, had arranged it all for him.

It was this dynamic and outrageously sexy young maverick who was moving Brandon's career along at breath-taking speed.

After Brandon had signed a contract with the agent, Bruce had created a special group of his talented agents to handle just Brandon's career. A major art exhibit in Washington, DC had received major media coverage. The paintings and the sculptures sold out overnight. The result was over $250,000 for its creator.

But it was the fashion work that Bruce asked Brandon to concentrate on.

"Your art work is great but it only goes to a collector. With fashion your work can be brought by everybody in America. You give me the sketches, your prototype designs and I'll take care of the rest for you. Leave it to me and my staffers."

So now, Brandon was working hard on designing one piece dresses with comfortable pockets in all colors—black, grey, magenta, cobalt, and crimson—with sparkling trims of silver and gold. Matching sweaters and hats were worn with the dresses. They were loose, comfortable but colorful. Housewives, working women would love them.

For the dress up or glamour gowns, he used magazines from the 1920's—The Jazz Age—to pull together slender, sheath dresses, with trains at the rear. Each creation was covered with bugles, fringes and flattered the female figure. Matching cloche hats that were all the rage during the Roaring Twenties were perfect as crowning the head of the wearer.

Those modeled on catwalks in different cities were wildly praised and purchased. Bruce took the sketches to a team of dress makers. These items were then taken to Sunshine Industries, an expert producer of clothing, and now hundreds of duplicates were being shown in exclusive dress shops.

"Think of accessories," advised Bruce "Large cloth flowers, scarves, men's summer wear. Think big. Maybe even a toiletries line we could call Brandy's."

As Brandon threw off his clothes and wrapped an old terrycloth robe around him, he was in a good mood because of a rave profile that had appeared earlier that week in the campus newspaper.

"Brandon Flores was called a child prodigy back in his hometown of Fairview when his artwork was noticed by visiting artist, Florabel Rousseau. She predicted a brilliant future for him and it seems like he has fulfilled her wishes. As a freshman here at Blackwood Tech, his paintings and sculpture and fashion design are turning this handsome, blonde-haired genius into a one-man industry. And he's only eighteen! Stay tuned."

He was naturally pleased at the recognition of his work. He was also aware of the growing hostility of faculty members whose annual salaries he easily surpassed. His enemies were outraged that here he was, not yet twenty and he was already gaining national fame as well as a very healthy income. Bruce had even predicted that before the end of the year, his brilliant client could become a millionaire.

Before he sat down to begin hours of intense creation, Brandon poured himself a goblet of chilled Chablis and went to the window of his den and looked down at the rushing river right outside his loft building.

I don't have anything in common with the other students, he thought. They obediently study and attend class and they're cut off from reality for four years—smothered in an unreal cocoon. I'm already meeting and interacting with famous artists, news makers, with the backing of an internationally powerful talent agency.

He knew this infuriated his haters. Since they couldn't attack him in the dorm any longer, they made a point of shouting insults and threats on the campus. When he lived among them, gangs of boys would pound on his door, try to set it on fire, break into his room while he was gone and throw his clothes out of the twelfth story window into the mud below.

They tripped him, knocked his books out of his hand and threatened to lynch him.

Since leaving the dorm, life seemed safer. And Bruce had persuaded his rising star to purchase a big new car.

"You're on your way," explained Bruce. "You'll be meeting important people at the fashion shows, in their offices. You don't want to appear as a young, starving artist. You're the new blazing star of tomorrow. So show them you've got some wealth. Always knock 'em dead with what you wear and how you live. Get a big car to begin with."

So Brandon was delighted to purchase his first vehicle, a gleaming Chevrolet, the color of moss green. He paid cash for it, too, surprising the salesman who had never seen a student at the school do something so unorthodox. In fact, few adult buyers brought their vehicles with a stack of paper money.

As Brandon headed to his main work table in his "fashion room," he surveyed the beautiful cocoon he had created here in this old loft.

The walls in his bedroom/den were draped in transparent curtains of aqua, emerald and persimmon silk. His huge bed was covered with an imitation lion and leopard skin comforter.

The kitchen shelves and the large fridge were stocked with wines, canned hams, cheeses, cold slices of ham, potato salad and pimento cheese. Bruce Jasmine had created a snazzy looking bar, "because you'll want to offer your guests something besides tea or lemonade. Corporate and art people like to drink."

Now Brandon bent over his desk as he emptied a large box of watches from Japan. They were all cheap but looked expensive. He ripped out the bands from all the items but kept the time piece.

For each one he created striking, sparkling bands from silk, durable cotton in all colors. These watches could be tied on wrists instead of having to be snapped on manually.

For men, the artist chose tree bark colors, imitation zebra, tiger, and reptile cloth. For women, they had choices of crimson, copper, black, silver bands. Sequins and imitation stones were sprinkled over them. When these designs were showcased at his exhibit in Washington, all two hundred models were snapped up at one hundred dollars each.

When Bruce Ramsey saw this happen he went: "Wow, Brandy, baby. We'll buy hundreds more and my staff will find some college kids who can turn them out. You'll get rich just with your watches alone."

Bruce had brought him a handgun and they had practiced at s shooting range. Brandon surprised himself by being a good shot.

"You need protection when living alone out here on this little traveled road."

At ten o'clock, an exhausted Brandon Flores settled into his bed with a cup of hot cocoa and turned on the TV at the foot of his bed.

He was dozing off when suddenly he snapped to attention.

On the screen appeared a woman reporter. She stood before the State Mental Hospital in Raleigh with a strong wind whipping around her.

"Have you seen this man before?" she asked dramatically.

The photo of a man's face was shown. His dark hair, beard and moustache gave him a religious look. His eyes of pale green startled in their raw confusion and fear.

"This man is known to the hospital staff as John Sparrow. He was discovered by a group of loggers wandering around in freezing snow near the Mouria Gorge. He swears he has no memory of the past. The doctors have examined him and discovered scars on his feet and hands—as if a sharp metal object had been driven into his flesh.

"But what makes this case shocking to both the hospital and law enforcement is that John Sparrow looks uncannily like the long lost Emmanuel Trident, the so-called Naked Jesus who was crucified by Ku Klux Klan members in February of 1941. His body vanished from the crudely made cross within hours. His wife, the famous artist, Diana DuPree, was lynched. Their twin infant boys vanished. The town was decimated by a bizarre plague right after the massacre."

A photo of Emmanuel Trident was next shown beside that of John Sparrow. There was no mistaking the incredible resemblance the two shared. How could two men have such electrifying eyes the color of the ocean?

The reporter concluded her report by stating that John Sparrow was wearing a white priest-like gown when the loggers discovered him.

There were blood splatters over the material. When it was studied the physicians discovered that the blood was nearly nineteen years old.

Brandon was astonished by this news. He dragged out his large scrapbook devoted to the Vesaria Massacre. Over the years he had clipped out every magazine and newspaper article about the tragedy. Especially treasured was a stunning color photograph of Emmanuel Trident's face. Those laser-like eyes the color of lime, stared back at the viewer.

"I've got to meet you, John Sparrow."

Brandon had a better chance than most in accomplishing this feat. He had visited the nearby hospital several times to give art lessons to the patients. He had become good friends with the facility's manager, a feisty, red-headed lesbian, Deidre Fuller. The two had enjoyed some great, bawdy meals in her private office.

He called her office several times throughout the following day and finally reached her around five o'clock.

"You want to meet John?" she whooped. "So does about a thousand reporters and a thousand curiosity seekers. Be here at one o'clock tomorrow. Drive to the rear of the building and look for a red door. This is a visit you'll never ever forget."

#

Deidre Fuller greeted Brandon effusively and whisked him to her office.

"First, I want you to watch this filmed interview we did with John Sparrow about two weeks after we admitted him. It's an amazing thing to watch."

She clicked on the TV monitor in an adjoining room and left Brandon alone.

A title appeared on the screen:

Interview with Patient 1801 - John Sparrow by Drs. Martin Gordon, Harry Goodwin, Miriam Ledbetter and Hospital Administrator, Deidre Fuller... Date: February 20. Place: State Mental Hospital, Raleigh, NC. Time: 3:20 p.m.

Several hospital staff members sat around a long table. At the head was John Sparrow. Brandon leaned forward to study this fascinating figure. He was slender and very tall with unusually broad shoulders. A hospital robe covered him. Large hands were clasped together on the table.

Black hair hung to his shoulders. His eyes were deeply set and his lips were full and voluptuous. A strange aura of intensity emanated through the camera lens. After the interview began, his expression displayed confusion, uncertainty and his eyes nervously darted around the room.

Then he studied his hands clasped before him. He seemed like a man trying to concentrate, to remember. His lips moved occasionally—as if he were talking to himself.

Dr. Gordon: "My name is Dr. Martin Gordon and I will be the lead interrogator for our interview with Patient 1801. His name is John Sparrow. To give you a brief history of our patient: the name of John Sparrow was conferred on him by a group of mountain loggers who found this gentleman wandering around a desolate part of a thick wood near Mouria Gorge located on Mt. Mouria. On the other side of this gorge is the ghost town of Vesaria. There are no houses or people around for six to eight miles.

"This village was struck by a mysterious plague in l941 that decimated the population and animals. Believed murdered was Emmanuel Trident, the young minister. He was nailed to a cross by the Ku Klux Klan but his body vanished hours later. His wife was lynched, his household brutally murdered, his two twin sons also disappeared.

"We'll now proceed with the interrogation of our patient. The rest of you will please wait at the end of the interview to ask your questions. For the record, I'll ask the patient his name, please."

John Sparrow: "I don't know my name. When I was found by the loggers, they named me John Sparrow. So that's the name I'm using."

Dr. Gordon: "Mr. Sparrow, do you remember how you came to be located in the woods and dangerously close to the Mouria Gorge?"

John Sparrow:" I have no memory at all. It's like I was suddenly awakened by the loggers and I was shocked to find myself out in the woods. I do recall terrible pain to my head. When I was first examined, the staff in the Blue Mist Clinic found dried up blood at the back of my head. When the loggers first found me, I could not understand their words. It was like they spoke a foreign language. And then slowly, I began to comprehend. It's like there's a huge, black door of steel in my memory. I can't go beyond that door. I need a key to unlock it. My hands and feet are very painful."

Dr. Gordon: "Do you know how you received the curious scars on your hands and your feet?"

John Sparrow: (he studied his hands and his feet)." No, I have no idea at all. When it rained last Sunday, there was a pulsing pain. When the rain stopped, the pain left me."

Dr. Gordon: "I'd like to inform the rest of you interrogators that our doctors have carefully examined those scars. They agree that these punctures were caused by some sharp metal objects. Perhaps nails. Mr. Sparrow, I want you to look at these photos we'll show on the screen here of Emmanuel Trident. He was a religious leader in Vesaria. They called him the Mountain Jesus. He created a church there called the All Souls Church of the Mountains. Do you see a resemblance between yourself and Emmanuel Trident?"

Photos of Emmanuel Trident appeared on the screen. He was shown wearing his Cossack robe in a pose with members of his church. Another picture showed him naked except for a brief sarong as he addressed his congregation. Another image presented Emmanuel Trident with his bare back facing the camera. A striking tattoo of the face of Jesus Christ covered all of his rear portion. After studying them, the patient looked back at the physician.

John Sparrow:"I'm—I'm amazed! We do look exactly alike."

Dr. Gordon: "Mr. Sparrow, would you please stand and remove your robe and pajama top for us and then show us your back? I'd like for my cohorts to notice something very unusual."

The patient stood and removed his robe and then his pajama top. He turned to reveal his well-muscled back.

The amazement of the doctors was perceptible. They stirred slightly because John Sparrow revealed a stunning tattoo of the Messiah on his back. The colors were extraordinary in their glowing hues and in detail.

Dr. Gordon: "You may be seated. What do you think happened, Mr. Sparrow? The state police have been investigating the Emmanuel Trident case since l941. That's nineteen years ago. Because of intense public interest, the search for Emmanuel Trident has been on-going. The case was never closed. Don't you find it extraordinary that both you and the missing holy man both bore identical tattoos on your back? You have extraordinary eyes of green—identical to Emmanuel Trident. Not many, if any, have eyes as dramatic as yours."

John Sparrow: (Staring down at his clasped hands). "I cannot say who I am. When I try to mentally go beyond that black door, I receive a very sharp pain in my head. It's like someone stabs me with a sharp dagger if I try to think back. So I try to avoid the pain. But—I will say this. In the five weeks I've been here I've discovered I'm very religious. When I read the Bible, it seems familiar. I can read passages and passages and it all comes back to me."

Dr. Gordon: "So you think you may have been a religious leader at some time?"

John Sparrow (smiling slightly). "I can find no other reason for my interest in the Bible—and my desire to help others. Since coming here, I've talked to many patients. It's like they gravitate to me and I listen carefully."

Dr. Gordon: "Before we close this interview, the staff has noticed how amazingly fast you put on weight. Your appetite is quite voracious. When we first saw you, you were like a scarecrow. But now, you're gaining weight and muscle tone at just a phenomenal rate. Would you mind taking off your robe again so I can point out to the others proof of your weight gain?"

John Sparrow once more stood and doffed his robe and top. Dr. Gordon went up to him and had the patient to bulge his biceps and flex his limbs. He looked very sleek, slender with muscles already appearing, especially his toned stomach.

Dr. Gordon: "Do any of you have any further questions for Mr. Sparrow?"

Dr. Miriam Ledbetter: "Sir, I'm curious about something you told the initial investigators who questioned you."

John Sparrow: "Yes, ma'm. And that was--?"

Dr. Ledbetter: "You said you were looking for something but you've lost it. You also said, and I'm quoting, 'It's too early! I came too early!' Were you referring to someone or something? Emmanuel Trident had a wife and two infant boys. Are they whom you were referring to? And when you said, 'I came too early'—are you suggesting you were sent out into the freezing cold by someone or something?"

John Sparrow: (he bowed his head and shook it slowly) "I wish I knew. If I were the real Emmanuel Trident, I'm sure I would wonder what happened to my family. And yes, I do think I came too soon for whatever it was I was to appear."

Dr. Gordon: "Mr. Sparrow, I want you to look at this picture. It shows Emmanuel Trident with a very rare appearance of his wife, Diana DuPree. She wasn't seen in public very much because we know now that she had a number of enemies. These enemies were convinced that she was actually physically half-man and half-woman. A hermaphrodite, if you will. Please look at this."

On the screen appeared a magnificent and glowing Emmanuel Trident wearing a white robe. Next to him shimmered a stunning blonde woman. She was dressed in a white dress of peach silk and a matching wide-brimmed bonnet with violets. Both people were smiling.

Dr. Gordon: "This is Diana DuPree. Have you ever seen a woman that looks like her?"

John Sparrow: (He stared intently at the images and then closed his eyes). "I'm sorry to keep disappointing you. She's a very beautiful looking woman. I don't know if I ever knew someone like her."

Dr. Ledbetter: "Mr. Sparrow, I'm going to do something very unorthodox and I hope you won't be angry or take offense. This is only my personal thought. But I'm convinced that you *are* Emmanuel Trident—"

Dr. Gordon: "Now, Dr. Ledbetter, let's not—"

Dr. Fisher: "No, wait. I'm with Dr. Ledbetter. I'm convinced that Mr. Sparrow can't recall the past because of some terrible violence he experienced. I believe that in time, we'll prove that you are our long lost Mountain Jesus. If this were to prove true, though, our biggest question would be: where have you been for the past nineteen years? How did you emerge so dramatically in the wilderness with no houses for miles around?"

John Sparrow: (Speaking very softly) Perhaps you're correct. The similarities between me and Emmanuel Trident are extraordinary. I want to have a name and a past. (He suddenly pressed his face against his hands on the table and shook with sobs. The others looked on quietly. For several minutes, the film contained only the passionate weeping of the patient. Slowly, he raised his face. Deidre Fuller passed him several Kleenex tissues.

John Sparrow: "I'm sorry. I apologize. Only—I *sense* I've lost a great deal somewhere in my life—and I can't remember what it was."

Deidre Fuller: "Mr. Sparrow, please remember that we here at the hospital are going to do everything we can to protect and help you. It'll take time. But we're behind you all the way.

The others all agreed.

Dr. Gordon: "This ends our recorded interview with patient number 1801 John Sparrow."

Brandon didn't move for several minutes. His face was wet with tears after witnessing the emotional breakdown of this patient. His weeping was real.

All of this new information was so amazing he had trouble taking it all in. Whoever Patient 1801 was, he was still a fascinating person and now Brandon was more excited than ever to meet with him.

To think that if this man was incredibly Emmanuel Trident, then he had once been the husband of Brandon's patron saint: Diana DuPree.

#

"He looks and acts like a religious leader," Deidre Fuller said. She and her Brandon hurried along the corridor to room 1801. "That tape you saw was made one month ago. A lot has happened to our patient since then. None of us think he's acting or putting on a great performance. He's been interviewed by numerous law enforcement people, lawyers representing Diana DuPree. They all reluctantly agree that he's sincere. He's been hypnotized. We've given him the truth serum. Experts have tried to trick him and they can't. He's totally sincere in what he says is the truth. It's like he keeps saying. There's a big, black door of steel that he can't unlock. His memory began the day he was found by the loggers. Other patients are finding him out to talk about their problems. There's this air of radiance about him that makes him literally glow."

"Wouldn't it be amazing if he does turn out to be the long lost Emmanuel Trident?"

They had come to the end of the long corridor where the room of John Sparrow was located.

"You can't stay long now," Deidre whispered. "If the doctors discover I've let you up here instead of teaching art, then my tit will be in the wringer. If anyone comes in and demands to know what you're doing, open your bag and show them your art supplies. Just don't upset him."

"I'll be Florence Nightingale."

She knocked firmly on the door and opened it.

Standing in front of the window with his back turned to the door was the patient.

"John, I've brought you the visitor I mentioned yesterday. His name is Brandon Flores and he's a student at Blackwood Tech. He's also a rising star in the art world. Turn around and say hello."

John Sparrow turned around with an expectant expression.

His surprise was visible. His eyes widened and he held out his hands:

"You—you're—"

"What is it, John?" asked Deidre Fuller...

"I—I'm sorry. The visitor was standing in the shadow and for a moment I thought—it was a memory struggling to come out. I'm sorry, Mr. Flores."

"Call me Brandon—or, as my good friends nickname me: Brandy."

"Brandy," smiled John sparrow. "I apologize. Come in.""

"I'll leave you two alone for just thirty minutes," said Miss Hall and shut the door.

Brandon felt dizzy from excitement and something more.

John Sparrow was tall, massive and totally stunning.

Long, shoulder-length hair framed a square, virile face that glowed with an inner radiance. His mouth was full and sensuous. A dimple in his chin made him Hollywood handsome. It was his body that truly stunned.

He could easily have played an ancient god, like Jupiter, in a movie. Beneath the thin robe and pajamas, his powerful shoulders, chest and arms bulged. He moved beautifully like a wild animal.

Yet, his dramatic eyes startled for being so out-of-place here. The color of emerald crystal, they hypnotized.

John's big, strong hands took Brandon's and led him to a chair by the window.

"You're trembling," John sparrow said softly. "There's nothing to be nervous about. I feel like I'm ready to explode but—never mind. Sit here and let's talk."

"I've brought you some things I thought you would enjoy."

Deidre had told him how much the patient loved sweet things. Brandon handed him a box of bakery brownies, donuts and pecan cookies. There were also copies of the current issues of *Life*, *Look* and *Time*.

Outside was visible a frozen landscape covered with wetness and mist.

After Brandon sat down, the patient took a chair directly across from him and leaned toward him: "Do you think we've met before, Brandy? My memory is so terribly confused. It's like I'm reminded of something in my past—but if I try to recall it, that horrible, intense pain shoots through my brain like a knife."

John Sparrow took his visitor's right hand in his and squeezed it. "People tell me they've met me before but I think they've mixed me up with Jesus Christ. I look like him, I know."

"This may sound crazy—but could you be the resurrected Jesus whose come back to earth? Could you be the one?"

"Am I the one? Why would Jesus return here—unless there's a reason? I don't know who I am. No one believes me. They think I'm a fake or a quick-buck charlatan who's a hoax."

"I believe you, John. There's nothing fake about you."

For the first time, the ghost of a smile softened John Sparrow's sensual mouth. It suggested the phenomenal charm that lay dormant within him.

"You're a beautiful boy. When you stood there in the shadows, I thought you were a beautiful girl—maybe someone I knew. Am I embarrassing you? I'm sorry if I did."

"You don't embarrass me at all, John. I think you're beautiful, too. I've heard you have a fantastic tattoo on your back."

"Would you like to see it?"

"Oh, how wonderful that would be! Please!"

The patient stood up and turned his back.

With a flourish, he suddenly threw off his robe. He wore just his pajama bottoms. But his bare back was even more powerful than in the video.

A tattoo of the patient's face was rendered in amazing colors and beauty.

On the smooth surface, lustrous hues of red, emerald and gold were arranged to perfectly capture the owner's features.

"I'm totally amazed! How extraordinary!"

John flexed his muscles so that the portrait appeared to be move.

What made this image especially striking was that it showcased John Sparrow's amazing torso. No flab was visible. The patient turned so his visitor could see the front of his physique. His pectorals were enormous and bulged over his flat stomach with chiseled abs. John undid the cloth belt to his pajamas and stepped out of them.

He was completely naked. Brandon stared spellbound at the man's enormous endowment. It swung heavily between muscular thighs as if it were a pink plastic shopping bag, filled with goodies.

He grasped his manhood with both hands to shake it.

"My man thing seems to have attracted a lot of attention here, Brandy. I wonder why? Do you think there's something wrong with it?"

Brandon could barely speak. "I—uh—no, there's nothing wrong with it, John. I'm sure anyone would want to give you a sponge bath after seeing what Mother Nature gifted you with."

"You think so?"

He slipped on his pajama bottoms just as a knock on the door preceded the arrival of Deidre Fuller.

"Time to go," she smiled. "I trust you both had an enjoyable visit."

"I'd like Brandy to come back real soon," John Sparrow said. "We got along real good. I think he can help me."

"Please let me come back," pleaded Brandon. "We really like each other."

"I'll see what I can do. I need to dash. I'll see you two another time." She hurried down the corridor.

John Sparrow came up and embraced Brandon tightly. Brandon felt like he were drowning in a wonderful cloud of intense virility and intoxicating scents of clean male flesh. The patient's hips pressed against him so that Brandon could feel the pressure of John's manhood.

"I can't get over," whispered John Sparrow, "the feeling that we've met before. I've got to figure this out."

"John, here's something to think about. I was adopted at birth. I was found on the steps of a charity hospital, just hours after the Vesaria Massacre, in late February, 1941. I had a twin brother who was adopted by another family. Diana DuPree is my patron saint. I'm in college because I won the Diana DuPree Art Scholarship. I think I resemble her. Yes, even to being both male and female. Feel?"

He took John's hand and brushed it over his chest. His breasts had become more pronounced

"What in the world?" gasped John Sparrow? "This is amazing. If they can find proof that I'm Emmanuel Trident, then you would be—"

"Your son. Crazy, isn't it? But that's something to think about in the coming weeks."

John embraced him tighter and kissed Brandon for a long time. The patient's lips were soft, warm, and delicious.

"If you are my son," whispered John. "Then I need to show you my love."

"And should you prove to be my father, then my mother is Diana DuPree."

John's hardness was becoming enormous. He pulled out his erection and thrust it into Brandon's hand.

"I wish we had a private place, to show you—"

Outside the door, they heard food carts being pushed close by.

"John, I'd better go now—but I'll return."

"My son," nodded John Sparrow. "That would be like Christmas."

#

For the next three weeks, Brandon found it almost impossible to fully concentrate on his projects. Because he thought of nothing but that amazing kiss, embrace by the most beautiful man he had ever fantasized about.

The body heat of John Sparrow's torso was intense. He carried a haunting body scent—like warm, clean flesh, with a suggestion of citrus, musk and wood.

When his handsome agent, Bruce Ramsey, took Brandon out for lunch, he said:

"You look luminous today—and far away. Want to talk?"

His client regaled him through the meal about the wonders of John Sparrow, describing the farewell kiss and embrace.

Brandon had already told his agent about his fantasy that he might well be one of twin sons of Emmanuel Trident and Diana DuPree.

"That would be the most amazing story ever told," nodded Bruce. For several moments, he said nothing as he studied his young client. Brandon was showing all the signs of being someone outstanding. His true heritage had to be extraordinary: not only was he unusually beautiful, but charismatic as well. And his talent was so unique that it stood out in the faddish, short-lived artists in the world of art and fashion.

"Well, let's put that on the back burner. We got a lot of things going on that we need to jump on right now."

Brandy's, the first fashion and art boutique, would have a grand opening in the state capitol of North Carolina—Raleigh—in two weeks.

Not only was this a strong media city because of the state government being there. There were powerful bankers, multi-millionaires, a fashionable set of women who traveled everywhere for the next hottest thing in clothes and accessories.

Bruce had already taken care of everything—from the publicity, seeing that this staff put the final touch on the pink, gold and emerald color motif of the interior.

Food and drink would be furnished by the prestigious Ham and Ale Food Company. Male and female models had been selected to wear Brandon's colorful fall outfits.

The women would be attired in wool and tweed dresses with matching jackets. The colors were basically persimmon and chocolate. The jackets would be trimmed in abundant faux fur.

The men would model tailored slacks, boots, and sandals with vibrant sweaters of striking cobalt, ruby and emerald.

"You'll be the center of attention," Bruce pointed out. "So wear something kicky, showy and very elegant. You'll knock'em dead."

Brandon's designs were going into mass production within a month. This would be a major step upward for the artist. Already beauty editors across the nation were showing sharp interest in the stunning work of this "Blonde Picasso," as Brandon was being dubbed.

The "Blonde Picasso" was always excited when in the presence of his rugged agent, Bruce Ramsey.

A mop of sandy-red curls topped a large head. Bruce was a powerful looking man although he was only twenty-eight. He dressed in colorful and beautiful tweed suits, bow-ties, and suspenders. In casual mode, his attire were snug slacks that showcased his best feature—as he put it—his posterior. Sweaters of bright colors emphasized his muscular torso.

During their first lunch at the fancy Beefy & Barley restaurant in Blackwood, Bruce had regaled his attentive client over champagne cocktails with his wild exploits before settling down as the head of his family's century old legal empire.

He had been a brawler, a boxer, had explored the world and fought alligators and monster snakes, climbed the highest peaks, and had been a finalist in the national search for a new screen Tarzan.

But the main producer didn't want a "red-headed" guy portraying the King of the Jungle.

One weekend, he confessed, he and some buddies had answered an ad in an underground newspaper in the big city and frolicked in several stag loops—naked and hard and crazy.

"God only knows what happened to those sex movies," he laughed. His partners were both male and female.

He was often photographed for slick magazines in the South as he escorted various Southern belles to Dixie entertainments. In one picture, he wore a brief black bikini on the luxurious ship of a multi-millionaire, Andrei Shoshawna. Bruce explained to Brandon that he and the mega-rich Greek tycoon had enjoyed a three month journey along the water ways of Europe.

They lived for another three months in Mr. Shoshawna's palatial castle on the French Rivera. Neither Bruce nor his host nor any of the many guests wore any clothes.

"Some days I can't remember—there was so much wine and hashish and flesh. We all need an orgy like that in our youth."

"So now, I've settled down to make you world-famous, as I think you deserve," he once said.

The agent drove his client back to Brandon's place.

Bruce had removed his jacket and muffler and stood before the roaring fire. Brandon thought the agent looked unusually ravishing in just his tight sweater of white and the snug khaki slacks.

"Let me fix you a drink, Bruce."

"First, I think I'd like to take a brief plunge in that sparkling river."

"It's freezing! You'll catch pneumonia."

"I love it like that."

Quickly, he stripped naked and ran down to the pier where he jumped off into the wind-swept river.

Brandon wasn't surprised by his agent's actions. The agent had already said he was a nudist and delighted in visiting a colony of clothes-hating hedonists in Florida.

Bruce bounded into the den and its roaring fire and took a towel from Brandon to dry off. After doing so, though, he didn't put his clothes back on.

"I want to be naked here," he said quietly as he sipped brandy. "I never want to wear any clothes."

"I don't mind at all, Bruce—just so I can stare at you and drool."

"You like what you see?"

Bruce Ramsey possessed a muscular but natural looking torso. His body wasn't ripped or shredded like the models on physical fitness magazines. He was firm but fleshy in all the right places.

"Look at what I got swinging between my manly thighs."

Bruce grasped his uncut phallus with both hands and squeezed it. His sac bulged with large testicles.

He put his drink down and moved closer to Brandon.

"Let's forget I'm your agent for an hour or two. Let me show how much I enjoy having you as my client."

He embraced Brandon, kissing him wildly and then picking him up and carrying him to the bed.

"I've been wanting to fuck you since I first met you," muttered Bruce Ramsey. He had helped Brandon get rid of his clothes.

"Holy shit!" he gasped when he beheld Brandon's impressive bosom. The breasts had grown larger. The nipples were thick and extended.

"You really are like Diana DuPree!"

Greedily, Bruce suckled and licked his partner's breasts before parting Brandon's legs and sliding his phallus into place.

"I'm a virgin, John!" whispered Brandon. "Please go slow. Be gentle, will you?"

"You'll feel like magic with my love making."

Brandon prepared for a painful experience—but it proved to be like magic when his partner slowly and carefully entered him.

This is my first man, thought Brandon. I'm thrilled it's someone as dynamic and glorious as Bruce Ramsey.

Bruce offered his hard, powerful body to Brandon to do with what he wished. The artist became an eager student, as he enjoyed caressing and tasting his visitor's outstanding posterior, playing with the impressive endowment and caressing the over-sized testicles.

Bruce proved to be a resilient lover. He came several times that passionate afternoon.

When they enjoyed white wine during a break, Bruce pulled Brandon close against him.

"I worry about you out here in this isolated area," he muttered. "I worry that those homophobes might cause trouble for you out here."

"So far, it's been okay. I'd feel safer if you lived here with me."

"Tell you what. Should anything weird happen, call me. I'll be here in a New York second, with my mighty muscles and body to protect you from harm."

#

The Grand Opening of Brandy's in Raleigh proved a major triumph for both Brandon and Bruce.

The media gave it full coverage because one of the news 'hooks" was that Brandon Flores was only nineteen years old. Yet, already he was steadily amassing a fortune with the high price his paintings and sculpture was bringing in.

Now, here he was, with a line of fun, sharp looking fashion for men and women. His creations were classically simple: well-tailored clothes with a startling splash of color...or bolts of gold lightning...red stars...copper hued belts.

On display were fifty of the hot-selling Brandy's watches. Both men and women buyers brought all of them at one hundred dollars each and store representatives ordered hundreds of them.

Brandon's own outfit created much comment. A gleaming tunic and slacks of silver-gray silk sparkled. His bracelet and ring consisted of the same motif.

Jet and cobalt stones of glass sparkled as trim around his neckline and cuffs.

The front page headline in the *News and Observer,* declared:

Young Fashion Mogul Triumphs!

"Last night's triumphant opening of Brandy's brought out the city's leading figures from the worlds of art, media, politics and industry.

"Everyone was excited to see the latest creations of an artist who many critics are describing as 'The Dixie Rembrandt.'

"Brandon Flores is only nineteen-years-old and attends Blackstone Institute on a Diana DuPree Scholarship. Brandon says the tragic artist, who was murdered in 1941, in the village of Vesaria, along with her husband, Emmanuel Trident, was an extraordinary creator whose work has unjustly been forgotten.

"The artist's trademark 'fun' fashions for both male and female, were wildly popular. What really proved to be the hits of the store were the daring and fun watches with dramatic bands of faux fur and imitation tree bark and bands with living, tiny fish swimming around.

"Brandon says there are other Brandy's on the drawing board. His agent, the dashing Bruce Ramsey, stood close by. Ramsey, dressed in Scottish kilts and attire, was listed in *Southern Living* as the number one bachelor, voted on by Women Who Love Dixie Men, a high-fashion social club for females in New Orleans, Savannah, Charleston, Atlanta and Asheville.

"Mr. Ramsey, by the way, proved true to his reputation of impish shenanigans when he went around the crowd and asked: 'What do Scottish men wear under their kilts?'

"Without waiting for an answer, he would turn his back and yank up the skirt of his kilt—and proved to us that his much-admired and now uncovered posterior was in great shape."

CHAPTER TWO

"Come along this way," Deidre Fuller said. "I think we'll find our Greek god at the pool. When he's down there, that's where you'll find a traffic jam. Everybody wants to see our Naked Jesus—as everyone calls him."

Brandon was thrilled to be able to visit the hospital again. His thoughts had been consistently filled with John Sparrow—the man, the lover and who might well be his father.

To get through the entrance, Brandon had to pass a dozen or more news cameras and reporters. Deidre Fuller had managed to get him admittance because patients wanted their artist friend back to give classes.

The mystery of John Sparrow was proving to be the biggest news story of the day.

. People couldn't get enough of it. The very idea of a movie-star handsome man, who has no past or identity and who many believed returned from the dead, proved too good to ignore. The really religious were convinced that this enigmatic figure was actually Jesus Christ, who had returned to earth for reasons only he knew.

Letters from the public flooded newspapers offices regarding "The Man with No Past," as he was often called. Everyone had an idea as to who John Sparrow might be. The most popular theory was that he had returned from the dead and he was really Emmanuel Trident. But if this should be he, then where had he hidden for nineteen years and why was he barefoot in sub-zero temperatures"

"Our biggest problem with John," continued Deidre Fuller, "is protecting him from these desperate widows and rich women determined to take him to bed. The worst is Grace Cowan, a multi-millionaire who's brought our John thousands of dollars' worth of clothes. She wants him to be the minister in the new church she's built."

She and Brandon entered the steamy swimming pool area. A large crowd had gathered at the diving area.

"Just as I expected," snorted Deidre Hall. "John's fans are all here."

Brandon couldn't see him because of the swarm of people surrounding him.

And then, as John Sparrow pushed his way through the mob, he began to ascend the ladder that led up to the highest platform.

Brandon wasn't the only one who sucked in his breath.

The magnificent torso of the man poised there, on the tip of the board, hardly resembled the handsome patient that Brandon had talked to nearly two months before.

This man stunned with his powerful, golden torso. He was totally naked—except for the sliver of black nylon wrapped around his hips.

The chest had now filled out with rippling muscles. The pectorals had billowed out into twin hubcaps of flesh. The shoulders, arms and thighs amazed with their power.

If he weren't a patient here, Brandon could clearly see him as an in-demand model—movie star. Brandon turned to Deirdre Fuller... "Wow! Am I seeing the same guy I talked to a month ago?"

She nodded. "It's absolutely stunning at the transformation. We keep thinking that some magician sneaked into the building one night and exchanged the old John Sparrow for this one. And look at all those people! It's like they want to climb into his lap."

The figure on the diving board suddenly bounced up and down and then plunged sharply into the water.

When he climbed out, he could have been a merman of legend.

Deirdre led Brandon through the panting and squealing admirers.

"John, your friend, Brandon, has come to visit you again. Can you come with us?"

"No, no, he's staying here!" one of the female patients screeched. "We need to talk!"

Brandon was just inches away from John Sparrow and breathed in his beauty.

Water sparkled on his golden flesh. His hair was now a helmet of jet that he swept back. His startling eyes were luminous and warm. Dark stubble was already shadowing his lower face.

"Yes, Brandon, I want to talk to you, too."

He turned around and waved a hand: "Sorry everyone. I have a very special visitor."

Deirdre landed closer: "Go and change, John, and we'll wait.

"No, I want Brandon to join me in the locker room."

"Well," Deidre said with a roll of her eyes, "whatever you say!"

In the warm and smelly locker room, John quickly stripped off his briefs and jockstrap.

"I thought you'd like to see me naked,' John said simply. "Most people do."

If he were a professional model, his days of fame would be assured.

Looking up at his face, Brandon saw that John's eyes were still suffused with a quality of sadness and frustration. Despite his fantastic physical transformation, he was still bedeviled by some tragic shadow.

John saw his look...

"Do you think I've changed since you last saw me?"

"Good God, but yes, it's the most amazing transformation I've ever seen."

John ran a comb through his hair but paused.

"Something deep in my mind says this has happened before, in other places, maybe in other worlds."

His eyes darkened and glowed, as if he were plumbing the depths of his soul.

"It's like a voice keeps warning me: 'Too soon, John. You've returned too soon.' But I don't know where I came from or what my purpose here is. I look around me—and it's like I've been in crowds before with people clamoring for my attention."

"Perhaps as a powerful religious leader."

John's face clouded over, as if this idea was disturbing.

"I don't know. Perhaps as a religious leader, trouble came after me. Maybe it led to my tragedy."

He slipped into a pair of gray silk boxer shorts. They clung to his lower torso like coconut oil which he smelt of. His every movement was like an entrancing dance. Everything about him, thought Brandon, dazzled with its beauty.

Maybe this is why Jesus was so popular and powerful in his brief time on earth.

Dressed in a beautiful sweater of cocoa cashmere and tweed slacks the hue of wheat, John resembled an old-fashioned glamour star of the thirties.

"John, you look incredible! I love your outfit."

He smiled at the compliment.

"People have been very generous. There's one, Grace Cowan, who's brought me a very sharp wardrobe. She's been talking to me about heading her church."

"So I've heard."

John looked at him curiously. "You're jealous," he smiled in a way that suggested he was used to people being jealous over him. "There's no romance there although I think she expects it."

#

The two men arrived in Room 1801 and again Brandon was fascinated by the dramatic change. John's anonymous hospital room had been transformed into a swanky little chamber of luxury.

Stacks of new books and magazines and baskets of fruits and candies crowded the corners and shelves. A big screen TV sat in the corner.

The closet was open to reveal new coats and sweaters and shoes. One of the overcoats was a magnificent fur coat with a matching hat.

On his dresser were the most expensive colognes that Brandon had drooled over in New York's perfume boutiques. Even with his growing bank account Brandon was hesitant in paying $250 for a small bottle of *Candy Dreams*, or $175 for a vial of *Tuxedo*, or $300 for *Royal Bain* de *Champagne*.

Deirdre entered the room and clapped her hands.

"See, Brandon? Our patient here is so popular he might be forced to find a larger place. John, you have another guest to join you."

Behind her emerged a short, heavy woman…

"John, my boy, you're looking so happy today."

"Brandon Flores," said Deirdre, "I want you to meet Grace Cowan. She's building a big, new church in Blackstone and so she's naturally looking for a dynamic minister to head it."

Grace Cowan was dressed expensively but not attractively in purple silk. From beneath a small, straw hat trimmed with fake daisies, her dyed orange curls brimmed over a round face. Her features were thickly covered with make-up. Purple mascara made her eyes look like those of a raccoon. A cherry red lipstick gleamed on thin lips. Her throat and wrists were encrusted with pearl jewelry.

"Brandon I've been hearing so many nice things about you! You are already a best-selling artist and clothes designer. That's wonderful!"

"That's nice of you to say so. And this might interest you. I won the Diana DuPree Art Scholarship. She's become my patron saint. I pray to her all the time for providing me with all my college expenses."

"Oh, that is very, *very* interesting," sighed Grace Cowan. "That whole Vesaria thing is so fascinating, it just never ends. And because of Vesaria, I'm convinced our John here has a link to it—because he's the very embodiment of Emmanuel Trident."

"Miss Cowan," cut in Deirdre, "please. I've asked you not to bring up the name of Emmanuel Trident."

"Oh, it doesn't bother me anymore," John said with a shrug of his handsome shoulders. "Everybody seems to think I am he. That somehow, I've been dead for nineteen years and have chosen now to be resurrected."

He lit a cigarette and sat on the edge of his bed. His dark curls had dried and now they framed his face. Brandon saw the naked expression of emotion on the woman's face. She opened up her briefcase.

"I brought along some photos of my church. It's all completed except for a few of the bathrooms and the dining hall. It's in Blackwood, right on a hill, near the college. You may have seen it, Brandon?"

"That's your church?" he answered in surprise. "I knew something big was being built but I had no idea what it was. I thought it might be a hotel because of its size"

Grace Cowan spread the pictures on the bed.

They presented a big, gleaming structure of modern design. It was built into the side of a mountain. Its scope was impressive with a spacious auditorium, thick, red carpeting and stained glass windows.

"And here's our office where the minister would have a staff of ten. We'd have a public relations person, a music director, and several television consultants. I would want to make a video of every service held in the church. I'd like to film mini-movies about religious figures—like Samson, Adam, and Goliath— similar to what evangelist Buster Scoggins has done. He stars this amazing young Adonis named Tommy Barnes who could be a double for our John. I think he would make a marvelous Samson, wearing just a brief loincloth. Hmmmm!"

She collected the photos and looked at John who had been very quiet. He stared at the floor with a cigarette between his fingers.

"I've also given our friend here copies of sermons made by Emmanuel Trident and I've shown him home movies that were made of his services."

"Oh, I'd love to see those!" Brandon said. "Could I?"

"Of course. We'll arrange something. John here would be spectacular."

The face of the patient had become grim. He shot her a glance:

"Have you thought about the public and media reaction if I took this on? They'd call me The Man with No Name. The Man from Nowhere."

Grace Cowan squeezed his arm. "Your worshippers wouldn't care a bit. They'd see you as someone very beautiful and inspiring."

She turned to declare dramatically: "I was only twelve when I was taken to Vesaria to see the Naked Jesus. That's what people called Emmanuel Trident."

"You actually saw him?" gasped Brandon.

"Oh, yes!" she smiled, pleased that he was so impressed. "I've never seen a man so beautiful. As we all know now, he began his services wearing a striking white gown, then he tossed it off. He hated to wear clothes. He wore these beautifully made panels of glittering silk to cover the front of his hips, so he wasn't really naked—but he was when he turned around and proved that nothing covered his rear. And that incredible tattoo of his face—or of Jesus Christ—on his back, that really astonished all of us."

"Much like our adorable boy here. And it was like a movie. A lone spotlight shone down on him and that powerful torso of his. Ah! That's something no one ever forgot. He was bigger than life with such a tremendous physique. Well, John? Are you any closer to giving me your decision? You can't stay here forever. The doctors are thinking of letting you go any day. You'd have no place to go."

"Now Miss Cowan," cut in Deirdre, "there are numerous churches and groups who want John to live with them."

Grace Cowan had lit up a cigarette and gave the woman a withering look.

"Humph! And be beholden on them for his existence. If John becomes my preacher, he would be independent. I'd pay him a fabulous salary. All his living expenses would be paid for. He'd have his own car, charge accounts at all the stores here and in nearby big cities. John would simply enthrall church members! He'd be Emmanuel Trident all over again. John? What do you think?"

Brandon couldn't stand looking at Grace Cowan. Her eyes stared intently at her handsome prey. There was such naked longing in them along with naked lust.

"I can't answer, Grace" he said softly. "I'll have to think about it."

"Of course, of course, I want you to. I have a few other candidates for minister—but you're at the top of the list. I simply have to leave. So many things to do—like interview some candidates for minister of my church."

She mashed out her cigarette in an ash tray and touched her fingers to her orange curls.

She looked coolly at Brandon. "You're leaving, too, aren't you?"

"Later," he drawled and enjoyed watching her face tighten.

Grace glanced from him to John and left the room stiffly with Deidre Fuller.

Brandon went up to John who was studying him.

"John, she wants your body. Badly. But then you're probably used to that."

He sighed. "You've got her figured out, eh? Yeah, you're right. But that offer is most tantalizing."

"I shouldn't try to influence you—but I think you should take it! I can see you so vividly in front of a congregation. Maybe you could copy your namesake—Emmanuel Trident—and wear almost nothing. That'd really get the people in the pews."

John snorted. "Yeah, if I let everything hang out, that'd really liven things up, wouldn't it?"

"Well, with that said, I've really got to go."

"I wish you wouldn't go, Brandy."

John had closed the door and came close to his visitor.

"It's late—"

"I know you'd like to feel of my muscles," the patient whispered. "Don't feel embarrassed. I can sense these things. Go ahead. I want you to. Slide your hand up under my sweater and feel my chest."

John had rapidly undone his belt, his pants buttons and pushed them down. His erection was enormous and he wrapped his hand around Brandon's which had grasped and squeezed it.

Brandon was so dizzy from this sudden onslaught of erotic delights that he had to hold on to his partner to keep from collapsing. As John's kiss became more intense, his phallus suddenly erupted.

Brandon stepped back to witness the thick streams of whiteness that squirted out. He grabbed a towel and John used it to dry off his organ.

"Whenever I'm around you, I go a little crazy—like I want to take you right here."

Before Brandon left, John leaned down to whisper: "In the future, no matter what you see on TV or read in the newspapers, take it with a grain of salt."

#

Bruce Jasmine urged his star client to quit college to take care of his rapidly growing career.

Brandon said he couldn't drop out now—this would mean terminating his scholarship. It would be a blow to the memory of Diana DuPree.

"I'm dropping all my courses except those in art," he explained. "I can easily handle those."

Yet, he discovered that because of the recent spate of newspaper and magazine articles about him, especially the opening of his first store, Brandy's, in Raleigh, the air of hostility among the faculty had intensified.

His instructors, who had at first been gracious in their critiques of his work, now smiled politely without warmth. His fellow art students didn't invite him to join them in visits to the local beer and pizza hangouts.

When he was heading to his car one afternoon, two familiar figures confronted him.

"Well, look at the cocksucker," jeered Gene Schmidt. He was a flabby, acne-faced bully who always led these attacks. "Thinks he's hot shit because he now owns a fag store for muthafuckers like him."

"Ain't she pretty?" simpered Harold Goins, the roommate of Gene Schmidt. "Bet she's giving lots of BJ's to her agent. Has he fucked you yet, maggot? Looka his chest! Is she wearing a bra or what?"

Brandon reached inside his jacket and yanked out his Billy club.

"You losers sure seem to have me on your mind. What's the attraction? Bet you're wanting some of my cocksucking. And that's a pleasure you'll never enjoy."

Suddenly, he slammed the club against the heads of his attackers. They stumbled around and then leaped for him—but suddenly, a snazzy red sports car squealed to a stop just inches away from the attackers.

Bruce Jasmine jumped out. He swung a baseball bat back and forth as he approached the group.

"Hey Brandy. Are these some of the goons you've been telling me about?"

"Goons!" snarled Gene Schmidt. "And just who the fuck--?"

His words ended in a shriek as Bruce Jasmine suddenly slammed his bat on the heads of the duo, zinging them fast and hard on the rest of their bodies. He kicked them, shoved them and pushed them away.

They limped away, glaring at the agent and his client, with Gene Schmidt shouting; "You're gonna pay for this, cocksucker! Just you wait."

Bruce pulled Brandon close against him.

"You okay? Something told me you might be in trouble and I'm glad I showed up."

"You're wonderful Bruce—but we haven't seen the last of those jerk-offs. They'll try again and they'll probably have more of their goon buddies with them."

Bruce stood back and shook his head. "Brandy, you don't need any of this shit. You shouldn't have to worry about people trying to destroy you. You're going to be very famous someday soon. You're on your way. These cockroaches will be forgotten. Nobody's going to miss them."

"Let's go to my place for something cold to drink, Bruce. We can talk it out there."

#

At Brandon's loft, Bruce once more stripped naked, jumped into the cold waters of the river, and when he trotted all wet and shaking into Brandon's den, a warm mug of rum awaited him.

Brandon rubbed him down with a large towel. Bruce grabbed him and threw him on the bed.

"Before we talk, we need to communicate this way."

He was more passionate in his love-making than ever before. His partner marveled at the warmth of his agent's ripping body.

"Treat me like a sex doll," panted Bruce. "Take my dick and squeeze it, lick it, suck it. Make love to my ass."

Bruce ravished Brandon's growing breasts and mounted him.

"One day you'll have your cunt," he whispered. "And I'll be the first one to fuck you."

For Brandon had described his goal of eventually having a sex change operation that some people were already doing.

After a simple meal of hot clam chowder, pimento cheese sandwiches and wine, the agent told Brandon that the media coverage of his big opening of Brandy's had gone out across the nation. Other cities were clamoring to have a Brandy's.

Time Magazine had even contacted the agency about doing a layout of Brandon and his many projects.

"We need to think about expanding our staff to help you out," Bruce said. "Those watches you made are fucking hot. Everybody wants one of those. You should think of making more accessories for your fashions. Big, cloth flowers, pendants in the shape of animals, butterflies, symbols like hearts and eyes. Scarves, hats, jewelry, maybe even down the road toiletries. You would have your own brand. Soaps, perfumes, after-shave, powder. Wow, we're gonna see a Brandy's Empire down the road. I can see it damned fast!"

#

Three weeks passed and although Brandon saw his enemies several times in the classroom building, they merely stared at him with hard, dark eyes.

They're too quiet, he thought. They're definitely planning something.

He wished he had taken up Bruce Jasmine's offer of moving in with him for a while. At least the presence of his agent's powerful, young body would ease his worries of being the target of thugs.

#

Brandon enjoyed working with the reporters and cameraman when they did stories on his career. He gifted his favorite male journalists with snazzy Brandy watches with zebra or imitation rock pebbles as bands.

His favorite women reporters received an eye-catching hat or scarf that was sprinkled with sparkling sequins and paste jewelry.

Brandon sensed that one key road to public notice was through the media. One article on him would often result in other articles from competing rivals.

One of his closest press allies was Abigal Corning, the top reporter for the local television station. Around seven o'clock one night, she called:

"There's something coming on at ten o'clock that I think you will have to watch. Can't say anything more. It'll knock your socks off."

At ten, he sat before his TV, while eating a hot fudge ice cream sundae when, Abigal Corning appeared on the screen

"Tonight you will be given an exclusive tour of the brand new and very controversial opening of the All Souls Church of the Mountains. This multi-million dollar structure was fully financed by famous philanthropist Grace Cowan who says she wants to bring something brand new and adult and controversial to Blackwood. And to make sure the controversy begins before it opens its doors, she has tapped the mysterious Man with No Name—John Sparrow, to be the minister. Let us now go into the church and meet our two newsworthy subjects."

Standing before a dramatically lit altar were two figures in striking attire.

Grace Cowan was dressed in a flowing purple robe with a wreath of lotus leaves encircling her head. Beside her was Jesus Christ—or someone who could have been his twin brother. John Sparrow had grown a beard and moustache during the past month. His white gown flowed over his powerful figure and on his head perched a garland of thorns.

Reporter: "Good evening, Miss Cowan and Mr. Sparrow. Miss Cowan, some would say you're taking a gamble on this church that you're financing one hundred per cent with your fortune. Why do you think this area needs another church when we have so many?"

Grace Cowan: "I know, I know, I've heard the same questions. I think that every community needs diversity in their worship. I have nothing at all against the traditional churches: like Baptist, Methodist, Catholic, Episcopalian and others. My church will not be tied down to one set of beliefs. I want to excite and stimulate people to enjoy their bodies through a positive way. Haven't we all gotten just a little tired of hearing the same lectures in churches since we were little?"

Reporter: "Mr. Sparrow, I understand you were very hesitant about accepting Miss Cowan's offer to be the minister here. Why is that?"

John Sparrow: "I believe many people are familiar with my case. I suffer from total amnesia about my past. Since being admitted to the state mental hospital, many people have told me that I have to be none other than the tragic Emmanuel Trident, who was violently murdered and then vanished twenty years ago, along with his family, when he was a powerful minister in Vesaria. I've seen his pictures and read up on him and all I can say is that I think he was a great man who tried to do good in an unorthodox way. I hope I can equal him."

Reporter: "Emmanuel Trident was also called the Naked Jesus—because he used such shock tactics as appearing stark naked in front of his congregation. He also used a hand whip to punish so-called sinners. Will you, Miss Cowan, be doing the same thing?"

Grace Cowan: "We'll have to wait and let the public find out for themselves."

#

On the Friday before the big Sunday that would see the doors opening to the All Souls Church of the Mountain, the *Blackwood Times* ran an in-depth article on the new house of worship and Grace Cowan and John Sparrow.

It was headlined:

One Church That's Guaranteed to Draw a Crowd

— By Starr Reynolds

When the doors to the brand new All Souls Church of the Mountains opens Sunday morning at ten o'clock, you can be assured there will be a line worthy of a movie premiere.

The church's founder, wealthy philanthropist, Grace Cowan, has sunk a reputed six million dollars into this venture. Just from a quick tour by this reporter, you will feel like you're in the lap of luxury.

Everything imaginable for those able to get into this religious temple has been done to make it the ultimate in comfort. Magnificent furniture and decorations will be waiting, along with an extravagant buffet.

But that's mere icing on the architectural cake.

Certain to be a bonanza of interest will be the preacher chosen to reign over his flock.

John Sparrow, the mysterious figure called The Man from Nowhere and The Man With No Name will be in charge. His resemblance to Jesus Christ is so striking that when you first see him, you may find it difficult to say anything. When this reporter caught up with him, he wore a beautifully designed gown of almond linen. Dark hair touched those incredibly broad shoulders.

His face was radiant and when he talks, he mesmerizes. Those stunning eyes of green that has caused so much comment in the media really are galvanizing. When he looks at you, be prepared to be hypnotized. They are truly amazing.

He carries with him a profound air of sincerity. No matter what his background is, his sponsor, Grace Cowan, has discovered a million dollar treasure.

As has been pointed out in the media, Miss Cowan and many others are convinced that John Sparrow and the legendary Naked Jesus, alias-- Emmanuel Trident--are actually the same.

#

When the doors opened that Sunday, Brandon was accompanied by Bruce Ramsey. Both had agreed to wear black for this religious experience. Although they arrived at seven o'clock in the morning, they were surprised to find a long line of people already waiting at the entrance. Three hours later, the doors opened. Visitors were greeted by two husky young male ushers and Grace Cowan. All three wore tunics of gun metal velvet.

The trio greeted each person. When Brandon came up, the philanthropist nodded her head and whispered: "John and I want to talk to you next week about something important. We'll call you."

The interior matched the gushing descriptions in the media.

Magnificent stained glass windows cast a cascade of brilliant hues over the dark pews with crimson cushions in the seats. Brandon had read that these windows were imported from an ancient cathedral in Italy and had cost more than a million dollars.

A haunting scent of burning incense wafted musk, sandalwood and tree bark. This, along with the eerie but soothing music, performed by an organist, a bass fiddle, a flute and a kettle drum, enhanced a sense of mysticism. Reality seemed far away.

By eleven o'clock, there was no more room. The doors closed and a choir attired in gleaming robes of gold and ivory preceded down the aisle. A larger orchestra was used and the music was again unlike anyone had heard. Miss Cowan had told the press she was using the original music written by Emmanuel Trident. The music was curiously muted and had no conventional rhythm. Stanzas began, paused, and continued with an occasional drum beat.

There was much neck craning as worshippers looked around to see who all had come. Brandon was surprised to see that many of the worshippers were young, some from college. The older visitors were neatly dressed and conveyed a quality of sophistication. The die-hard Christian types were noticeably absent. Perhaps all the discussion in the media that this church might prove controversial had obviously repelled the Bible thumpers.

Two television cameras were present. Brandon recognized several of the reporters who had interviewed him for profiles on his accomplishments.

Miss Cowan appeared on the stage and held her arms out:

"Welcome! Welcome all of you for this first service in the brand new All Souls Church of the Mountains. Without wasting any more of your time, for we have a busy schedule, let me introduce to you your Holy Man! John Sparrow!"

Lights all dimmed to near darkness.

A side door opened and suddenly, there he was—the star of this sermon.

There was a gasp at his entrance. John Sparrow was Jesus Christ brought to life in his wheat tinted robe.

Only a gold spotlight shone down on him and this bathed him in luminous radiance.

He walked slowly and deliberately up to the podium. He conveyed intense power, mastery, and self-confidence.

John Sparrow raised his hands above him and said:

"Welcome! Welcome to the first service to ever be held in this All Souls Church of the Mountains. We are dedicating this church to the memory of that legendary Mountain Jesus: Emmanuel Trident. We do not know where this religious pioneer is buried today, but wherever it is—you are not forgotten."

He came from around the podium and approached the congregation.

Then, with a dramatic flourish, he threw open his gown and cast it off so that it collapsed at his bare feet.

There was a louder gasp of shock—because John Sparrow was completely nude, except for a very brief panel of copper-hued silk that hung down before his manhood.

Everyone was now spellbound—because the sight of his magnificent torso bathed in amber from above enhanced his image as surreal. His pectorals were enormous and billowed over the rest of his body. His powerful shoulders, arms and thighs were bigger-than-life. Not even movie Hercules could compare to this dazzling specimen of male hood.

"I am a man!" he shouted and beat his fists against his chest and raised them upwards. Copper bracelets encircled his powerful biceps and wrists.

"Until Jesus Christ is resurrected again--look at me as your Messiah! Believe in me—yes, I, here in my earthly environment—and you will have a life beyond your wildest dreams."

As his words boomed out, Brandon was as electrified by this performance as everyone around him.

It wasn't just words that moved him so profoundly. It was the intensity of John Sparrow's words and the constant flexing of his body that created a totality of physical magic. Many realized that standing before them was someone phenomenal—and not just a mere preacher who had shown up to give an hour long sermon quickly forgotten--but a creature who meant every word he said.

Behind him, Grace Cowan smiled and nodded her head as if she was finally letting the world discover what she had realized all along: John Sparrow was a gift from heaven.

Later, no one could quite remember exactly all that this blazing new religious figure had talked about. All they could agree on was that they had never been so electrified by a speaker.

He had stressed that the Bible teachings were a cover—that life hadn't been created by a God. No, it was an ancient deity named Mouria who had flourished as all-powerful, millions of years ago. She was a hermaphrodite as were all of her citizens.

She shared her powers with a group of actual males who were famous for their bigger-than-life torsos and beauty and sexual energy.

One of them was Jesus Christ.

After a titanic cataclysm of the world, the civilization of Mouria was destroyed except for a branch had thrived on a North Carolina mountaintop until the late seventeenth century. They were forced to flee because of a marauding mob of vicious pioneers. There was no Adam or Eve. There was only one creature that possessed male and female attributes. This was the person Mouria wanted to live in the world. But aberrations occurred until the beings became a separate woman and a separate man. That's when all the troubles in the world began.

When John Sparrow finished his sermon and vanished through the side door, the congregation sat still for a moment—as if still too stunned to move. What they had seen had been so astonishing they would tell their grandchildren for years to come the day they first saw John Sparrow in action—and how they had realized the meaning of his words. His appearance—and sermon—was like nothing any of them had seen.

It was more than being present for a sermon. Through a dynamic transformation of the preacher's conventional role—John Sparrow had transcended a traditional Sunday morning ritual into a phenomenal life-changing moment for all that beheld him. Share your love for one another. Never judge. Support your family and friends in positive ways.

And then the applause began. Like the reaction to a masterful performance by a blazing artist, the applause continued until John Sparrow re-appeared. Dressed now in his white robe, he thanked everyone and then invited them to lunch in the basement dining hall.

Brandon looked over at his companion, Bruce Ramsey. He also looked dazed.

"I think we've witnessed something here earth shaking. This man has got to be either the real Jesus Christ—or Emmanuel Trident."

A mature looking woman in front of him turned and smiled:

"Emmanuel Trident *was* Jesus Christ—and now he's returned again—hopefully for the last time."

#

The shimmering glow of that unforgettable sermon carried on down to the magnificent dining hall.

This was no mere eating area found in most churches.

Four long tables groaned under the steaming dishes of succulent treats that were rarely if ever seen in a church buffet line. One table was laden with steaming pots of coffee, iced tea, fruit juices.

Servers wearing white hats and jackets filled platters with abundant servings of salmon, steak, pasta, lasagna, candied yams, broccoli casseroles, tuna fish casseroles, yeasty rolls and cornbread. The variety was staggering

Worshippers had a bewildering array of desserts to choose from: pies, cakes, puddings, cobblers and numerous containers of ice cream that set in bucket filled with ice.

Large round tables were quickly filled with visitors who eagerly shared their impressions of the morning. Everyone tried to explain their feelings but few were able put into words that could describe the whole electrifying experience. John Sparrow was looked upon as the second coming of Christ.

To their delight, he appeared now, attired in a robe the color of pearl and proved to be a powerhouse of charm. He smiled, laughed, posed for pictures.

Some of the visitors wept as they held his hands and he talked to them. They were certain he was the Christ who had returned. Some of the young ushers had to lead several people out of the dining room. They couldn't control their emotions.

When John Sparrow came upon Brandon and his friend, he stooped down beside him.

"Well, how'd I do?"

Brandon introduced the minister to Bruce and then let out a long sigh.

"John, you will never know just how much you smashed through to everyone. When you tore off your robe and everyone saw what you had, and what you said, it simply rocked everyone."

Still on his knee, the new minister studied the bronze-hued title on the floor before looking up at Brandon and smiling at Bruce… Although his manner was sociable and warm, that same sad quality could be seen in his eyes.

"Something very strange happened to me when I stood there. It was like I had done this many times in my life. I heard the music, I saw the worshippers and thought: you've been here before—and more before."

"Perhaps you're remembering things now—and closely related you are to the real Emmanuel Trident."

Before he stood up, he put his hand on Brandon's shoulder and smiled at Bruce.

"Grace may have told you this—but she wants you to paint me. It will be a big, special portrait by the most gifted artist we can find. I've chosen you."

Brandon pretended to faint. "How simply fabulous! This is such an honor! Can we start like mid-week? I've got exams on Monday and Tuesday."

They set up a time and John Sparrow said that money was no object. Brandon would be richer by tens of thousands of dollars.

Brandon made one stipulation: The painting would be done at his loft.

Bruce Ramsey was charmed by the young minister. Later he said: "He's the real thing. There ain't nothing phony about him. I've seen my share of charlatans but this guy is no shyster."

The diners were delighted when the choir sang softly more tunes written by Emmanuel Trident. The lyrics and the music were strangely soothing and uplifting. No one could be depressed with worries with this beguiling sound.

#

The first service in the All Souls Church of the Mountains created a media whirlwind.

Brandon prepared spaghetti and wine for Bruce that evening so they could watch the news coverage of John Sparrow and the new church.

"Good evening every one" began anchor Abigal Corning, "and we begin our newscast tonight with the sensational opening of the All Saints Church of the Mountains here in Blackwood. Let's go now to our reporter on the scene, Stephanie Albright.

A blonde haired woman appeared with her microphone standing a short distance away from the church where a long line wound past her and into the parking lot.

"As you can see from very early this morning, we had more than three thousand people to show up. Only one thousand of them made it into the church."

The scene changed to show the interior of the building.

Viewers were treated to the nearly nude figure of John Sparrow as he delivered his sermon. Then, a short segment of the crowded dining room and the hostess and her protégée moving around.

Several people were interviewed after the service.

"I came mostly out of curiosity but also to see if this church would be worth switching over from my old one," said Billy Andrews, a construction worker. "After seeing and hearing John Sparrow, I'll be here every Sunday

"I was simply electrified by Preacher Sparrow," said Sudie Carmichael, a housewife. "I've never enjoyed a service more than this morning. I'll definitely be here again." But there was at least one critic.

"It was just a lot of foowey macgooey!" grumped Abner Jacobs, a farmer. "I was amazed to see this preacher giving us a bunch of guff while wearing hardly anything. I was frankly embarrassed."

#

The news about the new church and its dynamic preacher grew steadily through the week. Now, everybody wanted to see what all the shouting was about. The hint of nudity was a big factor now in ordinary people making plans to attend. John Sparrow's fame grew far beyond the small confines of Blackwood.

TV crews from bigger cities like nearby Charlotte, Asheville and Raleigh did sensational programs on The Mystery of John Sparrow. Brandon read one feature in the *Asheville Citizen-Times* that showed the minister in his robe—and out of it.

"The Hercules Preacher!" shouted one headline that was accompanied by John Sparrow flexing his powerful muscles.

"If Jesus was a Mr. America," said one caption, "this is what he would look like."

One high school girl, Sadie Van Houten, had started a fan club for John Sparrow.

"So what if he is a minister," she declared. "John Sparrow is the sexiest man alive."

She was shown with her bedroom walls covered with newspaper and magazine pictures of her hero baring his body for religion.

#

With much excitement, Brandon welcomed into his loft the object of his painting.

John Sparrow immediately filled the big room and the air seemed as if it were cleaner with a silver sheen.

A uniformed chauffeur accompanied him. John had warned Brandon ahead of time that Grace Cowan was nervous with his choice of artists but he was in command. She was afraid the two men might end up in bed.

She was not happy at all, either, when Brandon laid down the law: she was not to accompany her dazzling discovery. The artist wanted her to be surprised and delighted with the final product.

She sent in her place her trusted chauffeur, Amos, who would report everything that happened straight back to the source of all this wealth.

"Mr. Sparrow, welcome!" smiled Brandon and made a mock bow. He turned to the rugged figure of Amos, who looked slightly sinister in his black chauffeur's uniform with the knee-length boots. He was a well-built man in his early fifties and also did duty to Grace Cowan as her personal bodyguard. It was also reported that Amos performed stud services for his employer and was found highly satisfactory.

"I've heard many things about you, Mr. Flores," Amos drawled.

"And everything you've heard is true," answered Brandon. "I'm as notorious as they say. Okay, let's get to work then. Amos, I do my work in private so I'll take John into my studio. I've got all kinds of magazines you can read out here on the balcony. As you can see, too, my bar is well stocked. In the fridge are all kinds of beer. See below? I've got a deck where my guests enjoying stripping naked and jumping into the water.

Amos made appreciative sounds. "It is pretty warm today and maybe a beer…

John caught on and spoke up: "Amos, a beer's not going to hurt you. While Brandon and I are working, take you a beer or two and go down to the pier. We saw it on the way up. There's lounge chairs and a table.

"Take off that hot uniform, have a few bottles, and enjoy that cool, brisk water. Go naked. Just like John here will be."

"You men get to work then," Amos snorted. He took off his chauffeur's hat and went to the bar. "It is pretty damn warm out there."

#

The young artist had worked carefully the night before to create the perfect setting for his celebrated subject.

Debussy's *La Mer* played on the record-player. A large fan blew a vivifying current through the studio.

Against a screen of dark gold, a comfortable stool with a cushion was arranged. Candles flickered here and there and a haunting scent of orange blossoms kissed the air.

"You," Brandon said pointing his finger at John "will instantly strip naked and you will don a special loincloth I made especially for you."

John lacked the quality of sadness that bothered Brandon so much. This afternoon, he was greatly enjoying this experience and pretending to be a male stripper. He took off everything, piece by piece, until he was naked.

"Here I am. Ready to be immortalized. And you have a piece of material you want me to wear?"

The artist was strangely silent as he saw up close the amazing torso of John Sparrow.

His flesh had become a gleaming golden tan, all over, and had sheen to it all.

His enormous pecs had grown even larger than the last time Brandon had seen him. His stomach was flatter, and even his stunning genitalia stood out.

It hung heavily, darkly, but glistened with sweat.

The phallus looked unreal—as if the subject had tied on an artificial dildo. But, it stirred and flipped up and down slightly while behind it, the huge testicles hung nearly halfway down to his knees.

"Wow!" gasped Brandon. "I don't know if I can get all that man stuff onto the canvas! I just hope my costume for you will cover the essentials—but you've got a lot to hide."

He had created an attractive concoction of egg-blue velvet with a spattering of stars, along with a big pouch. As John tried it on, he and his artist doubled over laughing. Even this spacious attire was too constricting for the heavily hung model.

It was agreed that he didn't have to wear it—just placed it over his privates to give the illusion he wore it.

Finally, John posed on the stool, his head thrown back and his hands griping the back of the stool.

Before he began to paint, Brandon took a roll of pictures of John Sparrow in various poses. John tossed aside his costume and playfully went into numerous poses. At one time, in high spirits, he grabbed his phallus and shook it at the camera. Then he braced his back against the wall, and wrapping both hands around his erection, he feigned to be in extreme sexual ecstasy.

There was a knock on the door and Amos stuck his head in.

His eye grew big when he saw John's sexual pose.

Brandon, afraid of what Amos would report to his employer, threw John his loincloth.

"Holy Mary," gasped Amos. "Mr. Sparrow, you do look unreal. I've never seen a man with a body like you have. I mean I've seen you in church with your sarong. But now, wearing nothing, its—its surreal..."

With a still stunned glance at the holy man's sexual apparatus, the chauffeur backed out of the room.

Alone now, Brandon went to his easel and picked up his palette.

"John, I'm going to try and be a good little boy and work very intensely. Afterwards, we can have some fun."

The model smiled and nodded his head.

"You're the boss here. And I'll try and behave myself, too."

Through the week, the posing sessions raced by. Brandon felt like he were under a spell as he did some of his best work.

John seemed to know exactly how to pose and to remain still although it could be disconcerting at times—as to when his manhood would stir and become fully erect.

"Sorry," he grinned. "I just can't help my little John from misbehaving."

"I'll certainly include him in our portrait."

"And Grace will have a heart attack."

Amos, the chauffeur, would poke his head in now and then—as if to catch the artist and model in a hot embrace. But he enjoyed stripping off his clothes and jumping into the river.

Although Brandon allowed no one to visit him during these sessions, he made an exception for Bruce Ramsey, who had wanted to see the much discussed torso of John Sparrow up close.

He was quiet as Brandon placed his oil paint on the canvas. He seemed spellbound by the spectacular nudity of John Sparrow.

Later he would tell Brandon that it was like viewing a living Greek statue of a god. John's torso was proportioned so stunning that it seemed to call out: Enjoy me. Touch me. Caress me.

Brandon enjoyed the wine breaks they had, where John could unburden himself. He lounged naked and relaxed as he discussed his bizarre situation at the church. Bruce had gotten into the spirit of these sessions—so he stripped naked, too.

The artist paused now and then and thought; I've got two of the most sexual and beautiful men to be found. And they're both only a few feet away, naked, very sensual and with just one word, they would both eagerly hop in bed.

"It's such a relief just to be out of the church and away from all those worshippers who want a piece of me," the holy man admitted. "People are always watching me. Grace is getting so aggressive about me bedding her down."

"Yuk!" Brandon gagged. "That's a situation I couldn't tolerate for a moment."

"She's so convinced that I've returned from the dead—that I'm the actual Emmanuel Trident. It's becoming impossible."

"I can see you joining the faculty of a university—to teach religion."

"No one would want to hear me preach about Mouria—that would go against established religion."

For the last posing session, Brandon took a roll of film showing both Bruce Jasmine and John Sparrow naked and embracing each other affectionately.

In several of them, they pretended to fight each other with throbbing erections. Then Bruce insisted Brandon pose with John Sparrow.

On this day, Brandon allowed Amos, the chauffeur join in the fun. That rugged man also took off his clothes, and with a beer in hand, let himself be pulled hard against the preacher man.

The other men had teased John about his perpetual erection.

"I'm used to it," he joked, "but since it might shock others, this is what I can do to make it soft. Just watch."

While Brandon, Bruce and Amos watched, John put his hands on his hips—and then his phallus flipped up and down several times and then he ejaculated. His audience whooped loudly and Brandon said he had got it on the Polaroid.

They all studied it.

"John, it looks like you're pissing white cream!" Bruce teased.

"You would make a fortune giving your male cream to a fertility clinic," Brandon added. "Just think. There could be hundreds of John Sparrows in the future."

"I don't need a hand or a body to arouse me," he laughed.

Bruce reluctantly dressed and prepared to leave.

He had an important meeting in Asheville with several high-profile moneymen who were very interested in investing in Brandy's.

Grace Cowan had called twice that afternoon to know if Brandon had finished his sessions with "my John."

John Sparrow shuddered and slowly put on his clothes. He sent Amos down to the car, to turn on the air-conditioner to prevent a smothering steam bath in the vehicle on the trip back to the church.

John pulled Brandon close to him, kissed him passionately, and whispered: "We've got to get alone. You're driving me crazy, little Brandy. You might well be my son. I want to take care of you."

"We will John. You know where I live now."

After his guest left, Brandon sipped some Chablis and looked around his studio. John Sparrow's powerful masculinity could still be felt. There was a spot near the posing area that still gleamed with the outpouring of John's semen. Brandy wanted it to stay there.

His male scent still lingered—a sultry combination of clean flesh, touched with musk and his favorite cologne: *Royal Bain Champagne.*

#

Seven days later, Brandon and Bruce Jasmine brought the painting over to the private office of Grace Cowan. Both John Sparrow and Amos were there to see the unveiling.

Bruce set up the covered portrait onto a sturdy easel.

Bottles of champagne chilled in vessels. Trays of delectable appetizers were set out.

While John smiled and Amos grinned, Grace Cowan looked tense.

"And here we have, John Sparrow!" announced Brandon and pulled away the clean white cloth that covered the canvas. With Bruce's help, Brandon had found a striking frame of wood and copper leaves and flowers to frame it.

Amos gasped. John grinned. Grace Cowan's eyes grew large—and then she smiled big with a delighted laugh.

There was John Sparrow in all his physical splendor.

Brandon painted him as he really was—yet, a stranger would have thought the artist had greatly exaggerated the male form.

The charismatic minister was shown with his face slightly tilted upward with his dark mane of hair touching those powerful looking shoulders. His expression was radiant, almost unearthly as if he saw something spectacular just beyond the edge of the canvas.

His tremendous body glowed, as if lit by an inner light. Each of his muscles was lovingly rendered with his chest bulging as if it were ready to explode.

The loincloth only covered the essentials. Clearly outlined was the man's manly equipment, although not graphic enough to shock.

Behind him, it was like he sat against the dawn of a new world. Gold radiance infused the sky, shot through by rays of burning crimson and jade.

John Sparrow looked exactly like a fresher version of Jesus Christ.

Grace Cowan stood up. She faced Brandon. Her face glowed.

"Mr. Flores, I'm sorry if I had any doubt in using you as our artist. You've caught our John Sparrow exactly the way I see him. He is a radiant, phenomenal person—and now here he is forever on canvas."

John came over to Brandon and looked serious: "I knew you could do it. You more than most know what and who I am. I salute you."

Amos looked from John to Brandon. "By God, that is some painting that will live forever. And I was there—to witness its birth."

"You were there in body," snorted Grace Cowan, "if not in mind."

Then she burst out laughing and the others joined in. Brandon had triumphed. John Sparrow was immortalized and now he filled the crystal goblets with champagne.

"To a great artist—Brandon Flores—we salute you."

"And to John Sparrow," the artist responded, "for providing me with such a magnificent person and spirit to paint."

Bruce had called in for a professional photographer to capture this intimate event. The images would be eagerly snatched up by the media.

They filled their plates with cold shrimp, lobster, cheeses and slices of beef before going into the den.

At Brandon's eager beseeching, Grace Cowen had taken out her collection of rare film clips that showed Emmanuel Trident in action.

It was a spellbinding experience. From twenty years in the past, the phenomenal Mountain Jesus could be seen at his peak. It was like watching John Sparrow. In the fragments of home movies, Trident was naked except for a loin cloth. He stood before a congregation and galvanized everyone.

One segment had been filmed just a week before the massacre. The religious leader was shown bare-chested on a sunny day. Wind tossed his hair, his arms were folded across his chest, and he smiled. Closer the camera moved so that his startling eyes filled the screen.

The screen went blank. No one spoke for a moment.

"John," murmured Grace Cowan, "that was you."

The object of her affection said nothing. His face was serious and taut. He got up quietly from his chair and went to his private quarters.

Before Brandon left shortly after, Grace Cowan came up to him and pressed an envelope into his hand.

"Here's my payment for the beautiful portrait of John," she smiled. "I hope its okay."

"I have no doubt it will be."

Bruce accompanied Brandon to his home.

After the agent fixed them dry martinis, he joined the artist on the couch as Brandon opened the envelope from Grace Cowan.

"You created magic on your canvas," wrote Grace Cowan. "John and I are both thrilled."

The check was for $50,000.

"Wow!" whooped Bruce. "You're rich, Picasso."

Bruce predicted that within a year, his client would have more one million dollars in his bank account.

#

When Brandon attended church that Sunday, he was delighted to see his painting of John Sparrow hung in the main foyer.

It caused a traffic jam. Everyone was struck by the radiant beauty of the subject and by the expanse of flesh revealed. Preachers were never depicted like this one. Other men of the cloth were always fully attired. John Sparrow was almost always naked.

No one complained. It was like having a human god in the pulpit here each Sunday. The physical sight of him was enough to inspire the worshippers to believe that heaven was right here in this church. What other place in the world had a minister who looked like an immortal sent down from heaven above?

Several newspaper photographers were present and took pictures of Brandon, Grace Cowan and John Sparrow standing below the painting.

The next morning, the artist was happy to see on the front page of the *Blackstone Messenger* a well-lit photograph of himself, Grace Cowan and the subject of the painting. The portrait was displayed between them.

The caption read: "Popular artist, Brandon Floes, stands with Grace Cowan, the force behind the new All Souls Church of the Mountains, and John Sparrow, the controversial pastor. They're shown studying the portrait of the minister created by Mr. Flores and which will be showcased in the lobby of the church. The painting is already creating controversy because of the nudity of the subject. The artist is said to have pocketed a staggering fee for his work. He was named by *Time Magazine* last month as an artist on his way to the top, not only in the art world, but in the cut-throat environment of fashion design."

#

Nearly midnight.

Brandon moved around his loft, shutting down the light and blowing out the candles after an intense evening of work on his paintings, his sculpture and his fashion designs.

It was still like a dream—the way his talent was paving the way to a steadily increasing little fortune. And he was now intimately involved with two ravishing men.

He had never fantasized this ever happening while growing up with a diabolical mother and a small town that seemed to always be asleep beneath a scalding sun.

His agent, Bruce Ramsey, was in talks with his New York City branch to find a place on Fifth Avenue or Madison Avenue for a possible luxurious boutique for Brandy's. Several top magazine and television fashion editors had shown interest in running major features of the young visionary.

Bruce had already asked Brandon to consider the very real possibility of moving to Manhattan within a few months. This was here a hot young artist should be, where his growing business prospects would grow much bigger and faster. The Big Apple was where Brandon could meet the sharp and talented people in the art and fashion industry.

His clothes boutique in Raleigh was packed with sharp looking men and women, snapping up his clothes and his accessories. Brandon was now creating striking scarves that could be worn by either gender. They were silk and satin. Colors of caramel and holly and black were spattered with colored stones. Matching belts would soon be available.

The Sunshine Production Company was working steadily to keep up with the demand for his fashions. Women appeared to be delighted with the Jazz Age touch to dresses, with abbreviated trains attached to the high fashion look.

Brandon took a shower and fixed himself a tangy gin and tonic drink in a long tumbler. Bruce had turned him onto alcohol, as a relaxer. Sometimes Brandon had a stiff drink when he experienced a rare mental block. The fiery flow of whiskey or scotch removed the barrier and his work improved. Yet, he was careful not to let drinking get out of hand. Even here at school he had seen some of the faculty drunk—and several hid bottles in their desks to sip on through the day.

He selected a robe of velvet, the color of a winter sunset and spritzed on some *Eric's Perfume*, a wonderful scent that Bruce Ramsey had given to him. It was made only occasionally by a close friend of Bruce's, an elderly chemist named Appolonius in Greenwich Village.

Brandon got beneath the velvet comforter on his bed and turned on the TV. That night's Late Show was telecasting a Bette Davis movie he had long wanted to see: *In This Our Life*.

Just before the movie began, someone knocked on his door.

Brandon's heart jumped. Few knew he lived here now. Bruce Ramsey was in New York City. Maybe it was one of his enemies? A TV segment had visited him here to show how he worked. The windows were opened so that some viewers could locate his address just by the landscaping and the flowing river.

He grabbed his revolver from his nightstand and cautiously approached the door.

The knock was repeated—firm and insistent.

"Who is it?"

"It's your Mountain Jesus—John Sparrow."

Throwing open the door, Brandon was enveloped in powerful arms.

"John! I'm so thrilled to see you!"

Saying nothing, the minister held Brandon closer. He wore a long, luxurious fur coat and matching Russian hat. He smelt like the outdoors—cold, clean and invigorating.

"Can you do me a big, big favor? It'd mean everything to me."

"You know I will. What is it?"

"Tomorrow morning—could you drive me to Vesaria?"

"Vesaria? Well, sure. I'd love to. I'm free tomorrow—but I'm not sure how to get there."

"Amos drew me a map. It's pretty easy. Its three hours on the new highway. If we leave early we can get there by noon."

"Yes! We'll leave by eight. My car's just had its tune-up. John, why do you want to go now—so suddenly?"

They had gone into the den. Brandon saw that his visitor was greatly agitated. He paced back and forth in his great coat and rubbed his fists while staring at the floor.

"I've fallen into a trap, Brandon. Grace is convinced I'm Emmanuel Trident. Lots of others are, too. All I hear is his name and Vesaria! Maybe if I go and see what's there, things will come back to me."

He stopped his pacing and pressed a hand to his head. His face scrunched up in pain.

"It's that damned black door that I can't unlock. I can see it. A massive barrier of black steel, all locked up. And behind it is my past. The doctors have hypnotized me, given me truth serum, they've tried everything—but my past is just hiding there, until the right time."

"When do you think the right time will be?"

John looked up at him and squinted his eyes.

"I came back too soon! Too soon!"

"You need some sleep. Why don't you take a long hot shower and I'll fix you a mug of hot buttered rum and I'll rub you down."

The visitor nodded his head slowly. 'Yes, yes, that's a good idea. That's what I need. Some sleep. And we'll go to Vesaria tomorrow morning? Grace is out of town this weekend with Amos. She's shopping for some new draperies for the church."

"We'll leave bright and early and I'll fix us a big, old-fashioned breakfast. Come, darling. Step out of your shoes and get under the shower."

The big man had become almost childlike in his passivity. When he threw off his coat, Brandon was surprised to see that Emmanuel wore nothing beneath it. String-up sandals covered his feet. He kicked them off.

John bent down and kissed him lightly on the mouth.

"You're wonderful, Brandy. It's like—you're someone I should know. I'm glad I do know you."

"Into the shower, big boy!"

When John dried off, Brandon had a red wool blanket to wrap around him.

"Come to bed, John. Here's your drink. Drink it and then I'll rub you down."

"Ahh, you're much too nice to me."

He had calmed down a little and when he finished his drink, he tossed off the blanket and stretched out on his stomach.

Brandon felt dizzy from this exhilarating sight. He had seen his visitor naked before, had been kissed and embraced by him. But there was never the right moment to physically enjoy each other.

Now, they were alone, in a warm, sensual setting. Outside, a bitter wind howled against the window. The river below looked icy and treacherous.

John's vast body glowed from its bath. As Brandon ran his fingers over the warm flesh, he felt his subject growing looser and more relaxed.

When his hands moved over the spectacular tush, he could see the large equipment bulging between the muscular thighs. Arousal was visible and by the time John turned over his phallus pulsed against his flat stomach.

"Your hands feel like magic, little boy," murmured John. "I can sleep with you tonight?"

"You'd better!"

With that, John Sparrow pulled Brandon hard against him. His mouth was hungry as he kissed and licked and pushed his partner's gown away.

From the first moment Brandon saw this man, he had dreamed of this happening. Now it was. He wanted to forget nothing about it—but John was moving so fast to slake his desire that Brandon had no time to contemplate and memorize each movement.

John's flesh tasted clean and slightly salty and very warm. He lay still as Brandon used his lips to suckle the large nipples, then to lick and savor the flat stomach, then lower until he tasted the tip of the phallus which pulsed like a thick, meaty heart.

Brandon used both hands to hold the enormous testicles, as if they were melons. They churned in their pink sac and the erection continued to swell.

Through that memorable night, John taught Brandon all there was to know about love-making with another man. He had learned his extraordinary prowess somewhere in the past. A man like this, thought Brandon, had to have had countless men and women. His body was made for sinning.

Like some exotic foreign land, Brandon explored this remarkable terrain thoroughly. Nothing disappointed. Everything thrilled. It was like John's sweet, luscious mouth was starved for flesh. He couldn't get enough.

"You've got a woman's bosom," whispered John in awe. "Mouria! You're a man, yet you're a woman. This is something extraordinary just as I always knew you were."

He got on top of his partner, parted his legs and prepared to enter him.

'John, you're so enormous—I don't think I can take you."

"You can. You will. I'll dazzle you."

And somehow, he did just that. He inched his hardness in very carefully, pausing to see if he were causing pain. Brandon felt none. He felt like an enchanted force was slowly entering him. Steady strokes built up an exhilarating sensation until he cried out.

"The cry of joy," whispered John Sparrow.

#

Just as dawn was beginning to break, Brandon awoke.

A big, powerful arm was thrown around him. Beside him, John slept deeply. His pink mouth was parted. A silver trickle of spit gleamed on his chin.

His body lay on its side, still in repose. Up and down moved his brawny chest. Those mighty pectorals swelled out, the nipples fully erect now.

Brandon couldn't resist sucking the right one, his favorite. It tasted warm and tender. Rising from his partner's hips was his half-erect manhood.

Brandon was enjoying playing and massaging this remarkable organ, when John stirred and opened his eyes.

"Still having some fun with John's play toy?"

"I couldn't resist."

John pulled him up and hugged him close. Brandon didn't want to ever leave the intoxicating warmth of those big arms wrapped around him and that solid chest where his face was pressed.

"You're both man and woman," murmured John Sparrow. "Yet, you don't have a female opening. If you did that, it would put you on an extraordinary status."

Brandon told him it was his dream to be operated on—where he would finally be both genders.

"For me, one sex isn't enough. I want to be like Diana DuPree—who had both and was lynched for it."

#

The day was cloudy and cold for driving. A vicious wind whistled around the windows of Brandon's new car.

Inside it was toasty and cozy. Both he and his passenger sipped hot coffee from the big thermos Brandon had prepared. He had also put together a classic mountain breakfast of ham, scrambled eggs, grits, gravy and homemade biscuits slathered in butter.

Still clad only in his fur coat and sandals, John's restlessness had returned, though. His hand kneaded his knee and he sighed long and sadly. He was so big, he filled up the front seat. His body heat was so strong that the driver had to turn the car's heater down.

The map was easy to follow. They skimmed along the new mountain highway until they turned off to the rural exit that led toward Mt. Mouria.

Overhead, the sky had become steadily filled with a thick layer of dark clouds.

When they came to the sign, Vesaria 9 miles, snowflakes were appearing on the window shield.

They drove through thick woods, past decaying houses and farms where machinery lay rusting in the fields.

And then they came to what was left of a once thriving little community. Brandon guided the car to the little main street.

"We're finally here, John—we're now in the village of Vesaria."

This was now a ghost town. Nothing lived here. No people, no flowers, no animals.

All that moved here was the whirling of dead leaves. Old store signs creaked in the moaning wind.

A rusted can rolled along the gutter. The glinting of shards of ice and glass gleamed coldly from the watery light of winter.

"It's like a town from a horror movie," whispered Brandon.

John looked increasingly anxious.

"Oh, God, Oh, God, this is Vesaria! It's a place for the dead! So many died here. All that hate—just exploded!"

Slowly, the car passed by a brown and empty Polly's Little Snack Shop...a U.S. Post Office...Ben's Beer and Spirits...Best Tools and Hardware...Becky's Bakery.

Dust from many years caked the cracked window. Rotting hoses from the fuel pumps writhed on the ground like dead snakes. The two men got out and began to walk slowly and thoughtfully along the cracked sidewalk.

Wind shook furiously the branches of the old trees that lined the main street.

Dead leaves swirled around in macabre dances. A rusted can of *Linda Green's Tomatoes* scuttled around the broken sidewalk.

"It's hard to think of this place once being lively with people," Brandon said sadly.

"This place was all a hell hole, a dump, until this Emmanuel Trident arrived," muttered John, half to himself. "He tried to do good here. And what did he get in return? They crucified him! They lynched his beautiful wife. God knows what happened to the boys. Like you said, you could damned well be one of them."

They came upon a small mountain of stubble and rock. Brandon's finger followed a line on the map and rested on an X.

"It says here that this was the church set up by Emmanuel Trident. And look what happened to it. It was destroyed by the monsters."

An almost palpable veil of gloom and dashed dreams lingered over this dismal area. Brandon could imagine mountain people wearing their best all streaming into the church on cold, fall mornings and balmy days of summer. Where were the choir members? The school kids? The smell of a covered dish supper?

What fury had pushed the church's enemies into demolishing it? What had they said to each other as they slammed into rubble the walls and floors and windows?

"Let's get out of here," muttered John. "It's too sad. Let's find the home of the Tridents..."

As they drove to the house, it was like the powerful wind was trying to push them back. Overhead the dark clouds raced with an almost supernatural rapidity.

The home of the Tridents was another pile of blackened rubble.

The two men got out and stepped up to the edge of the destruction.

They were struck by the modest memorial that had been erected to the memory of Diana DuPree.

It was a polished slab of marble. Skilled hands had created from the same material the bust of the tragic artist. Somehow the stone conveyed the image of a delicate, petite woman with large eyes. Beneath, words were cut into the stone:

Vandals had chipped away enough of the memorial that it looked ruined. Graffiti had been etched here and there: "Burn in Hell." "Goodbye freak!"

"This is all that's left of Diana DuPree," Brandon said bitterly.

"I'm glad the plague killed everybody here," muttered John. "They deserved death in the worst way."

His fingers delicately traced the features of the bust.

They pawed through the bricks and rocks. They found rotting remnants of books, of crushed china and stained glass. The dead had eaten off these once exquisite items, probably on a long table with a linen tablecloth. Jugs of wine, beer, baskets of rolls and biscuits. All that was beautiful and beloved were destroyed.

"Why?" whispered Brandon. "Their hate for the holy man must have been frightening to behold."

"It wasn't just for him and how he conducted his services," John said quietly. You've got to realize their hatred and fear of the golden-haired woman. Or man. Diana DuPree. I've read where the haters called her the Unclean Thing. The White Nigger."

"I've been called that."

John looked sharply at his companion. "You've been called white nigger? How strange. First Diana DuPree and then—you. She should have worn that label with pride. It meant she was different. Special. You should feel the same one, my son."

He became silent and thoughtful as if, thought Brandon, something traumatic was going through his mind. They poked around the destroyed place when Brandon suddenly let out a gasp.

"John, I've found something here. Look!"

Using his foot, he pushed away fragments of rock and cement to uncover a small, narrow case. He picked it up.

'Look, John. It's an Indian holster for a knife. But where's the knife?"

They both began digging with feet and hands when John stooped down and picked up something.

"Brandon—here's the knife for your holster. Look, it's not just an ordinary knife. It's ancient."

They both studied the dirt-covered blade and the striking handle. It showed the symbol of Mouria. The handiwork was priceless.

"John, this must be the Mourian Dagger that Diana DuPree used to protect herself!' gasped Brandon. "I've read where one eye witness said she had this amazing knife that had a life of its own when she was fighting the Klansman. She told someone that the dagger was found in one of the caves by her mother."

John handled the weapon thoughtfully.

"It's incredibly light," he murmured. "And see this workmanship around the handle? It looks damned ancient!"

"Just imagine!" murmured Brandon. "Diana DuPree actually clutched this dagger when she was fighting the ghouls. It's no telling where this weapon came from."

Brandon tried to slide the weapon into its sheath but something prevented it.

He shook the holster and a small object fell out. He and John both studied it after wiping away the dirt. It was the photograph of a man's face. A strong shell of plastic enclosed it.

"John, look at it! It's a man's face and he looks uncannily like Jesus Christ—or you!"

"Good God!" whispered John Sparrow. "It's amazing. I wonder what its significance is?"

"Maybe it's Emmanuel Trident!"

He glanced up at John's face and was shocked by the wild confusion in those remarkable eyes. It was like a soul in hell was staring out.

Brandon took his hand and squeezed it.

"Let's go, John. This place is disturbing you. I can tell."

John walked to the edge of abyss and tossed aside his luxurious magnificent coat. A furious wind tore at his hair. He stood there naked, heroic, like an unearthly being with his astonishing height and torso.

He stared up at the dark sky with the fast moving clouds of prune and umber and shook his fists:

"Why Mouria? Why God? Whoever you are up there? Why did you allow this happen?"

#

That Sunday, the *Blackwood Times* ran two eye-popping pieces about John Sparrow. Both were calculated to create an explosion of controversy.

The first one instantly jumped out for it was a full-page ad, bordered in black, with the names of six local ministers as signatories at the end of a brutal blast.

CAST OUT THE NAKED CHARLATAN!

"We the undersigned have had enough of a charlatan and a religious imposter who has invaded our God-fearing community and made it a mockery.

"We have become the laughing stock around the country. No one can take us seriously because of this evil-doer who uses every cheap trick of show business to attract gullible, morally adrift persons into his expensive new church.

"We will not name any names but this shameless jade has attracted many of our former church members by creating sensational stunts to draw attention. Like some cheap, sleazy carnival barker, this evil doer actually uses nudity to attract the young. Immature women who should know better are in his congregation every Sunday. They have no interest in discovering God's power. They sit and palpitate and drool like diseased heifers in a barnyard as they behold their strutting male peacock who shows off everything that should be kept private for the marriage chamber. This is the cheapest sort of snake oil chicanery that we had hoped had died down at the turn of the century.

"Beware of this disgraceful exhibitionist and return to your churches where you'll see where the true spirit of God resides. Amen and May God forgive this Hitler with no clothes."

Brandon saw the signatures and had heard from both Grace Cowan and John that the usually staid, boring churches in that area were in an uproar. Their attendance had all fallen down to half the usual worshippers. Everyone wanted John Sparrow to entertain them on Sunday morning.

In the newspaper's Sunday magazine, the editors had cleverly published on its cover a picture of the new movie Tarzan, Gordon Scott, with his muscular torso—nude except for a brief loincloth—smiling out to the readers.

Next to it was a sensational picture of John Sparrow, totally naked except for his slender panel of silk covering the essentials. He was shown with his hands thrust above him—with his gleaming torso on full display.

Both images glowed in luscious color.

The headline read:

"Meet The Tarzan of the Pulpit: John Sparrow"—the most controversial minister in the business.

Under the byline of Joyce Kamarosa, the article quickly got down to business:

"No one knows much about John Sparrow—the controversial and red hot new minister of the All Soul Ministries of Blackwood that began two months ago. But one thing everyone agrees on—and that's that the incredibly handsome and charismatic Mr. Sparrow-- has brought in an explosive new ingredient to his church and the name for it is good old fashioned sex.

"This is why there are now thousands who seek entrance to the dazzling new church just outside of Blackwood. They know they'll be guaranteed an unforgettable performance by Mr. Sparrow that will consist of him stripping off his robe and displaying nearly all of his eye-boggling physique. Except for a flashy variety of revealing front panels, Mr. Sparrow would be completely naked. Not that this would bother his mostly young congregation—and especially a growing league of followers, mostly young girls, who hang pictures of their hero wearing very little in their bedrooms. They call themselves The Sparrows and have an ever-growing membership.

"Without exaggerating, his torso is staggering. Many have thought him more than capable of winning a Mr. America title. His face alone, though, would make him an international heart-throb. His features are Slavic, with a luscious set of lips, jet black hair that touches his strong-man shoulders and eyes that are so electrifying in their blazing lime color that when one meets him, the lucky person is too stunned to speak at first.

"He appears to enjoy the sensation he creates when he reveals nearly all of his flesh and often laughs at the consternation of the easily shocked. He says: 'You see more nudity at the beach. I'm always covered up in the area that society demands be hidden in public."

"Mr. Sparrow is a man of mystery. What is known reads like a fantasy story in a comic book.

"He was found six months ago, wandering around a remote logging trail in a desolate mountain area. The loggers said he was near death, terribly emaciated, wearing a strange white monk's gown of white. It was spattered with blood which later proved to be eighteen years old.

"At the state mental hospital, his recovery was considered phenomenal. He consumed vast meals and his torso quickly filled out. Within four months, his transformation was total, and most of the staff said he was as powerful and big as super hero like Superman or Spiderman.

"Yet, he claims to be totally lacking in knowledge about his background.

"One examining doctor said it was like this extraordinary person just fell out of the sky."

#

Brandon had cleaned the strange dagger found at the home of the Tridents. He put it into its holster and made a belt that he could wear beneath his clothes. He was glad he had done so because three days after his trip to Vesaria, he awoke to find the front door of his loft painted with a slogan: "Faggots Go to Hell."

His new Chevrolet had been vandalized. Someone had broken into his garage and torn off the side-mirror and sliced open all four tires.

When he reported this to the visiting policeman, he was asked: "Do you have any enemies who would do this?"

'Yes, I have quite a few enemies. Those on the faculty who're jealous of me and there are those who know I'm close to the new minister, John Sparrow."

The young cop looked up with interest at this name.

"You know him? I go to his church. He's the greatest. I feel secure with him around. Man, I wish I had a body like his! He makes me think of Superman."

By now, Brandon had dropped most of his classes except for those on art. He would be moving to Manhattan by fall anyway. Bruce Ramsey had found him a cozy, one-bedroom apartment in the fashionable area of the city known as Sutton Place. He would be just a few blocks from a main subway system. Bruce would be moving to New York himself to expand his firm.

There was no question now that he was facing a hostile art department and some students. The bigots would yell out obscenities whenever they saw him. No invitations were being extended to him for potluck parties at the homes of the older students or faculty.

One bright spot was when the local TV station did a feature on him: "Blackwood College Has Its Own Coco Chanel."

Brandon's good friend there, reporter Abigail Corning, highlighted his fashion line and said how the two boutiques—in Raleigh and Charleston, South Carolina-- he had were selling out. New York fashion editors were showing sharp interest in his line. On top of that, his paintings and sculpture were now in hot demand. The big Commercial Bank of Charlotte had just commissioned two large paintings and an exhibit of his work in Raleigh had sold out.

Brandon told the reporter that he was moving to Manhattan by fall.

"I've moved ahead on my own," he said frankly. "What I'm doing doesn't need a college degree. I feel like I'm wasting my time all day while in class. I want to work!"

That Sunday, he arrived early at the All Souls Ministries of the Mountains. Although the line to get in was long, the ushers knew him now as a close friend of John Sparrow and saved him a choice seat near the front.

He was anxious about contacting John Sparrow. The poor man had been terribly nervous and withdrawn all during the ride home from Vesaria.

He had clutched his head with both hands and moaned: "Oh, Brandy, my head is killing me. A thousand razors are there. I'm trying to remember the past—but that black, steel door remains locked!"

The lights dimmed slowly and now only a golden radiance illuminated the podium. The music lulled the worshippers into a relaxed, soothing mood.

Grace Cowan took her seat. Brandon saw immediately that she was not in a good mood. Her slight smile was missing. Dark glasses hid her eyes and she stared straight ahead and sat stiffly. Something was definitely amiss. She welcomed everyone but her voice was tired and dull.

A narrow door in the wall opened and in walked the man everyone had longed to see.

Strong applause greeted him and he smiled and held up his hands for silence.

Brandon leaned forward for he saw that like Grace Cowan, there was something disturbing about the John Sparrow who loomed over everyone.

His face was pale and his eyes stared out like two haunting cavities. His facial hair had grown longer but it was untrimmed.

Although he smiled and greeted the worshippers, he did this through slow motion. It was like his blazing energy had left him.

He stepped out in front of the podium and let his robe drop to the floor. Although Bandon had seen this several times by now, it was still an erotic shock to see this Adonis go from robe to near nudity—and this was in the sanctity of a church.

All that protected him today from being totally naked was a swath of silk that was the briefest yet. His dark pubic hair even peeked over the top. It was as if he were saying to everyone: See, I'm giving you more to look at today than ever. And the next time, you may not even see me hiding my assets behind a thin strip of delicate fabric.

He ran a hand through his long hair and stared hard the floor.

Then he began to speak quietly about human evil.

"It's always here," he nodded. "You can't get rid of it. If Jesus were to come down today, do you think he would be welcomed with open arms? Many would rush to pay him homage with their love. But— like a man who did that in l941 in a little village named Vesaria, he found out that all that love just hid a slithering horror that was waiting to strike. Emmanuel Trident came that village to clean up this armpit of the mountains, as it was called. It was a place dominated by barbaric mountaineers who delighted in trading their own children with their neighbors. They raped these youth and the little daughters would become pregnant by their own fathers, or their brothers—and this went on for centuries. But this Mr. Trident, he cleaned that place up good for a while. Then he did the unthinkable—he married the town freak, Diana DuPree, and that was the beginning of the end."

His congregation sat transfixed for all this time, the minister paced back and forth, staring hard at the floor, like he were trying to see into the ground below. The copper bracelets that encircled his bulging arms gleamed eerily in the muted light. The minister's voice grew louder with words jumbling into the next one. It was like he had forgotten all others and was conversing with his conscience.

"Before the Klansmen struck and destroyed all that was good, a sizeable part of the village knew something terrible was going to happen. And they did nothing. They just sat back on their porches and let hell visit the Trident home. This is where people were butchered, scalped, castrated, crucified, and lynched. And these good souls just sat fanning themselves and did nothing because it might upset their supper plans. Even the sheriff in nearby Asheville knew what was going to happen—and he didn't do a goddamned thing!"

Grace Cowan shifted uncomfortably in her seat. Others looked at each other. Where was this sermon going?

Suddenly, Preacher Sparrow startled everyone when he covered his face with his hands and sobbed.

"That poor, tragic family!" he wept. "Murdered. Destroyed—by a bunch of Neanderthal monsters. They're still with us. Where was God when this happened? Why did Mouria, the deity worshipped by the Tridents, desert them?"

"Why do we even pray to a God who allows atrocities to happen—again and again...in the North Carolina mountains...in Nazi concentration camps...in our nearby wooded areas where men in bed sheets string up innocent black men while laughing...yes laughing and whooping it up. Mouria! We need Mouria!"

The minister dropped his hands and raised them in the air before stumbling through the side door. For a moment, there was silence, then Grace Cowan stood up and went to the podium.

"Reverend Sparrow had not felt well for some time. I'll lead us now in morning prayer."

Brandon's heart dropped. His fear had been proven right. John Sparrow should not have visited Vesaria and the Mouria Gorge.

As he was leaving he encountered Grace Cowan.

'You're responsible for John behaving like this!" she seethed.

"What do you mean?"

"I know he went to Vesaria two weeks ago because you'd been pestering him to go! And that's one place he should never have returned to."

'I did? Where did you get that idea? I was as amazed as you were when he wanted to go there. I knew it was bad for him."

"Ha! Some story! But your kind is good at lying. Oh, yes. I know your kind."

"My kind? And what is my kind pray tell? Because I could turn the question back on you and say, oh, yes, her kind is responsible for this."

'You know what I mean! You homo! You Unclean Thing! I've met your kind before and you should be afraid to show your face in public! The things you do are ungodly and unnatural! I warned John to stay away from you."

Brandon pushed his face closer to the wrinkled old face of Grace Cowan.

"And I know that John Sparrow had too much class to fuck a banged up old bag like you."

Brandon was too enraged to think straight and only afterward did he understand that he would never be allowed in the All Souls Ministries of the Mountains.

#

Brandon's growing sense of despair became stronger when he read in the newspaper that services at the All Souls Church of the Mountains were cancelled that week due to "the illness of Reverend John Sparrow."

He called the parsonage but the secretary said that John Sparrows was being treated for overwork and that he was expected to return that Sunday. He and Grace Cowan were out-of-town.

What could that mean?

Brandon's puzzlement was shared by everyone who had seen and heard John Sparrow's last sermon.

He was the living embodiment of good health. His glow, his powerful physique symbolized vitality and strength.

Now, the anti-John Sparrow faction grew louder.

A local radio talk show featured call-ins from listeners and a heated topic, as it had been several times, was the strange illness of John Sparrow that kept him from preaching.

Bandon listened to the different call-ins and was appalled at how hated his boyfriend was by many of the yakkers.

"He should be run out of town," fumed one woman. "He's a charlatan. Plain and simple. Imagine, a preacher stripping naked—right there in front of children! And the thing he preaches—urging nudity and saying there's no sin."

"I'll bet he's just a cheap imposter from a carnival," seethed a man with a high voice. "He sure doesn't look like a preacher. He looks like a circus strongman or some pervert from a big city where he gets paid to show off his body. No telling what he does in that church after dark. I know women are nuts about him but it's all sex. Dirty sex. And he says to understand homosexuals. They oughta be locked up in prison."

But, there were the John Sparrow fans.

"He's the greatest thing to happen in Blackwood," cried Joani Tanglewood. "We're all sick of hearing the same old guff in church every

Sunday about sinning and going to hell. Reverend Sparrow believes in hope and love. I think he's gorgeous."

Brandon grabbed the phone and called into the station. After a brief wait, he was "on the air.

"As to John Sparrow having orgies in the church, ha, that would never happen. You'd be on camera. There are security cameras in every room—yes, even the bathrooms. And as for his asking people to understand homosexuals, isn't that what Jesus Christ would have asked?"

#

His phone rang later that night.

"Brandon, this is Abigal Corning? Have you heard?"

He recognized his buddy who had interviewed him recently for her television show.

"Heard what? Tell me!"

"It's our friend—John Sparrow. He's vanished."

"He—he what? Abigal, what are you talking about? What do you mean he's vanished?"

Abigal had a good source at the police department who informed her that John Sparrow just abruptly disappeared. There were zero clues as to his whereabouts.

He was supposed to have presided over a business luncheon at twelve noon yesterday in the church. When he didn't appear, Grace Cowan checked his private quarters in the rear of the building.

It was empty. The bed had not been slept in. Further investigation showed that nothing had been taken—except some clothes from the closet, including his magnificent fur coat, and the keys to one of the cars.

"I was afraid something had happened," Brandon said and told the reporter about the trip to Vesaria the two had taken.

"Why would he be so upset about visiting a ghost town?"

"Why? Because I'm convinced he really is Emmanuel Trident! Everything adds up. His appearance, his personality, that amazing tattoo on his back. I think he really was suffering from amnesia and remembered none of that. But how he could have remained hidden for nineteen years is a real mystery."

Abigal said that the state troopers were contacted to be on the lookout for a Cadillac and license plates.

Even though it was early, Brandon called up the private line of John Sparrow. He knew that Grace Cowan shared this number.

Grace Cowan quickly answered.

"Miss Cowan, this is Brandon. I just heard about John. We've got to talk. Let's get over our problems for now. This is urgent!"

A moment of silence passed when she said: "Drive up to the rear of the church where there's a private entrance. Ring the buzzer and I'll answer."

The church's parking lot was packed with police cars and media vans. Reporters milled around and when they saw Brandon, they gave chase. He was recognized as the artist who had painted the revealing portrait of the missing minister.

When he rang the bell at the private entrance in the back, the door quickly opened.

Grace Cowan looked like an old woman who was on the verge of death.

Dressed in a pink, quilted robe, she poured him a mug of coffee in her private office and sat across from him. She lit up a cigarette.

"Miss Cowan, let's try to forget our nasty words to each other. I greatly apologize and beg that you forgive me. Can we just talk a little?"

She studied him and then shrugged. Her usually coiffed curls were matted now and brushed back into a gray helmet. No make-up hid the wrinkles and the crowfeet now. She could have been any old mountain woman in any small town.

"I forgive and ask the same from you. Nobody knows how much this church means to me. I've spent my life planning for it. On his deathbed, my father made me promise to construct a place like this. I was so happy when the church was finished. Then I found John. I was certain fate had meant for us to meet and he--he just transformed everything. You see, Emmanuel Trident had agreed to come here in 1941 when my father invited him here. Daddy was going to build him a church—just like I've done. But then, that horrible massacre happened and all my father's plans were killed. And now—John's up and gone. I hate to think he might be dead. Yet, something tells me he's alive."

"Why would he just do this so abruptly? It's like everything was coming up wonderful for both of you!"

The woman covered her face with her hands and groaned.

"Now I know when people say they're destroyed by life. I feel destroyed. Yet, I can't hate him. I really loved that man—in my own way. It was like having Jesus and a brother and a father all rolled up into one man. He made me laugh. I felt alive. I knew he couldn't love some old hag like me. I have no illusions. I think something profound happened to him mentally. He wasn't the same for the past few weeks."

"---ever since he returned from Vesaria."

Grace Cowan stood up and went to the wall. She pulled a cord and the large cloth that covered the portrait of John Sparrow was lifted away.

"Look at him!" she whispered in awe. "Just think that he was alive and well just two days ago. It's like he's looking at us—"

A gold spotlight highlighted the portrait. The sparkling jade eyes seemed to stare directly at both Brandon and Grace Cowan.

"It's like," murmured Brandon, "he wants to tell us something."

"Oh, John!" wailed Grace Cowan. "What is it? Tell us! Dear God, talk to us."

"Did he not suggest anything of what was bothering him?"

She shook her head and walked away.

"He's not coming back. He kept muttering, 'I came back too soon. Too soon.' I have no idea what he meant by that. Where did he come back from?"

#

With the disappearance of John Sparrow, each day seemed shadowed with darkness for Brandon, even when the sun shone.

He had talked to his agent, Bruce Jasmine, several times but that dynamic young man was scouting for property in New Jersey and Massachusetts for possible Brandy's boutiques.

Bruce had already found the perfect spots in the beautiful coastal city of Wilmington, North Carolina and another one at Virginia Beach for the next Brandy's. His scouts still sought a good location in the heart of Manhattan for the flagship store.

The fashion editors for both *The New York Times* and the *New York Daily News* newspapers both wanted to interview the young artist for major interviews.

"I've got a bad feeling about John Sparrow's vanishing like that. I don't think he'll ever return again."

He told Bruce about seeing strange cars driving slowly by his building. They may have been curiosity seekers who had read the articles about him---but Brandon sensed they were up to no good.

Bruce said he would be back home in two days. In the meantime, he urged his client to remain vigilant. His enemies were still out there.

#

There was no doubt now. His loft was being watched by hostile eyes. Each morning, he found threatening notes stuffed under his door. His tires were slashed. Someone tried to start a fire under his porch but it failed. When he went for a walk at night, some driver tried to run him off the road—twice. Police were getting irritated at having to come out so often.

He was happy when his door-bell rang, followed by several impatient raps and Bruce stood there.

He was naked but his arms were full of presents for his boyfriend.

"Oh, Bruce! I'm so terribly happy to see you."

The dashing young agent had dropped his gifts on the floor as he embraced Brandon and kissed him with hungry, hot lips.

"This has been waiting for your magic touch," he whispered and guided his partner's hand down to a pulsing erection.

He picked Brandon up and threw him on the bed.

"I've been hungry for you," murmured Bruce.

"I've been starving for you, too!"

Several hours passed before they relaxed with cocktails and the sushi that the agent had brought. The other packages yielded imported chocolates from Switzerland, *Monsieur Duffy* and *Barky Bark* perfumes and a beautiful bracelet of silver and precious stones.

"Bruce please stay with me for a while. Like several days. The bigots are at again. Slashing my tires. Trying to run me off the road, all kinds of shit."

The agent said he urgently needed to take care of business in his Asheville office—to discuss the plans for moving to New York City in fall. He promised to return as soon as possible and would stay as long as Brandon needed him.

#

Mystery Surrounding Missing Minister Deepens

— By Janice Dorfman

If possible, the mysteries surrounding the bizarre vanishing of a popular religious leader in Blackwood only deepen.

On the afternoon that he vanished, John Sparrow left behind a half-consumed meal he was eating. Police say that it looks as if the missing man left in a sudden rush. The sermon he was typing up in his typewriter was only half finished. His notes were handwritten. He had let his staff off early that afternoon. He gave no reason, only to tell the five administrative workers that he was giving them all a short day.

Kay Edwards, the senior secretary, said that just before she left, a female stranger entered her office and asked that she see John Sparrow. She had no appointment. The woman gave the secretary a small box and said that if she presented that to John Sparrow, he would definitely see him.

Miss Edwards stated that the box was unusually heavy for its small size. She heard nothing rattling within. She knocked and entered the office and John Sparrow stood at the window, looking out. He wore a plain white shirt stuffed into dark slacks. He turned and received the box. He opened it, said nothing, but his mood definitely changed. He said quickly:

"Send the lady in!"

The stranger entered the office and there were sounds of muffled voices. It was like they were talking in a foreign tongue, stated the secretary. The voices became louder and then abruptly stopped.

Miss Edwards left and that was the last anyone saw of the minister.

She described the visitor as a very tall female, who wore a striking gown that came to her feet. The attire was copper in color. Strange symbols splashed the material.

Her skin was much bronzed suggesting that she may have been foreign, or Native American. She spoke with a slight accent. The secretary added that her breathing was very harsh. It was like she had trouble getting enough air. The woman also wore a slight perfume which Miss Edwards described as unusually nice. Very large dark glasses covered half her face. Investigators have been unable to track down this mysterious visitor, the strange box she had delivered to the missing man nor does anyone remember anyone driving up in a car.

#

Brandon was questioned by detectives and he told them frankly about his visit to Vesaria with John Sparrow.

"We should never have gone there," Brandon said bluntly. "It really upset him."

"And why do you think that?" asked Detective Myron Hudson, a young, bright looking detective.

"When he saw the rubble of the church that Emmanuel Trident had preached and the home where he lived with his life and two little boys, he was stunned. He said several times, 'Why? What did these innocents do to be destroyed like this?'"

Detective Hudson leaned forward:

"Were you and John Sparrow lovers?"

The question was aimed to shock and it did but Brandon managed to shrug it off.

"No. John Sparrow was a very loving, sensual man who embraced everybody: men, women, old, and children. It was just his nature. There were all kinds of sordid rumors about him because of the way he appeared nearly nude when giving his sermons."

"You painted him nude for the church."

'Yes. Grace Cowan ordered the painting. We were never alone when he posed."

"He was seen entering your house late at night and staying all night."

Again, Brandon gave an elaborate shrug. "Yes he did. We talked about many things—about the fact that people considered him to be the actual Emmanuel Trident, the legendary holy man who vanished with his family. Many people were convinced that John Sparrow was actually the real Jesus Christ."

"You talked all night?" asked a plainly skeptical detective.

"Yes, it's possible to talk all night when the person is as extraordinary as John Sparrow."

The detective reached into a folder and withdrew a stack of Polaroid pictures.

"I understand you took these photos."

Brandon saw the nude pictures he had made of John Sparrow for the painting.

"Yes, I took these for my painting. I wanted to find the best pose because this was a portrait that would be seen by thousands."

"Oh, you mean, pictures like these were supposed to help you?"

Detective Royce shoved over several photos showing John grasping his enormous erection with both hands and aiming it playfully at the camera.

"John was always doing stuff like this. It meant nothing. He delighted in shocking people. This would look pornographic to a stranger—but this was just John being John."

"Oh, sure," sneered the detective. "I can see myself being delighted when one of my cop buddies gets all naked and jerks off for me."

#

Bruce Ramsey drove up in his new Lincoln Continental and brought a suitcase.

"Bruce is here so never fear."

Just his presence alone instantly stabilized the atmosphere in Brandon's loft.

He embraced his host tightly and murmured: "I don't want anything to bother your work. I've brought my typewriter and correspondence and my own phone. So we can both work without any worries of red-neck bigots or the cops bothering us."

Feeling secure again, Brandon worked intensely on new dress designs, this time giving the frocks borders of glittering stones and silver bolts of lightning.

For the men, he drew out slacks of all colors with matching shirts and sweaters.

As a joke, he went to his electric sewing machine and turned out a very brief speedo of black.

"Bruce, dahling, would you be a wonderful stud and model these briefs for me?"

The agent put his glasses down and burst out laughing at the flimsy little garment.

"Sure!" he whistled. "Anything to help out my brilliant young prodigy."

He stripped off his clothes and tried to fit his privates into the swath of silk.

Brandon laughed when his lover stood, bow-legged and just his testicles nestled in the swimsuit.

"Sorry, babe, that's all of Bruce's Mighty Wonder that can fit into your newest creation."

Instead of dressing, he said they should stop work for the day and have supper.

"I'll just take my usual river dip," he grinned, "and I thought we could drive into town and have a beer and pizza night."

"Yea—sounds great to me"

#

Brandon had never visited the small village of Blackstone at night and was relieved to get away from his loft for a while.

Both he and Bruce dressed in warm sweaters and jackets for it was unusually chilly.

It was a Friday night. The streets were packed with cars and bikes and after trying to find a place to park, Bruce told Brandon to get out of the car.

"Wait here for me and I'll be back soonest after I've found a place to park."

"Hurry up Bruce. I don't like being alone here."

Brandon leaned against an empty building where a street light shone.

A few blocks away were the favorite college hangouts for pizza, burgers and beer.

He touched the Mourian Dagger that he wore on a belt.

Just having this gleaming weapon gave him confidence. Diana DuPree may well have been my mother. And John Sparrow was my father.

Suddenly, strong arms grabbed his throat from behind and more arms fastened themselves around his legs.

"Our rich-bitch cocksucker needs to see the countryside," jeered a man's voice.

"I need some fag pussy tonight so let's get it on boys!"

A car had screeched to a halt and Brandon's attackers dragged him over where three more men waited.

They threw open the door of the backseat: "Get his ass in here."

Just then, a whirling column of energy jumped into their midst.

Bruce wrestled and knocked down two of the attackers but Brandon suddenly felt the car he was trapped in race away into the darkness.

As strong rope was twisted around his wrists and legs, as a hand kept slapping his face hard, Brandon heard the wail of a police car very faint and faraway.

PART FOUR
Tommy Barnes Discovers Life

CHAPTER ONE

In his comfortable hotel room on Times Square in New York City, the magnificent young man lay naked on his bed and read the want ads. On his nightstand gleamed several bottles of tomato juice and an array of nuts and fruits.

Bananas, oranges and grapes were arranged neatly on the metal tray. In a plastic trashcan filled with ice rested several quart bottles of beer and wine.

Tommy Barnes had gotten drunk a few times during his early years in the Marines but gradually knew when to get his warm glow and then stop it.

Next to him on the bed was a well-worn pocket sized pad sheathed in leather. It wasn't the Bible like everybody thought. It was his own journal dedicated to researching the legacy of Mouria. He had started it as soon as he became a Marine. What he was looking for couldn't be found in the Bible.

Mouria was there, waiting for him to explore and worship her, but he sensed it would be years before he could compile a history on this fascinating god.

And next to his Mouria journal was a hand whip. The handle was beautifully crafted out of wood and ivory. The thongs were dark and soft from much use.

Strange, smiled Tommy Barnes that he wasn't in the jungles or in the mud-filled trenches anymore—shooting and killing and smelling like a Marine who hadn't showered in two months.

Or polishing his boots and lying in a tent with mosquitoes or poisonous snakes or scorpions trying to find an opening in his netting.

Tommy had been a free man since leaving the Marines two years ago.

He had been careful in saving his money. His still close buddy, Evangelist Buster Scoggins, had helped see that his adored protégé's investments would grow over the years.

He had been thrifty, too, in stashing away his military pay.

So right after being honorably discharged, he brought some new stylish but durable clothes and a good leather bag and began to see the world.

Buster Scoggins had given him tips on where to go and what to look for. The evangelist's advice on where to go to find the best whippings certainly came in handy during Tommy's experience around the world.

The former Marine was always flattered at being occasionally recognized from his *Buster's Bible Tales* appearances. In Hong Kong, in Morocco, Rabat, in Australia, someone would come up to him and sing out: "Samson! Adam! Autograph please?"

The television episodes were especially popular in the Orient and in Budapest. In Italy and Spain, in particular, *Buster's Bible Stories* were rabidly popular.

He went into a bar one night in Alicante, Spain. The bartender kept looking at him as he served the other customers and suddenly he shouted, with a big grin on his face: "Is Samson! Is Adam!"

Tommy was treated like a super movie star that night. Everyone wanted to buy him a drink—or take him home to see if his phenomenal torso was as extraordinary in person as it was on the TV screens.

He was naturally good with his hands and could lift and carry things that would ordinarily take six men to do. It wasn't necessary he did this. He had plenty of money for a young, single dude. He just liked the exercise and working alongside people he would never have met if he hadn't left Pineville.

He knew by now that he was what people called a real Macho Man. Dark stubble on his chin and cheeks and neatly trimmed sideburns gave him a virile quality. No matter how closely he shaved, the beard began to grow again within hours. This proved to be quite attractive to people who prowled for spectacular looking hunks like him.

With his body and face, he realized that everyone—male or female—would pay big bucks to play or adopt someone like him.

He felt awkward at first in accepting money for his company but he also discovered that those who offered him money and gifts were hurt when he refused them. They were used to paying fortunes for jewelry, cars, homes and they only wanted the best. This included an extraordinary human playmate.

To them, this young giant was better than any screen star. His little-boy expression of innocence and especially those sparkling, mint candy eyes seemed to cast a spell on these flesh seekers.

He had been lucky that his procurers were very attractive and very wealthy. Yet, after only a few days of being a "kept" boy, it had become deadly boring. He was not used to having someone slobbering over him, demanding his attention through the day, of being watched and worshipped and obsessed over.

He discovered he had a quality that made people go a little crazy with him nearby. They would literally have guards and domestic help watching him 24 hours a day. If he smiled at someone else, his keeper would go berserk. The physical demands were not great. He had outstanding stamina when it came to sex.

So he stopped playing these games after the tenth person, a wealthy Austrian woman, threw herself into the Danube River when he announced he was leaving. He was forced to jump in and save her and all her friends were thrilled with the drama of it all.

Because of his large size, he stood out wherever he went. If he was in an elevator, his head nearly touched the ceiling. He had to stoop slightly when entering a room. In a movie theater, he usually sat against the wall. If he sat in a regular seat, those behind him couldn't see the screen.

When he took a swim anywhere, people gathered around to watch him. He carried with him his specially constructed black speedo. Even with this skimpy bathing attire, he saw people nudge each other and grin as they stared at his crotch. The leather and rubber sewn into the cup still bulged out like he had stuffed an egg plant in there.

The brief was cut low enough in the back to show a generous portion of his lower hips. His ass crack was visible at the top.

While a Marine, though, he had much time to think about his life and he concluded that he did not want to live a life that was normal. None of the conservative, Christian values of Pineville had touched him. He knew he possessed the qualities that would provide him with a wild, romantic life that few could attain. He wanted to do something in front of a big crowd. His memories of being part of the Evangelist Buster Scoggins Revival Show made his face light up. That had been fun and fulfilling.

In the Marines, many of the men were faithful fans of Evangelist Buster Scoggins. With great excitement, they finally realized that in their midst now was the stunning star of the Samson and Adam episodes on the *Buster's Bible Stories* series.

A group of twenty-two men hurried to Tommy's part of the barracks one night. He was just emerging from the showers and when his new-found admirers saw him—wet, his amazing body gleaming and rippling with power, they were dumbstruck.

He signed autographs and after he dressed, he posed with his new fans for pictures. The Samson and Adam star declined, however, to pose naked for the cameras.

"I'm not on stage anymore guys," he explained. "The next time I use the pool, I'll let you know and you can snap me there."

So whenever he visited the base's large pool, a crowd would always appear with their cameras. Their girlfriends and buddies back home were thrilled to see their men posing with this spectacular looking Adonis.

He didn't like to pal around and get drunk in bars and go to brothels and get into drunken brawls that his macho buddies thought you had to do to be a normal cigar-chomping jarhead.

When his fellow Marines pulled out their wallets to show him pictures of their parents or girls or wives they left behind, Tommy felt strangely removed. That type of existence just didn't connect with him.

He'd never had any of that and so he couldn't see himself all teary-eyed about home sweet home. If he did think of home, which was rare, he never thought of the Barnes. They had been there but they were always wary and scared of him. He sensed it in the way Myrtle Barnes regarded him. When he came near her, she began to hyperventilate. She would get up and leave or move to a different place.

No, he wondered about his real parents. They had to have been special because he sensed from the beginning that he was extraordinary. His outstanding torso, his thoughts, none of it fitted in with the conventional way that he was supposed to have evolved.

The idea that he could actually be the son of the late Emmanuel Trident and Diana DuPree grew steadily stronger. Countless people told him how his resemblance to Jesus Christ was amazing. And a few even compared him to the lost Mountain Messiah. The cult of Emmanuel Trident was especially strong in Asia and Germany.

He visited with one group in Berlin. It was astonishing to enter a darkened chapel, crowded with men and women wearing wheat-hued robes, and giant photos of the Naked Jesus were everywhere. And there were numerous oil paintings of the deity Mouria.

When Tommy appeared, these cultists crowded around him, gasping in amazement that he was the exact replica of the missing holy man.

"You—you have to be related to him!" said countless people. "Your eyes, your big build, your charisma—you must be one of the missing twin boys."

When Tommy left the chapel, he was followed by fifty or more of the worshippers. All praised and made signs of love to him.

This made him swear to discover who he really was—and if he was a descendant of Emmanuel Trident and Diana DuPree, he would have to prove it.

Even in high school, fellow students and even a teacher were certain that he and the doomed Tridents had to be connected. His resemblance to the lost Mountain Messiah were dramatically similar.

As Evangelist Scoggins told him: "Tommy, there are not many men on Earth who have eyes as stunning and the color of emeralds as you and Emmanuel Trident."

Many times in his young life he dreamt the same dream.

There was always an electrical sense to his vision, of an intense energy, a blast of beautiful warmth and there stood two nude figures.

The man resembled Jesus Christ. He was heroically constructed with mighty body and limbs. His companion was a ravishing woman with gold hair and beautifully formed—although she possessed modest genitalia of both male and female.

Both stared straight at the dreamer. A wind blew their hair, behind them and the background was luscious crimson, streaked with tangerine colored clouds.

The couple beckoned to him, both smiling and nodding their heads.

Although their voices were silent, Tommy was thrilled when they said: "Come! Hurry! We're waiting for you."

And when he awoke, it was always with a sense of depression as he looked around his ordinary narrow bedroom, walls decorated with a few framed oil pictures and a tepid breeze, stirring the white curtains.

Sleeping one floor beneath him were two people who were his foster parents and who were total strangers to him on every level.

#

From his first day in boot camp, until he was discharged, all others—from the grunts to the top military brass—were in awe of him.

He might be only eighteen, but his extraordinary physical gifts made him envied and respected. Nobody had any wish to fight this bulging young bull.

His manhood was certainly noted in the showers. Men from other barracks would find an excuse to take a shower when he was there. His sexual equipment had become legend.

During his first week in the barracks, he showed all the others why it wouldn't be wise to involve him in the usual drunken brawls.

A dozen or more roaring jarheads had staggered back to the barracks where he was reading his Mouria journal that he had just started. They thought it was a Bible and called him Jesus freak, Jesus Boy until finally he cleared them out by knocking out each one.

Then he went back to making notes in his journal about the legacy of the hermaphrodite deity named Mouria—and whether Emmanuel Trident had survived all those centuries as a high priest of this very ancient god. And if Mouria had sent him to Bethlehem on one of those flying machines they had at that time—and he was adopted by a couple in a manger who named him Jesus.

One of his most fervid admirers was a handsome Italian, Tony, from the Bronx.

"One night there were fifty or sixty of us men and women sitting in a bar in Virginia Beach watching the Buster Scoggins evangelical show," Tony said. "It was your last night with his revival. You wore black slacks and a white silk shirt, opened halfway down your chest. And you sang *Nearer My God to Thee*. Tommy, you had us all bawling our eyes out. You sang it with so much intensity. And the choir came in. We never forgot you or that song. Will you sing for us for Talent Night?"

"Yes," Tommy smiled. "I would enjoy singing again and appearing before a big crowd. I miss the spotlight."

Tommy's platoon held a talent show twice a month. Anyone who wanted to do anything was asked to participate. Anything to alleviate the long days where nothing happened.

A group of smart, talented musicians had found each other and formed a sharp-sounding little musical group called The Jar Heads. Tommy rehearsed with them for some of the tunes he wanted to present when he appeared in the show.

There was Donnie on piano, Zach on violin, Peter on guitar, Carson on sax and trombone, Harold on bass fiddle and Rufus on drums.

Yet another bunch of both black and white recruits had created a singing group. They modeled themselves on the Ink Spots, Billy Ward and the Dominoes and the Hilltoppers. They would provide chorale backup for

Tommy and they greatly enjoyed the idea of doing some fancy dancing, too.

The show was highly anticipated. It was the only entertainment for the thousand or more men.

There was always a problem in the delivery of motions pictures. Television was non-existent here. Radio was good for listening to but all the men wanted to see something live, raw and usually funny as hell.

For this show, hundreds of men crowded the benches with their cigarettes and Cokes and watched some of their cohorts appear in drag as they mimicked a recording of the Andrew Sisters belting out "The Bugle Boogie Woogie Boy of Company C."

Some of the Yankee guys did their comic shtick of Italians singing "Oh, My Papa," and "Ole Solo Mio."

A sultry, Brazilian tune and beat began by The Jar-Heads and the spotlight shone down on Tommy Barnes as he danced and swayed upon the stage. All the men greeted him with enthusiastic applause and whistles.

His body gleamed with coconut oil. A brief sarong encircled his hips. He shook mariachis as he began to croon a popular tropical infused hit song, "My Golden Place."

"Come along

"And let me take you to a golden place,

"Where we'll sip some wine,

"Then you'll be mine

"As we dance and sway

"Because that's the Brazilian way…"

Behind him emerged a dozen nearly naked men, also dressed in sarongs, as they joined in the music. They harmonized and tapped small drums as Tommy stole the spotlight with his sensual movements and his undulating hips.

When they finished, the applause was stronger and there were shouts of more. More!

For the second number, Tommy had chosen that rock classic, "Shake Rattle and Roll."

He and his dancers threw themselves into the music as they humped and swiveled their hips. Tommy caused a roar of laughter when he playfully untied his sarong and shook his bare ass to the audience.

For his final number, he went to the edge of the stage. His mood was serious when he said:

"I think we're all thinking of home tonight. Christmas is three weeks away. I'd love to have you join in if you recognize these songs."

"I'll Be Home for Christmas," and "Have Yourself a Merry Little Christmas" were the holiday standards that caused many a man to weep that night.

For his final song, Tommy came to the edge of the stage. Behind him, his background singers moved close in.

"O Holy Night" was the final song. Tommy and his vocalists had practiced this number over and over until the harmony and presentation were perfect.

When the last words were sung, there was a moment of silence. And then the audience stood up and cheered and applauded. Like Tommy Barnes, tears streamed down their faces.

For the next few days, those who had attended this musicale could talk of nothing but Tommy Barnes. He was better than any musical personality they had ever heard.

Just as entranced was the top brass on the base who were in the audience that night.

When the CBS network contacted military officials if they had any musical talent that could be showcased on the big Christmas Special that would be televised on December 25th, Tommy was immediately offered.

When asked what music he would like to perform, he said: *"Ave Maria."*

He had already performed it several times with his High School choral group. He sang it to himself many times.

He would be backed up by a sixty-member military choir. A fifty-piece symphony orchestra would perform with him. Tens of millions of viewers would be watching him live around the world.

When the camera switched over to him on that special night viewers were spellbound by the magnificent figure of a young man, dressed in his military uniform, sing *Ave Maria.*

He didn't perform this classic music in an operatic way. His beautiful voice rang out in strong, intense notes that seemed like it came from the heart.

As the camera moved closer to the singer's face, watchers were spellbound by the beauty of Tommy Barnes. His jet curls were combed back from his angelic face. The camera moved even closer so that one saw the full, pink lips, the cleft in his chin and his stunning eyes. They were wet with emotion.

When the choir joined in, the camera had shone some of the vocalists wet-eyed from the emotional impact of the music.

The sequence ended as the camera pulled back to show the singer standing powerful, alone with an amber spotlight illuminating him in radiance.

Tommy Barnes was a sensation.

His segment of the program was replayed many times by the network during the holidays. CBS was flooded with letters and phone calls, demanding that Tommy Barnes be brought back.

In Pineville, Woody and Myrtle Barnes suddenly became mini-celebrities. Everywhere they went, strangers came up to them and poured out their emotions for their foster son. For once, the Barnes felt lucky that Tommy had lived under their roof.

It showed that he had been brought up in a good Christian household, as they told the local media.

Those who read these interviews laughed aloud. They remembered well how the mother had spent more time in bed during those eighteen years when their foster son lived with her—than she did acknowledging his presence,

Evangelist Buster Scoggins was beyond thrilled. As was his faithful congregation who adored Tommy and still missed him badly. Buster even got permission from CBS to replay Tommy's performance of *Ave Maria* on the preacher's syndicated show.

The military brass received numerous letters from talent agents and recording studios who all wanted to sign up this blazing young talent to their rosters.

Handsome, young crooners were all the rage. There was the sizzling sensation of Elvis Presley, along with Paul Anka, Frankie Avalon, Johnny Mathis and Pat Boone. The mature male vocalists like Perry Como and Dean Martin were too mature for the hip teenagers of America. None of these teenage heart-throbs could compare with the spectacular beauty, muscles and voice of this spell-binding young jarhead.

The word went out, however, that Tommy Barnes, still had two years to go before he could be honorably discharged.

Although happy to have made such a powerful impression with his television appearance, Tommy had a strange reluctance to enter show business. It all sounded like fun where he could make good money.

But he had read enough true life tales of young stars who blazed white hot at the beginning but quickly flamed out. Even if he should sign up with a top talent agency after his discharge, he was turned off by the the prospects of the relentless campaign to stay popular, to do commercials, be worshipped by screaming fans, to live a fake existence that all depended on a teenager's attention span.

No, his energies would be devoted to traveling the world after his discharge, studying other cultures, seeking the answer to the Vesaria mystery that haunted his dreams.

#

Military entertainments like the Talent Show came only occasionally.

There was still the grueling, grim days of having to exist in close quarters, sleeping only inches from snoring men. Since Tommy slept in the nude, he became used to knocking away the curious hands that tried to inch under his blanket in search of his manhood.

There was one big, bellowing senior officer who had heard about Tommy's sexual gifts and demanded he come into his private office one afternoon.

"Drop your pants, jug head," the big, bellowing man had commanded. "Let me see what I've been hearing about."

Tommy let his britches drop so this obnoxious old ass-hole could see his manly gifts.

"Come 'ere officer and sit here on the edge of my desk so's I can get a feel."

"No, sir--sir!"

"WH—what? Did you not understand my order?"

"Yes, sir! But as for what you asked, no sir!"

The old geezer's face turned blood red and he screamed "I could have you thrown into the brig, because of this!

"Yes, sir! I know, sir! But I don't think your superiors would approve of you wanting to suck my cock!"

"Get out of here!" screamed the old pervert.

What Tommy really missed were the thrilling whippings he received from Buster Scoggins.

The young Marine often wrote his mentor about how much he had loved about having his ass flogged by the sharp, nasty nips of a leather whip.

The evangelist eagerly replied, too, that he had never punished a posterior that was as outstanding as his former protégée.

In the Orient Tommy was happy to find master whippers. He paid them a little money, and they cracked the whip expertly on his backside. These sessions had him ejaculating repeatedly, always astonishing whatever man held the whip.

Tommy got out of his hotel bed and stood in front of the dull mirror of his dresser.

He tensed and bulged his glorious muscles. A beautiful bronze tint covered his whole body. This was another strange thing that happened to him—because he never sunbathed while in the Marine Corps.

It was like his body kept gradually evolving in a way he had no control over. After leaving the military, he never bothered to work out anymore. His torso didn't need it. His musculature remained strong and firm and attractive.

The amber tint of his flesh seemed to come from within. There were no tan lines of any kind on his body. This very attractive coloring was just there.

After he left the military, he visited places where he could lay naked outdoors, especially on the Rivera where his nudity created a sensation.

The usually blasé French people had never seen anyone as fabulous as he.

#

Tommy turned his back to the mirror and smiled in delight at the image that was reflected. He had no idea what inspired him to have a portrait of Emmanuel Trident embedded into his skin. Tommy just knew it was meant to be.

In Singapore, Tommy had heard about this tattoo artist, an old man named Sessue, who was considered the best skin artist in the world. Word was that he had trained in Tibet from a young age and was now legendary in his skills and the exotic ingredients that went into his tattoo colors.

For an American military man, the old man would create a work of art on any part of his body—as long as the recipient let the old artist pleasure himself with one's torso. He was terribly picky. The candidate for a tattoo had to strip naked. If Sessue liked what he saw, then he would create a lasting treasure—in exchange for a memorable sensual experience.

Tommy went to the shop on a busy side street in Singapore and was ushered into a shadowy chamber crammed with Oriental lamps, rickety furniture of bamboo, dozens of metal and crystal mobiles. Several little feminine boys sat around at their artwork. When Tommy entered the chamber, they dropped what they were doing and stared at him with awe. He resembled a beautiful young giant to them.

"I speak little English," the old, white bearded man said quietly in his private chamber. "But you are very, very big. I like big American boys. Will you disrobe for me? Just put your clothes on the chair there."

Tommy enjoyed an offbeat experience like this. You didn't find this in America. He sniffed the air and was charmed by the sandalwood incense...by the colorful silk tunic worn by the master tattoo maker...by a radio that played the high, whining voice of an Oriental pop singer...at the giggling little fairy boys who crowded into the chamber and looked up at him as if he were a giant.

His clothes came off and he stood there, just inches away from Sessue.

The elderly man's eyes had become large and incredulous. He glanced up at Tommy's little boy face and then back to the incredible chest, shoulders, arms and thighs and of course—at his outstanding manhood.

Sessue reached forth and wrapped his hands around the limber phallus.

It was by far the biggest he had ever handled. It flowed from his hand like an enormous package of white muscle. He unrolled the foreskin away from the tip of the organ. A huge mound of gleaming pink slid out. From the large opening, a big bubble of translucent honey gleamed.

The skin artist put his hands under the oversized testicles. He jiggled them slightly. They were larger than some of the melons the artist enjoyed. His fingers squeezed each one, like he was feeling up cantaloupes at one of the outside fruit stands.

All this handling made the mighty organ begin to swell bigger.

The artist glanced up at Tommy's face and saw that he was red-faced from arousal.

Sessue nodded his head and laughed happily. He clapped silently.

"Ah, yes, you will get your tattoo."

In order to get it, though, Tommy agreed to have a massage from the elderly artist. He lay nude on his stomach on the soft bed covered with purple velvet. The massage was sensuous in the extreme. Oil-laden fingers were quickly replaced by a warm mouth so that it felt like silken butterflies skimming over his flesh.

This oral sensation centered on the cleft of his rear-end, the hole, then several tongues that licked his scrotum, groin and the smooth phallus.

The young bull had never experienced anything so arousing and then he felt other lips and when he raised his head to look around, he saw the delicate assistants devouring their fill.

All night this went on—yet, Tommy wasn't exhausted. The way he was aroused by the others was an art—one perfected over thousands of years. They would gradually build him up—then stop for exotic drinks and fruit.

And then the process would begin again until he writhed in sexual pain. It felt like his whole male package was going to explode from tremendous pressure. When he orgasmed, it was tremendous. Several towels were used to mop up the warm cream.

There was another break and then the massage would resume and each ejaculation was more powerful than the first one.

The next day, he got his tattoo. The ancient artist propped the sketch of Emmanuel Trident on the wall above Tommy's naked form.

Sessue worked on the tattoo all that morning with four mature assistants helping him. That night, the portrait was finished. During all these hours, six of the pixie like boys fed Tommy a steady array of Oriental delicacies. The wine he sipped was memorable—and it left no hangover. It made him forget the pain of the needle.

When the old master finally finished, he had Tommy to remain on his stomach until the fleshy rendering had healed. A pleasant smelling oil was sprayed on the still tender flesh. Over this was draped a very light cotton covering. This was also soaked in an herbal concoction to prevent any infection. A fan kept the small chamber cooled and refreshed.

The artist skimmed his hands over Tommy's buttocks. The gentle fingers massaged them and he asked if Tommy enjoyed getting spanked.

"Most definitely," grinned Tommy. "I did not bring my whip."

"Ah, just as I thought," smiled the ancient man. "The surface of your rear has that certain quality of having been flayed many times—most unusual in a young boy from America. I have many whips"

A girlish little boy brought to the old man a velvet cloth upon which were arranged several hand whips. A middle one was chosen.

Soon, Tommy hurtled to heaven when the leather tongs nipped at his posterior. This was done so expertly that the boy became aroused to the point that he erupted into the terrycloth towel beneath his hips.

As the whipping continued, Tommy ejaculated several more times. A crowd had come to watch this miracle. There were many gasps of wonder and delight as Tommy unburdened himself with gusto.

When the cloth was removed from his back, Tommy was asked to stand naked before several floor-length mirrors.

There he finally saw the image on his back that he had long dreamed of. It was like having this Mountain Messiah literally with him at all times. If anyone should ever ask him to describe Emmanuel Trident, Tommy could just whip off his shirt, turn his back and let the questioner see close-up what the holy man looked like.

By the time he pulled on his clothes, the group of boy workers and admirers had grown to nearly a hundred. All of them bowed and made sounds of awe and delight—not only for the magnificent tattoo now permanently on his back of Emmanuel Trident—but to a torso the likes they had never beheld.

They gently touched Tommy's rear and made kissing sounds. Tommy smiled sweetly and to show them he loved them all, he undid his britches and pulled out his manhood so that the crowd could enjoy touching and kissing it.

Later, he heard that he had become a legend there. He was called Big Sweet Tommy with the Biggest One on Earth.

CHAPTER TWO

The young vagabond wanted to have fun in New York City but not the usual kind one associated with someone of his power and beauty. He wanted it to be as off-beat as possible...

He wanted no conventional job. He had plenty of money saved up so that he could play with the different employment ads. He could work as long as he wanted, or quit at the first sign of boredom.

So when Tommy scanned the want ads that night, the first job he checked off was that of a bouncer in a disco bar on Forty-Second Street. The bar was called Dante's Inferno where mist was belched out now and then to give it a smoky ambiance. The people who came here wanted only one thing and dancing was the least of them.

The men and women wearing party clothes from a discount warehouse crowded around the bar and the tables. They came desperate to hook up or to have sex in the backroom's many cubicles.

Tommy was fascinated by this side of life. He didn't judge. He just wondered why people would spend hours each night, determined to get banged by somebody they didn't even know.

He watched many women performing oral sex on men and men doing other men. They all acted frenzied and out of control. Tommy wondered what it was about the male phallus that generated such ferocious connections—with squeals, growling, and deep throat gagging— like the person doing the gobbling was having a heart attack.

Dressed in black with a gray turtleneck jersey, his very size kept everything under control so well that the owner asked Tommy if he could train other big former Marines to be bouncers.

But he discovered that when people drank a lot, they lost their respect for him and others so he was forced to throw them out into the streets. He became bored by the relentless sexual propositions from women and men. Some of the men were straight but as they drunkenly gurgled, "I'll gladly be a queer if you'd let me play with you. I'll bet you got some monster hangers."

One night, a very tipsy man vomited all over Tommy's new suit. He quit on the spot, stripped off his clothes and threw them at the club manager. With just a tablecloth to cover himself, he returned to his hotel room, past the amazed look of the counter clerk, and scanned the Want Ads for something else.

The Village Voice newspaper offered him a second shot at offbeat employment.

The ad read: "Auditioning for important single male role in the adult drama, *My Last Chance*. Role is non-speaking but requires extensive nudity. Must be eighteen to 40-years-old, good shape. No prudes."

Tommy found The Albatross Theater in a converted warehouse near the waterfront of the Hudson River.

The auditorium was half full with male hopefuls. The young man at the desk near the entrance looked up at Tommy and his eyes grew big. He whistled as his eyes went up and down Tommy's torso. For this occasion, the hopeful wore snug khaki slacks, a white turtleneck sweater and a leather jacket and biker's cap.

The man gulped: "You're over eighteen?"

"I'm twenty-four."

"Have you acted before?"

'I appeared as Samson and Adam in some religious programs. I was naked in both except for a really brief pouch."

"Great. So I guess it wouldn't bother you to appear totally naked, no pouch, in front of hundreds of people?"

"No problem. I like being naked."

'Yeah, I can see why. You're number 13."

As soon as Tommy left to take a seat, the man zoomed down to the front and whispered to the director, Claude Harrington: "Wait until you see number 13."

"Why?"

"Take my word. You've found your stud—and this kid is big!"

After a half hour, the director stood up and faced the applicants and the crew:

"Thank you all for coming. I'm the director Claude Harrington and I'll be helming *My Last Chance*, written by award-winning Jaime Sheraton and it'll be starring Christina LaMonte. We've cast the play with the exception of one very crucial male role. Jim Masters. The story is the sex fantasy of the heroine and her sister. All this performer has to do is to appear in the dream sequences and he won't be wearing anything. Everything you were born with will be on full display. Now if this is not your cup of tea, I'd like for you to leave now. We don't have much time. So don't waste ours. Also, have your shoes off before you go on stage. If we're all ready, I'd like to call to the stage Number One."

The stage only boasted a few items of furniture. A table and a large bed covered with a single sheet. Propped up on the bed was a human-sized female doll that could be found in the sex shops of New York.

Onto the stage ambled a pleasant looking all-American type who said his name was Eddie and he attended Columbia University.

"Okay Eddie," said the director," "now I'd like you to remove all your clothes. Do it like you're alone in your college room."

Eddie blushed slightly. Awkwardly he did his strip and neatly piled up his clothes on the table. Clad now only in blue boxer shorts he slid those off.

He stood bashfully with his arms dangling beside him. Tommy thought the kid resembled a high school bookworm. There was nothing sexy about him.

And so it went for another hour. For some of the candidates, this was strictly a lark they could tell their buddies about. They came on stage, chewing gum, dressed in grungy jeans and dirty socks.

And then it came time for Tommy to make his audition.

He strolled out confidently and even from the stage, he heard the gasps and the excited stirring of the play's personnel.

"Your name is Tommy Barnes? You certainly fill out your clothes well, I'll say that. Would you mind removing them as the others have?"

"Don't mind at all."

He pulled off his jacket and turtleneck sweater. Now came time for his slacks to be unbuckled so that he was clad only in a black bikini brief.

He slid his fingers under the waistband and peeled this off. He turned and casually posed.

"Woooo!" several people gasped and applauded. "Woo-woooo!"

"Mother of God!" muttered Claude Harrington. "We've found our star. Tommy would you flex those gorgeous muscles of yours and turn around?"

The young Adonis went into some strong man poses. He turned and rippled his back. The voyeurs got an extra thrill when they saw the extraordinary face of a Jesus Christ like image beaming back at them. When Tommy made his back muscles dance, it was like the face smiled and beamed at them. Tommy turned forward and rested his fists on his hips.

With an impish gleam in his eyes, he made his penis flip up and down. He cupped his enormous balls in one hand and pretended to be amazed at their size. Everyone watching him whooped and some yelled: "Bravo! More! More!"

Director Claude Harrington rubbed his eyes in mock disbelief.

"Whew! Tommy, has anyone ever told you that you have one absolutely fabulous torso."

"A few people!" grinned the young sex god.

"Would you now get on the bed there and pretend you're fucking the doll. Boys bring the bed closer to the edge of the stage. We want to see every inch of our young stud bull."

Several stagehands dragged the bed to the floor lights.

"Now Tommy just get up there and pretend that you're making love to our main star. Make it as real as you can. Don't try to be pretty or graceful or sexy. Just be!"

Tommy brought the doll down beneath him and straddled it.

Into the opening between the doll's legs, he guided his penis and he gasped—because it felt like the real thing. Slowly, he ground his hips. He thrust and grunted and pumped steadily. Behind him, he heard people whistling, whispering, clapping and making sounds of astonishment.

"Tommy, could you pull out and show us what you've got?"

The stage lights were hot and sweat sparkled on Tommy's body as he turned over. His erection was full blown.

There were more gasps and whistles of disbelief since most of the hopefuls had stayed behind to see who their competition was.

"Tommy, could you do this every night of our run."

The young stud nodded and suddenly groaned as he grasped his erection and it erupted with its copious burden. He had managed to hide it behind his hands but thick streams of semen spattered against the floorboards. There was more raucous whistles and whoops of amazement. One of the stagehands quickly handed him a roll of paper towel.

"Sorry," Tommy grinned sheepishly. "I wasn't prepared for that."

"Neither were we," laughed Claude Harrington, "but if you could do that every night, minus the cum shot, we'd have the most popular show on off-Broadway. You're hired. Be here tomorrow at one for rehearsals."

#

Within a week, New York's incestuous theater world hummed about the sensational young performer who was to appear totally nude for the quirky *One Last Chance.*

One heard that the leading lady had threatened to leave if Tommy was cast. She was said to have screamed at director Claude Harrington: "who'll be looking at me when we've got that big-cocked stud swinging his hard-on all over the place."

The femme star was a petite woman of fading looks. She had once been a promising starlet in Hollywood, appearing in several romantic comedies for two years. And then her luck ran out and critics derided her "Rom-Com" career. Her last job was on a daytime soap, *To Each His Own*. This sexy play was her big chance to make a comeback and had agreed to partial nudity for this production.

In their big sex scene together, she dreams of a handsome hometown farm boy who had once worshipped her when she was a Home Coming Queen at the University of Alabama. She had turned him down when he wanted sex. Now, as an aging spinster, she dreams of seeing him again and this time she wants to bed him down.

With the stage dramatically lit, Tommy walks out naked and joins his co-star in bed. They make passionate love and then silently, he leaves her. Then he appears again naked when the heroine's sister, Hilda, also dreams of this fabulous farm boy and Tommy has sex with her.

The director closely directed the love sequence. When Tommy appeared to be passionately having intercourse with his co-star, his privates would be nowhere near the woman's vagina. He was instructed to fuck the mattress because everyone on the front row could graphically see every movement of his oversized male package.

By the time the show opened, expectation was at fever pitch. Ads showed the star and Tommy in a passionate embrace—with the word "Hot" covering the essentials. The gay press showed a sizzling picture of Tommy with his hands behind his head, naked, and a two word caption of "Last Chance" just barely covering genitalia...

When he first appeared that night, the theater went wild. The gay men and the female swingers whooped, clapped and shouted. When he stepped off the bed, with his penis half-hard, there was more pandemonium.

The bed was pushed right up to the footlights. When he mounted his co-star, those in the front row could see his equipment in action. Although he never penetrated the actress, his phallus was thrust repeatedly against the mattress. This always got him hard. When he stood up, his semi-erection still caused people to gasp in amazement.

As one gay columnist wrote, "Tommy Barnes with his enormous manhood and ultra-fabulous torso brings a new dimension of sexual fantasy onto the stage. With his spectacular torso, his stunning ass and of course those phenomenal jewels swinging all over the place, the theater should give out paper towels to all its male audience members."

And so it went for his every appearance—much to the rage of the female stars. To them, the play was hijacked by this amazing young warrior who said not one of dialogue...

For two months the drama was sold-out. Tommy had become a fascinating young sex god. In interviews with the local media, he was always covered up. In no way, did he act like the usual sex performer that were now everywhere in porno movies. These triple-X entertainers usually carried on interviews while totally nude—and often aroused.

Readers couldn't get enough of that beautiful, innocent face and that spectacular torso and equipment.

Tommy turned down numerous requests for nude pictorial layouts for the straight and gay media. If his cock was plastered all over the media, then his sexual mystery would vanish. He knew most people were filling up the theater just to see his naked body and especially his scandalous male equipage.

At that time, several hit Broadway shows featured male and female nudity. *O, Calcutta, Hair, Boys in the Band* were just a few productions where your ticket brought you live and uninhibited performers who gave you live what you fantasized about. In one red-hot stage hit, *Fleshy Titbits*, audience members were encouraged to strip naked and jump up on the stage and enjoy an actual orgy.

#

Away from the stage there were riots of fanatical fans desperate to grope the red-hot sex idol or strip him naked.

He discovered this when he attended an exclusive party given by Broadway dynamo Chris Tunson, who had made his millions by road-showing musical classics that endlessly traveled the country. He and his wife were famous for their penthouse parties atop the Waldorf-Astoria.

Tommy went along with the director, Claude Harrington and was immediately surrounded by a dozen or more stage stars. At Claude's suggestion, Tommy had worn a pink V-neck sweater of cashmere and snug white slacks that clearly outlined his lower regions.

The penthouse had a huge swimming pool and the Tunsons insisted Tommy don one of the many extra bikini briefs in the poorhouse and take a swim.

The swim suits were all much too small for his proportions but he finally pulled on a flesh-colored brief that looked as if he wore nothing."

When he appeared, everyone applauded and whistled.

"Jesus H. Christ!" was heard from several of the men. "Talk about a stud that's got the meat!"

When he jumped into the pool, the water made the tiny brief more restrictive so he stripped it off.

"Claude" he shouted over the din, "could you get me a towel so I can come out! I ain't got no bathing suit."

Several of the bathers had pushed up against him. He felt his equipment being grabbed and stretched and the more he fought them away, the more insistent they became.

When he climbed out, there were more whistles and bawdy shouts when everyone saw his jaw-dropping erection. Only by escaping into a bedroom and putting on his clothes was he able to escape mass rape.

#

Tommy gradually found this job boring, too. Every night it was the same. A growing mob of gay men and queens appeared every night and screamed each time he appeared on stage. They flooded his tiny closet-sized dressing room with boxes of candy, expensive bottles of *Red Fever* cologne, silk underwear and pictures of themselves in sexual poses.

Fans discovered what hotel he was staying in and knocked at his door at all hours. Mobs of males and women would corner him on the street at night and grope him.

Several gay and straight tabloid editors were beginning to write negative columns about his refusal to attend the city's orgies, the gay hangouts or pose for nude spreads in magazines or to appear in porno movies.

"Tommy," wrote one columnist for *Gay Blade*, "if you're reading this, be aware that some of us are getting tired of your precious, superior attitude in keeping yourself private. Your fans naturally had hoped you would attend some of the parties you've been invited to. To visit the gay bars, to strip naked at the Gaiety Burlesque. You have a God-given body that drives your admirers crazy. Can't you just be generous for once—let your ordinary man-on-the-street fans enjoy your astonishing torso and your manhood. Be generous to your following. It's almost Christmas. And they're the ones who made you famous."

When Tommy told the director he was quitting, the poor man pleaded and begged him to stay on. Without Tommy as the sex star, the play would surely close. Yet, since Tommy had signed a three month contract, nothing could prevent him from leaving. The two female stars were thrilled that their enemy would no longer be there to hog the spotlights.

At the farewell party thrown for him in My Buddy's Italian pizza parlor in the village, Tommy was cheered by everyone—including the femme cast members because even they had to admit he was an adorable cub.

He laughed as hard as the others when a special cake was wheeled out and he was asked to cut it. The confection was designed as a giant phallus. Two enormous balls of ice cream represented his now famous testicles.

Tommy sliced into the cake and to the surprise of everyone, handed the plate over to co-star Christina LaMonte...

Everyone howled, though, when they saw that to the dismay of the actress, Tommy had presented her one of the ice cream shaped testicles.

All this time that he was relaxing, goofing off, there was a strange inner conviction that all this was leading to something tremendous in his life.

An image had become fixed in his mind: that he stood naked before worshippers. He was extolling the reasons why Mouria had once reigned over the Earth, and why Mouria would one day return.

Tommy didn't think this resurrection would be a cataclysmic event.

Perhaps Emmanuel Trident, and someone who was physically like Mouria, would make their come backs at the same time.

#

He worked for a month as the strongman in a traveling carnival. People came to stare at him with open-mouthed amazement. In his brief little leopard skin speedo, his body all oiled up, he bulged and flexed his muscles.

For three dollars extra, customers could stand beside this young muscle man and feel his biceps while having their pictures made. Many of his female admirers became frisky while posing with him. Just as the flashbulb popped, their hands slid down over his ass, over his crotch. One over-eager women actually yanked the front of his briefs down. When the crowd saw his equipment pop out, there were gasps, laughter and many, "Oh, my God! Oh, my God!"

After the show, Tommy waited his turn to cleanup by using the outside shower behind the big tent.

The first time he stripped naked to shower, he suddenly heard cameras clicking and giggling. Hiding behind bushes and hanging from tree limbs were dozens of customers who had paid extra just to see him bare-assed.

But after several weeks, Tommy grew depressed with the tawdriness of the circus. He couldn't stay clean, his clothes always needed washing, everybody wanted to touch and feel him. When he pushed away the questing hands, people got nasty and angry. When he used the toilet, he never knew if somebody hadn't rigged up a hidden camera to catch him in the act.

Some of the women, especially the hoochie-coochie girls, were determined to bed him but Tommy had become expert at blocking sexual advances. He had spent his whole life doing so. These strippers would invade his tiny trailer completely naked and throw themselves on him. There was always an audience when these encounters occurred. The woman was sent flying out the door to land on her ass.

Tommy felt sorry for the poor yokels who came to this carnival and got suckered in.

Those young kids and couples made him pity them. Out in the Deep South, people who came to the carnivals were usually poor farm folk. They'd scrapped up all their money just to have a night away from the drudgery of farm life. It was depressing to Tommy to see people live like this.

Yet, there was one carnival star that fascinated Tommy and they became good friends.

Her name was Mary Ann and she was hailed as the Man Woman.

Her costume was designed so that one half was a tuxedo for a man. The other half was a tawdry chiffon gown to show that she was a woman. The bodice was cut so that her small left breast was exposed.

Tommy discovered Mary Ann was unusually well read and educated. Her small trailer was piled high with books. She always had a pot of hot coffee simmering on her little hot plate.

One night he discussed intensely his search for the secret of Mouria and the legacy of Emmanuel Trident.

"The Naked Jesus?" gasped Mary Ann. "I actually saw him way back in 1941. My grandma took me. I've never forgotten that incredible experience, of sitting there in the All Souls Church of the Mountains. And he was like—like a living, breathing god. A giant."

"And when he tore off his robe, everyone gasped. Bigger even than those muscle men like Steve Reeves. He was buck naked except for a silken panel that hid his privates. He preached about the duality of Mouria, the ancient god. By being half-woman, half-male, like me, this deity could see the world through the eyes of both sexes. Wish I knew about Mouria."

In another conversation, Tommy listened as Mary Ann discussed her many experiences on the road.

"You know, Tommy, something very weird happened to me when the carnival appeared in Fairville as part of the state fair. There was this adorable boy there. His mother insulted me by laughing at me and telling her son that he was like me. I jumped on her and beat her lousy ass. But you know—the boy and I exchanged smiles—and I just knew that he was like me. But he was still growing and hadn't fully developed—but he was a beautiful kid: gold curls, big blue eyes, trim body. I've always wondered whatever became of him."

When he went to bid her goodbye on his final day with the circus, Mary Ann embraced him and said:

"You know something, Tommy, I've been meaning to tell you this. But you look so much like Emmanuel Trident I had thought at first that when I saw you, it was like had returned from the dead. You're destined for something big. Really big!"

#

He worked in the oil fields.

The work was hard, the hours terrible, but Tommy enjoyed in a way using his body to bring in a paycheck. He still had fifty-thousand dollars in his bank account but he didn't want to touch that until much later.

The men he worked with were too busy focusing on their jobs so they didn't stand aside in awe when he worked with them.

He discovered a tavern that specialized in spotlighting local talent. A small, but expert orchestra, was there and Tommy appeared one night.

Dressed in black, he rehearsed with the group of musicians and when the spotlight later hit him, he crooned the beloved ballad, *At Last*. He had watched this number introduced in the old movie classic, *Orchestra Wives* that was shown several times on television.

The packed tavern were thrilled—not just because of the stunning voice of this newcomer—but with Tommy himself. They stomped and applauded, whistled and demanded he be given an encore.

He became an in-demand singer but after a few more appearances he left his job and moved elsewhere.

"I'm getting close to where I should be going—but not quite."

#

As a cable repair man, he got propositioned so many times by both women and men that he quit. He got tired of pushing their hands away and listening to them threaten to report him for sexual harassment if he didn't share his goodies.

He traveled extensively in an old Ford pickup he had brought from a farmer in Omaha. Tommy painted it a bright red, a gesture that meant that every time he looked at his truck, it jolted his spirits upwards.

But no matter where he went and found work and tried to blend in, his physical attributes quickly set him apart. He could wear baggy jeans and old tee shirts and beat-up boots but it was never enough.

He carried himself like a king. His torso, his height, his physical beauty brought him looks that were admiring, lustful, fascinated, curious.

If he took off his shirt while working in a field of cotton, his muscles and the blazing tattoo on his back instantly made him the center of attention.

If he wore just regular bathing trunks to a beach, other bathers saw him, nudged each other, and moved closer. Sometimes gangs of psycho boys tried to start trouble but he finished them off without barely breaking into a sweat.

When he got a job as a lifeguard at a public swimming pool in Atlanta, the pool became a mob scene in just hours when word got around about the "gorgeous giant."

#

In Austin, Texas, he took guitar lessons from Amanda Butler, one of the most outstanding guitarists in the nation. The student learned quickly for he had "played" around with this instrument while in Pineville.

When his teacher asked him to play and sing something, he crooned the old British Ballad, "Leaves They Go Green."

The trees they grow high

The leaves they do grow green

Many an hour I've watched him all alone

He's young but he's daily growing...

When he finished, Amanda Butler looked stunned.

"Good God, Tommy—you sound incredible. Your voice was so beautiful—but there was something powerful beneath it."

She talked to him about recording some songs for a label she worked with Prodigy, and he put his voice on several old mountain and British ballads. "On the Banks of the Ohio" "Silver Dagger," "Black is the Color of My True Love's Hair."

When his music began to be heard on that city's radio stations, listeners were thrilled. They wanted to hear more—but the singer had already left town.

#

While exploring the mountains of Colorado, he came upon a large community named Winter that was composed of naked people.

Over one hundred nudists lived in a pastoral setting. They all had long hair, the men beards and moustaches, and they grew lush fields of vegetables, wheat, and fruit. Their chickens produced eggs and later the chickens provided food for the inhabitants.

Tommy discovered that these men and women were nearly all college educated. There was a panel of men and women who governed.

What astonished Tommy was that when they held religious services, they faced an enormous stone carving of an ancient deity.

This was Mouria.

Tommy had just entered this community when he saw this wondrous sight.

By this time, the whole population of this little village had gathered around him. They were amazed that someone so big and beautiful had just suddenly appeared.

"Please stay for a little while, or longer if you wish," said a mature giant named King Edward.

Tommy removed his clothes. His unclothed torso elicited the usual signs of amazement but after a few minutes, he was treated like a much desired visitor.

Edward was the "king" of this community. He was majestically built. His neatly trimmed hair, moustache and beard were the color of snow although he was only forty-two years old.

"You'll be my roommate while you're here," he said.

King Edward enjoyed a snug log cabin with one large bed, with periwinkle blue curtains at the windows, an actual bathroom and bath.

"I'll show you our praying place," he said and took Tommy's hand.

A large area of the grounds was cleared and wood benches surrounded the circle.

"Mouria is our god," Edward explained. "We've all read what little we know about her. Dr. Norma DuPree was the great historian who described how Mouria reigned over a vast civilization. They were all hermaphrodites like her. The people were described as beautiful beyond description. A group of super men—white, almost giants, with astonishing bodies and powers—advised Mouria on everything. One of them may well have been Jesus Christ. He later appeared in Vesaria in 1940 and revitalized the place but his enemies tried to destroy him."

"That carving I saw when I came in," Tommy murmured. "Who did it? It looks amazingly ancient."

Dr. Norma DuPree had brought the huge stone back from her trip to Tibet in the early 1930s. Before she died, she presented her discovery to the Black Mountain Museum which was trying to acquire enough curiosities to attract the public.

In the mid-1940s, though, the museum went bankrupt. Nearly everything was acquired by other museums but this particular piece was purchased by a wealthy philanthropist. He had come to Winter to become part of its society. He brought along the Mouria stone.

"We don't worship any deity," explained King David. "But Mouria is the only power we know of that includes all people and all genders. We don't judge people if they're attracted to members of their own sex, the opposite sex, their family members. That's not for us to even consider. We believe in harmony and affection."

The newcomer was surprised that Winter was like a micro- village, like Vesaria. Among the population there were two doctors, a nurse, a dentist, and several teachers who left academia to live the "natural life."

A number of the inhabitants were also musicians. In the main cabin, a piano and other instruments were present where the players would entertain the others during meal time.

The new visitor was delighted with the abundance of freshly sliced vegetables, fruits, and fried chicken and veal dishes. Freshly baked loaves of breads were present at all meals. Both men and women took turns working in the kitchens and doing the cooking.

Tommy was urged to appear at their next religious gathering and explain his journey in life—and especially why Emmanuel Trident—and Mouria—meant so much to him.

It was his third night there when he stood before the small populace of Winter. Torches were lit and flickered over his powerful torso. Like King Edward, he was letting his hair grow once more. His always dark stubble now formed the beginning of a beard and moustache.

His audience was spellbound by his uncanny resemblance to Emmanuel Trident.

Tommy enthralled them all with his search for the meaning of his life—for he was almost certain that his parents were Emmanuel Trident and Diana DuPree.

Everyone gasped, for most had thought the same thing when they saw him.

"You are our next Naked Jesus!" shouted King Edward.

Tommy glanced down at his nudity and grinned: "At least you got the naked right, my friend."

The newcomer's popularity rose even higher when he sang for them.

His unclothed audience were delighted with his rich, intense voice, while he strummed his guitar.

He explained that he was vocalizing the very songs that were recorded by The Tridents of Vesaria before they were murdered…

Most audience members had heard these tunes many a time and so they joined their voices to Tommy as they sang "Banks of the Ohio" "Silver Dagger" and." Black is the Color of my True Love's Hair."

#

On Tommy's fifteenth night in Winter, the weather had turned grim and cold. A hearty fire crackled in the cabin of King David. Both he and his guest lay relaxed with each other, their arms embracing the other. Several glasses of the home made whiskey made them feel warm and sensual. They had made passionate love together all that evening.

King David was heroically constructed with an impressive set of privates. Both he and his new companion enjoyed studying each other's manly attributes, caressing them and loving them.

Now they studied the flames in their crimson and jade shadowing.

"Tommy, I sincerely think you're heading for something big. Really big. Have you ever felt that your parents—and I'm pretty sure they are—Emmanuel Trident and Diana DuPree have been guiding you along your life's path?"

Tommy closed his eyes and smiled: "Yes! Yes, it's always been there. That conviction that I'm going to do something big. Not sure what it is now but I'm moving toward it."

His host advised him to find a good college that taught religious history and past civilizations.

"Emmanuel Trident came from another dimension or he somehow existed in a supernatural trance for centuries," opined King David. "I'm convinced those legends are true: that he could well be asleep in one of those caverns within Mt. Mouria. You should go on an exploring expedition someday soon and study those openings in the mountain. You might just find your father there: unchanged, still very much alive but in a spiritual sleep."

Excited over this possibility, Tommy announced the next day that he was leaving for "profound reasons."

There were pleas for him to stay but as he got into his red truck, he said: "I'm going to find my father."

#

He returned to New York City and went straight to the great library on Forty-Second Street.

Tommy studied stacks of college catalogues and with the help of a librarian, he narrowed the list down to two.

He wrote to these colleges for their catalogues and as he waited in his hotel room, he decided to change his name, too.

"I'm starting a new phase of my life—and now I'm moving faster to my destiny."

PART FIVE

"We're Brothers"

CHAPTER ONE

Brandon stared out the window of his office in the Teacher's Building of Sterling College.

Although only noon, the day was dark with the promise of snow.

A frigid wind whistled against the cracked window and he kept telling himself that he had only one more month before he would complete his stay here as Visiting Professor of Art/Fashion.

He had agreed to come here for three months just as a favor to the dean, a close friend from Blackwood Institute, who wanted to build up her weak art department. And what better way to stand out than hiring one of the hottest names in art and fashion: Brandon Flores of New York City!

He was impatient to begin the biggest change of his life and it would all begin when he entered the Gender Transition Center in Birmingham, Alabama.

At last, he would finally have that operation that would make him a woman—a woman who would still possess her male genitalia.

His name would be changed, too.

World—meet Diana DuPree!

And then he would return to his luxurious penthouse in Manhattan. He knew his home there in the big city was destined to be his—because this was the very exclusive apartment building in the ritzy Gracie Square section of the Upper Eastside where Diana DuPree had planned to live.

In fact, Brandon was astonished to discover that the magnificent home of the dead artist had been kept in perfect condition through all those decades. The executors of her vast estate had agreed that nothing there would be changed. It was kept like a rare sanctum of a dead woman who was now undergoing a renaissance.

A young landlord had allowed Brandon to explore the luscious living quarters that was locked away from the public.

For one entire rainy afternoon, he was like someone in a trance as he stepped into this marble and crystal paradise on the top of the building. Glorious lamps, statuary, tapestries and Persian carpets began his tour. Diana DuPree's kitchen had all the modern appliances she had installed back in 1940.

Her art studio featured floor to ceiling windows that looked down on a sparkling East River. Her bed was covered in a bronze-hued comforter of silk, with turquoise pillows.

In her huge closets, her clothes still hung there. Fur coats, hats, dresses and gowns and scarves—all the luxuries from decades ago. All were protected in plastic coverings. Her king-sized bathroom still smelt faintly of gardenia soap.

The shelves were filled with perfumes by Coty, Caron and Trezetti.

Brandon had become good friends with the young male manager. He was startled that his new tenant had gone to school on a Diana DuPree Scholarship and that she was his veteran saint.

The manager listened to Brandon make a plea of buying the apartment of Diana DuPree. His past history proved that he would honor her name and her home.

Now Brandon was hoping to hear from the manager. Brandon would keep his present apartment there while living in the home of the mythical Diana DuPree.

#

His art and fashion careers had now made him a multi-millionaire at the age of twenty-six.

Brandy's now had twelve boutiques, spread in exclusive enclaves of fashion. His Madison Avenue store was a wild hit with New York's elitist and wealthy. Opening night was a media sensation where he and his adorable agent/lover, Bruce Jasmine, greeted and performed for the rabid reporters and photographers.

The handsome Bruce impersonated Tarzan. Only a large fig leaf of green velvet covered the essentials. The rest of his handsome torso was visible to everyone.

Brandon naturally appeared as Tarzan's lover: Jane.

His skimpy clothing of faux leopard left all of his trim body exposed—except for a swath of material across his breasts. They were already obviously bigger than those of an average male. Although Bruce knew of his boyfriend's chest development, they thought it wise to keep it hidden until after Brandon underwent his sex change operation.

#

The young artist and designer winced as he remembered an interview by the media in Fairville with his mother.

The opening of the Brandy's on Madison Avenue had made large headlines in the Southern media—but especially in Brandon's home town.

Edith Flores was shown in a rocking chair, holding a picture of Brandon when he was fourteen. Behind her stood Reverend Flores.

When asked about how she felt of her foster son's amazing success in the fashion and art worlds, she smiled wetly.

"Oh, I always knew that my beautiful boy was going to be somebody. When he seemed depressed or exhausted from his painting, why I would bring him a nice cup of hot cocoa, pat him on his head and tell him that it was all worth it. Someday he would be rich and famous. And he certainly has."

One reporter cut in: "Mrs. Flores, some of your neighbors say you were reported to the police several times about possible child abuse? Your neighbors claim they heard your son scream numerous times over the years."

"How dare you insult me—a preacher's wife?" snarled Edith Flores who then stuck out her tongue at the camera. "Those are just a bunch of goddamned hypocrites who were always jealous of me. Those fucking old snoopers. My boy would hug me all the time and say to me that I was the best Mommie he could ever have. Yes, he did. The best Mommie in the world. That's what he said."

"Then why hasn't he visited you since he left Fairville?" asked another TV reporter. "Several eyewitnesses say he knocked you down in your driveway on the day he left. We have a picture."

One of the neighbors had been snapping pictures that day, explained the reporter, and one of the images was of Edith Flores lying on the driveway with her panties exposed.

"Get out of my house!" screamed Edith Flores. "I'm a goddamned preacher's wife. How dare you insult me? If it wasn't for me, my son would have ended up digging ditches."

#

His chalet here in the Virginia hills was big enough where he had continued to do much work. It was New York, though, where he got his stimulus and his security. He had enjoyed working with the students in his art classes here at first—but he saw no one who showed the passion and stubbornness that would give them a career outside of academia.

#

His memory was haunted by his mother, Diana DuPree, and her tragic fate.

In fact, he had written several articles about *The Art of Diana DuPree*. She was being rediscovered by a new generation of artists and historians. Her fantasy views of the world—which she committed to canvas in dizzying contortions of pastel and violent colors—were being reexamined now by modern art collectors. She had assumed cult status. There were now attempts to collect her work from private owners and have them displayed in a major exhibit in the Metropolitan Museum of Art in New York City.

Connected to her was the personal history of Emmanuel Trident and naturally that of the long lost John Sparrow.

There were no longer any searches for him. He had vanished as completely as Emmanuel Trident. So bizarre and compelling were these two mysteries that they had been examined on television in documentaries. There were numerous articles and even several books about the incredible history of the whole Vesaria mystery.

An off-Broadway play had won awards and critical praise because it had brilliantly dramatized the astounding saga of Emmanuel Trident, Diana DuPree and their lost two boys.

Brandon collected everything he could find about these three legendary figures—Emmanuel Trident, Diana DuPree and John Sparrow-- into large scrapbooks. He now had video tapes of John Sparrow in the pulpit.

Grace Cowan had the foresight to film his every sermon. She had died a year ago. After John Sparrow vanished, no one was interested in attending her church and watching the parade of handsome, dynamic ministers who attempted to replace the dazzling minister. Finally, Grace Cowan shut the doors and donated the property to Blackwood Institute.

Before she died, though, Brandon received one afternoon in his Manhattan penthouse a large crate. Its return address was the town of Blackwood. When he opened it, he was stunned to see the portrait of John Sparrow that he had painted for the church.

Included were the video-tapes of his sermon and even several of the robes he had worn. Brandon pressed these garments to his face and could smell the faded scent of citrus, musk and wood bark that the minister favored.

For hours, Brandon sat in front of the picture, with a bottle of champagne, and wept as he remembered everything about that extraordinary figure, the likes of which the artist had never met. "He destroyed me for all others. I'll go through life looking for a replacement—and that'll never happen."

Each time Brandon watched these filmed performances of John Sparrow in all his naked glory, he couldn't control his emotions.

. John had given him just a whiff of what he could do—and then he vanished at his peak.

#

Brandon glanced at his clock and put the exam papers into his portfolio.

It was almost time to supervise the Living Art class.

He certainly didn't need his salary as a famous visiting art professor. He was now getting such big money for his paintings and his fashion designs that he would never have to work anywhere. His bank account contained millions of dollars.

His boyfriend, Bruce Ramsey, had moved his agency to Manhattan and it occupied a complete floor in the famous Flat Iron Building on Madison Avenue.

This brilliant dynamo and his small army of brilliant professionals had invested Brandon's fortune into real estate: apartment buildings, restaurants, hotels.

The dynamic Bruce was also busy representing several new "stars" to his agency. One was an eccentric artist—Swampy Sam—a primitive painter who lived in the deadly Dismal Swamp near Georgia. His canvases of wild looking images of serpents and crocodiles and demon faces were attracting much public interest. Bruce said the man was a "novelty" and would be forgotten in a year but at the same time, art collectors were going wild for him.

Another new star signed up by Ramsey and Associates was Ozuzeko— a petite actress from Japan—who had just signed a contract with Alfred Hitchcock to star in his new thriller, *The House*.

#

In most articles and television reports about John Sparrow's connection to the Vesaria Mystery, Brandon's name was often cited as being one of the last people to see him alive. Many cultists and investigators were certain the young artist knew a lot more than he was saying. The incident of the cops discovering a stack of Polaroid shots of a naked John Sparrow in Brandon's bedroom was often cited that they may have enjoyed more than an artist/model relationship.

With John's vanishing, it was like a dark cloud hung over everyone who had known the holy man.

When Brandon and Bruce Jasmine had set off to eat pizza and drink beer that fateful night, a gang of vicious thugs had attacked them.

Two of them tried to overthrow Bruce but he fought them off. Two more threw Brandon into a car and raced off into the night. In the meantime, numerous onlookers who had heard the commotion had called the police.

With Bruce's information, several police cars had raced in the direction of where the getaway car was last seen...

The attackers had dragged Brandon out of the car and tried to strip him naked but Brandon fought wildly—gripping his Mourian Dagger and slicing flesh all around him.

There must have been something scary about Brandon that night because his attackers had backed away, staring at him in amazement, as he whirled around and used his blade like a wild person.

Then the thugs tackled him, throwing him to the ground and Stripped off his clothes with one of them hollering:

"Let's see if the freak is man or woman!"

Just then, two police cars appeared along with Bruce Jasmine.

The thugs tried to escape but they were arrested, followed by a sensational trial. The four criminals were charged with kidnapping, attempted murder, torture and several other crimes. Two of them were the bullies that had hounded Brandon from the beginning. The other two were off-campus buddies who had a reputation for "beating up faggots," as they confessed. They really wanted to teach Brandon Flores a lesson.

The trial was covered by the national press. This actually enhanced Brandon's media profile. He came across to the public as a feisty, brave young talent who would take no more intimidation from thug-like men.

#.

A knock on his office door shook Brandon from his reverie. His attractive young assistant, Brenda, entered.

"Ready to face reality?" she grinned. "And see some naked male flesh?"

"Oh, boy, to see a live, naked boy!" he joked. "This will be my last one—here."

"Ah ha!" she laughed. "The last one here, but I'm sure there will be many more when you return to New York City."

"They're all lined up now," he teased, "panting for my affection."

Brenda threw her head back and laughed again.

"By the way," she said, "our scheduled model, Devon, won't be here. He hurt his shoulder playing football. So he's sending in a replacement. Not sure who it is. I think he's a jock, too."

"That's okay. I just hope the newbie isn't frightened of being bare-assed and facing fourteen panting art students."

Brandon picked up several boxes of freshly baked donuts and pastries.

"Mmmm, they smell good!" said Brenda. "Especially on a freezing day like today. I've already got the coffee on"

Brandon always enjoyed figure sketching class because it was always a kick to have an ordinary young guy sitting there stark naked for all to drool over.

CHAPTER TWO

A group of fourteen art students were gathered around the coffee klatch in the corner of the drafty old studio when Brandon entered. They all made appreciative sounds when he spread his pastry boxes on the beaten-up table.

"Dive in!" he ordered. Someone else had also brought along a platter of ham and cheese sandwiches. Brenda put the Greek Spinach Pie she brought on the old woodstove that belched smoke in the center of the room. Another student uncovered a metal bowl that brimmed with warm biscuits and butter. Jars of honey and fruit preserves were on display, as well.

The scent of strong coffee perfumed the air and since Brandon enjoyed the smell of tobacco, several of the students lit up their cigarettes.

A relaxed and convivial atmosphere pervaded this old corner studio.

Brandon nodded and smiled and chatted with some of the boys and girls and they all studied keenly his clothes.

Each day, he wore a different outfit for dressing up was one of his rare pleasures. Never did he wear the same clothes twice. That day he had donned a striking, over-sized sweater of cobalt blue, with patterns of burgundy, gold, crimson and jade interworked into the fabric.

On his wrist glowed a large watch with a ruby red band—one from his vastly popular Brandy's time pieces.

He went to his desk in the corner with Brenda and she handed him a stack of essays she had helped him critique.

He looked around. The model's stool was empty.

"I hope our model hasn't forgotten about today?"

"Jimmy said he might be a few minutes late because of football practice."

Brandon tried to hide his irritation when Marsha, his most neurotic student, hurried up to him and from her expression; he knew she wanted advice on her latest ill-fated crush on a fellow female student.

"Mr. Flores," she began, "I know I should wait until after class..."

While he listened and continued looking through the term papers, the door opened behind him and Brenda leaned over to tell her boss that the male model had arrived.

"Oh, goodie. Would you tell him what to do, my dear. I'll be right with him."

"I think you'll want to see this guy, sir."

Surprised by her words, Brandon shooed Marsha away with, "I can't listen today. See me next week."

At first, Brandon couldn't see much.

This model was big!

His back was turned but just from his size alone, he certainly had to be a football player or weight lifter.

Brenda had guided the new model to the posing stool and handed him a mug of steaming coffee and instructed him on what to do.

"Just take your clothes off and put them there on the chair."

It was the way the model was stripping off his clothes that held everyone spellbound.

First off was the green ski cap that revealed jet-black curls.

Next, came a thick red muffler. The black leather jacket hit the floor next and this left revealed a powerful back covered with a navy blue sweater.

Gradually, the sweater, the black boots, the red socks came off. Curiously, he kept his sleeveless tee shirt on.

By the time the snug jeans and black boxer shorts joined the rest of the clothes, except his tee shirt, Brandon and his students realized that here was a young man of extraordinary power.

Turning to face everyone, he slowly peeled off his tee shirt. He was totally naked and completely at ease. A pair of tortoise glasses framed eyes of a glistening emerald. They were surrounded by double-thick lashes of coal.

"Hi," smiled the young Hercules, "I'm Jocko Shaun. I'm your model today because my buddy Kevin is out sick."

Wearing nothing now, he sat on the edge of the stool and braced his hands behind him on the seat. This thrust his massive shoulders, arms and chest forward.

None had ever seen a man's pectorals as enormous as those that bulged out from the incredible chest. They were bigger than a pair of women's buttocks.

His stomach was flat, yet chiseled with beautiful abs.

Icing on this formidable cake was what hung so heavily between his powerful thighs.

His genitalia was almost grotesque in its size. The testicles bulged enormous in their silken sac. The uncut phallus, while soft, gleamed thick and long as a big thermos bottle.

A shadow of beard darkened the square jaw. A light covering of hair dusted his amazing chest and only a little was visible on his pubic area.

Brandon had become transfixed, for sitting there was the very twin of John Sparrow, if he was fifteen years younger.

For a moment, no one attempted to sketch. Brandon looked at the faces of his students and they were transfixed in amazement.

Brandon blinked his eyes and thought: this couldn't be John Sparrow! He's too young. Yet, how many males could have the identical muscularity of that missing man.

"Mr. Shaun, eh, can I get you a platter of our food?" Brandon finally asked. "Its plain ole fare: sandwiches, biscuits, donuts."

The answering smile was warm. "That'd be a real nice little treat, sir."

This broke the spell and the students now bent over their sketch pads but their eyes kept returning to the sensational manhood of this young Samson. He accepted the refreshments from Brandon with a sweet smile.

Where in hell did this kid come from? Was the thought of nearly everyone in the room?

They were used to seeing ordinary young guys with modest genitalia and average bodies.

And now, here was someone literally bigger than life that sat naturally and relaxed, as if he were used to being naked among clothed strangers.

After several minutes, Brandon asked: "Mr. Shaun, would you mind getting up and turning your back to us and brace your right knee on the stool's seat. And place your hands there, too, so we can sketch your back."

"I'd be happy too."

His voice was deep, pleasant and very Southern which another charming plus was for him.

He put his coffee mug and empty plate on a chair next to the stool.

With his back now to the room, he lifted a knee and rested it on the stool, like a jogger prepared to sprint.

Now, Brandon had to sit down on the nearest chair.

For there, astonishing everyone with its beauty was the face of someone who resembled Jesus Christ, tattooed in stunning colors that one rarely saw on inked skin.

It glowed supernaturally in the muted light. The features were drawn brilliantly. It was as if the face was staring back at them and welcoming their stares. The portrait was etched on skin that gleamed a champagne bronze.

It was after this shock vanished that everyone noticed, once again, the awesome package of male sexuality that hung down so heavily.

And staring at them all was a spectacular tush—one perfectly white and rounded with an unusually deep cleft. They could even see the pink opening that bore no hair.

Brandon tried to control his emotions. Fate had brought into this old, smoky room an extraordinary visitor who almost certainly had to be related to John Sparrow.

Could Jocko Shaun be the holy man's son? If so, how was that possible?

When Brandon asked him to pose with his face forward and his hands behind his neck, it confirmed that this Jocko Shaun had to be related to the missing man.

His face enchanted for its male beauty. Full lips were perfectly shaped. His magnificent physique rippled with every movement. With his glasses perched on his nose, It made him look exactly like Clark Kent, the alter ego of Superman.

Calm yourself, Brandon cautioned himself. Wait until the class is over and then move in and see what the fuck is going on here. You don't want to have an emotional breakdown in front of everyone.

But it was like some of his students, especially the girls, were having their own breakdown. Their faces were flushed and their eyes glittered in frank desire. A few of the boys, who Brandon suspected were queer, were having the identical reaction.

This sizzling young Samson would most definitely remain in their minds forever.

His virility was so powerful that one could feel his body heat. He nibbled indifferently on cookies and stared at the window that was covered with ice and snow.

His fingers occasionally slid down to his privates and he scratched them. They were slightly darker than the ivory white of the rest of his body and muscular as if they had received an unusually large amount of attention over the years.

At last the bell rang, and the students reluctantly gathered up their belongings and left. Several of them paused to say, "Thank you!" to their model who smilingly accepted their compliments.

Now, Brandon was left alone with this masculine treasure who called himself Jocko Shaun.

The powerful young athlete seemed to be in no hurry to dress or leave. Without putting his clothes back on, he strolled naked over to the coffee klatch.

"I hope you don't mind?" he smiled as he filled his paper plate with more chocolate chip and the rest of the sandwiches. "I didn't have time to grab lunch because of football practice."

"No. Not at all. Take all you want. Please have some more coffee, too. Your mug must be cold by now. Here, let me do it?"

Brandon felt like he was babbling moronically as he took the cup from the big hand of this beauty and filled it with fresh coffee. He turned and handed it to him and looked up into a pair of sparkling eyes. They were the color of tree leaf, only strained through vinegar—light and luminous.

They stared down at Brandon curiously with a warm glint. His lashes were so thick they looked almost false. The tortoise glasses added an exciting dash of sexual allure for he suggested that he was brainy in addition to being a fabulous athlete.

When Jocko accepted the cup, the muscle of his right arm bulged out dramatically, like a softball had suddenly emerged.

He smelt like clean sweat and hot flesh and a whiff of Old Spice Aftershave. His body heat was incredible.

His nipples were hard and as thick and big as the tips of his thumb. It was with difficulty that Brandon didn't lean forward and start sucking on them.

Brandon caught himself before he leaned forward and blurted: "I hope you don't mind my staring at you—but—you look so much like someone I was very close to that I thought you had returned from the dead. He—he had the same amazing tattoo on his back as you. It's totally uncanny."

"Wow! That's interesting."

The way he talked, his expression, the sparkling light lime of his eyes—they were all John Sparrow.

"Could you come to my place for supper tonight? I don't want to talk here. It's much too important. But I think this might be quite significant for you, too. I am firmly convinced that you simply must be related to this person—who met so much to me."

Jocko stuffed the last cookie into his mouth." Well—I did have wrestling at the gym. But this seems to be a lot more important."

"Please! Come by at six thirty. I'm a good cook. I have lots of beer. You won't regret it. Don't dress up. It'll be very casual. And—could I ask just one little favor?"

"Sure. If I can help you out."

"Could—could I feel of your arm muscle. It's so amazingly big—just like my friend's bicep was."

"Help yourself."

Jocko forced his right bicep to bulge out again like a small melon. Brandon squeezed it, closed his eyes and swayed slightly. Jocko grinned, as if this were a request he was used to granting.

"Ah! Amazing. So, until tonight, Jocko."

After the student dressed and left, Brandon went to the stool where the naked Apollo had sat and posed.

It smelt like a man had been there. The top of the stool was slightly moist—where the enormous testicles and phallus had rested. Brandon pressed his cheek against the surface and groaned in delight. He could see that tremendous set of genitalia again, exposed and relaxed with no sense of subterfuge. Where most boys were hesitant to expose themselves in public, this sex god had done it as casually as if he were home alone in front of the TV.

He had no trace of modesty or inhibition. Brandon was certain there was a strong streak of exhibitionism in him—just like John Sparrow.

#

He heard the gravel in the driveway crunching as someone drove up. From the window Brandon saw below his guest parking a red Ford pick-up truck.

When the knock came on the door, Brandon closed his eyes for a moment, took a deep breath and opened.

Jocko Shaun filled the doorframe.

He wore a dark leather jacket with the red scarf and black biker's cap.

He looked down at Brandon and smiled.

"Hi. Here I am."

"And I'm so happy to see you, Jocko. Take off your things."

"You mean everything—like I did in class today," he teased.

Brandon pretended to faint. "Eh, not right now! I might pass out."

Jocko laughed like a naughty little boy.

He doffed his jacket and cap. A white turtleneck sweater and snug khaki's outlined his formidable physique. His very presence filled the darkly lit den.

Brandon grasped his hand and drew him into the den.

Jocko's fingers tightened on his and an electrical pulse surged through them.

Then he gasped: "Wow! This is damned nice! Looka the view!"

They went to the enormous plate glass window that looked out at the jewel of a city in the distance Lights had come on and twinkled. Directly beneath the chalet ran a stream.

The sun was sinking on the horizon in a glowing mass of fiery crimson, purple and gold.

"And these paintings!" the guest whistled. "I've heard about your place here. Are these paintings and sculptures all yours?"

"Half and half. I hate a blank wall. They're all originals, though."

Small tables with crystal tops sparkled with paste jewelry and watches and Indian and Oriental figures.

"And see," laughed Brandon, "I'm wearing one of my fashions. It sells well in Atlanta, especially with men."

Brandon had put on his favorite creation: a wheat-hued robe that was cinched at the waist by a gold lion's head. Eyes of crimson red glinted from the animal's face.

"Nice. Very nice."

"Would you like a beer—or a Russian Bloody Mary? Or, a martini."

"I'm not fancy. I'll start out with a beer."

Brandon brought him a bottle of Gold Dreams which was made especially for him by a brewery in Asheville.

Jocko took a sip and made a sound of appreciation. "Woo! Nice beer. Doesn't taste much like my Old Milwaukee."

"Let's check out some food over here. I hope you're hungry."

"I'm always hungry and will eat about anything."

They went to the long buffet table beneath another window.

Brandon's cook came in three times a week to whip up gourmet meals and appetizers that were frozen so they could be microwaved. Now, Jocko filled his platter from piles of shrimp, oysters, barbecued chicken wings, cheeses, olives and pickles and made himself a monster cheeseburger covered with a mound of guacamole sauce.

They put their meals on red lacquered trays.

"Let's go over here by the fire."

They settled down on cushions before a large coffee table. This area was made even plusher because beneath them stretched the magnificent fur of a white bear. Jocko rested his arm on the head of the stunning animal whose black eyes seemed to watch them intently.

Behind them crackled a fire in the hearth that was shaped like a Gorgon's mouth. In front of them was an enormous color television.

A small white screen had been set up and on a nearby table were several reels of film.

In the background came the soothing choral music from a record player. They were recordings that Grace Cowan had sent him before her death of the All Souls church of the Mountain choir.

Brandon pretended to eat, to keep his guest company, but he felt so breathless as to what was happening that he was afraid he sounded retarded. Not since John Sparrow had he had a guest in his home whose size dwarfed everything around him.

"Your music," Jocko said softly. "It's very beautiful—and soothing. I've never heard anything like it. What is it?"

"Its part of the reason I asked you here tonight. It was created in a special church I attended while a student at Blackwood Institute. The All Souls Church of the Mountains. But let's enjoy the food first. Tell me something about yourself."

His real name was Tommy Barnes but he had always hated it and so he had re-named himself as Jocko Shaun. He wanted to create a brand new personae because he hoped to be doing big things.

"Could you be the same Tommy Barnes who made some recordings in Austin, Texas and then vanished? I heard one of your songs this afternoon called 'The Trees They Grow High'"? "Hey, that's interesting. I did make some recordings. But I thought they never went anywhere. How did you hear me?"

"Brenda Holiday played it on the air today. I heard it. It was fabulous. Your voice sent shivers up and down my spine."

Tommy laughed. "I'm glad I had such an effect on you."

"Out of the colleges you could have chosen, was there a reason you chose this one?"

"I had several catalogues I ordered. Three of them sounded interesting-- so I closed my eyes, tapped my finger one of the catalogues and it was this one. I'm majoring in religious history and anthropology."

"Then you're religious."

"Not in a traditional sense. Have you ever heard of the Vesaria Massacre? I believe in the religion of Mouria. I want to return to Vesaria, which has been a ghost town since 1941, and revive it as a minister of Mouria."

His words had an electrifying effect on his host.

"Yes!" whispered Brandon. "I'm fully aware of Vesaria and Emmanuel Trident and Diana DuPree. That's why I asked you here."

Jocko didn't move. For a moment, he was silent and then he asked quietly:

"Tell me. What is it?"

"I have something to show you. Maybe you'll understand why I'm acting a little crazy because—well, wait and see these pictures I have."

Brandon pulled out a huge scrapbook from beneath his coffee table and opened it.

Staring out was a vivid India and ink drawing of the deity Mouria.

A color photograph presented two faces: a shimmering woman of silver and gold features pressed against the head of a man who resembled Jesus Christ.

Jocko said nothing for a long time as he looked at these originals.

"That's Mouria—the Indian God. And those two people—they look like Diana DuPree and Emmanuel Trident."

"So you guessed," smiled Brandon. "You're getting close to why I invited you here."

Jocko sat up in great excitement.

"This--this is amazing! Mouria—and Diana DuPree and her husband, Emmanuel Trident—they've both played big roles in my life!"

Brandon clasped his hands together.

"I was right all along. Keep looking. Don't stop. I think you'll be astonished at what you'll see."

.A glossy color photograph was the next one in the album. John Sparrow and Brandon smiled out. John wore a white Cossack robe and his dark curls touched his shoulders. A slight beard and moustache outlined his square jaw. His arm was wrapped affectionately around Brandon's shoulders.

"That could be you, Jocko."

"Who the hell--?" Jocko gasped.

"Keep looking and maybe you'll be as shocked as I am."

The next pictures showed a naked John Sparrow, clad only in a narrow panel of silver silk, standing before a congregation. The following picture caught with his back to the camera. His amazing torso made one sense they were in the presence of someone extraordinary. The radiant tattoo of Jesus Christ glowed prominently.

"Oh, wow!" gasped Jocko. "Who is he? He looks enough like me to be my father."

"He *has* to be your father, Jocko. His name is John Sparrows but I'm convinced he was actually Emmanuel Trident and John had just suddenly appeared in winter, wandering near the Mouria Gorge. He told everyone,

'I've come back too soon.' And he eventually vanished but before that, we became lovers while he was preaching in the All Soul's Church of the Mountains in Blackwood."

Brandon pressed the "on" button of the projector.

On the TV screen, John Sparrow came to life.

The lighting and camerawork was excellent and the holy man resembled a bigger-than-life creation from Hollywood. Standing with his bare feet apart, only a brief panel of aqua silk covered the front of his hips. His arms were thrust upwards and he spoke with fire and power.

His audience was spellbound. Just as the two men watching this were. Brandon looked at Jocko:

"John Sparrow must be your father—and mine, too! I was adopted in February of 1941. I heard I was found—with my twin brother—just hours after the Vesaria attack. Were you adopted, too?"

Jocko made a sound, like a gasp, and sat back with a stunned expression on his face. Then he jumped to his feet and paced around while running his hands through his hair.

"I—I can't believe this is happening! I, too, was found on the steps in February of 1941 and learned later I had a twin brother. My foster parents meant well—they just didn't know who I was."

"So was I! I have no doubt that my father was Emmanuel Trident. My real mother was Diana DuPree. And Emmanuel Trident was resurrected as John Sparrow."

Jocko fell down beside Brandon on the floor. His face was flushed, his breathing fast and his beautiful eyes sparkled with excitement.

"You are my brother! We've found each other! You and me—we're here, right here and not separated any longer. I'm your brother and you're mine!"

Jocko grabbed his sibling and squeezed him tight against him. Both began to weep. For a long time their bodies shook as they tried to stop their sobbing.

"I've dreamed of you—of my unseen brother—ever since I found out I had one," wept Brandon. "All those years in my miserable home, I kept thinking if only my brother were here with me."

"And you lived just fifteen miles away, all that time," Jocko pointed out. "While you suffered alone, I lived with people who I had nothing in common with."

The bigger brother pulled away slightly, to study his twin's face while pushing the curls from his face.

"You're beautiful, little bro," he smiled. "You look like an angel: the blonde hair, those big eyes of blue, your boyish body."

He leaned forward and kissed Brandon lightly on the lips. Then his kiss became more intense as Brandon pulled his brother tighter against him.

Saying nothing, Jocko picked Brandon up in his arms and carried him to the bedroom. Quickly they stripped off their clothes and fell onto the goose-feathered mattress.

No words were needed as Jocko began to make passionate love to his beautiful brother. His lips tasted his mouth and when he saw the developed breasts, he licked and suckled them as he prepared to enter him.

"Jocko, be careful!" gasped Brando. "You're so huge!"

"You'll love what I can do," whispered his lover. "You'll want more—and more before."

Although Brandon had enjoyed the love-making of several men by this time—especially the hours with John Sparrow and Bruce Jasmine—his over-sexed brother made him forget everything around him.

Jocko was tireless, resilient, as he ejaculated multiple times and still kept going. The sheets were soon damp with sweat, with warm semen and saliva.

When the twins began to simmer down, a pink and emerald sunrise was just appearing outside the snow covered window.

"Don't move," Brandon smiled to his smiling brother. "I'll make us breakfast in bed. Just lay there and relax."

Jocko glanced down at the large rise in the sheet that covered his lap. "Hurry, brother, hurry. I've got something that needs to be taken care of. Get to work on it soon. That's what brothers are for, right/"

#

Jocko had fallen back into a light sleep when Brandon brought him a tray of an omelet, creamed spinach, yeast rolls, a bowl of strawberries and a bottle of champagne.

"We'll eat this together," the host smiled, "and then we'll discuss our future. But I don't want you covered up, my sexy sibling. I want to feast my eyes on all that you bring to the table."

"And after we eat our breakfast, perhaps you'd enjoy feasting on my male steak. That comes with gravy and two very large potatoes."

"Oh, you!" laughed Brandon.

After he consumed both feasts—the one on the tray and the bigger one beside him—he and Jocko began to talk.

"We're living at an extraordinary time in our lives," Brandon murmured. "Our missing parents are doing all this. They've brought us together for a profound reason."

"They want us to return to Vesaria," Jocko said. "I think we should go there as soon as we can. There's something there they want us to see—something that no one's seen before."

Brandon reached over to his nightstand and held out his Mourian Dagger and its case.

"Hold this, brother. I found this knife when John Sparrow and I visited Vesaria. This is the dagger our mother used as a weapon against the ghouls. Her mother had given it to her when she explored a certain cave there. And now look at this."

Brandon shook out the small black and white photograph.

Jocko's eyes widened at the long ago image of a man's face.

"My God, that's Emmanuel Trident—or Jesus Christ."

"How did Diana get this? I told John Sparrow it could have been him? He had no answer."

"I've read many articles on the Vesaria happening where the writers are convinced that there is an astounding cavern in the side of the mountain that could be a resting place for the Mourian priests. Just think, Brandon, our father—Emmanuel Trident—could well be up there right now, sleeping peacefully, just awaiting a signal to awaken and come back to Earth."

"That does it. We'll leave for Vesaria tomorrow. My car's in good condition. I know exactly how to get there. It'll be a three hour to and from here. Are you game?"

Jocko jumped out of bed and still naked, he mimed someone climbing a rope up a steep surface.

"I've found the cavern!" he shouted. "And I can see someone—someone whose our father!"

#

Jocko had insisted he drive because "I worked as a trucker in Alaska for a few weeks when I was traveling around America."

The snow had stopped and after they reached the interstate, it was smooth driving.

Both he and Brandon had dressed warmly for their trip. A large basket of sandwiches and thermoses of hot coffee and steaming soup would also help the two men enjoy their journey.

By the time they found the sign, "Vesaria—9 miles", a powerful wind moaned against the car.

And then they finally came to the outskirts of the little ghost town.

"I remember all this when I was with John," murmured Brandon.

"I was with Evangelist Buster when I was here."

They drove slowly down the empty main street. For Brandon, it really did resemble a grim, ugly ghost town.

For Jocko, there was nothing living or hopeful about this desolate place.

He parked the car in front of Abe's Seeds and Spices.

Bundled up, the twin brothers walked together in the street.

"Just think," Jocko whispered, "Daddy used to walk right where we are."

"I can see him so clearly because I was with John. Big, towering, his shoulders thrown back, his long hair blowing in the wind, his special fur coat whipping against him."

"Let's go see the church. There's not much time. It's already growing dark"

The map showed that they were only a few blocks from where the All Souls Church of the Mountains was once located.

It was a shock still to both visitors to see it again in ruin.

Jocko had taken Brandon's hand and pulled him closer.

They dug around with their boots to see if there was anything interesting of note. As before, only shattered rock and glass was visible. Scavengers—both human and animal—had removed everything of interest.

"And now—home," muttered Jocko.

The pile of ruins that could have been their birth home still stunned them.

"I don't find it hard to imagine that you and I were born here," said Brandon. "I feel a bond with this place."

"Yeah, me, too. I wonder where Daddy was taking us that night?"

Jocko took Brandon's hand and led him to the pathetic marble tablet that marked the grave of Diana DuPree.

Dirt and dead leaves nearly obscured it. Jocko read aloud her epithet. The crude graffiti made a mockery of the tribute to the butchered woman. "Burn in Hell" and "The Freak is Dead" were scrawled in hate.

On the slab were inscribed the simple words:

Both young men wept at the sad little tribute to a person they considered their doomed mother.

Silently, they stood up and resumed their ramble through what was quite probably their first home.

'She once had a flower garden so beautiful that people came from all around to look at it. Now, it's nothing but weeds."

"Are you sure, Jocko? Look back over here."

In the midst of deadness, a rose bush had flourished.

'Oh, my Gosh!" gasped Jocko. "That's where I fucked the ground!"

"You—you what?"

He told Brandon what he had done—creating a big hole in the ground and thrusting his member into it and humping the ground until he ejaculated.

Brandon howled at this story and he looked at his brother anew. Jocko was like a dynamic life force—like John Sparrow had been, like Emmanuel Trident was before him. They were all capable of doing something sexually outrageous.

"When the weather gets better," Brandon teased, "you'll have to return and fuck the whole ground so more flowers will flourish."

Jocko laughed in delight. He snatched a rose blossom and playfully placed it behind Brandon's ear.

"From my seed, I give you a beautiful flower."

They walked a few feet more where the ground ended and the enormous canyon began.

Brandon held Jocko's arm as they peered over the edge into a mist-shrouded abyss below.

"It's so hard to believe that the Mourian Indians had built caves in the walls of the canyon," mused Jocko. "If you look closely at the walls, there are narrow ledges and places to put your hands and feet."

"Our father could be resting in a magical temple right now as we stand here."

Jocko lay down on his stomach and peered over the edge of the ground into the abyss below.

"I'm damned sure," Jocko said with meaning, "that if we could just get down on the face of the canyon, we could find the cavern that holds the secrets of our lives."

"We'd need all kinds of mountain climbing gear, Jocko, to do that! It could take months, years, to do it right."

The light was fading fast and the temperatures were dropping faster. It would soon be freezing out here.

"First thing tomorrow morning we'll look around. We may have to return with more people to do this justice."

"Okay, but let's get back into the van. It's freezing, my brother."

#

They found a clean little motel at Mountain Mist on the nearby highway.

After a big, mountain breakfast the next morning at the motel's coffee shop they were chatting with the friendly desk clerk, Patty Hamilton, when she surprised them both by saying:

'You say you're gonna try to climb the side of the Mouria Gorge? My brother, Ian, is a nut about mountain climbing. He's been exploring Mt. Mouria since he was a kid. If you need a good man, he's the one. He runs a farm just behind the motel here and can create his own schedule."

"Great! I could pay him whatever he wants."

When the brothers found him, Ian turned out to be a slender, friendly man who was tickled to earn some good money by helping Jocko to climb.

"I'll follow you in my truck," he said.

Pulling his cowboy hat lower over his forehead, he turned up the collar of his jacket and hurried to his truck.

When they pulled up to the edge of the canyon, Ian hopped out of the truck and immediately started to secure the ropes and gear that he fastened to the rear bumper of the truck.

Before Ian and Jocko went down the mountainside, they discussed what they wanted to do.

The young farmer said he had explored this mountain ever since he was a little boy. His parents had warned him about its history but this didn't bother him.

He and his mountain buddies had been real careful at first. They only dipped into the small caves near the top. But over the years, they grew more daring and were fascinated by the hiding places made by the Mourian Indians.

As they climbed further down, the openings grew bigger. One day Ian was with two friends when they came upon a narrow slit in the mountain wall. It looked too artificial and man-made to be a natural opening.

Inside they entered a gigantic cavern. One would never know from outside that it was here. As they turned on their lights, they saw instantly that this was an important chamber made by the Indians.

The floor was amazingly smooth with no debris. It was like it had been used recently. A strange illumination made it unnecessary for even flashlights.

From this main chamber it divided up into several well-used trails and these in turn led to more chambers.

One could easily become lost. On some of the walls were inscriptions in a different language. And there was one path that led downward with handmade steps.

Something made the group scared. It was a definite quality in the air. It was like they were all being watched. Then they heard a bizarre roar. It came from some tremendous creature.

They ran like hell. Months later, Ian returned alone—but he couldn't find the opening. It was like it had been covered up.

"That's what you would want to find," he suggested. "I think something really big is hidden down there. I never told any of those geological groups that came to explore."

Now, Brandon watched the two men descend the face of Mouria's Gorge. They looked helpless against the terrifying abyss beneath them. All had walkie-talkies and at least once or twice an hour, Jocko would tell Brandon what progress they were making.

As the day passed, the climbers entered several caves but they proved to be useless and caused by nature. While waiting, Brandon looked around this eerie, haunted landscape and thought: how strange it is that here I am, in the place where my parents may have lived and died, and now I'm sitting on the edge of an abyss.

The sun had not set when Jocko and Ian reappeared. They were dusty and sweaty and disappointed that they had not found the magic cave.

"I'm coming back in a few weeks and I'll find it," Jocko vowed. "Will you join me, Ian? You'll be paid well for your time."

"Not only will I join you. I've got a dozen climbing buddies who would be thrilled to join us."

"Great! I really think we're getting close to uncovering the mystery of Emmanuel Trident and Diana DuPree."

Ian had glanced curiously from Brandon and Jocko and he said: "I know this sounds kind of Twilight Zone like, but both of you could be the spitting images of Emmanuel Trident and Diana DuPree. I've seen their pictures in magazine articles about the Vesaria Mystery. You, Jocko, are an exact duplicate of Emmanuel Trident and Brandon, if you had long, blonde hair and wearing a gown, you could be Diana DuPree."

"And the twin sons?"

Ian rubbed his neck. "Now, I never saw them. They were kept from public view. And the big mystery is what happened to them? I heard one of the killer's wives rescued the babies from death and placed them in foster homes."

Brandon said quietly: "Jocko and I were both found on the steps of a charity hospital in Alabaster. That's just an hour from here. This was back in February, l941, and just a few hours after the massacre. We never knew our parents."

Ian suddenly stared at the ground. His face paled. He looked up and his eyes went from one to the other.

"Oh, Jesus! I'm looking at you and I'm trying to figure this out—"

He whirled around and clasped his hands before facing the two men. "I can't believe that just maybe I'm staring right now at the twin sons of Emmanuel Trident and Diana DuPree! Lord have mercy! This is just too, too much."

The young man covered his face and broke into sobs. "You're alive!"

Jocko and Brandon closed in and embraced him.

The three young men wept for all that had happened—and what was coming down the turnpike.

#

CHAPTER THREE

Events Now Raced to a Climax for Both Men

Jocko had exams to take at college but he was determined to return to Vesaria and explore the caves.

Brandon had already resigned his post at the college. His work there was finished. Now, he began packing up his chalet and prepared for the shipment of his own belongings back to his swanky apartment on Gracie Square, high above the East River.

Brandon's faithful housekeeper in Manhattan, Mamby, was in charge of seeing that his apartment would be ready for the arrival of both Brandon and Jocko. From experience, Brandon could count on her for everything—from making certain the fridge and the pantries were stuffed with food and that the beds were prepared with Egyptian threaded linen and pillows. She would do this with the help of six other maids and a butler/chauffeur.

But before he returned to Manhattan, there was the all-important event that would change his life around.

He would be entering the Gender Transition Center in Birmingham in a week where he would be transformed into Diana DuPree. He would spend a week in the clinic before being released as this vibrant and exciting creature.

And then Jocko would join him there and they would live together forever as two loving brothers.

On the last weekend before school closed, he invited select members of the faculty and students to come by. They were curiously intrigued of course to find Jocko there and it was obvious to the visitors that the two striking men were more than friends.

For this last festivity, Brandon wore a glamorous robe he had made of burgundy velvet, studded with small mirrors and precious stones. Jocko, at Brandon's urging, attired himself in a very brief sarong of tropical colors. When he greeted the guests at the door, there was a moment of shocked delight.

By now, Brandon's most intimate friends knew what he planned to do and were totally behind him. He had never discussed in detail the pain of his life, but they sensed it had overshadowed the high points of his existence.

A lavish buffet was prepared with Jocko acting as bartender, enchanting everyone with his near nudity. Many of the twenty-eight guests had certainly heard about this raging young beauty with the fabulous torso.

Now, they were able to see what all the shouting was about. Many agreed that he surpassed gossip. He simply stunned with his animal hotness.

The abundance of outstanding dishes was much remarked upon. Brandon explained that he had to empty his fridge and freezers of all the food stored there.

In the backyard, near the river, Brandon had taken nearly all of his male clothing. While he kept a few necessary outfits, most he had given some away to his friends but the rest he put on a bonfire.

He set a match to it and to the cheers of visitors, declared: "This is the end of my old life!"

He had packed up his most ravishing female outfits to wear while in Birmingham. His closets in New York City brimmed with beautiful clothes just waiting to be worn.

His lingerie was the finest from France. His other garments were those he had created and others he had purchased at Manhattan's most chic boutiques.

His perfumes now were the most haunting—and unforgettable. There was *Captain Molyneux, Kandy Kristmas, You, Mt. Jupiter, Kippa Tiger.* Each was unique and made especially for him.

There would never be any grunge, casual and denim garments in his wardrobe.

A wire service feature did a retrospective on his work and at the end, left an intriguing statement:

"The dynamic young artist will enter a hospital in Birmingham, Alabama for treatment of an undisclosed condition. His many friends wish him well."

#

In the meantime, Jocko passed all his courses with flying colors.

He interviewed a number of his jock buddies to help him and his mountain friends explore in depth the secret of Mt. Mouria. This was turning into a major expedition.

Media began to spread the word that this was an intensive attempt to solve, at last, the mystery of Vesaria and would include top explorers.

Word spread fast about the impending journey and pleas to be included poured in from not just the campus residents but from outside, as well.

Three of those who Jocko chose were from the Department of Geology. They had long been fascinated by this strange area of the South. They all waived away any offers of money. This was to be a volunteer task of passion. The expedition would certainly add luster to their backgrounds—whether anything was found or not. One of the professors was an expert cameraman. His filming of the project would certainly be of interest to television stations.

Still, Brandon tried to leave Jocko with a hefty sum of money to be used when necessary. Jocko refused the funds, since he had his own stash and this was to be for him, a religious expedition. He wanted to be beholden to no one should the trip be a success.

Among the team was the brilliant and gung-ho young professor, Dr. William Rothe. He had already appeared on the pages of the *National Geographic* for his sensational work he had performed on the mysterious Nazca lines in Mexico. He had written and lectured brilliantly that these fascinating designs and roads created thousands of years ago by the Nazca Indians were actually signs to be seen from above by flying spacecraft. Ten thousand years ago, he wrote, there were no flying machines—except for those from outer space.

Like Jocko, he was convinced that phenomenal findings were waiting to be discovered in the Mouria Gorge. He believed there was a temple within a vast cavern where the high priests could "store" their leaders and mighty warriors even when they had died—and bring them back with sacred texts. The Egyptians used this device, although their sacred temple had yet to be discovered.

"When it is found, you may find figures of men, thousands of years old, looking as they did when they were induced into a trance. I think we may find the same thing in the Mouria Gorge."

Jocko had already promised to join Brandon in Birmingham after the operation to give him support.

The night before they left the campus, the brothers visited a young minister, Reverend Todd Adair.

He was thrilled when Brandon and Jocko asked that he marry them.

The handsome young minister had done this secretly several times in Boston where he had studied. Now, to find that he had two brothers who wished to be united in marriage, was an exhilarating experience. It was like he were pioneering in a ritual that might one day become accepted as a norm in America.

He performed the ceremony with his young wife, Celia, beaming and smiling at this extraordinary union.

Afterward, she served them some homemade wine and listened in astonishment at what these two stunning young men were planning to do.

"I'll be a man and a woman within a week," Brandon explained.

"And I'm going to find my father, Emmanuel Trident, where he's resting in eternal sleep until awakened by a psychic signal—in Mt. Mouria Gorge."

When he identified his father as Emmanuel Trident and his mother as Diana DuPree, both man and wife gasped.

This fabled couple and the Vesaria Mystery were hot topics of discussion in countless college courses. Emmanuel Trident, especially, was looked upon in awe.

Many students were convinced that he was actually Jesus Christ who had returned to do good on earth. That he was literally crucified by mountain vermin was fact.

After the newlywed couple left, Celia and her husband discussed for a long time this amazing visit.

"Did this really happen?" the woman whispered to her husband in bed. "It's like a dream."

"I predict a tremendous battle looming for Brandon," warned her husband. "His kind can kindle murderous feelings from the ghouls of the world. I hope he keeps a weapon handy."

Before drifting off to sleep, the wife asked: "What if their father really was Jesus Christ? What does that make them?"

"Extraordinary," answered her husband.

#

Jocko drove his brother to the airport the next afternoon.

Brandon studied the people milling around and wondered what their reaction would be if they knew what he and Jocko were planning to do?

He saw wives with husbands, some with children and then he saw young couples. They held hands, some kissed each other, and they were unafraid to show their affection.

Maybe one day I'll have that. I'll have Jocko who I can show my love in public for and no one will blink an eye.

Jocko seemed to read his thoughts for he moved closer to him and threw an arm around his shoulders.

"Nobody's going to say anything," he smiled. "Because if they do--?" He made his hand into a fist. Dressed in black leather, he resembled a possibly dangerous athlete—either a champion boxer or wrestler.

"When you see me next time, my heavenly brother, I'll be Diana DuPree—the sexiest and most ravishing blonde to be found in New York City."

Jocko rolled his eyes with a laugh. "Woo, and will Diana be jealous of a certain sissy boy, named Brandon Flores, that I'm hotly in love with."

"No jealousy there. You've got wonderful taste."

Over the speaker, Brandon's flight to Birmingham, Alabama was listed as ready to board.

Jocko kept his hand around his companion's waist. And right before he was checked in, the handsome young man leaned down and gave Brandon a kiss on his mouth. It was a deep, probing kiss. Several passengers looked at them in shock.

"You'll keep in contact with me?" Brandon asked. "You have my number at the hotel. Great luck, dear Jocko. This is a time we'll never forget."

Tears brimmed in the eyes of the powerful young man.

"I know. I'll be thinking of you."

They hugged briefly before Brandon vanished into the plane.

#

Before he left the airport, Jocko dipped into an airport bar and ordered a pitcher of draft beer.

His excitement was so great that he could barely sit still.

Just in the past three weeks, his young life had hurtled at jet speed along a path that exhilarated him—for he was certain this was the way that had been planned for him all along.

All the doubts about some of his choices in life now vanished. Everything he had done so far had led to this plateau.

At no time in his turbulent young life could he have imagined he would actually meet his twin brother again—and fall passionately in love with him.

He had discovered that Brandon was a phenomenon. It was like he were both woman and male, his drive and extraordinary talent had already made him rich at the age of twenty-six, despite those many attempts by his mother to destroy him.

Brandon's love for him had transformed the way Jocko looked at things. He no longer wanted to drift, to move aimlessly and waste his days doing stupid things.

He didn't know what he would end up doing but he thought now of spending his life with Brandon. Maybe one day they could adopt children. They'd be a regular family.

Or—and this was the ultimate fantasy—maybe someday soon, he and Brandon could return to Vesaria, help it become reborn, and he could be a powerful preacher—like his father.

Perhaps this was the real reason Emmanuel Trident had cursed the village—wipe it clean of everything and to make it virgin for a new beginning.

I'll be with Diana DuPree, we can rebuild a chalet like she had—and maybe like our parents, we can have a miracle birth!

PART SIX

Diana Lives Again!

CHAPTER ONE

"Any messages for 801?"

The desk clerk swiveled around in his chair and stuck his fat hand into the mailbox of 801.

"No ma'm. Not a thing."

"Has anyone tried at all to reach me? I'm expecting a very important call at any moment?"

The slug-like clerk, wiping sweat from his brow with a handkerchief, shook his head.

"No, ma'm. It's been real slow today. Hardly any calls at all for anybody."

"Have they fixed the air-conditioning yet? My room's a steam bath. I don't know if I can stay there another day?"

"They're still working on it, ma'am. I know it's uncomfortable, especially now with our heat wave. It should be up and working by tonight."

"By tonight? If it's not fixed, then I'm moving elsewhere."

"I'm sorry, ma'm. I wish I could help you out."

The stunning blonde woman dressed in a beautiful dress of champagne colored linen left the shadowy lobby of the Hotel Sun and went out into the scalding sunlit sidewalk.

The desk clerk, Jeremiah Walker and the two black bell hops, watched her with keen interest. This shimmering guest was the wealthy Diana DuPree from New York City.

They had never seen a customer so attractive and radiant. She moved in a voluptuous gait, as if she were a fashion model or movie star. Her shoulder-length hair was such a light blonde it was almost white. She stood out from her surroundings like she had just been born.

"She so looks like Marilyn Monroe it's amazing," sighed Jeremiah, as he used a new handkerchief to wipe away the dripping perspiration from his face and neck.

"Oh, boy, she is such an angel," nodded TJ Wood, an ancient bell hop who had worked at the Hotel Sun for sixty years. "Prettiest gal I've ever seen. Looka that hair. Like spun sunshine."

"She could be a movie star," smiled LeRoy Wood, the forty-year-old son of TJ.

Jeremiah McCrutcheon wondered if this Diana DuPree would consent to having her picture taken as a publicity gimmick so he could put it in the lobby window.

She would be shown smiling and beneath her the words: "I couldn't imagine staying anywhere but at the Hotel Sun!"

#

Diana DuPree hated this old hotel in Birmingham but the hospital staff had asked that she stay here for her transformation.

She could easily walk to the Gender Transition Center six blocks away. Four days ago she underwent the major part of her change. The undeveloped vagina, which had always been there, had been engineered until it now worked perfectly.

"We're amazed none of your other doctors didn't discover it," observed her surgeon, Dr. Alfred Steele. "It's always been there but it was covered by a thick membrane."

She told him of the ever increasing sex drive that made her want to literally climb the walls. That area of her body would throb at times but her fingers couldn't bring her relief. While at the same time, her penis rarely got erect.

"That's because you've always been more of a female than male. Your penis was just there to urinate and you probably got erect now and then and orgasmed. Now, your female parts can function in that sense."

Dr. Steele cautioned her that the first time her vagina was used for sex, it could be painful. She was taught how to massage the inner part with creams and lotions. She was also given a flesh-covered dildo that resembled the male organ to practice with.

Diana smiled when she thought of the lusty Jocko Shaun. The first thing he would want to do was to make love to her—and her new orifice. He would be gentle, though, for his love-making had left her breathless and wanting more when she was Brandon.

I'm still Brandon and always will be, she thought. But now, he'll have his other half to accompany him through life.

The new Diana DuPree thought of all these things as if they were still a fantasy. She had only been here for a week but her life was transformed forever. Mentally and emotionally, she felt more alive and alert and her perspective of the world was changing.

It was like a new personality had entered her, for now colors were much more radiant. Ordinary scents like the gas fumes from the passing traffic were sharper. The perfume she put on was like champagne to her nostrils.

My mother is here with me. She's watching out for me. She had arranged the profound meeting with her twin brother.

"Thank you, Mother!" Diana whispered as she stood in the white heat of the afternoon and waited to cross the street.

She crossed over to the enormous city park.

She had never seen one so large and now, at midway, in the broiling sun, it was packed with workers enjoying their lunch.

A haze coated the ground with a pearl-like hue so everything had an air of unreality. The air simmered with the smells of frying chicken from a nearby Chicken King shop, gas fumes from the slow-moving cars, the smell of freshly cut grass.

Her sunny ensemble drew much attention, she noticed, since most people were dressed down in grunge. A row of construction workers, eating sandwiches and sipping Pepsi's as they sat on the curb, made appreciative remarks and whistled at her.

She had stiffened in fear the first time this happened. In college, her enemies often whistled and cat-called insults, but now, she realized it was sincere. She touched her face—thrilled at wearing actual make-up and perfume in the real world.

When in New York, she had spent several hours with an outstanding make-up artist, Danny Hummingbird. He had taught her how to choose the perfect base and pancake to use on her. "Very little," he had advised.

It was her eyes that he concentrated on.

"Stunning eyes" Danny murmured. "Crystal light blue."

So she was instructed how to blend in mascara, eye lash darkener, and then for her mouth, Danny gave her several choices: either a fiery orange/crimson or a frosted cherry.

Her blonde wig was one of several she had made by Madame Rupunzel on Madison Avenue, just a few blocks from the very popular Brandy's Fashion Shoppe.

Today her whitish yellow tresses touched her smooth shoulders. Diamond earrings and a copper bracelet gave her glitter.

Her agent, Bruce Ramsey, had telephoned her several times to tell her that all of New York's fashion world and the media were going crazy to find out what she was up to.

Bruce had teased the press agents with intriguing hints: "Brandon is resting up—so that when he returns to all this madness, he'll be a brand new person."

Already gossip columnists knew they were onto something and Pauline Pearl, in her syndicated column, "Pearls of Pauline," had penned: "What red-hot young fashion prodigy may be changing both his name—and his gender—as I write this. This famous artist may soon be signing his name on his work under a very different signature. Mr. or Miss? Let's wait and see…"

#

The hospital had told her to stay close by the phone since she needed to return for minor surgery. This would be to tweak the major operation. She would be examined thoroughly, have some stitches removed and given more hormone shots. After that, she would be free to return to New York City where Mt. Sinai Hospital would resume any medical needs if necessary.

This shimmering woman now paused at a large fountain in the middle of the park. Water sprouted from the sculpted pitcher of a woman who had two little children and a dog pawing her skirt.

Diana stared up at the metallic face of the mother. There was nothing there although the mouth was upturned into a cold smile.

Like my foster mother, thought Diana. Edith Flores was a widow now since Reverend Flores had passed away. She gave out an interview where she said her famous son would have nothing to do with her.

"After all I did for him for eighteen years," she wept. "So cruel and cold-hearted."

The newly made woman walked gingerly because the new opening between her scrotum and anus was still tender. Occasionally, a streak of sharp pain would almost double her over. The doctors told her this was natural. She looked at men hungrily and if they were handsome or sexy, she smiled.

What was happening to her? Her naturally shyness had vanished. She fantasized about having sex with many men—but then after having a lover like Jocko, she was afraid they would all be disappointing. And Jocko was already her husband.

He had asked to be present here for her transformation but Brandon was adamant.

"No! The next time you see me, I want to be Diana DuPree. It's my gift to you. Brandon Flores will be a wonderful memory to us both. From the moment you see me, I want us to start new lives. We're going to do wonderful things together, you and me. So don't visit me until I'm the new and dazzling Diana DuPree!"

#

CHAPTER TWO

She found a shaded park bench beneath some ancient oaks and took out a paperback from her pocketbook. It was one of her favorite classics, *Rebecca*, by Daphne DuMaurier.

But she didn't read a word.

She couldn't get over the astonishing phone call she had received right after she had recovered from the operation and was in bed.

Jocko called her from a pay phone booth alongside the road between Vesaria and Blue Mist Motel.

The connection was horrible but what she managed to understand was a story so astonishing that it was like he were describing a science fiction fantasy.

#

The twelve man expedition had searched numerous natural caverns in the walls of the canyon.

Just before nightfall on the third day, one of the men shouted; "We've found something! This might be the opening!"

The men all scurried on their ropes to the area. Sure enough, what they saw was a narrow doorway that from a distance could pass for a natural cavity.

With everyone using their lights, they filed into a large chamber. The floor was so smooth of any dust or debris, it was like someone had just cleaned it. A fresh stream of cool air refreshed the explorers.

Curious illumination came from an unknown source but there was no heavy darkness. The men were able to put away their lights.

From this room radiated several passages. These, too, proved to be incredibly polished. On the walls, someone had painted surprisingly sharp pictures of human like figures and strange animals, some of them so huge they looked like dinosaurs.

Among these images were the figures of beings that resembled both man and women in one body.

Carefully, each group of men took a tunnel but tied one end of wire coil to a rock at the entrance to prevent getting lost. The three groups each had a hand cranked siren to use should they find anything unusual. Each unit also had a walkie-talkie which kept them in constant communication with the others.

Within an hour, one group sounded the alarm: they had entered a tremendous chamber.

All the other men hurried with excitement to see what their cohorts had found.

They all gazed around them in amazement.

The man-made vault rose so high up until they couldn't see the ceiling. Steps led deep down into an abyss. The air stream was stronger here. It was cool and sweet and they noticed it made them unusually clear-headed and filled with energy.

As they all gathered to plan their next move, Jocko had entered a smaller room off the steps to the right and came upon a huge room where the walls gleamed like they were covered with silver paint.

There was one ledge that stuck out from the wall.

Jocko moved closer and froze: the large figure of a man in a white robe lay there, as if asleep.

Jocko shouted for the others to come and see this astounding sight.

"Mother of God!" gasped Dr. Harry Thorn. "This is too unbelievable! If you guys weren't with me, I'd tell myself I've gone crazy."

They stared at this person and saw that he was nearly six feet five at least, his skin had a yellow cast to it so that he must be Asiatic. His breathing was steady, his eyes were closed, and his hair was pulled back into two braids.

Who was this sleeping inhabitant of the cave?

Could he really be one of the fabled high priest of Mouria?

A steady stream of cool air was evident here, as if this vivifying coldness was part of the magic that was keeping this man alive.

Although dumbfounded by this discovery, Jocko realized that this man wasn't Emmanuel Trident. He didn't come close to the photographs that his son had branded upon his memory.

The finding of this strange figure would certainly make for sensational headlines.

As he stood apart, staring hard at the sleeping giant, Jocko saw a tall, narrow door to his right. It would be missed if one just glanced at the corner of this wall.

He moved toward this opening—but suddenly, the eerie illumination suddenly went dark.

The explorers found themselves in a darkness that was almost solid. Their lights could barely work. It was like a secret signal had darkened this room—as a defense mechanism.

"Men, let's move out of here right away!" shouted Jocko. "Something's happening here and we don't want to be trapped."

The explorers needed little urging to move as fast as they could upward where the same extraordinary darkness awaited them.

When they entered the outside, it was refreshingly light, although it was actually nearly dawn.

"Whew!" said one of the men. "That was like a horror movie. We found something incredible—but it was like some unseen power wanted us out of there before he found something else."

"Emmanuel Trident is hidden away way down there," Jocko declared. "I can feel it. I'm damned certain we'll find him. Let's get back to camp and we'll try it tomorrow."

When Jocko and his team arrived back at their trucks and tents, they discovered several TV vans parked there. More than fifty journalists were there to greet them.

The Vesaria expedition had become a sensational news story.

All around the world, hungry seekers of unsolved mysteries were greatly excited that something amazing might be uncovered with this project.

When Jocko got hold of Diana DuPree later that night on the phone, he said: "I am certain that within a day or two, I'll find our father and we'll be reunited again."

"You will, Jocko. And then we'll be a happy family again! Because I'm now Diana DuPree."

Watching Diana DuPree from a distance was a striking looking man who stood out because of his heavy resemblance to Jesus Christ.

His mane of dark hair touched his broad shoulders.

His eyes were deeply set and a beard and moustache covered most of his face.

He would have been considered attractive except for the strangeness of his mouth.

An accident of some kind had caused the right corner of his lips to lift upward into a grin—or smirk. The scar was permanent and made a different impression on each person who saw it. Some were offended because it looked as if he were trying to hide a grin which was especially uncomfortable at a serious occasion—like a funeral.

Others thought he was always happy and carefree.

The park people and the homeless called him Jesus Jr. because of his uncanny resemblance to the Savior. Others didn't want to defile the legacy of Jesus Christ so they called him the Sidewalk Preacher.

He much preferred Jesus Jr. He experienced triumph when the homeless would stop and cry out: "It's Jesus Jr.!" He forced himself to eradicate from his mind his real name which was Nathaniel Giddens.

Now, he studied the golden woman sharply. He saw her when she came out of the entrance of the Gender Transition Center yesterday. That's where you could see firsthand the physical abominations who went around pretending they were women. A very few were women who had changed over to the male gender—but the fake women were the easiest to spot.

They had a nervous habit of touching their chest, or their thighs and moved a little uncertainly—because they'd all gotten fake pussies!

He saw that this one had now come out of the Hotel Sun. So that's where this abomination was living.

She was one of them--an Unclean Things.

This thing that moved around wasn't really a woman, nor was it a man. It was one of those "in-betweens" that he had been warned about and now he warned others about. They were fleshy scum that had no business living on the face of God's earth.

His Daddy always called these creatures White Niggers.

They were worse than a damned, black nigger.

These were God's outcasts and had been all through history. The Bible stressed how unclean and despised they always were. History couldn't be wrong, seethed Jesus Jr. God was never wrong. Hitler had made a mistake during World War II, thought the fake preacher. Instead of rounding up Jews, he should have concentrated on lapping up all these cocksuckers and fake homo-monsters. The slave camps had held only a few. There should have been millions of homo-monsters sent to the gas chambers.

The Sweet Lord had made two separate human beings: Adam and Eve.

A Man. A Woman.

Those who didn't fit into either gender were things of evil. The Bible said so all through it. Yet, these things were all around and more were appearing. Jesus Jr. realized that as a mere man, he couldn't eradicate them all from the face of the earth. But he had worked hard in his own strange way to do just that.

These things had worn women clothes and paraded around the fag area on Third Street like they belonged there.

That's what really burned him up! He saw them cackling and flipping their wrists and making exaggerated jokes about each other. They lived at night at the Gay Paree Bar. The police shut it down every few months but it always opened up again. There was also that homo-monster coffee shop they liked to use, too.

He often visited the queer area where he searched for potential victims and knew the bar there and the habitués and many flirted with him. They seemed to like his Jesus look and asked him why he always wore a black suit, white shirt and dark tie.

He jokingly told them he was a preacher but that he had learned to love everyone.

He bothered no one and the faggots and the Unclean Things thought he was cute and that he was a self-styled preacher gave him some color.

He never lectured them. If they passed him on the sidewalk, some wanted to spill out their problems. He listened quietly and offered a few consoling words and always concluded by murmuring: "Jesus saves. Remember that. Jesus is watching over you."

Yeah, if Jesus were watching, he'd probably encourage me to slaughter more, more!

He lied easily. It came as easily to him as spouting a passage from the Bible.

He could barely resist yanking the straight razor from an inside pocket and letting them all have it. His Daddy had shown him pictures of what happened to men who had gotten diseases from queers and whores. That VD ate their mouths and private parts like acid. Junior had gotten so sick looking at those pictures that he couldn't eat anything for two days. Why didn't God punish those diabolical things and wipe them off the face of God's earth?

His father jabbed his finger at the pictures and hollered: "That's what queers and whores do! They were sent to us by the Devil! They oughta be exterminated! Every dang one of 'em! They deserve no respect. Treat'em all like garbage because garbage is what they are!"

So it thrilled him to mutilate those cock-suckers two months apart. It had been so easy. They merged in his mind with the six other butcheries he had committed in other Dixie places—in Florida, Georgia, and Texas. The law never really took those murders seriously, either. They were like him—these abominations should be shipped off to hell. Their very presence on Earth defiled the very air people breathed.

They had seen him around that area and flirted with him and he had acted like a country bumpkin, like he had no idea what they wanted to do.

He ejaculated as he looked down at the butchered face and torso of these Unclean Things after he'd finished them off with his razor.

He had to do it again.

And sitting right there on that bench, glowing like a radiant gem in her shiny gold beauty, was his next victim.

#

Before she could fall into the spell of *Rebecca,* she noticed the good-looking man who walked past her. He resembled Jesus Christ—but one who grinned a lot.

She saw him yesterday when she came out here. It was obviously a place where he liked to hangout.

What made him stand out was that he wore a black suit, white shirt and dark tie. A lot of men were wearing their hair long now along with beards and moustaches but this man stood out. In a bizarre way he suggested Emmanuel Trident in his close resemblance to the Savoir.

His fingers grasped a dark book. So, thought Diana, he's probably a teacher.

She lowered her volume as she saw several street people come to the man and shook his hand.

Diana couldn't hear what they said but then she watched the stranger place a hand on the head of a red-faced woman with crimson, matted hair and a pink dress sprinkled with strawberries.

The woman clasped her hands and nodded her head as the man said something to her. They moved out of sight and Diana tried to resume her reading but she was struck by the scene she had just witnessed.

What kind of teacher was he, Diana thought, where street people all seem to know him?

To her surprise, the man reappeared, this time without his followers, and although he didn't look at her, she was certain he was aware of her.

He sat down at a park bench a short distance away. He opened his book and appeared to be lost in thought.

Diana was intrigued because he made her think again of John Sparrow in his hair and facial hair alone.

He stood up and came towards her.

"You look mighty cool and comfortable sitting there," he said.

He stopped before her and smiled.

"I'm really burning up," she sighed. "I had to get out of my hotel room because it's just as hot there. The air-conditioner's broke. It's like a steam bath."

"You mind if I join you? I promise not to interrupt your reading."

"Please do."

He sat down and crossed his knees, with one black shoe jiggling up and down.

"You must be terribly hot in that black suit you're wearing," she noted. "I mean, it's a very nice looking suit but I think I'd take off my jacket, if I were you."

"This is the way a preacher is supposed to dress," he shrugged. "I'm a man of the cloth—and my worshippers wouldn't like it if I didn't wear some cloth."

"You're a preacher?" Diana asked in surprise. "You're so young."

At first she had thought he was grinning at her. But as she saw him close-up, she realized that his mouth was set into a permanent smirk because of some accident. This made her feel sorry for him.

"You can find God at any age. But I am a preacher and I must say, a very successful one. See? I carry the book of the Lord with me at all times. They all know Jesus Jr."

"Jesus Jr? Now that's a very curious name."

"Don't you think I resemble the Savior? Everybody does. I'm proud when people think of me so highly. Some think I could be Jesus Christ resurrected from the dead. They say that I'm the one."

"You're the one?" she repeated slowly. "I was once told by a minister that if Christ should ever return to Earth, and if we suspected he might be the real thing, then we were to go up to him and ask him to his face: 'Are you the one?'"

"Would you say that to me?" the killer asked hopefully. "If you did, you'd make me a very happy man!"

"I couldn't say it unless I believed it and let's be frank I know nothing about you. I said this to one man a long time ago and he proved to be the devil."

He turned to her in excitement. "I'll let you get to know me and then you'll surely say, 'You're the one!'"

"Please," she snorted, "don't hold your breath."

Yeah, he thought gleefully, I'm the one who's going to slit your throat and cut off those fake tits.

#

The Five o'Clock Bar and Grill was a dark, cool, hole in the wall near the park where the air was moist with old beer.

Diana DuPree was amazed to find herself here after Jesus Jr. persuaded her to have a drink with him.

She had stopped by her hotel first to check for messages but to her frustration, there were none. With the air-conditioning still down, the thought of returning to her steam bath of a room was too nightmarish to contemplate. A visit to this bar seemed a pleasant alternative. She was glad that Jesus Jr. was with her. She was tired of being alone in this strange city that looked like all its color had been burned up by the heat.

She was also intrigued with this new mind-set of her's that began the minute her operation was over. Now she studied the men on the streets, in the park, in the lobby of her hotel with renewed interest.

No one had ever made love to her as a woman before. Diana sensed that with very little encouragement, with just a smile or a raised brow, she could get nearly any male into her hotel bed very easily.

She would never do it, though. Jocko commanded her thoughts and feelings of love. She missed his powerful, big body, his boyish expression, the intense way he had loved her—the complete security she felt with him close by.

And what was he doing now in that cavern? She could barely sleep thinking of the outcome of his exploration of the Mouria Gorge. Imagine finding a man's body sleep alive but asleep, wearing a white robe, Asiatic, his hair in two plaits.

The nervous little waitress, an old woman with red curls, had brought them their bottles of Old Milwaukee Beer and said to Diana: "You look so much like Marilyn Monroe I told my boss, Henry, that you could be her twin sister. He looked out and said: 'You are damned right.'"

"Oh, please!" laughed Diana. "That's very sweet of you. People tell me that a lot."

"She's going to be in movies," joked Jesus Jr. "It's going to be called, 'I'm The One.'"

When the waitress left, he continued staring at her so intently, that she felt uneasy.

"You've been studying me all the time we've been together," she observed. "What is it?"

"You're so beautiful!" he sighed. "Guess people have told you that all your life."

"No—not until recently," she smiled—for it was true. It was an exhilarating new position—to have, for the first time, people actually telling her how stunning...how lovely...how beautiful she was.

Visions of this freak lying on the grass of the park, with her eyes gouged out, her fake titties sliced off, and her mouth slashed into a Halloween grin, made Jesus Jr. lean forward eagerly.

"I want you to see my church. It's in the park at the far end where there's not many people."

"You've got a church—in the park?" scoffed Diana DuPree. "How can you do that in a public park? Wouldn't the park rangers close it down?"

"They know me. They like me. They're glad I can keep those homeless people in control. My church keeps them in line. You'd like my church. I call it the House of Rebirth. People can come there and begin a brand new life. They may have had done a lot of things in the past—or life did things to them. I help them resurrect themselves."

Yeah, I kill 'em, grinned Jesus Jr.

Resurrect? Diana DuPree was struck by his words. Strange that here she was, starting a brand new life as a woman, and this strange young man was helping others begin a new life.

I am resurrected, she thought in surprise. From my old life, I've been reborn.

"That's so interesting what you've just said," she said eagerly. "Have you seen many others, who've decided to bury the past and begin a new life?"

"Not that many come to my church," he said frankly. "But enough have—that I help ease them into this new groove of life."

Diana glanced at her watch and quickly picked up her pocketbook. "I'd love to see your church—but I have to get on back to the hotel. I'm expecting a very, very important phone call. I shouldn't be here now."

Jesus Jr. was furious that his plans for murdering this freak were all for naught.

"Come on, please. Alright then, I can visit you in your hotel room."

"I don't know," she said slowly. "You can walk me back to the hotel if you'd like."

As they moved along the steaming sidewalk to the hotel, Diana wondered if her operation was affecting her mentally. She would never invite a strange man she didn't know into her living quarters. Yet, here she was, being escorted down the street by a man who could be Jesus Christ himself.

Could this intense young man actually be Jesus Christ, she mused.

Ever since her traumatic experience with Dick Brown, she had met only one man who would definitely qualify for the honor of being The One. And that was John Sparrow.

Her brother, Jocko Shaun might be another contender but he was still a mere baby compared to John Sparrow.

When the couple entered the lobby of the Hotel Sun, the fat clerk motioned for Diane to come over and handed her a slip of paper.

"This call came in just a few minutes ago. The guy said it was urgent. An emergency. He would stay at this pay phone until you called."

With Jesus Jr. following her, she rushed into her room and dialed the number.

Before the second ring, Jocko had grabbed the phone. The connection was so bad it sounded like he were on a landing field at an airport.

"Jocko, I—"

"Diana!" he gasped. "We've found something so goddamned amazing you can't believe it."

"What is it?"

"It's a surprise! We're keeping this top secret. Don't breathe a word of this to anyone."

'Jocko, tell me what you've found!"

A clicking sound was followed by silence.

Diana stared at the phone, her heart racing, and tried to make sense of what her husband had just told her.

"Good news?" asked her visitor.

"I—I think so," she answered faintly. "A friend of mine is involved in something and can't tell me about it."

She strongly wanted to discuss this extraordinary event with this young man but Jocko had stressed that not a word could be breathed for the time being.

The air-conditioning had been repaired. Yet, the room was still warm and stuffy

She was suddenly glad to have company at this momentous event that Jocko had said was already happening.

"Let's have a little drink to cool things off," she smiled. "Do you drink?"

"If I'm with someone as beautiful as you, I do anything."

At least the small fridge was working. She removed an ice tray, a bottle of tonic water and a bottle of Seagram's Gin.

She poured them drinks into plastic cups and handed one to Jesus Jr.

'Here's to our health and our future," she said. "And to the success of my friend's quest.

"To a beautiful woman who I find charming and mysterious."

"Mysterious? In what way?"

"You've been very nice—but you reveal nothing about yourself."

"I don't know you. We've just met. With the passage of time…"

"But you said you were leaving here any day."

She nodded and looked out the dusty window. "That's true. Or, I may be stuck here another few days."

The hospital had forewarned her that she would definitely need a post-operative examination that could take hours. She was waiting for the call to return to the center.

Jesus Jr. put his drink and began to unbutton his white shirt.

"Well, I know one thing. It's damned hot here. Would you mind terribly if I removed by shirt?"

"I'm not sure, Jesus—"

"Ah, pretend we're at the beach. It's warm enough. I wouldn't wear my shirt on the beach now, would I?"

"Okay. You've got a point. But just your shirt."

"Well, in that case I might take a little more off. Ha, ha."

That same curious detachment came over her that she had already experienced several times since her operation. It was like something had happened to her brain—she was acting like a stranger and she couldn't control it.

One part of her saw herself from above, standing by the window, still dressed up in dazzling amber.

In front of her was this total stranger who could well be a psychopath, who was jokingly stripping off his white shirt, and now—even his trousers.

And this didn't shock her. It was like—this has happened before—to somebody else.

But now, she broke out of her reverie because Jesus Jr. continued to startle. His front was covered in tattoos. It looked like he wore a jersey of black and blue and red figures.

Diana saw faces of the devil and scriptures from the Bible. Skulls and bones. Anchors. Hearts.

"Oh, my God!" Diana whispered. "I had no idea you were covered like this with tattoos. The last man I saw tattooed was someone I love..."

He grinned and flexed his muscles. He was lean and hard.

"Nobody does. It always shocks the few people who've seen me naked. This is only the beginning. Take a look at this."

He turned and made his broad back ripple but his muscles took secondary place to the beautiful sunburst that took up all of his back. Surrounding the sun were numerous faces of bearded men—each one different and alarmingly lifelike.

"Those are the disciples of Jesus and of the devil," he explained casually. "Yes, Satan has always had his advocates, too. See Hitler and Mussolini."

Diana used a finger to trace over the stunning reproductions of these images of evil.

"I'm simply amazed," was all that she could say. "This must have taken years of work."

"Yes, since I was little, I've had them put on me. But now, let me show you the real shocker."

The killer casually pushed down and stepped out of his shorts. Diana was even more amazed at what he revealed.

The face of the devil had been drawn around his genitalia so that it looked like his tongue was actually Jesus Jr.'s impressive penis. Sharp horns spread upwards from the shaved pubic area.

The young holy man grasped his phallus and swung it around.

"I like playing with the devil's tongue. Would you like squeeze the old demon's tongue?"

She didn't move. Again, it was like she were watching from above as she stood immobile. She felt eerily removed as if this were a dream and she had no will.

"Okay, that's enough. I'd like you to go."

His flushed face clouded with anger.

"I've shown you everything I am!" he seethed. "I don't do this with just anybody. Now, let me get a look at you."

She moved toward the door.

"Go!"

He snorted and began to dress.

"Bitch. Just as I thought you'd be. You're all ice and snow."

"You're getting nasty. I'm changing my opinion of you."

"Yeah?"

He buttoned up his shirt and stuffed it into his pants.

Dressed as he was now, no one could imagine the tantalizing surprise hidden away beneath clothes.

He stood and studied her for a moment with an unnerving intensity.

"I'm sorry," he sighed. "I got carried away. I thought we had a good rapport going on and understood each other. I'd appreciate it if you'd come to my House of Resurrection with me. I'll behave. I'm preaching a special sermon."

"Ha! Not me. You've shown me what you're capable of doing. You'd probably throw me to the ground and rape me."

Her words made Jesus Jr. start. His eyes widened in surprise—because he did plan on throwing her to the ground and butchering like a hog. He recovered enough to say:

"You, in particular, should find my sermon of interest. You'll see my true self there."

"I hope it'll be an improvement over what I saw here."

Jesus Jr. rolled his eyes and heaved a sigh of exasperation.

"I showed you a true side of myself. I can't apologize for that. You hide behind secrets and images and I don't think even you know who you are."

"No," she said. "I'm discovering it gradually. Diana DuPree has a lot to learn yet. Okay, maybe tomorrow afternoon. I have business to attend to. We'll meet out by the fountain."

He hesitated. The urge to butcher was powerful but this Unclean Thing looked totally in control now. It was like she had power but wasn't aware of it yet.

"Okay," he sighed. "Tomorrow afternoon. Sorry the way I acted. It's just that you're—you're so beautiful."

"That's very sweet of you. I couldn't stay angry long at someone who says I'm beautiful. Make it late. About five-if I can get there. And if I can't make it, you'll know it wasn't intentional. Bye Jesus. I enjoyed your company."

Saying nothing, he left and closed the door but not before Diana heard him murmur "Beautiful yes, but beauty isn't what we think it is. What did

St. Paul say: 'Whether in or out of the body, I cannot tell—but God knoweth!'?"

\#

She was glad she stayed because a half hour later, the hospital called.

They wanted her to be there for preparation at 8:30 a.m. the next morning.

\#

The next morning, she left word at the hotel desk to be sure and give whoever called, the number of her hospital room. It was urgently important. She also said she would be away from her room the whole day and probably two.

\#

She smiled in delight as she entered the beautiful Gender Transition Institute.

The very air was lightly scented with a haunting aroma of flowers.

Everything was in pastels: pink, gold, and emerald.

The receptionist for Dr. Alfred Steele greeted her warmly.

"Oh, my word, but you certainly do look a picture of dazzling beauty!"

Diana had chosen to wear a striking silk dress of honey-gold. It was trimmed with copper sequins. Belted at the waist, the material caught all the light so that it literally sparkled.

Her wide-brimmed hat was of the same colors and jazzed up with a large crimson rose above her left ear.

When her primary doctor, Alfred Steele greeted her in his office he also looked stunned at her appearance. When she had left several days ago after surgery, she was still woozy from the anesthesia and had no desire to dress up or apply her make-up. Today, though...

"I am amazed! I never say that about most of patients but you could easily be a double for Marilyn Monroe in a movie! Seriously!"

The famous specialist in gender realignment was not exaggerating. The case of Diana DuPree, formerly Brandon Flores, had the whole staff talking.

When he was first examined months ago, the specialists were astonished to find that the subject already had a vagina—but it was hidden beneath a fleshy covering. It had been there since birth. All they had to do was remove this membrane, irrigate the cavity with various fluids and lubrications.

His penis functioned normally although it was small in size.

In other words, he was now a fully functioning male and female. The patient refused the thought of removing his male parts. He wanted the sex organ of both genders.

"My mother was lynched because she kept the privates of both male and female," Brandon explained. "That's never ever going to happen to me. I'll become a crusader for people like myself—and I'm sure there are thousands out there. I'll become a radical gender change pioneer."

Sitting here, though, was a woman of stunning beauty. Her eyes were a brilliant, luminous azure, like sparkling crystal. Her features were striking and voluptuous. Lipstick enhanced the luscious lips and mascara illuminated those beautiful orbs.

Her bosom was full and eye-catching. It was the style of Diana DuPree, though, that was so extraordinary. Her outfits were always show-stoppers.

Matching costume jewelry added to her luster. Dr. Steele could never see this creature wearing casual or grunge. No, Diana DuPree was the type of beauty who wouldn't be caught dead in jeans or cheap tee shirts.

At 9:30 a.m. she was prepped and put under anesthesia.

The team of gender specialists surrounded her and intently examined everything they had done. Her new vagina was now perfectly functioning. It was still tender and delicate but it was already healing fine.

Since her female part was natural, and not artificially constructed, she could have intercourse now, if desired. The repression of her female side, though, contributed to her intense artistic genius. By not expending it anywhere, it was all forced inward, with no physical release.

Her breasts were already formed when she entered. They were then slightly enlarged and looked normal.

They tweaked, removed stitches, and repaired other nips and tucks.

When Diana awoke around two o'clock in the afternoon, she was then told she would be held another day to make certain everything was healing.

The following day was hideously boring to her.

She wanted more than anything to make contact with Jocko.

Her imagination ran riot. What had they discovered in Mouria Gorge?

The next day, Diana was put through a series of tests, given shots, was instructed on how to treat and care for her female addition, and advised on her diet.

"You must drink water, water, gallons of water," said Dr. Steele. "This will keep your whole body hydrated. Here's a list of the vitamins and supplements you should always have on hand. Stay out of the sun. Your skin looks fabulous. Keep it that way. Too long in the sun will eventually destroyed your beauty."

Then the doctor leaned back in his seat and said:

"My team has discovered something else extraordinary about your condition, Diana. You can have children if you want."

"Children!" she gasped. "I'm in shock. How wonderful!"

"Everything is there for you to reproduce. You would need to be very careful about your health, should this happen. It might be a dangerous birth. But it's all there—if you wish to use it."

She closed her eyes and wept.

"Children? Mine. Jocko and I can raise a family!"

#

At five o'clock that afternoon, she was released.

Dr. Steele walked with her to the elevator:

"Nothing can stop you now from being a woman—and a man, if you want it. You're our prize patient. You'll look wonderful in our brochures and ads."

She had signed a contract that she was willing for her case to be advertised in the media. Flattering photographs were taken of her—before and after. The media was already after her for this extraordinary story that was certain to make sensational headlines.

A famous male artist and designer named Brandon Flores—was now both Brandon and a woman named Diana DuPree. He took his femme name from his own, famous Mother. Or so he thought. Reporters were certain to demand proof that the fabled Diana DuPree of Vesaria, lynched and butchered, was actually his parent.

"You'll give courage to all the thousands who are dreaming of having this done—but they haven't the courage," said Dr. Steele.

Her medical records were already being transmitted to Mt. Sinai Hospital in New York City which she would use as her base medical facility in the future. Her days here in Birmingham would soon be only in the past.

Tomorrow, she would fly to the Asheville Airport where she would rent a car and drive to Vesaria to be with her beloved—and his astounding secret.

On her way to the hotel, she felt so giddy with joy that she stopped at Aunt Lucy's Steak House and ordered a bottle of champagne to accompany her meal. This was an eatery strongly recommended by Dr. Steele as a must visit if one desired an outstanding Southern meal

This was in celebration of having achieved her life-long goal.

Other diners noticed the radiant presence of Diana DuPree as she sat at her window table. Her glowing hair flowed around her shoulders. Her shiny dress with the crinoline skirts looked like champagne. Her gleaming hair and lustrous eyes made her the focus of many admiring admirers—particularly the men.

It was nearly dark by the time she entered the lobby of the Hotel Sun.

The clerk held up his hand to catch her attention.

"Miss DuPree, a man just called your room but it was impossible to understand what he said. The sound kept breaking up and there was so much static."

"You don't know what he wanted to say?"

"As I said, it was impossible."

In her dark room, she started to pack. Then she phoned her travel agency and they reserved a first class seat for her flight to Asheville. A car would be waiting there in her new name. It was only an hour's drive to Vesaria.

Tomorrow, her brand new life as Diana DuPree would go into high gear.

She would be with her wonderful Jocko—and hopefully there would be a surprise that would be life changing.

Diana showered and selected a fresh dress of white linen with matching slippers, hat and pocketbook. A new straw bonnet shaded her striking face. She spritzed herself with *Eau de Eric*.

Before going out into the dreadful heat again, she stopped by the hotel's bar and ordered an icy gin and tonic.

The place was half-filled with other travelers. They all turned to look at this shimmering figure who resembled a movie star.

The bartender, a slender black man named Parry, smiled at her.

"I think everyone here is wondering if you might be in movies. You look like a Hollywood queen."

She laughed and put her drink down.

"I'm really flattered—but I'm just a poor little fashion designer and artist. The drink was delicious. Could I have one more?"

#

She left the bar with a pleasant buzz and crossed the street to the park.

The heat was smothering and very few people were around.

A haze now covered the ground.

She had thought occasionally of her strange acquaintance, Jesus Jr., and despite his sometimes bizarre behavior, he intrigued her. What would he do next? This was one man who would never bore anyone.

By the time she came to the fountain with the steel woman and her three children, the sidewalks were deserted. She heard the roar of a crowd nearby and music blasting over a speaker. Someone at the hospital said there was a free concert that night in the nearby football stadium. The Beach Boys were giving a free performance for charity.

"So you didn't forget me, after all."

His voice came from behind her. When she turned, Jesus Jr. stood smiling down at her. "I kind of gave up on you," he said.

"Sorry. I was tied up with other matters since I'm leaving tomorrow morning."

His face looked unusually serious.

'You're—you're leaving? I didn't know. I thought you'd be here a few more days—"

"No. Sorry, but this is my last visit to the park. Now, I need to go back to the hotel and finish my packing and—"

"Wait!" he pleaded. "I so want you to see my little church here. It's only a few minutes away. You promised me. You can get a better feel of me."

She hesitated. Diana just wanted to relax in her room, take a cool bath and go to bed early for tomorrow was going to be hectic. Her flight left at 7:45 in the morning. She would have to get up by five a.m., dress, catch a taxi to the airport in order to board her flight.

"Okay. I'll go with you for just a few seconds. But I can't stay late."

"You'll be back at your hotel, tucked in your bed in no time. Come on now."

He held out his hand. She took it.

Within minutes, he smiled, this radiant creature would be a butchered carcass with no eyes or tits.

CHAPTER THREE

The park was empty of people tonight.

A mild breeze blew steadily, but not enough to wipe away the hideous humidity that made the sweat pop out and saturate her clothes.

"My last night in Birmingham," she murmured. Diana felt slightly dizzy. I shouldn't have drunk two drinks in the bar. I should have gone straight to my room.

The increasing mist gave everything here a ghostly quality. And a sinister one, too.

"And you're never coming back?"

"Not unless I have reason to. It's just not my kind of a place to live. It's too damned hot here."

Jesus had wanted to wait and savor the waiting game with this homo-monster, to enjoy her beauty before he sliced her up like a pig. His pulse quickened because he realized that within just an hour, he would see her butchered carcass on the ground.

It would look so pretty against that white dress she wore. He glanced at her and shuddered: this freak had all the white skin and gold hair and pretty features just like a real woman. Yet, he knew what was hidden beneath that lace finery.

"If this is your last night—here," he smiled, "I'll give you a special blessing."

"No Biblical scriptures now," Diana warned. "We'll keep it real quick and simple and then I'll have to leave."

"It'll be over before you know, my beautiful Diana! The end will come fast—for you, my beautiful sinner."

Something about his words and tone jolted Diana DuPree from her thoughts.

She looked around. Nothing moved. The air was thick with the rancid smells of overflowing trash cans, old fried chicken, old beer and old cigarette butts.

Jesus Jr.'s arm was firmly around her waist. Doubt made her hesitate. Those words of his—"The end will come fast—for you, my beautiful sinner," made a chill pass over her.

As she tried to pull away from him, his strong arm around her waist guided her forth along the path.

His behavior in her hotel room was too edgy for comfort. A person like him would have to be treated with care and caution. She pulled her purse up to her chest. A quick thrust into her bag and she would have her Mouria Dagger there to protect her. The thought of her weapon, the one her mother may have used when she was butchered, gave her a strange comfort. It was like the sensation of having a cross to ward off a vampire.

They came to a small, handmade stage at the far end corner of the park.

A chain fence separated this part from the roaring traffic on the interstate just a few feet beyond. Only the metal barrier prevented the cars from hurtling into the park.

A single gold light shone down on a man with a long beard and hair. He was playing a fiddle and behind him danced in strange, jerky steps another bearded man. He turned and held his arms out as his cohort sang a mountain ballad:

The mists have gone

We're here alone

To worship another power

When our end comes

May we dance and play

To that force that's so

Much higher

As he sang, he began to move around in a dance like that of his fellow musician. Both men did awkward whirls and clogging movements.

When the song ended, the singer nodded his head at Jesus Jr.

"Wish there was an audience tonight, Jesus. You got a quarter for the bus?"

"Both you guys hurry on down to the soup kitchen at the Biltmore before they shut down for tonight. They got chicken and dumpling, I hear."

"Oh, we does love our chicken and dumplings," the fiddler giggled. He and his buddy stumbled away into the darkness.

Now, it was only the man and the new woman who stood here at this isolated encampment.

"Right back over here is my very special praying place," cooed the killer. "Right behind those bushes there. I'll just give you a little prayer and..."

"No, please, I must get back—"

"Only for a minute or two—and then we'll part forever."

With his arm firmly around her waist, he guided her closer to the steel fence and behind a thick row of high bushes. The cars roaring along the interstate were so close, they were just inches from the fence. She saw huge rats jumping in the air onto the carcass of a mangled dog.

To Diana's surprise, Jesus Jr. quickly and silently removed all of his clothes except for his high black boots. The mass of tattoos on his body made it look like he wore a dark undergarment. His strange mouth made it look like he were laughing. Yet, his eyes were dark and intense.

He stood naked and straight, like someone about to perform a ritual. Diana backed up slowly to the path. There was something unnerving in the way he was acting. Maybe he was planning to rape her out here in this empty place. Yet, Diana felt a curious power moving into her veins. Her head was clear now and she prepared for battle, if need be.

He spread his hands in a sweeping gesture.

"It's time you said goodbye to all this. Say goodbye to it all."

"I am. That's why I'm—"

"No, 'the rebuke of the Lord cometh in flames of fire,'" he muttered. He swept his hands around him. "No, goodbye to it all. I mean to everything. I know something about you, my dear little Diana. You aren't really a woman, are you? You're all fucked up, aren't you?"

Instantly, Diana knew what was planned for her.

This had happened before—when some human monster had tried to annihilate what she was. It had happened to her mother and father by the ghouls in Vesaria. Now, it was like fate had set into motion for history to repeat itself.

It will not happen again, she thought. No, nothing in the world will allow this to happen. A rage poured into her veins to join her sense of power. It coursed through her body so that she threw her shoulders back and tensed for battle. Her hand slid into her pocketbook.

The knife of Mouria was there—finally, at last, to be used again, just as her mother had used it to defend her pitiful self.

Jesus Jr. sensed she was preparing for battle. He lunged forward and knocked her purse with the dagger from her hand.

She whipped a high heel from her foot and held it in both hands.

"Oh, you want to prolong your fate? I'm Jesus Jr. who wants to help God rid the earth of unclean things, Diana. You're an abomination that needs to be destroyed. You'll poison everything you touch, my pretty lady."

"You're a monster who should have been destroyed at birth," she spat. "You're scum that nobody will ever love. You should cleanse this earth of yourself, you sleazy little cockroach!"

His right hand shot out and grabbed her throat and she saw his left hand reach to his back where he had taped a straight razor. With the ease born from much use, he waved the weapon above her head.

"Say good-bye to all of this, fag scum, for—"

Suddenly, he gasped as Diana rammed her knee up between his legs. He doubled over and his would-be victim slammed her elbow into his neck.

Now, it was Jesus Jr. who was half way to the ground. Diana had seen where her Mouria dagger had landed. She ran and picked it up.

The killer wasn't about to admit defeat. Still on his knees, he grabbed her legs and yanked her down beside him. He rolled over on top of her and now used both hands to grab her neck.

"Fuckin' homo-monster! You goddamned white nigger!"

His words ended in a high yelp as the razor-sharp blade of the dagger swept over his throat.

The demonic preacher rolled off her, his eyes bulging and he holding both hands to his throat.

The sliver of steel rammed into his left eye, then into his throat, then into his heart.

'You—"he gurgled. "You—abomination."

He struggled to his feet but Diana shoved him back against the fence and slashed his face, his throat, and his privates.

He slumped moaning to the ground and shook.

"Not me, this time," she panted. "Not me, but you—you sonofabitch! I did this for my mother—my father—and everyone who died because of ghouls like you!"

She watched the thing that used to be Jesus Jr. thrash around and convulse. Beneath him crunched a bed of beer cans. His fingers curled and touched his throat. His face turned toward her, in horrified disbelief.

And then he lay still. His eyes were opened wide. They stared up at the stars as if shocked that his plans had gone bad. That never happened to Jesus Jr. whose real name was Nathaniel Giddens. Yet, the scar on his mouth made it seem like he were grinning at his fate.

"You told me you were the one," she groaned. "God knows, you were *never* the one!"

She flicked away the pine needles and dirt and debris from her dress.

Before she thrust her dagger into her pocket, she held the handle and kissed the blade.

"Thank you—Diana DuPree—and Mouria!"

She watched several of the enormous rats slowly creep toward the bloody figure of Jesus Jr. One of them leaped upon his throat, and then another one. Within seconds, his corpse shook as the ravenous rats found a tasty meal for the night.

Quickly, she ran out to the path. It was empty. All around her, the mist had covered the ground, so that it was like she was still within a nightmarish fantasy.

When she came to the fountain with the mother and children, she used the water to further clean herself up. No one had seen her.

She had savagely killed someone—and it didn't bother her.

Diana stared up into the smiling face of the metal mother and her two children.

She thought of her butchered Mother—who had been defiled and murdered by abominations. This time one of the ghouls lay at the fence for rat food.

#

The street was almost empty as she paused to see if anyone saw her.

She would have to sit in her miserable hotel room and wait until morning before she could catch her plane to Asheville.

Until she died, she would have to think of the young body of Jesus Jr. lying naked and destroyed out there in the park among the rusting beer cans and the leaping rats.

Just as she prepared to cross the street, Diana watched a dusty red Ford pickup truck move along slowly, as if the driver were looking for an address.

The street and the sidewalk were both empty when the truck rolled to a stop before the entrance to the Hotel Sun.

Outside lighting bathed the front of the old building with gold and crimson illumination.

There was only one truck like that in the world.

From the driver's side, Jocko stepped out.

He wore no clothes.

The passenger door opened. An equally powerful form emerged.

Emmanuel Trident/John Sparrow was suddenly there—in all of his magnificent glory. No clothes hid his god-like torso.

"Jocko! John!"

Father and son turned to look at her. Smiles of joy spread over their radiant faces as they crossed the street with their arms opened wide.

"Diana! Diana DuPree!" cried Jocko.

They watched as she stepped out of her shoes, discard her dress, lingerie and tossed aside her hat.

Like her father and brother, she was naked, too.

They studied her with amazed expressions and nodded their heads.

"You—are at last, Mouria!"

Jocko grabbed her hard against him. He turned to his father and said "We found him, alive, in the Indian Cavern, where he's waited all these years for you to become—what you were always destined to be."

Emmanuel Trident held out his phallus and that of his son to Diana.

"You'll have my children and those of your brother's."

"We'll return to Vesaria," vowed Jocko, "and start a new world there. And you'll be our queen again."

He went to Diana and they were pulled hard against the powerful torso of this man who had brought them into the world.

"Now," wept Diana DuPree, "I know that you *are* the one—Jesus!"

The End

About the Author

Jery Tillotson is author of the ground-breaking memoir, *I, A Man*.

Jery was a prize-winning journalist for fifteen years before he moved to New York City. Over the next thirty years, he wrote more than two hundred stories and novels under a number of popular pen names for the gay press.

Writing as 'Jason Fury', his story collection, *Eric's Body*, was published in 1993 and became an overnight sensation that still sells steadily today. It has been re-issued numerous times around the world and is now regarded as one of the major pioneering works of gay erotica.

Jery also writes as 'Andrea D'Allasandra,' 'Kandy Kristmas' and 'Big' Bill Jackson. He lives in a famous gothic residence in the mountain city of Asheville, North Carolina. His home served as the backdrop for his sensational autobiography, *I, A Man*. You can contact him at his popular website: www.jerytillotson.com

Printed by Libri Plureos GmbH in Hamburg, Germany